The Three Suitors

The Three Suitors

a novel by

RICHARD JONES

An Atlantic Monthly Press Book

LITTLE, BROWN AND COMPANY   BOSTON   TORONTO

LIBRARY OF CONGRESS CATALOG CARD NO. 68-13967

FIRST AMERICAN EDITION

First published in the United Kingdom as *The Age of Wonder*

ATLANTIC–LITTLE, BROWN BOOKS
ARE PUBLISHED BY
LITTLE, BROWN AND COMPANY
IN ASSOCIATION WITH
THE ATLANTIC MONTHLY PRESS

PRINTED IN THE UNITED STATES OF AMERICA

CONTENTS

1 Evening at Swanquarter   1

2 A Morning Visitor   10

3 Mignon Wastes her Credit   25

4 The Divided Estate   36

5 A Virtuoso Performance   51

6 Sir Arthur for the Masses   65

7 The First Suitor   95

8 Misunderstandings   120

9 The Second Suitor Arrives   158

10 Back to the Land   181

11 Patrick Finds a Home   203

12 Stratagems   222

13 Movements   239

14 A Prospect of Union   262

15 The Third Suitor   276

    Epilogue   Reconciliation   299

The Three Suitors

FOR
ELIZABETH SPENCE

1

EVENING AT SWANQUARTER

VERY often and especially in the evening when, with her brother, she walked out in the fields below Swanquarter, Mignon knew the meaning of old age. It was the bitter experience of departure without farewell, the nostalgia for voices and faces which had gone, the sadness of those whose children have died among strangers, the persistent disbelief that a lifetime could end in the minor key without real meaning or savour. In terms of the theatre it called for an actress standing on a darkened stage, one arm extended to hold off an unnamed enemy, the other held across her eyes to screen away the unmentionable.

The last lights in the windy sky commented ironically on their position: two old people watching the evening express hurtle by on its last lap to Port Rydal, with the grey walls and slate roofs of their home half hidden by trees as a backcloth. With their hands raised to their eyes, Mignon and Freddy summed up old age abandoned, archetypal old age waiting for the long-lost traveller's halloo; and under the spectacular sunset, which struck cloths of gold in the farmhouse windows, they became heroic in their fidelity, tragic in their passionate scrutiny. Then, as they moved homewards, one carrying a bundle of firewood, the other an apronful of crab apples, they were diminished. They were simply two old people, the last of a large family and a generous tradition, living out their years in seclusion; one might have said abandon. Was this all? she asked herself; but the question might have been addressed to the clouds piling up over Caeriforshire, to the fir plantations and windbreaks below them, to the last light caught on the surface of mid-August floods, to the sweep of pearl blue sky where, beyond the golden tumults and ribbons of vapour, the new moon trembled. It was the hour of reconciliation and homecoming for everyone but herself. She loitered in the fields while Freddy went on ahead and when she reached the stone steps which led to the kitchen door she stopped and turned back regretfully. Was this all there was to it? Inside the kitchen she heard Freddy strike a number of matches as he fumbled at the lighting of the lamps; from the courtyard she heard the water falling musically from an iron spout on to an iron grill; from the lonely house across the fields came the keen echoes of buckets and hobnailed boots as late tasks were finished by storm lantern; from the main road nearby she heard the farmboys racing down a straight, deserted stretch to Caerifor. Mignon was outpacing them all. She had moved away on the evening train on its journey through thin woodlands and outcrops of rock. The train left behind dissatisfaction and the fear of being forgotten (for the world rumbles on like a train and to get off is to be lost).

* * * *

Those were strange, uneasy days for Mignon and, to a lesser degree, for her brother. They were days spent equally in the resentment, hope and foreboding aroused by the decision of Mignon's only daughter to return home after an absence of four years. The daughter, married to a businessman in Rhodesia, had been unwell; she was to be accompanied on her trip by her only son who planned vaguely to become a vet.

Mignon usually tended to think of her daughter as a lost, beautiful cause and was sure that when she arrived they would frazzle one another's nerves to ribbons : hence the forebodings. Mignon was pessimistic because she had been, as she put it, "thinking quite a lot" about family matters. Pottering around the house, sitting in her rocking chair, dozing in front of the fire, she'd been reviewing the whole of her relationship with Nesta and had decided the girl was a washout. Freddy was inclined to agree, but for form's sake put in a good word for his niece, with whom he had never been able to have a satisfactory conversation.

"Oh, but, dearest, she's always been a washout. Everything was expected of her and she achieved nothing at all." A sigh. "One day I'm going to write a book about families, full of home truths not put into print before."

Freddy looked mildly sceptical.

2

"Think of it: we were seven children. Two died in the 1914 War; you never married; Getta had no children; and three of us produced solitary chicks, each as self-centred and selfish as the other. Look at Nesta! Hardly ever writes. Look at Muvvy! Living all these years in Caerifor and might as well be dead for all we see of her. And then the classical example of ingratitude: look at darling Edward, who's washed his hands of us in spite of all that his uncle and I did for him. Three of them and not a really generous impulse anywhere. Why, the way we're left here anyone would think we'd got the plague. Sometimes," she exclaimed, "it's just as though the family had been cursed by a crosspatch fairy. Nobody cares a fig whether we live or die."

Freddy had not lost faith in his nieces and nephew and that day he had a funeral oration on hand in which he was making the point that so long as there was life there was hope of change and renewal. He quoted himself to Mignon; he believed Nesta and her cousins would be moved by grace and would one day gather about them offering to share their lives and their hearts.

"Do you really believe that, Freddy?"

"If I didn't think that—" and his eyes had become big with earnestness, "I couldn't bear the thought of those children at all."

*   *   *   *

The day of the funeral, Mignon was left alone with the old corgi, Ianto. Towards six o'clock, she sat down in her rocking-chair near the kitchen window and looked out at another clear evening vanishing over the cornfields. She opened Meredith's short story about Lady Camper and Colonel Opie, and, having perched the old pince-nez (she was too ashamed to wear them in public) in the middle of her long nose, began to read. Meredith had long been a favourite author and whenever she picked up his books she observed to Freddy, "Fashion's a strange thing. Can't understand why Meredith is so neglected nowadays. Some of the things in this book are absolutely priceless." Her enthusiasm could not, however, compete with the fine print, the motion of the rocking-chair and the aroma of

3

simmering soup. Gradually the novel slipped into her lap, her head lolled forward on her chest, the pince-nez dangled unused on its black ribbon—and she slept.

Then, in a dream, the long-lost nephew Edward came into the room. He stood uncertainly at the door in a velvet-collared overcoat and looked at his aunt apologetically. He came forward slowly and held out both arms. "Aunty Micky," he said in his rich, theatrical voice, "I'm sure you think I've neglected you shamefully." She stood still for a moment and then opened her arms. The doubt and resentment of years passed away; whatever had happened in the past no longer counted. They kissed. They hugged one another; and the intensity of her joy awoke her and left her stunned. What remained, too, was the wonderful freedom from rancour that came after she had forgiven the man. It was an almost tangible sensation of goodness.

Impossible to say how long she sat bemused by the dream. She stirred only when she heard Freddy grumbling to himself because he'd stubbed his toe in the unlit hall.

"Do you want me to walk for you, Freddy?"

"Not at all, Micky, I only want a little light." He peered at her accusingly. "You've been asleep, haven't you, Micky?" They had a thing about sleeping in the daytime.

"I had a short nap. And after all my work in Nesta's room I think I'm entitled to one. And why are you so late? How your Jehovah must get a pain in the neck listening to all your supplications."

Freddy stood, perplexed, near the table where Mignon was trimming the lamp. Why was she so cross? He noticed, too, with what impatience she shut the window once the lamp was lit and how ungraciously she dashed the soup into their plates. He sat down without a word and tucked his napkin into his clerical collar.

"You haven't remembered what day it is today, Micky." She looked up in surprise. "Why, thirty-five years ago exactly Evelyn died."

"As long ago as that?"

"Thirty-five years. Yet she was close to me all day."

"The best of us all."

"The best. You know, it's this that is so touching about the

4

dead: they come back to you some days as vividly as though
one had only left them yesterday. You can almost touch them.
I could see Evelyn vividly. Do you remember that old dress
of yours which looked so well on her? The one with a sort of
cape over the sleeves? I recalled her in that."

"Fancy that, dearest! And to think that just now—when I
was dozing—" an odd look at Freddy—"I dreamed about
Edward most vividly. He came back to apologise for his behaviour."

"He did?"

"Wearing an Asquithian kind of coat."

Freddy credited Mignon with second sight and attached
great importance to these breakings-in from another level of
awareness. She herself was sceptical and this disbelief made her
gifts more genuine in Freddy's eyes: a parallel with genius
which flowers despite itself. "We may hear something yet," he
said.

"Poor Evelyn would have suffered had she known her boy
would let us drop as Edward has done. She could never understand ingratitude."

"His father's side."

"For sure."

"You and Arthur did all you could for the boy."

"For poor Evelyn's sake. For poor darling Evelyn."

"Believe me, Micky, Evelyn would thank you."

"Evelyn would thank us both. We've nothing to be ashamed
of. We've always been the same." She carried her napkin gently
to her lips. "Who could have foreseen Edward's behaviour?"

"Nesta said it was because there were no more pickings after
Arthur died."

"Nesta may have been right. Of course, she was the most
bitter about him. She once said she'd spit in his face if she saw
him again."

"Silly talk."

"She's forgotten it all now. She's been abroad. I don't suppose
she ever thinks of Edward. It's left to us to carry on these old,
painful thoughts because we're old and left so much alone. We
live with the past around us. We think as easily of the dead
as of the living—and, believe me, with far greater pleasure,
very often. So we go on playing the might-have-been game.

5

Were we living fuller lives or had the money to travel we wouldn't vex ourselves over these old matters, don't you feel?"

"Well, I can't say I brood as much on the past as all that," he replied softly.

"But you must do, a little." She pressed her crossed hands against the base of her throat. "It's our age, Freddy, that makes us think of these things. Really, there's no more interest in them and yet we've got to go on toting them around with us because we don't make new friends or see new faces. Why, twenty-five years ago the whole thing would have been pushed aside. We would have snapped our fingers at Nesta and Edward and Muvvy."

"Well, of course, twenty-five years ago we had our own lives."

"Exactly. One retires. One pulls up one's roots in London. One returns here. One by one old friends drop away or die, and there's nothing in the past to go back to. That's the nature of things. Where *we* are so defenceless is that we don't have the pleasures of continuing family life to interest us. Grand-children, great-nephews and—nieces, visits, new friends, family occasions. All those things would have given us new horizons, a part in the new generation. We've no one. No one at all. That's what's so hard. That's what I'd never foreseen when we were all here together as children. We've got nothing to show at all. We haven't even enough ready cash to save what's left here. Don't think I want Nesta or Edward or Muvvy to do any-thing for us. It's not that. It's just that the sharing of their lives would have brought us such pleasure and interest, don't you feel? If they took just a little interest in us at times. How long is it since Muvvy last called in here with Ashley? I can't even remember."

Freddy had seen her that very day in Caerifor. Believing she had meant to cut him, he had "fixed her with his eye" and she'd stopped for a few words. Mignon was unimpressed and waved the incident away. Freddy looked at her scandalised; it seemed in contradiction with what she'd just been saying. "But she's our own flesh and blood, Micky. I feel I must try. We must be ready to be friendly. After all, what you must face up to is that Edward may return—then what would you do?"

6

She rose and went to the sideboard where some wafer-thin slices of cold meat were lying on a plate. She divided the meat between them and sat down again.

"What would I do? I'd try to show him nothing had changed. I'd try not to look hurt or offended. With people like Edward it's a waste of time showing deep feelings, don't you think? Despite his cleverness and all that he's a shallow person. You make up your mind not to let him use you again."

* * * *

Then, without warning, she jumped up from the table and asked, "But why are we talking like this? That's past. Finished. A part of life that will never return." She walked back and forth looking for a jug of milk, too agitated to know what she was looking at. If Freddy only knew (she said) how much she hated being haunted by the ghosts of the past.

"Believe me, I don't want to live with regrets. And sometimes I could jump out of a window because our lives are so dull. I long to meet interesting people, don't you?" She grabbed the milk and stared at him aggressively as though about to pour it over him. His offence was to have finished his meat and deserted the argument for the remains of a dish of rice pudding. He licked his lips furtively, ashamed to be thought lacking in sympathy. He stopped scraping the sides of the dish and waited for her to sit down or move away.

"Ah," she cried, "if you only knew how I long to meet new, interesting people. To be part of a group of large, generous-minded friends. People who'd give one some real hope or belief in human beings."

She walked away and then returned towards the lamplit table where Freddy had resumed his scraping as dispassion-ately as possible. "Don't *you* ever wish for something big and generous to happen, Freddy? Something that would change us, transform us? Don't sit there stuffing yourself. Answer me."

"Look here, Micky, don't spoil my supper. I can't get churned up like you." He waved his spoon at her. "Don't put on these Edith Evans acts. Don't start shouting at me. Natur-ally, I want nice things to happen to you and to everyone else

7

in the world. I love to see happiness. You know I'm only really at home with happy people. What's more, the only difference between us, my girl, is that my idea of happiness is one that begins inside and goes out to the world. Yours comes from the world and ends in you. That's your way to happiness and I respect it; but it's not my way and I wouldn't want it to be. All the same, I hope very much for your sake that something wonderful will happen to us both—something big and generous, as you put it. And there's no reason why it shouldn't happen. Miracles happen daily. Despite everything you hear and read this is the age of wonder so I've no doubt at all but that you'll get your wish. Be prepared for it. I hope it brings you happiness."

"You're such a dear," she said impulsively. "I hope your little sermon turns out to be right. Sometimes I think nothing nice will ever happen to us again."

Her eyes softened, her manner mollified; Freddy could go on scraping his dish. "You could be wrong, my girl." He laughed at her as he chewed with a suggestion of endless reserves of good humour. Mignon, back at the window, smiled at him, impressed, despite herself, by the earnestness of his manner, and secretly quite pleased. She didn't inspire such eloquence every day.

*   *   *   *

Yet the bird trapped within her remained unappeased; the life within demanded some release. Abruptly breaking off what she was doing, she threw a cardigan over her head and shoulders and—with a few words of explanation—left the room and the house. She walked towards the main road holding the cardigan to her head not by gathering it under the chin but by holding the sides of her head with both hands, like a woman running away from a disaster. She reached the roadside where she stood a long time longing to see a little movement, to feel a little of the passing of the world. Standing there, near the spot where a biscuit tin known only to the postman, the baker and the household was hidden, the bird became still again for nature, like music, helped to pacify and restore. What, a short time before, had been intolerable—their isolation, their aban-

8

donment—had died away. In its place was gratitude. After all, she reasoned, she and Freddy could have been worse off. They had much to be thankful for, not least their good health, their simple tastes and, on the whole, their mutual respect. Those were things which no one could give or take away. And as she drew nearer to the house and saw Freddy's lamp shining through the leaves of the bushes and saw, even, the owlish beads of light on his reading glasses—he was staring ahead in a trance unaware that he was being observed—she remembered that compared with many people they were extremely cosy. Inside the house again and its special aroma of ripening apples, wood-smoke, old hangings and books, she could not imagine another shell for their last years. How could either of them have ever considered a life away from there satisfactory? The sense of their continuity, their rightness in that place sustained her, too, and she ended the day hopefully.

The next morning, though, she was vulnerable again. The shabbiness, the emptiness of the house depressed her. The rooms were sun-bleached, threadbare, the ceilings filmed by the smoke of too many fires, the floors worn thin by too many generations, the curtains too old even for cleaning. Everything called out for renewal; but where was the money to come from? She sighed and went on cleaning.

A MORNING VISITOR

ABOUT eleven o'clock Ashley Corbett called. He was the husband of the Caerifor niece, Muvvy, and was a good friend to the old people. Whenever he passed to view a property or on council business he brought them a little gift. That day because of the heat, he brought a block of ice-cream. Nothing could have been more welcome and Mignon, hot and flushed from her work, divided the ice-cream into three portions. Then they all sat down in the bleached white chairs in front of the house to eat and talk.

Mignon and Freddy were in Ashley's pocket. He could do what he liked with them. Mignon always said they were devoted to him and he was certainly the only person who could praise Tory prime ministers in her presence and get away with it. She indulged Ashley's politics on the grounds that he had never lived away from Caerifor for long periods and so, not having any vital experience of the world, was entitled to his naïve enthusiasms. It was within his capacity to hero-worship Tory leaders. On that side he was undeveloped.

The indulgence was easily understood. Ashley was their true friend and a generous one. In addition, he was a handsome man and Mignon liked handsome men especially if they were well-built, well-dressed and did not find gossiping with her beneath their dignity. She took as much pride in Ashley's appearance as she would have done had he been her own creation. Whenever he came, she arranged his handkerchief in his breast pocket, laid a napkin carefully across his knees to protect his elegant check trousers, even dusted his shoulders. Ashley got no attention at home and so relaxed, swelled out, became happy and self-confident and charming and was in every way a well-loved only son, knowing he could do no wrong, knowing that almost everything he did and said would be approved. While eating his ice-cream he asked them, in a

way certain to whet their curiosity, whether they liked surprises. "Nice ones?" countered Mignon.

"I should say so." He looked at them with a certain archness.
"My dear people, the fact is I've heard from your nephew."

"You mean Edward?"

He nodded. "Edward Lloyd-Ballantyne." The brother and
sister held their breath. "A brief note, of course, on college
stationery. A business letter." Ashley took the letter out of his
inner pocket. "He's willing to go up to five thousand cash down
for the right kind of house." Without bothering to look at his
listeners Ashley unfolded the letter and read it aloud to them.
Mignon covered her dazed eyes with a thin, slightly mottled
hand. "What makes him want to come back to this part of the
world?" Ashley had no idea. The question hardly bothered
him although his wife was sure the successful Edward wanted
to come back to his own country and cut a dash. Freddy said
the old roots might have begun to pull.

"Never!" Mignon said finally.

Ashley resumed his ice-cream. "I told them there were a
couple of properties on my books which might suit them but
the price is a bit more than the five thousand they're ready to
pay." He went into details with an estate agent's enthusiasm
while Mignon and Freddy, afraid to look at one another,
were sick at heart. They diminished. They drew into themselves. They buttoned up their eyes and their mouths. They
were both appalled that Ashley, who was closer to them than
anyone, could be so obtuse and could not see that Edward was
more than a business deal to them.

Mignon heard herself saying, "He must have money to
burn," to which Ashley replied lightly that if Edward's wife—
whoever she was—wanted a modern place she could have the
Corbetts' home for fifteen thousand. Mignon and Freddy were
both aghast. "You'd sell your new home?"

"Why not? We get nothing out of it and there's no one to
leave it to."

"But it's your home, Ashley. There are certain things that
aren't for sale, aren't there?"

"It's only a house, Aunty Micky."

"What do you mean. 'It's only a house'? It's your home."

"Muvvy and I—" he spoke slowly, as though to deaf people—

"I say, Muvvy and I have a house. We don't have a home. Neither Muvvy nor I can make a home."

"Dearest, that's nonsense. Nonsense. You and Muvvy disgust me. Truly, dearest, you don't try."

Even her outrage did not move him. Setting his dish aside he merely asked how anyone could feel at home in a glorified goldfish bowl. The house had been built to make Muvvy's friends jealous. It would give them another twist of the knife to shrug the whole thing off at a profit, to abandon the most modern, talked-about house in the district for, say, an old vicarage or an early Victorian doctor's house in Caerifor.

"But Muvvy wouldn't ever accept this?"

"You don't know Muvvy. Why, as soon as she saw Edward's letter she told me to be sure to get my commission. She doesn't think Edward's got the money, in any case. Do you?"

"How should we know? He never writes to us."

The division in herself caused her voice to break, to show impatience and disgust and Ashley realised the extent of his bloomer. In order to cover himself, he began to use the false-innocent voice he normally used when telling lies to his wife when she knew he'd been with a woman clerk, reputed to be his mistress. "Would you like to see him again if he comes down, Aunty Micky?"

Mignon had recovered her balance. "The question is, dearest, does he want to see us? A man who can let years pass without sending a word, only a miserable printed Christmas card, isn't deeply interested in us, is he?"

Ashley, crestfallen and crushed, said, "He owes you everything, of course."

"Everything!" Mignon said vehemently. "After Evelyn died, then his father, there were only Arthur and I to turn to. His father's family wanted to ship him off to Canada. He didn't want to go so we kept him, housed him, educated him and then, to give him a start, Arthur pushed him on to the Inner Circle and he's been revolving there ever since and finding it less and less to his taste to remember those who pushed him on. In old-fashioned language, it's sheer ingratitude. I say it to you in confidence. I wouldn't want anyone else to know I cared."

Ashley had been found shallow and thoughtless and his thoughts of an easy deal, cheap when set beside such deeply-felt resentment and hurt. He tried to apologise; Mignon brushed him away. "It doesn't worry me as much as it used to. I washed my hands of the family years ago—Edward, Muvvy, even Nesta—the lot. They're all poor stuff and we should have guessed that a few years on the Inner Circle would have corrupted Edward and it was also to be foreseen, too, that eventually he'd want to come back here to show off the money he's picked up. 'Up to five thousand' and all that. He's thoroughly vulgar."

She glanced at Freddy for encouragement, but he was looking into space, greatly shocked and pained. It was beyond his understanding how his sister could say things which she'd probably regret within a few hours—was probably angry with herself for saying them even as she spoke.

* * * *

Ashley wasn't quite sure what was meant by 'The Inner Circle'. "Oh, don't you know that expression? It was Arthur's. He used to say that to get on in England you've got to get on the Inner Circle. He rather made it his life's work to push as many deserving people on as possible in order to counterbalance the nincompoops who were there by reason of birth and privilege. By Inner Circle he meant the groups revolving around the sources of patronage. Get in and you're in for life. You get named for commissions, select committees, privy this, privy that, until you haven't a moment to call your own. Once all the Inner Circle trains were filled with lords, baronets and pushing lawyers; now they're getting overcrowded with scientific dons and people like Edward with one foot on the academic treadmill and the other in what our father used to call 'the demi-mondi'. You know, social climbers with a bit of specialised knowledge and influential connections."

Without knowing it, Mignon had talked herself into a good humour and when Ashley asked how people could get on to the Inner Circle, she wiped her mouth and laughed. "But that's what everyone wants to know. The essential thing is to want to. Like Edward. He was a real C. P. Snow character—fascinated by power for its own sake—not to advance a cause or an ideal, but simply for the pleasure of seeing the wheels go round and being in the swim. You know the sort of thing—to see that casual remarks at a dinner party can alter the course of events, to be able to write small notes on the right crested paper recommending people for jobs. Even as a young boy he used to listen to Arthur's stories about Whitehall, about the behind-scenes activities—the usual things—until he was spellbound. Arthur loved all this, too, but he was troubled by a radical conscience. He could never really accept that things were conducted in just such a hole-and-corner manner. While Edward was fascinated by politics and power."

In a minor way, Ashley had the same obsession and said defensively, "But these things are fascinating, aren't they?"

Mignon, at her most radical, asked bleakly, "Why?" She blinked. "The mediocrities who rise to power! Their passionate devotion to their own small careers! An awful world."

Apropos of this, Ashley said he was just finishing Lord Rugden's memoirs, published in London that spring. "As far as I can see he never once had an original thought."

Mignon's laugh sounded like dry biscuits snapping. "How right you are. We used to know him fairly well before he was kicked upstairs. In those days he was Tony Ripplesdon, the Member for South Kent. A good-hearted bore. Arthur said he was the only man who could put a prayer-wheel out of business."

Ashley agreed that the man's style was heavy, leaden. "Aren't all books by public servants like that?" asked Mignon. "*Jottings of a Queen's Counsel*; *Thirty Years in Whitehall*; *Memoirs of a Diplomat*. Deadly dull," she said. "And why? Because well-spent lives are dull. That's the hardest fact to accept, bar none."

Ashley laughed appreciatively. It was the sort of sally which bound him to Mignon. She knew this. With a realist's cold double values she also knew that the fact Ashley thought this so witty was the price he had paid for having remained a small-time man during his forty years.

"And tell me," she said, giving him his money's worth, "does Lord Rugden write a preface in which he says he hopes to instruct the public?" Ashley nodded. "Does he assert that the public ought to know how public servants work?" He nodded again, deeply amused. "And the more the average man knows

14

about the way he is governed the better it will be for the world?" She was right again. "I told you, dearest. They've been saying that for years."

This seemed to prove to her that it was untrue and Ashley protested mildly. He thought civil servants were right to make the effort.

"Well, you would, dearest. You've got the virus, too."

"Virus?"

"You're a public figure who's lost his way. I don't know why."

"But to come back to my point. The public must be interested in such memoirs or they wouldn't sell well. The authors seem to make a packet."

"Oh, Ashley!" There was real reproach in her voice. "The fact that such books make money couldn't possibly justify them. And in any case, you're wrong. The author usually pays towards the cost of publication."

"Money doesn't justify them, I agree. But the fact that they're published proves there's a need for them."

Mignon looked blank. "What need?" She was being spiky, so Freddy cut in briskly, "People's curiosity, Micky. Ashley said so."

"What could a Lord Rugden tell you that was new? A nonentity like Tony Ripplesdon had nothing of the slightest interest to say. Life was dead in him. He was a rural hoddy-doddy with a taste for other people's wives. Essentially a nobody and nothing he said could be interesting because nothing he experienced interested him really. He's dull, dull, dull, not living. Then, you must remember, he was a public servant— like Arthur—and I agree with Lord Grey when he said such people should shut up because they're only executives not initiators of policy."

* * * *

Both Ashley and Freddy, in varying degrees, were surprised by Mignon's passionate disapproval. Why was she so over-bearing about such a small point? Then, without being asked, she gave them a clue when she recalled that on her husband's retirement it had been his ambition to write his memoirs and publish his diary. She said this as though it proved the absurd-

15

ity of both memoir-writers and diarists and added, "I told him there were enough books in the world without adding to the number."

"Yes, Micky, and you made a big mistake. It could have given Arthur an interest in his last years. As it was he was like a fish out of water."

"The task was beyond him. He was tired by the extra responsibility of the war years. He arrived here from London tired to the bone. He had nothing to say."

"He had lots of racy stories."

"Arthur liked a good story and he could tell one well. No one better. Such stories don't make a book, and, in any case, they weren't all instructive."

Ashley supported Freddy. Even, he felt, if the diaries had not been published they would have made a good family document. Ashley was always talking about the family as though he was part of a dynasty. She reflected a moment on this point while he went on, "I don't suppose we'll ever get another member of our family into the Cabinet secretariat again."

"Don't be pessimistic. You never know."

"Who then?"

"Well, who is there? There's you, dearest. Well, in Parliament, perhaps if things work out properly. There are no children anywhere around but Nesta's Patrick and he seems not to be over-shadowed with grey matter—well, if what his mother says is true—although he's got enough charm for three. So he could get the women's vote."

"I may marry yet," said Freddy. "Marriage might cure my insomnia."

Appreciative glances from Mignon and Ashley inspired him to develop the theme a little and after a time Ashley said, "But it's the married men who can't sleep, you know. That's what Uncle Arthur used to say."

Freddy sniffed happily. "A question of conscience, I dare say." He realised suddenly what he had said and looked anxiously at his sister.

To steer the talk into safer channels, Ashley asked whether his uncle's diaries and papers were still kept in the old place.

"In the same place," was Mignon's abstracted reply. "That cupboard in the little sitting-room is filled with them along

16

with letters, notes, newspaper-cuttings: the hoardings of a lifetime."

"I thought they were to go to the National Library."

"There was a plan ..." Mignon was deliberately offhand.

"Nobody ever looks at them?"

"Freddy used to."

"They tried my eyes," Freddy put in defensively as though found guilty of neglecting the flowers on someone's tomb. "The writing was so small and finicking. Mind you, those diaries have got good things in them. Very good things." Freddy tapped Ashley's elegant knee. "They'd interest you. I mean with your interest in politics. I wonder you've never had a glance through them yourself. Arthur was at the centre of things for years, at the top of his particular tree for half his working life. Something of the stirring times he lived through brushed off on him. He seemed to know everyone and my impression is that everyone liked him. His great secret of success was that he never lost the common touch."

"I often wonder—" and Mignon's grand manner covered a sinister doubt—"I often wonder how much people really cared for Arthur as Arthur. He was a public servant; he had access to secrets. People wanted him for what they could get out of him. Junior ministers were the worst—always hoping for someone to canvass for them higher up. Not that Arthur was taken in."

"I said Arthur remained down-to-earth. His success never changed him. That was the remarkable thing about him. He was never taken in by the great people he met. He kept that peasant directness. He saw a man for what he was and no amount of education or outer trapping could ever take him in. But he got a lot out of his life. He had a phenomenal capacity for hard work, for memorising relevant facts, for getting to the heart of a subject." Freddy began to spit a little in his fervour and had to wipe his mouth. His sister carried on where he left off almost in the same tone.

"God knows he worked hard enough at one time. His work was his life. Then some years before his retirement he lost interest. It was quite sudden and I never knew exactly why. The glamour wore off and yet in some way it was deeper, more personal—like an actor who gets tired of a role. He was always an intriguer and as close as an oyster and it was not

17

until some time after his retirement, one day when we were sitting together out here and we were looking out over the fields—as we might be now—and young Philip Hugh was ploughing the field by the road, that Arthur said, 'You know, the man who's spent his life ploughing the same twenty acres has had more real satisfaction out of his life than I've ever had. I envy the man who finds his life's work on his own doorstep.' He was in a very strange frame of mind, very disturbed, unsure of himself, perplexed, without confidence."

Ashley was fascinated and listened as though to someone returned from the dead. He wanted to know why this was so. Mignon thought a moment, stroking the arm of her chair reflectively. "Regrets, dearest, regrets. Personal matters and other things. A sense of failure as a human being. 'I feel like a man who's been playing the wrong game all his life.' That was another thing he said. I asked him what he meant. 'Micky, we gave our energies to a world that was dying on its feet. I did nothing to bring anything new to birth. To have been midwife to a corpse!'"

"Poor Arthur," said Freddy emotionally. "Poor man. How I pitied him."

Mignon lifted her head, her mouth set in a Churchillian pose: "I said: 'That's also my belief. We lost our way early on and I don't know where; and I have had my father's precept before me and failed.' And Arthur said, 'We were a defiled generation. We didn't have your father's pure strength. We didn't have his certainties or his pureness of heart.'"

"Do you think he was right?" Ashley asked.

"How can such statements ever be proved right?—or wrong? They come from a lifetime's experience, a lifetime's looking at things and feeling. Such summings-up have nothing in them for the person who hasn't lived out the whole thing. Certainly, for Arthur, his summing-up was right."

Ashley, fascinated by this cynical-tragical Mignon drawing on the unforeseen width and depth of her experience and the intensity of her memories, asked what his uncle had meant. But Mignon's face was running with tears, a tissue of converging streams of water ran over the russet cheeks and she could not or would not say what she knew and felt.

"Uncle Arthur must have had some satisfaction from his

life." It was a statement not a question. Mignon made no answer. "But didn't he?" Ashley asked.

"Oh, precious little, believe me. Even the disastrous business with Mrs. Benjamin ended in grief. Everything went. In retirement he had a chance to serve on local bodies, people were always asking him to lend his name and prestige but he refused."

Freddy said his impression of his brother-in-law in his last years was of a fish out of water. He pointed to the empty white bench a little distance from them and recalled how the man had sat there wearing the very hat which Freddy himself (having inherited it) then wore. With his hands clasped on his walking stick in front of him, Freddy tried to swell out his winnowed frame and even tilted the panama over his eyes in the way his brother-in-law had done; but his eyes, childishly entranced by his own acting, were worlds apart from the dead man's bright, sensual eyes with their doubts, their trouble, their disillusion.

"Yes, indeed, he sat here hour after hour staring ahead, straight ahead at the hills over there. With what intensity. I never saw anything like it before or since. You felt he wanted" —he groped for an image, a phrase—"to draw the mountains into his soul. To pull the rocks and stones down on his head."

Normally Freddy's phrases amused his sister; that day she said nothing. They were all silent and all close again as if the foolish incident over Edward's letter had never happened, although the matter was not forgotten. When it was time for Ashley to go he felt he could leave without leaving any scars behind.

* * * *

"Oh, but you can't go yet," Mignon said, "you haven't given us any local news of any kind. You're our only lifeline, our Reuters. Is it true what I hear about Davidge's?"

He could not control his delighted smile as he nodded. "It's a record for a Caerifor sale. £26,000."

Mignon and Freddy were at an age when inflated property prices seemed a personal threat; they could only hold up their hands in wonder. Ashley gave them another dark thrill: there was a possibility that Harbin, the Port Rydal emporium king, would be buying what he called "ten acres of bog and a tumbledown farmhouse" for just over £3,000. "For a weekend retreat," he added heartlessly. "They're going to start a new sport—watching the bog eat money. You sit in a deck chair on the nearest piece of drained land: you get the contractors in and you see £150 an acre vanish without a trace. The point of the game is not to lose your nerve."

He stood up—having amused them—and said brightly: "Rubbish sells itself these days, whether it's houses, furniture— or memoirs." This last with a wink at Mignon.

"Wish I could get a good price for some of the old junk here," she replied.

"Such as?"

"I don't know. What would fetch a good price, do you feel?"

"You're not serious, are you? I warn you I won't do a thing to help you. Break up this place? Never."

She turned her head to look up at him, noting his deep feeling after his coolness about his own home.

"Oh no. Never. This house is unique in many ways. It means something. People have really lived in this house and then your father's name still means something. It ought to go to the nation," he ended dramatically.

Mignon was often surprised by Ashley's judgements and asked what was so special about Swanquarter.

"Piece by piece, nothing. As a whole, everything. There can be few places like it in the country." Mignon was not impressed, and, when Ashley praised the atmosphere of the house, she cracked back: "You mean that's your wicked estate-agentese for a decaying place."

"No. Really. I'm serious."

"If someone would like to buy some of it, they're welcome. I'd spend it all on repairs."

Freddy hated to hear his sister talking so lightly about their home. If she sold the things inside to repair the outside, he said, she'd have nothing left but a pretty shell.

"Well, at least, it might be pleasanter to live in," Mignon retorted calmly.

Normally, Mignon never referred to money in a personal

way; it was taboo. No one was more surprised than Ashley to hear this gay talk of selling up the family heirlooms and just before he left, when he and Mignon were alone together, he asked her whether any unforeseen difficulty had cropped up.

"Not at all, dearest. We're no richer and no poorer today than we were yesterday. The difference is that Nesta's coming home and it would have been nice to have the place done up for her return. It looks woebegone, so uncared for."

Ashley looked up at the long building with its unusual gable-end windows and did not contradict her. Privately he had thought the house in poor condition for a long time but felt it was hardly within his power or right to say anything. "All the same, I'd think twice before I began selling things. Remember that the house is perfect as it is. To let anything go would spoil its particular charm for ever."

"Yet why hang on to things, dearest? Who's to come after Freddy and me? And who cares honestly? Nesta?"

Ashley mumbled something vague about not being short-sighted. Then an idea came: "If it's only a question of a couple of hundred pounds why couldn't I lend you the money?"

Mignon lifted her upper lip imperiously. "And when should I repay you? When, do you feel?"

"Does that matter?"

"To me, very much."

"You're wrong. What matters is that this house should be done up. The rest's just a quibble. Let me give you the money for it."

She became flustered and insisted that she had been talking wildly. He repeated his offer. He said how easily his money came. *He* begged to be allowed to help her; *she* insisted that her mood would pass, that she had overtired herself cleaning out her daughter's room and had reached the point where she could walk out of the place and never return. "What keeps me here but loyalty? So long as Freddy and I are here something of the old tradition lives on. I know it's already slipped away from life."

"It's your duty to keep the place going. In a way it's my duty to help you. For God's sake, take the money. Why not be simple and say yes for once?"

She continued to shake her head. "I'm touched. I'd rather not, dearest, if you don't mind too much. It's a personal quirk, perhaps, but it's what I feel."

He got into his car and lowered the window. "You're making a big mistake. Think about it." She leaned through the window to rearrange his lapel and tell him how young he looked in his new hat, but she did not reply to his remark.

*   *   *   *

Mignon sucked a back tooth thoughtfully. She supposed Ashley had made a couple of thousand pounds on the Davidge deal. "I've never known anyone make money so easily—and to be so generous."

Freddy agreed enthusiastically. "He's our best friend, Micky."

Mignon plumped up a cushion and leaned back. "He wants to lend us a couple of hundred to do up the house." Freddy looked up quickly, his breath held.... "Oh, but I refused. Of course. I felt it was wrong, don't you agree?" Freddy's face said, "No." She thought a moment. "I felt he was covering up his gaffe over Edward."

"He meant nothing bad, Micky."

"He saw, all the same, that we felt deeply about the matter."

There was a curious pause. "Micky, I hope you thanked him for his offer."

"Of course." But she remembered that she had spent more time refusing than in being grateful, so added, "I'll drop him a note of thanks, too."

Freddy asked why she had refused.

"Because we'd never be able to pay him back. Two hundred pounds is nothing to Ashley but it's a big sum for us. I hate borrowing, in any case, and think what our darlin' niece Muvvy would have said. The news would have been over the town in two days."

"Does Muvvy matter?"

"Think what a handle it would give her. She hates his coming here already."

Freddy wondered whether it might be possible to borrow the money and repay so much every week... Mignon waved the idea away. "By the time we'd repaid in full the house will need repainting again and so it'll go on for ever and ever and ever."

"Yes, but meanwhile the house would have been painted once."

"We've managed very well up to now without any outside help and you know it well, Freddy. Neither of us has got much capital left but I'm determined that we'll get by without anyone's help. In any case, I hate putting our friendship on a mercenary basis. Ashley's visits mean far more to me than new paint on the doors. As it is he's always giving us things in a discreet way. His tact is perfect but a loan of £200 is too much. Believe me, Freddy,"—she wagged a finger at him like an evangelist—"believe me if we once got used to easy money we'd be *ruined*. Ruined! We'd want more and more. Yes, Freddy, we would. And the day might come when he'd resent our wanting his money and he'd stop calling and, frankly, that would hurt me far more."

How an isolated loan could corrupt them was not clear to Freddy and he found Mignon's refusal high-handed.

From under his brother-in-law's ancient panama Freddy was looking at his sister, admiring but perplexed. She was always springing surprises on him and he found himself staring at her as though she had been a new acquaintance. Seated opposite him in the old wicker chair, she had half-turned her head upwards towards the spot in the ivy above their heads where sparrows were making a lot of noise. As she turned, Freddy was struck by a sudden movement of truth and generosity in her face; it was a moment when twenty years fell away.

A kind of youth lingered mysteriously in Mignon and visited her face in sudden moments of excitement, absorption or rapturous recollection. Life's perplexities vanished; the charm of tolerance and achievement remained.

They were both reminiscences of their father: stern, Wordsworthian foreheads sprung with wiry and turbulent hair; deeply-set, changing eyes that seemed at times to have a tissue of veils across them and, at others, stood out brilliantly; long, slightly aquiline noses and distinctively full, lopsided mouths which appeared to close with difficulty over uneven, unstopped teeth; and both patrician in the American way with corded necks and diminished jawlines accentuating the fullness of the lobes of the ears. As they went indoors together the slope of their shoulders and the narrowness of their backs were identical. They seemed to have weathered in exactly the same way.

3

MIGNON WASTES HER CREDIT

THE same day, that afternoon, Ashley again called to offer them a cheque for £250 as an outright gift.

Freddy had hardly had time to form a first syllable of thanks before Mignon, with a strange, shocked gesture—as though someone had put his hand on her knee—repelled—there was no other word—the offer. Freddy was horrified. Mignon's manner, her expression, were both capable of wounding the man to the soul—and did so. He blushed and looked confused as though caught out in a shameful thing, as though, after years of acceptance as an equal, he had betrayed an inferior origin. The eyes—and they were good eyes, very honest and uncalculating—which had shone with such pleasure, scaled over with hurt. Freddy tried to protect Ashley and, at the same time, save Mignon from her own folly, but his sister ignored him. She was too busy making it absolutely clear to Ashley, Freddy, herself and the world at large that she wanted help from no one—not even Ashley. All he could say was, "But why?" An outsider would have thought he was asking for a loan.

"Because Freddy and I have talked the matter over and we've decided we could never pay back the money." Freddy tried to explain that he had never agreed to this but Ashley was himself too anxious to get in his point. "I'm giving you the money. I want to give it to you. Please listen to me."

"Unthinkable. Unthinkable. It's terribly kind of you, dearest, and we're more grateful than you know but ... not now.

"I admit there are difficulties," she added ambiguously, "but Freddy and I will manage somehow without fuss and bother."

Ashley had committed himself to the gift. His vanity, his idea of himself was involved as well as his pleasure.

It became clear that to refuse was also to hurt so Mignon started to invent: Freddy and she were no longer young, there were difficulties, there was so much involved and, in any case, she couldn't have the house cluttered up during her daughter's visit.

Ashley raised his arms in exasperation.

"Oh, believe me, dearest, we don't want to say no to your offer. We'll think about it."

"You won't," he retorted petulantly. "I know you won't. You're fibbing. Politely, of course."

"Ashley, I'm not fibbing. I mean what I say. Please don't talk like that."

They tried to smile at one another but both failed.

"And what do you think?" Ashley addressed Freddy.

"Ah," he replied quickly, "Micky decides." He was afraid to say more but his eyes were tragic for he could see Micky wasting her credit with Ashley, wildly, stupidly, unnecessarily. Ashley had been as set on making his gift as most people are on having a good time; not to have seen this was to fail to respond to human goodness.

As a last gambit, Ashley said: "The age of gold won't last, as I've repeatedly told you. If you don't benefit now you never will." His failure to smile took away some of the happiness of the remark and then they were suddenly becalmed, Mignon in obstinacy, Ashley in exhaustion and Freddy in gloom. Ashley, who had sat down across the table from Mignon, impulsively pushed the cheque towards her. "Here. Take it. You're being shortsighted. Think about it and know that it's yours."

This she reluctantly accepted. "Yes, Ashley. We'll think about it. It's terribly nice of you."

Then he retreated, feeling that silence and second thoughts were the better advocates. Mignon was left at the front door holding the buff cheque which she could not help examining helplessly as though it were a sentence of some severity.

Freddy stood behind her (they were both in the hall) and she saw little but disapproval in his manner.

"I know you want me to accept it, don't you, Freddy? I can't. It's rather unkind to force people to accept charity when they'd rather not."

"That's not charity," Freddy said, pointing to the cheque.

"What else but? Ashley knows we've hardly got a bean."

"It's still not charity."

Freddy disagreed entirely with his sister's approach and said

26

sinisterly: "You know it's harder to accept a gift gracefully than to give. Ashley wants us to share his abundance."

Like a lizard's tongue darting out to pick up a fly, Mignon cried, "Abundance from dishonest sales. That's about all *that* is! False values. Fake prices. I don't like money earned that way."

Freddy was shattered by this oblique attack on Ashley himself but contented himself with saying, "But you're raising a new issue now."

"I don't like to be beholden."

"Oh, Micky—" the words were forced from him—"you're just being vain." He insisted. "Yes, it's a form of vanity. You call it pride but it's vanity. No one will think more of you for refusing that cheque. Even if Muvvy sends a typed letter to every house in Caerifor no one could find anything wrong in accepting money for such a purpose."

Freddy's vehemence had an old-fashioned ring, but Mignon knew he was sincere. "The things you've said in the last five minutes are dotty things, silly things, the sort of things you ought to wake up in the middle of the night and blush about. Don't you see it's an art to accept such a rich present? Ashley was a most perfect, a most gentlemanly donor. He's done everything to make you feel the gift was a tribute to the old family home."

Mignon had never thought of this. "He's always giving us things... What do we give him in return? It makes me feel so beholden."

"Beholden to Ashley? Our best friend, the only relative we can ever talk to?" His voice was disgust itself.

Mignon sniffed, said nothing, and went on nursing the cheque awkwardly. Freddy said no more either; his courage had given out. The cheque was eventually placed in a small drawer and Mignon began to wonder whether there was any other way to raise enough money to by-pass the loan. To refuse £250 and then spend hours nail-biting on possible ways of raising the same amount was cockeyed; and Freddy told her so. He heard her going round the house, opening and shutting windows and he knew she was examining the woodwork. She found the tour depressing and was haggard when she sat down near him. They understood one another perfectly. No one needed to speak. Yet what to do? She and Freddy had not enough ready cash to do the work and were too old to attempt the job. The problem without a lump sum of money was intolerable.

In time, worrying about the loan gave way to worry about Ashley who did not call for over a week. Either (she told herself) he was too busy or he was offended. She missed the visits; she missed his little bits of news; she missed the sight and sound of a younger person. She missed their only real contact with the outside world.

* * * *

She went into Caerifor to see him. When she arrived at Ashley's office he was out. One of the surveyors, Randall, a mannerly, rather gushing man, invited her into his room and they chatted amiably about this and that until Mignon noticed a shopping basket on a sidetable with a couple of packages in it. Did that mean that her niece was around? Randall said Mrs. Corbett had left the basket there while she went to the dentist. She was expected back shortly. The conversation resumed but with less verve on Mignon's part; the idea of meeting her niece was disagreeable to her.

They did not meet because Muvvy heard her aunt's voice as she entered the office. Then, indiscreetly, she put her head to the glass-panelled door to hear what was being said inside. Mignon saw this equivocal outline and stopped in mid-sentence; had Randall not been there she would have called out. Randall, realising what was afoot, blushed, fiddled with his papers, tried to create a diversion. Then the niece went away without her basket, leaving Mignon and Randall to stare at one another in unholy embarrassment.

Randall's nerve broke first: "Wasn't that Mrs. Corbett?"

"It seemed so."

"She must have thought you were a client." Randall knew it was impossible to mistake Mignon's voice and accents; he knew the old lady was being avoided; yet he had to make an excuse. Mignon said sharply: "Why behave as though she had something to hide?"

Randall started the conversation again, but by the time Ash-

28

ley came, the atmosphere in the office was so odd—Randall so flustered and Mignon so put out—that he thought they'd been quarrelling.

"Not a bit of it," Mignon said inside Ashley's own room. "It's Muvvy. Why is she avoiding me?"

Ashley feigned a mild surprise.

"A most unpleasant thing happened." Mignon recounted the incident and Ashley said Mignon had been mistaken for a client.

"That I'll never believe."

Ashley raised his shoulders wearily. "You know Muvvy as well as I do. Her actions aren't entirely rational."

"I call it rude. Insulting."

"If she did snub you in that way, I agree. Anyway, forget Muvvy. How are you?"

Mignon pulled off her gloves and set them down together on the glass-topped table. "Rather humble and contrite, if the truth were known."

"Why? Have you burned one of Freddy's manuscripts?"

"I've been worrying about our last conversation."

"Oh?"

"Well, when you didn't turn up I thought you must have found me hard and ungrateful. I seemed so spiky. So ungenerous."

"Oh, forget it. I was cross. Sure, I was cross that you were so obstinate. I was more hurt than you'd believe. It was just as though you'd put up a barrier between us."

She saw he was not exaggerating. "But that's rubbish, Ashley. Freddy and I think your discretion was perfect. Most, most touching. Terribly nice. We have this horror of imposing ourselves. Please don't bear us any ill-will."

"You know I never bear ill-will," he said rather falsely, for he was still resentful. "I understand your attitude perfectly. Although I find it hard that, after all the years we've been related, you should be afraid to impose. What are friends and relations for but to give a helping hand? But as you don't want my little gift, that's that. You can burn the cheque."

And as he said that, she knew she had made a mistake. The lovely £250 had gone for ever. Her knees took the blow; her throat felt it; there was a pricking of incipient tears in her eyes.

29

The unreal debate about the morality of accepting the gift ended abruptly and she wanted the money as she had never (she believed) wanted anything else. Like an apple of luscious aspect swinging away into the blue, its departure dazzled, blinded, overwhelmed; and Ashley knew this, but made no effort to bring it back. He would be cruel, too.

He casually opened a drawer and brought out another letter from the suddenly communicative Edward in which he announced his plans for visiting Caerifor.

"Muvvy and I are putting them up and she thought you might like to come down to have a meal with us."

"That would be fine."

"So you'll come?"

"Yes. Oh, yes. We'll come."

He promised to keep them informed of arrangements and, as he spoke, misinterpreted her subdued face, the drooping mouth. "Do you mind that we have them to stay with us?"

She asked why she should mind. Ashley said: "You and Freddy have strong feelings about Edward—which are understandable—but Muvvy and I are indifferent. You understand that? We never expected anything of Edward."

Ashley struck blood.

"Expected anything? What did we expect?" Her fury was instant, uncontrollable, but he brushed her aside.

"I know what you mean. I know you expected nothing in the material sense. I mean that you feel neglected and cold-shouldered. You're entitled to feel this."

"Oh, Ashley, how could you speak of our expecting anything? That's the last word to use. You know we're not in the least grasping or self-seeking. Wait a moment. Please. Let me explain. What we feel deeply is that Edward has shown a complete lack of feeling or human warmth. Even you must see that."

"But you won't mind meeting them?"

She controlled herself. "We've nothing to be ashamed of. Perhaps, even, Edward would like to visit us. After all, our home was his for many years."

"That's entirely up to you."

Ashley's voice held no hint of helpfulness. He felt cold towards Mignon, partly because he was busy, partly because he was still furious with her for refusing his gift. Mignon thought he was behaving abominably; he seemed incapable of making the slightest allowance for her feelings.

They were of two completely different generations in their attitude to money. To Mignon it was still partly taboo; to Ashley the give and take of money had no more about it than the buying and selling of bread. Money had lost its magic years ago. And so he sat before her: handsome, well-tailored and business-like. His coldness gave his mouth a certain tautness and meanness, the mouth of a person who is avenging an insult.

Back home, Mignon ranted to Freddy. "I don't know what's come over him. The letters from Edward seem to have changed him. I suddenly saw him in a new light: calculating, common, a shallow person. He never attached any importance to what other people feel as though he can't understand delicacy or doubt. If it's something that can be bought or sold then it's good. God knows I think Muvvy is the dreaded end as a human being, but there are times when I think she's got a point of view, too, so far as Ashley is concerned." She almost spat with temper. "And think, dearest, we're being invited to meet Edward as though he were some sort of public figure we'd heard on the radio. It's so pathetically provincial and ignorant. I've never been so put out."

Freddy didn't know what to say. He was just hoping miserably that her anger would expend itself when the most surprising thing happened: Mignon sat down and began to cry. To see his sister crying from anger and disappointment was so outside Freddy's experience that his mouth dropped open. "You feel quite well, Micky?" She turned her head away. "Can I get you anything?"

She replied haughtily, "I'm perfectly well."

They were embarrassed into silence. She wiped her nose harshly and went into the kitchen where, in her agitation, she trod on Ianto's food-dish and broke it. "Damn and blast," she shouted.

When he went in to join her she turned towards him sharply. "It really wouldn't be much for you to prepare the tea once in a while."

31

He protested. How was he to know which bus she meant to take home? Ah, she retorted scornfully, there were so many! Freddy excused himself. He had no idea his sister felt unwell.

"I'm perfectly well. I'm cross and humiliated, that's all. I can see that everyone, even Ashley, lets us down in the end. It's awful to be the old, poor relations, especially if you've got some pride. Everyone feels you can be taken for granted. Have some money! Come to dinner! Meet Edward! Nobody thinks we've our own feelings. And even Ashley, the person I thought we knew really well, can behave like this. And doesn't bother to hide the fact that Edward is only another business deal."

Freddy would not accept this. Mignon said the only thing that interested Ashley and Muvvy was money. "They quarrel about everything else but they agree on money. They worship it. They respect it. And you watch: they'll butter up Edward and try to get all they can out of him."

"If you feel like that we hadn't better meet Edward or go to any party for him."

"I probably won't go, in any case."

Suddenly, Freddy took off his glasses and covered his eyes with the palms of his hands: a little trick for 'relaxing his eyes'. He uncovered his eyes and stared at Mignon myopically. "How I hate to see you making yourself ill over these things. Whatever happens, Micky," he put his glasses on again and focussed her severely, "we've got nothing to be ashamed about. We've done our duty. I want us to keep our dignity, too. It pains me far more to see you give way under these pricks than to suffer from them. Of course thoughtless people will always give you small pricks."

"Small!"

"What else are they?" He spoke softly, compassionately. "Think a moment. If Edward comes what can he do or say now that will make any difference to us? There's nothing he can do to alter either *your* life or mine or bring us much happiness or unhappiness. All that's past history. What is more important still is that we're at an age when we can leave the world to look after itself. This is the time to make our peace with the world and with ourselves and make our own souls."

"Oh, tosh. The world made my soul years ago. And yours, too."

Freddy looked at her comfortably. "The great difference between us is that I'm not satisfied with mine."

"That's your burden."

"I daresay, Micky."

In trying to sound reasonable and holy like crazy (way above the battle) Freddy irritated his sister, who thought him smug. "What exactly do you mean by 'making a soul'?"

"If you don't know what I mean at our advanced ages I'll never be able to tell you."

"They're all words, like free will and predestination and redemption. They don't mean anything at all. Free to do what? Predestined for what? Redeemed from what? My idea of a God of love is one who apologises for the sad, sorry mess he's made of the world. Making my soul, indeed!"

"Perhaps making your soul would include forgiving or accepting the sad and sorry mess man has made of the world and accepting your part in it."

"That's one thing you won't get from me. Looking back on a fairly long life I see only one thing very clearly: that for most of the time I've been dependent on the whims and fancies of others—from shouting at the Tories during Dadda's elections to making your tea after a tiring afternoon in town."

"Dadda never made you shout at the Tories. What a thing to say!"

"Maybe not, but I was conditioned by my upbringing. There wasn't much free will there. That's why I say the world made my soul years ago. I'm formed by circumstances which no longer exist; by people who died years ago; by events I've forgotten. Those are the things which made my soul and I'm damned if I'm going to pretend that I can do much with the mess now. I accept it because I have to, not because I see any shape or purpose in it, believe me."

"Your attitude makes your life more bitter."

"Well, that's *my* burden."

They supped their tea angrily and haughtily, both sniffing virtuously and looking askance at the other (for it was months since they'd had such a fundamental breach) and neither able to laugh. The evening might have passed in this half-war had not the post office rung up with a telegram from Nesta saying that Nesta and Patrick, having reached Venice, were on

33

their way to Geneva. No date for their arrival in London was given.

The regret that the house had not been redecorated for their arrival moved Mignon to think of other things apart from her recent humiliations. Freddy said the only solution was to accept Ashley's gift. Mignon started but kept silent. Freddy pressed his point and she replied: "I don't think we can depend on that money any more. Ashley more or less withdrew it this afternoon." She added hastily, "Not in so many words. He was on his high horse and told me to burn the cheque."

"In such a hard way?" Freddy's eyes were enormous.

"He simply turned his back on the whole thing. I knew by his voice the offer was dead."

"You offended him."

"Seems so."

"What a dreadful pity. I don't mean about the money only."

"I agree. I was wrong."

"You must learn to accept gifts nicely," Freddy began until she cut him short with a harsh, "Rubbish! I don't want to be beholden to anyone. Anyone. We'll keep our self-respect."

He watched her closely and she went on defiantly: "We'll get along and we'll manage the repairs on our own. Far better to keep a seemly distance in such matters, don't you feel?" Another Freddy-ish silence. "In any case, Nesta must understand our position. She won't be here for ever and if she doesn't like it she can clear out."

Freddy wondered how long she would stay. As long as it took to get Patrick into some university? Mignon thought until Christmas.

"Of course, she's completely out of touch with reality. There won't be a single university with a place vacant now. Anything that happens will have to be for next autumn. She's in such a dream and no one bothers to explain anything to her."

Freddy wondered whether Nesta and Edward, both returning to their old country at more or less the same time, would meet.

"Lovely thought." Quite abruptly the idea of this made Mignon laugh. On the one hand, there was the long-lost Edward hoping for a house on the cheap (along with Ashley hoping for a good sale); and, on the other, was Nesta wander-

34

ing around Europe without a clue about anything. What a collection they made!

"Family relationships, my foot. Self-interest dictates everything, don't you feel? Sordid little arrangements." That was Mignon's summing up: "Sordid little arrangements." She decided it was absurd to worry about such people or their designs. It satisfied her grand manner to have this proof of her invulnerability even though she had cried with vexation.

Other people, she told herself, would have been pettish or distant. She would show nothing because she had grown indifferent. People were like animals; they changed from day to day and the thoughts of yesterday were no more than the skin the lizard puts off in the spring. Double-faced animals, sly, self-seeking but human only in their boring sententiousness and censoriousness, their desperate attempts and pretences at morality and discipline. Expecting nothing, nothing could hurt her and hence (she told herself) her hardness.

"People have no connecting principles of any kind," she said to Freddy. "Has that ever struck you? They say one thing today and another thing tomorrow. It's hardly worth one's time listening to them. They're all acting out a part."

It was a resolution of the problem which pleased her enormously. She summed up grandly: "One thing is sure, Freddy. We've battled on well enough together, don't you feel? That's about as much as we can expect from life at our age. Whatever these people do they can't really alter our way of life or thinking or contribute anything to our hopes. And we'll show wisdom by not expecting anything. Don't you agree?"

Freddy had said more or less the same thing only a couple of hours before, but when he heard the same sentiments from his sister he was not convinced. Certainly such a point of view offered a nice, comfortable solution, a sort of dream of indifference and invulnerability, but they were human beings, dependent largely for their joys and sorrows on their own kind; and they were suffering because of this and Freddy knew it. He also knew that if great joy entered their lives they would rise to this, too.

Why, he suddenly thought with a shock, joy would transfigure them as much as when they were twenty.

4

THE DIVIDED ESTATE

ASHLEY never forgave Mignon for refusing his gift. To show his disapproval and, perhaps, to let a little air into their relations, he stopped calling at the farm. Mignon knew he was huffed but was sure he would relent for, with all his faults, he never bore grudges for long. In the meantime his boycott deprived her of an up-to-date account of plans for Edward's visit. To satisfy her curiosity Mignon was obliged to resort to Effie Johns, a well-placed observer of local life, whose daughter was supposed to be one of Muvvy Corbett's close friends.

Effie Johns had lived in partial retirement for years but knew more of the ins and outs of Caerifor than a thousand more active people. Having developed a sophisticated news sense she had lost interest in the Edward saga for the time being. He was coming, the date was fixed, so the story would become interesting again once he arrived and everyone had a chance to see him. In the meantime there was a far more significant matter to hiss into Mignon's face as they sat together near the bay window of Effie's parlour.

"So that's what *I* was told," she said, replacing the lace curtain which she had just slightly deranged to watch a strange couple pass down the street. "There's this young, very attractive woman, the wife of someone in the County Planning Department, and she and Ashley have been seeing a good deal of one another on the sly. Until the husband came home one day, caught them in bed and is suing for divorce."

Mignon still had the mud from Swanquarter on her Mrs. Baldwin shoes and still had a kind of rural innocence in her thinking. What she heard could not be true. Shock, disbelief and instincts of generosity moved in waves across her face while Effie Johns went on blandly, "And there are two young children, who are very fond of Ashley, call him uncle and that sort of thing. Ashley used to call when the husband was there. On Council business, naturally."

There was a lot more circumstantial evidence which sounded wickedly true, yet Mignon could not accept it. She knew Ashley had got a reputation as a lady-killer (no difficult task in the narrow annals of middle class Castivorians) and his friendship with the young couple had been misinterpreted.

"The curious thing," Effie Johns went on, "is that Muvvy doesn't know. Yet. But I guarantee she'll be told and then there'll be fat in the fire. Of course, I haven't told a soul but you. I know how close you are to Ashley."

"He's a dear friend," Mignon said loyally, but flustered and afraid.

"He's a man I've greatly admired. A self-made man who's never grown above himself," was Effie's verdict. And she continued to praise Ashley while supervising the laying of the tea table, occasionally breaking the thread of her talk to advise or admonish the ancient housekeeper. "I always feared the marriage between them would go on the rocks (Use the yellow plate for the cake, dear!) and it's a miracle it's lasted so long. They're a well-known case (Lady Benson-Williams likes lots of butter on her toast); a well-known case. In my opinion neither of them has tried."

"I believe I agree with you, dearest."

Mignon had to tell Freddy as soon as she got home. Without the stage effects of Effie Johns' drawing-room—the heavy lace curtains, the fantastic Victorian ornaments, the birds and fruit under glass, the penumbra like a nicely cooked fruit cake —and without the Effie Johns voice, shocked and hollow, and the Effie Johns eyes, large and calculating, the story seemed improbably dramatic. Freddy was not, in any case, a good listener: he had to be dragged back from golden-tinted worlds of his own—his natural habitat—and it took minutes of question and answer to establish him in the here and now where such a story could hope to have effect. He promptly dismissed it as a wicked rumour and gave Mignon a lesson in loyalty: "Ashley would never deliberately break up a young family with babies. Never. Poor Ashley, what has he done to attract that sort of reputation? Why do people say such things?"

Once Freddy gave his mind to a problem he adumbrated its

37

many aspects with a ponderous openness of mind worthy of Henry James; but most of all he had his own vision of Ashley, built up after years of friendship, and he could not see him, a rich, successful, potent man, preying on a young ménage with a view to stealing the wife from her husband and children. Mignon agreed that such a thing was unlikely but she had knowledge of the destructiveness of the sexual drive, which was the most unknowable thing in any person. "If it ever turns out to be true I shall say one thing in Ashley's favour : he's married to that arch-bitch Muvvy which should explain everything. I don't think I've ever understood how a good-looking, virile man like Ashley could ever have saddled himself with such a drear. A drear of the first water."

A thought struck her. "It would, of course, be awkward if this scandal broke just as Edward and his wife arrived. And with all Caerifor invited to meet them at a buffet supper."

Freddy, who had already wandered back into his own world, came to with a start. "What's all this?"

"A big reception to meet our distinguished cousin the historian, dearest. We're not forgotten. I'm told by Effie we'll get an invitation and on the same terms as Commander and Mrs. Truthin and the Town Clerk of Caerifor."

* * * *

In time, they received the gold-edged invitation card marked R.S.V.P.—which made Mignon crackle with irritation; and a day or so later Ashley made his first call for a long time. Despite themselves, the old people could not forget the rumour and their guilt about it gave them a strange half-smile of anticipation, as though they expected him to confess. Ashley had got over his pique and looked well after a short fishing holiday. He had stayed at a farmhouse and was rhapsodic about the virtues of the simple life, about bacon on the hook and log fires in the evening.

He had brought some trout and hoped Mignon would cook them for him as his wife, who hated fish smells in the house, refused to do so. Towards midday they went into the kitchen and while Mignon prepared the vegetables Ashley gutted the trout. With an old apron around his middle, he was absorption

38

itself, working away peacefully like a good, domestic animal, not at all like the villain of a bedroom farce.

Freddy and Mignon enjoyed the fish even more than Ashley and were lavish in their thanks; but the way they watched him from the corners of their eyes, and the way they were suddenly startled into speech as though recalled from some troubling obsession struck Ashley unpleasantly. Mignon rattled on about Nesta and her not writing and then went on to Edward's party.

"Muvvy won't expect us to reply to her invitation, will she, dearest? She knows we'll turn up."

"Don't know why she sent one to you," Ashley replied. "She tends to overdo the formalities on these occasions."

There was a pause. "Who prints your cards?" Mignon asked drily. He told her. "That firm must be making a small fortune out of you if Muvvy sends out cards for a simple little supper. I thought you only used cards these days when something really grand was under way."

Ashley looked up artlessly. "It'll be quite a big do. We thought Edward's coming ought to be marked. The return of the native. You know what I mean."

"Quite."

"Anyway, don't be put off by the cards. You know Muvvy as well as I do. Don't mistake the formula for the good heart behind it."

Was that the remark of a man who had betrayed his wife with Mrs. X? Mignon thought, and retorted darkly, "I know Muvvy."

Ashley went away troubled.

Freddy, who knew his sister's storm signals, looked at her very doubtfully after Ashley had gone. Something was on the way, he knew, and without realising what he was doing acted as conductor to the lightning. He hated fuss of any kind and said he preferred not to go to the party if it were too formal. This general sort of remark brought the stunning reply, "We're not going. I never meant to. On the day itself, we'll both be ill. A touch of food-poisoning or something that will keep us both out of circulation for a couple of days."

Although not above a little mild malingering when it suited him, Freddy had always invented on the spur of the moment. Planned malingering seemed sinister and could tempt fate to inflict the imagined sickness with real force. Not to worry, said Mignon; she would do all the talking. "You'll simply stay in bed so that I can show you to Ashley. He's sure to call. I'll totter round looking martyred with my hair dishevelled."

Mignon was so thrilled to have thought up this simple 'one in the eye' for her niece that she smoked a cigarette. She was an incorrigible amateur when she smoked, whiffing away like a schoolgirl and finding scores of imaginary pieces of tobacco on her lower lip. Inspired by the cigarette she told Freddy her counter-plan: she would invite Edward and his wife to the farm. She was sure Muvvy would refuse to come, but even if she did not Mignon would meet Edward on her own ground and not in the role of demoded elder among the Chamber of Trade slickies.

Freddy went away, cracking his knuckles in agitation and wishing his sister had a simpler nature. "Oh, dear, these small things that get her!"

Ashley called and in the course of his conversation said thirty-five people had accepted invitations and, he added, there were to be four kinds of wine. Mignon felt these remarks came from his 'undeveloped' side and was embarrassed. Once alone with her brother she chewed the facts over.

"Four kinds of wine, Freddy." A significant silence. "Buffet supper for thirty-five." Another silence. "Here's two less already." A slightly longer silence. "Tell me, when we gave our receptions in Rutland Gate how many wines were there? Did you ever count them? Oh my God, these provincial lives. What do they know about anything?"

Freddy protested against her sneering and Mignon cried back, "Don't think I'm jealous of Muvvy. What gets my goat is the sheer impertinence of the whole thing. The colossal conceit, don't you feel?"

"It's unworthy of you, Micky. Laugh at the whole thing. Vanity Fair was never worth taking seriously."

"But I can't get over the colossal cheek of it: the gold-edged cards, the four kinds of wine, the buffet supper for thirty-five. And what is it all for, after all? A damned business deal. There's no more real feeling in it than in a dead chicken."

The day before the party Mignon was less angry because she could act and seizing the telephone as though it had been a gun, she told Ashley they were both ill and both needed medicine. As might have been expected, Ashley brought out the medicine himself and sat on a chair by the side of Freddy's bed. What had they eaten? Would they be fit by the next evening? Mignon, who was walking around in a dressing-gown with a cup of thyme infusion in one hand, was pessimistic. She went through all the meals of the day before and then spoke of the minute amounts they'd been able to keep down. Freddy grinned artlessly over the bedclothes and watched her arrange in a bowl the fruit which Ashley had brought them. When he rushed away again—still not sure whether their illness was diplomatic—the oranges, bananas and grapes remained behind to reproach them.

"I feel rather bad about the fruit," Mignon said. "Damn."

Freddy's contrition was deeply felt. "We've nothing against Ashley, have we?"

"Of course not. That's why I feel so bad."

To ease her conscience, she telephoned Ashley to say how much his kindness meant to them; how they would enjoy the fruit; how hard they were trying to get better.

In fact, Ashley's goodness, his niceness, his simplicity of heart, almost made them change their minds. This melting mood lasted until Mignon realised that Muvvy herself had not telephoned. "Shows you how much she thinks of us, don't you feel? She probably thinks we're putting the whole thing on."

"Well, my dear girl, what else are we doing?" Freddy turned pink with astonishment.

* * * *

But Edward rang. Almost the first thing he did on reaching the Corbetts was to ring up to ask how the invalids were.

By the ease, the unhurried richness of his voice, Mignon could see that his long absence called for no explanation. He might have seen them the day before.

"I doubt if we'll be well enough by tomorrow. It's risky to play around at our age, you know. To put it bluntly, Freddy and I have the squits and we couldn't meet Muvvy's sophisticated friends in that state, could we?"

"You haven't changed," he replied, the line shaking with his fat laughter.

"Why should I change, dearest? We're always the same. A bit more wintry than when you were last here, I suppose."

"Do your best to come. It might be good fun. What odds if you have the squits?"

"Not to you, dearest. You'll take us as we are. Is Muvvy like that? As it is she's ashamed of us. Imagine how she'd suffer if her poor, old, broken-down relations kept jumping up to go to the loo."

Edward laughed again although he was embarrassed. Mignon asked coolly, "When are you coming here? Come to lunch tomorrow and bring Muvvy and Ashley if they want to come. Fine. We'll expect you."

The conversation ended there.

"I don't suppose it's ever struck him that we feel vexed," Mignon said. She was thoughtful. Despite the incredible casualness of her nephew, hearing his voice had brought her great pleasure and it had essentially been the voice of a successful and friendly person.

She jumped up. "And now to think up the menu. We must give Edward something special. Roast lamb and onion sauce," she said. "Edward's favourite meal." She glided away into the kitchen and shortly afterwards went out to see what the local butcher could offer. She spent the evening preparing the meal, humming and vocalising tunelessly at the same time. She was too busy to stop to speak to Rohama Lloyd when Rohama came over for her evening journey for water. In any case, she didn't want Rohama to know what was happening.

Rohama came over for water twice a day although she had a supply of her own, because she maintained the Swanquarter water was better. Certainly, in the hot weather it was cooler because it rose from a great depth. Rohama was a kind of stepdaughter to Mignon, the child of a liaison between Mignon's husband and a Port Rydal woman known, like eighteenth-century actresses, simply as Mrs. Benjamin.

Under the terms of the Benson-Williams will Rohama had inherited a small farm attached to Swanquarter, which had been farmed with the larger holding for many years. She had taken possession of her legacy on attaining the age of twenty-five to the great scandal of the old people who would have bought her out had they had the money. The farm, with the fanciful name of Caebarcut, the kite's field, was too near Swanquarter for the old people to ignore Rohama entirely and a viable sort of relationship had gradually grown up between the two households. Rohama had arrived determined to be friendly. She had no relations of her own living near and longed to be accepted as part of a family. When she saw how neglected the old people were she had grown to feel responsible for them and took an interest in their wellbeing that was not always well received by Mignon for whom the Benjamin episode and the division of the estate were vivid realities. She was often prickly and resentful.

The circumstances in which the estate was divided were not happy. Mignon, Freddy and Nesta were betrayed in word and deed by Sir Arthur into thinking that Rohama had been left some money in trust. Instead he left her one-third of the estate and although everyone had been shaken by this decision there was nothing that could be done. There was vague talk of fighting the will and its conditions, which laid down that neither party could sell any part of the estate without the consent of the other, but Mignon wisely decided that legal charges would have taken what remained. The real grief of the will was not that Sir Arthur had remembered his daughter by Mrs. Benjamin but that he had given her land which, in the family's opinion, was not morally his. Swanquarter had come down from the Roberts family and had eventually been divided equally between Mignon and Freddy, the last remaining children. Then Freddy sold out his share to his brother-in-law at a generous price at a time when farms in that part of the world were not making much. Sir Arthur already had joint ownership of the other half and paid off the mortgage which went with it. In terms of cash he more than did his share in holding the place together, since their farming had been wacky for years and the County Agricultural Committee took over most of the land during the war; but Mignon maintained he had no right to tie them up with Rohama.

When the newly-married Rohama and her husband arrived to take up their share both failed to appreciate the real nature of their position and approached Mignon with the openness and freedom—the cheekiness even—of those who feel their lives are charmed. Rohama was well aware of her origins and had come to the conclusion that as neither she nor Mignon were guilty of any crime there was no reason why they could not be friendly. She could not understand why the brother and sister were not more natural and free with her and yet she did everything she could do for them.

*　*　*　*

On the day of the Lloyd-Ballantyne visit, she went over for water in the late morning and while her buckets filled under the spout ran up the steps towards the kitchen carrying a bowl of blackberries. The kitchen door was open, the kitchen itself was empty but saucepans simmered, meat spat in the oven, fruit and cheese were arranged on the dresser. It was clear that a more elaborate midday meal was planned than usual.

All Rohama's sense of injustice at the way she was kept out of the old people's lives rose in her as she saw an array of silverware for six people, polished and inviting on a tray. She set down the bowl and looked around, uncertain what to do next. Then she heard Mignon in the corridor beyond the kitchen and walked through into the dining-room. There, Mignon was stacking the Royal Doulton dinner service and dusting it with a yellow cloth. Rohama would have known at once by her expression and by her dress alone that something was on; the dinner service confirmed it. Partly curious, partly resentful (the keynote of their relationship) she asked Mignon if she was spring cleaning. Mignon ignored the question and simply said, "How you made me jump!"

Rohama repeated her question and Mignon's "In August, dear?" vexed her. She insisted: "Somebody coming?" Mignon paused, hating to share her secret. "As a matter of fact, somebody is." There was a further pause. Both waited. Rohama refused to put another question for fear of a direct snub and left the matter to Mignon's conscience. The old lady set down the meat dish and said carefully, "You must have heard of our nephew, Edward Lloyd-Ballantyne, the historian?"

"You mean the son of those in Maesglas once? The one whose father died of drink?"

Rohama's calculated briskness diminished the person of Mr.

Edward; and Mignon, careful not to show vexation, said grandly, "Our sister Evelyn's boy. He's now a professor. He and his wife are coming here today."

"You mean to stay here?"

"For luncheon. He's staying with Mr. and Mrs. Corbett."

Rohama with her arms folded and nostrils a-flare wanted to know why he wasn't staying at the farm. No answer. She tried again: "What made him turn up after all this time? Is it because your daughter's coming home?"

Mignon was regally offhand. "Not at all. His visit is very brief. He wants to show us his new wife and look over the old place."

She sighed and began to dust a tea-service, setting one cup affectedly before the other. She flicked a saucer saying, "Don't be surprised, dearest, if you should see us all walking round the fields. Edward will want to look round."

Rohama was afire with suspicion and unsure whether to invite the visitors to call. Having never met Edward her instinct was to be friendly, but again she feared a snub. Because of mutual mistrust she would probably end up glowering at the visitors from behind the plants in her kitchen window, thus making everyone feel as ill at ease as herself.

"This will be a sentimental journey for Edward," Mignon went on. "I gather," (she invented) "that he wants to show off to his new wife who's expecting a baby."

"How old are they?"

Mignon was vague. Edward was about eight years older than her daughter; his wife would be much younger.

"She'd better be if she's having a baby," was the brisk reply. "How long have they been married?"

Mignon thought about a year and added (still inventing) that this explained why they were in the romantic stage.

"Well, a good God, they should have got over that by this time. How old did you say he was? Older than Nesta? At that age he should never have silly stages. They could be bad for his health." Rohama laughed harshly, hating to see this simpering, affected Mignon, normally grateful for her attentions, trying to keep her at a distance. As Rohama had intended, Mignon blushed. Any mention of sexual matters seemed to hint at Rohama's dreadful origins; a child of love carried the odour of the bedroom with it everywhere. To hide her embarrassment Mignon pushed back a wisp of hair with the curve of her bony wrist.

Rohama had not finished. "I suppose you've heard about Ashley Corbett?"

Mignon knew what was coming but did not flinch, "What should I have heard?"

"Oh, it's all over Caerifor: somebody called Carter working for the County Council found him in bed with his wife."

"Are you sure that's true? There never was a place like Caerifor for rumours."

"Everybody's saying it. They also say there's going to be a divorce and then it'll all come out in the papers. I'm sure Muvvy won't like that. That won't suit her book."

"Well, it wouldn't suit anybody's book, would it? Would you like all your private life turned out in a divorce case for the benefit of the newspapers?"

"Of course," Rohama seemed well-briefed. "They don't put the full facts into the papers if the case is undefended." She looked knowingly at Mignon. "They'll probably not defend it. Unless, of course, this man Carter is going to sue for damages. As he well might according to what people say. They say she's a beautiful woman."

"With all due respect to yourself, Rohama, I don't think there's a word of truth in what you say. Ashley Corbett comes here often enough and he's never breathed a word of his troubles."

"Well he wouldn't, would he?"

"What do you mean?"

"You're the last person he'd tell. He thinks of you as his own mother. And you *are* Muvvy's aunt, even if you don't have a lot of time for her."

"People's lives are their own business. I don't think it matters to us, dearest. Don't you feel it's better to allow people to go their own ways?"

Rohama thought a while and then, seeing to what state of discomfort she had reduced the old lady, became magnanimous. "People will put anybody into bed these days. I think they get a pleasure from it. Don't you?" Mignon looked baffled. She had never thought about the motives behind gossip. "It's as

46

though they get a thrill out of that sort of talk. Anyway, if I can do anything to help you get ready for the visitors let me know. I've brought you a bowl of blackberries and they might like a tart." Mignon regretted she had no time to make a tart—since Edward liked them—and hardly had the words been said than Rohama offered to make one there and then. Mignon, quite won over, washed the fruit while the younger woman, with deft movements, rubbed shortening into flour and, in her own words, "knocked up" a pair of textbook tarts, complete with roseleaf decoration. Then she hurried away, begging Mignon to go up to the quarry to pick as many blackberries as she could before they rotted. She hurried home with her water, as Mignon well knew, to report everything she had seen and heard to her husband.

Both Rohama and Martin had a fixed idea that Mignon and Freddy would do something legal but obnoxious with their property and the news of Edward's return, by some fluke kept from her until that moment, was a threat. Could the old people be making over the place to him as a place for his retirement? The idea had dropped into her head like a divine thought in a Byzantine painting, complete with star and golden thread; there must be something in it. Martin pooh-poohed the idea, but largely from habit; he was often having to cut down his wife's fanciful notions. Even while he said there was legally nothing the old people could do he remained restless, such was the degree of mutual suspicion between the two groups thrown together at Swanquarter.

Rohama made things worse by having an obsessive interest in the old people's lives. She was always observing them and whenever she called at the house she issued a report to her husband. The most trivial things were reported: that they were eating mushrooms and bacon; that Mignon had bought a thirty-five-shillings pair of slippers for her brother. If she tried a mood picture, Rohama would say, "They look grumpy today. They're getting on one another's nerves. They must have heard from Nesta. I've noticed her letters always depress them." Martin was not indifferent to this small chat but he was much colder towards the old people, sometimes openly contemptuous and hostile. All he really cared about was the future of their part of the property and was feverishly seeking ways and means

47

to encompass them with a situation in which they would have no choice but to sell out to him.

Martin was a man of medium height but powerfully built, his head set well on his shoulders, his body well planted on sturdy, peasant legs. He had the narrowness, the intensity, the strange fire of ambitious men in the prime of their physical strength who know that they must succeed—that is, that they must make money and become someone of consequence—but who have not yet found the avenues through which their success is to come. He was searching all the time for the opening, the chance that would set him on his way, and, in the meantime, had pushed almost everything else aside. He was willing and anxious to push the old people aside but they were beyond his reach; so he watched them with this mixture of contempt and resentment that Mignon found hard to bear.

On marrying Rohama he had at first been vaguely impressed by her half-relations, as though something of Rohama's own vision of them had affected him. To her they were distant people who had a role to play in the fairy-tale fantasies of her life; her imaginative hopes went out to them as to saviours and benefactors: an unreal assessment which only a child of two worlds and a citizen of neither could have dreamed up. Gradually, Martin's manner, his cheek, grated on the brother and sister and they rebuffed him; then Martin, feeling rebuffed, suspected them of being snobs and he began a campaign against their haughtiness and coldness which always wound up with the rhetorical questions: why did Rohama bother about them? Why did she butter them up?

Then there was the matter of the electricity. Swanquarter had been one of the first places in the county to have electricity: Mignon's father had installed at some expense a private supply produced by a machine. During the 1939-45 War the machine broke down and could not be repaired. The house reverted to oil lamps. After the war a new machine was not bought because of a promise of electrification for the whole region. When the electricity came in the middle 1950s Mignon said the cost of installation was too great and that was that. Shortly after Rohama and Martin took over their farm they raised the question of an electricity supply and suggested that they and Mignon should go halves in having the current brought from the nearest mains. Mignon refused and said she could not afford the money. Martin went ahead with his own scheme and eventually installed electric milking machines as well as household gadgets while Mignon and Freddy remained stuck in the past.

Martin had never forgiven Mignon for refusing to go halves with him on the cost and soon developed this refusal as proof that the old people were hoarding their money. How was it, he asked his wife, that her father had left only some derisory sum of money? Wasn't it likely that he had made over enormous sums to his wife and daughter, before he died? Rohama, naturally, had no answer; she was left with doubts and resentments.

There was little sign that the old people had any plan for the farm or for the better use of the fields, which were all let out, or for the maintenance of the outbuildings, which were in need of repair. The whole thing bothered Martin deeply and the present decay and uncertainty about the future provided an inexhaustible topic for conversation. And what would Nesta do? Surely, they reasoned, she had grown used to a different way of life in Rhodesia; she would never return to Swanquarter. Perhaps she might sell them the farm; at least give them the first refusal.

To make the matters worse they could not discuss this subject with Mignon, the only person who might have put their minds at rest; the subject was one of many that could not be broached. The upshot of all this frustrated ambition and covetousness was that they could not respect the old people's reticence and soon gave the impression of pushing, ambitious people for whom delicacy could easily be the same thing as snobbery. To make the situation more complex, Rohama had all the illegitimate child's anxiety to vindicate itself and a rather exaggerated sense of her own worth; and if she fluttered at the least movement from Swanquarter it was part of her tragedy that she never understood what Mignon and Freddy felt. Rohama never realised, too, that the old people, especially Mignon, were equally obsessed by what she and her husband did. Despite themselves, Mignon and Freddy were aware of everything that went on at the farm. Each day, for example, on rising, Mignon would peer through her window at The Other Place, as she used to call it in

49

her letters to Nesta, and comment on what she saw. A line filled with washing before eight o'clock or the tractor in the fields before nine were major events in this lost souls' game of 'I spy'.

This obsession was the bane of Mignon's life. She hated herself for prying and, having grown used to the fuller, bigger life in the great houses in London, at the centre of imperial diplomacy and politics, this proof of her moral and social poverty was dreadful. She realised, too, that her manner towards Rohama was absurd, that she was behaving like a dirty snob, and yet she could not help herself. It was not enough to be good neighbours and to treat the girl and her husband with respect; something was missing: simplicity and openness. Rohama's kindnesses were enough to melt concrete but the brother and sister refused to let down the last barrier; they would not surrender.

They ought to have invited Rohama and Martin to meet Edward; it would have been natural and friendly. Mignon could not bring herself to do so and all that Rohama saw of him was by accident: while she was scraping potatoes at her sink two cars went by, one containing the Corbetts (Muvvy in a big blue hat), the other containing a fatherly looking man and a girl young enough to be his daughter in a pale green headscarf. Rohama flung down her scraper and rushed upstairs to get a better view from the landing window.

From this point she saw the cars bumping slowly down the lane towards Swanquarter. They stopped in the courtyard and the four passengers got out and walked round the gable end to the main door. Before they reached the door, this opened wide and Mignon and Freddy almost fell out, arms wide with greeting. In two seconds they were kissing everybody right and left. Even Mrs. Corbett, who criticised Mignon severely each time she met Rohama in Caerifor, was kissed, and Mrs. Edward, who had offered a large bunch of roses, was kissed a second time even more powerfully than the first. They spent a little time talking among the wooden chairs in front of the house before going slowly indoors, talking, laughing, nodding like mad, and completely unaware of the young woman watching them with wonder and amazement and nostalgic for similar returns in her own life.

5

A VIRTUOSO PERFORMANCE

It was quite simple. Once Mignon had the guests at Swan-quarter on her own terms she took everything as read so that there was neither comment, questions nor complaint about Edward's long absence. They arrived. She kissed them. She overwhelmed them at once by sheer force of personality. She poured warmth and affection over them all, even Muvvy, and there was no conscious breaking of ice. If Edward and his wife found this too much they could retreat towards Freddy who kept offering chairs to people who were too excited to sit down.

If there had been any fears in the old people's minds that Edward would greet them as strange apparitions out of some provincial and demoded limbo, the reality was quite otherwise. His response was so immediate and sincere it was clear that, to draw a comparison from baking, he had carried over some real, fermenting dough from their last meeting. It helped, of course, that he had no complex about his long absence and he did not expect his relations to have any. The fact that he had turned up was all the proof they needed that they had never been forgotten.

Physically he had changed without appearing to age. He was plumper and greyer but because he was brown, in good health and unwrinkled, his face was not that of a middle-aged person and he had retained the youthful sparkle of his smile.

"Now," he said turning to his wife and her bunch of roses, "I've told her that this is a folklore-free zone. She's got all sorts of illusions about the place: beautiful heiresses locked up in garrets, ghosts, family secrets, dark hints over the port—you know?"

"Ah," said Mignon (suddenly inserting with no pretence at originality: "She's a perfect English rose, your wife.") "It is we who are folklore, Freddy and I. I sometimes feel we've been here for so long that we embody past, present and future. Suddenly, about the age of seventy you get the sensation of having lived a long time." She laughed her patrician, lop-sided laugh.

Edward left the two women together and sat down next to Freddy. "They tell me," he said in Welsh, "that you're now at the height of your powers. Never written better."

Freddy was ecstatic. "I've had more calm to think and write these last few years than ever before. That helps."

"And what have you got on the stocks now?"

"I've been tidying up odds and ends all through the summer and I'm hoping this winter to get down to a few recollections."

"That should be interesting."

"That remains to be seen." His eyes opened wide. "You know, I've had a very, very narrow life to the outsider: just here and most of the time at Croswardine (where Freddy had a living) and the whole of my travels abroad can be summed up in ten pages *but*—" and he tapped his chest, "in here I've lived very fully and instructively. And as time goes on I seem to be the only link left between the present and the old days. So many of my old friends have gone; so many pitifully reduced by the grip of old age; so many I would go so far as to say deformed by old age. And as they go the magic of their old world goes with them. It struck me the other day—I was doing an appreciation of Alderman Owen Williams, one of Father's stalwarts in the southern end of the county, he died aged ninety-two—and I thought, 'Well, you're really singing the swan-song for a way of life.' That's why I want to put down some of my memories for those to come after."

The young wife sat next to Muvvy, a parched, formidable beauty in a high witch's hat, whose sharp, bitchy eyes wandered over the room, assessing, disparaging.

She leaned across to Norah and, in a stage whisper, pointed out the signs of decay. "I haven't been here for ages. It always gives me a shock to see how it's going downhill."

Norah drew herself away. She was a good-hearted, spontaneous girl who had been touched by their reception. "It was wonderful once," Muvvy said, "all the china used to shine and glitter. Now I don't suppose it's been washed for years."

She turned to Edward, who had been left alone. "Don't you find Aunty Micky's changed?" she asked treacherously. "Don't you think she's got that real apple look, like a russet? I've noticed that as old people get on they revert to the family style. Aunty Micky looks like a real old countrywoman, almost a 'bodo', you could say, although," with a hint of derision, "she still keeps that grand manner, that 'Don't you feel?', that 'Dearest'. She likes to remind people she's been somebody although she looks such an old countrywoman."

Edward looked at Muvvy lucidly and said calmly, "Then you must say the same thing about me. I've got the sort of face you can see every day in Caerifor. Sometimes I think I get to look more and more like a farmer as I get older. And, do you know, I don't find that strange. We're all country people, aren't we? Our roots are here among the peasantry. There's nothing odd that we should look like peasants."

"I didn't say peasants. I said 'country people'."

Edward's voice was arched with contempt, "What are peasants but country people? What are country people but peasants? Except that one sounds a little harsher than the other. The reality's the same."

"Not to me," Muvvy said, vexed, "I make the distinction."

"It's beyond my understanding," was Edward's reply.

"I think they're delightful," Norah put in. "I've never understood what was shameful in growing old."

Muvvy's voice grew sharper. "I didn't say there was. You've quite misunderstood what I said."

"I think we understood you very well," Edward said ripely and was saved from elaborating his remark by the return of the others.

"Ah," said Mignon, "if you knew the difficulty we've had in opening the sherry. The cork was rotten."

"Oh, what a fuss, a lot of fuss, you've been to," Muvvy said. "We expected a simple little lunch. Some cold meat and salad."

Stung for his sister's sake, Freddy said, "That was not our idea of a meal for visitors." Mignon ignored the remark and sat down regally next to Edward. "You've got a charming wife. I hope you deserve her."

Ashley recognised a fellow spirit in Edward's surprisingly gnarled, lewd grin. "I hope so." Edward lifted his glass. "To our happy reunion. It's a pity Nesta isn't here, then we'd have the whole clan."

"We haven't been all together for years," said Mignon.

53

"And I feel I've never been away. Nothing has changed, you know, except, of course, that Uncle Arthur isn't sitting outside looking at the far horizon over the top of his cane."

Despite Muvvy's presence, despite the fact that she wore her hat, like a provincial grande dame, to show that she had other, more important engagements later on, the meal was a real success. Edward appreciated the mutton and the onion sauce; the blackberry tart crowned his joy.

"Do you know who made it?" Mignon asked. "Rohama."

Having heard lurid stories from Muvvy, Edward was surprised by this proof of Rohama's closeness.

"We get on quite well, dearest. Extremely well when you think of the background. Rohama finds us a bit old-fashioned and touchy and I try to be friendly with her ... there are reserves ... the past keeps coming between us and what can we do? After the upbringing she had she's turned out a straightforward girl, down to earth, devoted to her home and husband. Between them they're making a go of their side and I sometimes think they'll have the whole place one day. Oh yes, Rohama impresses us in many ways, doesn't she, Freddy?"

Freddy agreed.

"We'd have been closer to her, I think, if her husband had not been so uncouth. He's a disagreeable, rather common sort of man. Good-natured, I suppose, and he treats Rohama like a queen. There's no refinement or breeding, of course. He's not our kind of farmer at all. What do I mean? Well, his family have a place the other side of Port Rydal. And over there it's common for the men to work in the steel mills while the women carry on the farm during the week. The men farm during the week-end or according to the shifts they're on. There's something un-farmerish about them with that common herd touch as though half-way into the industrial classes. It's not that I'm a snob; it's simply that I don't know how to meet such people half-way. He stands out among the farmers around here who've still got that natural gentlemanliness you get from years of farming. Perhaps I'm unfair. All I know is he'd like us out of here."

"He's very what the people round here call 'having'," Freddy added.

His sister agreed. "You can't misunderstand what he's think-ing and he's got an ignorant, ill-bred way of talking about money. He seems to think we've got a fortune salted away. But on the whole he's nice enough to me. He knows I can give as good as I get. He always makes his cracks at Freddy, who's too slow to reply. My God, I wish we'd got some money salted away; we'd leave this place to them like a shot."

Edward was surprised so Mignon asked, "But what have we got to keep us here? I'm often very bored, I assure you. I really haven't enough to occupy my mind and the house is full of the past. Freddy has his poetry, his writings, his friends, but I've got no one really of my own kind. Frankly I find so many local people narrow. They've seen nothing and don't want to. Oh yes, it's well known that I'd love to spend my last years in new surroundings." She smiled at Norah winningly, sure the younger woman would understand. "We've been rusting here, year in year out, with the same faces, the same routines, the same preoccupations. When you reach my age even your memories get boring."

Muvvy wondered whether Nesta would like to take the place over. Mignon showed a calculated indifference. "I suppose she's outgrown us by this time."

Muvvy said she would give a lot to see the meeting between Nesta and Rohama. Nesta had usually referred to her half-sister as the 'slut's kid'. Mignon chose not to recall this.

"She was very bitter," Muvvy said happily.

Edward moved the swathe of thick hair from his brow with a heavy hand. "Not as bitter as she might have been."

Muvvy retorted: "Rohama had a point of view, too."

"We've always allowed for that," Mignon said acidly.

Matters brightened when Muvvy said she had to leave and dragged the unusually silent Ashley away with her, although he longed to stay. They quarrelled all the way back to Caerifor about Mignon.

"But don't you see that underneath she's good-hearted and a very lonely, dispirited person? I don't think people realise just how near the end of her tether she is."

"Whose fault is it she's lonely? Even Nesta can't get on with her mother. She's impossible. Why she couldn't even accept a gift from you though the place is falling to pieces."

55

"Why in God's name did I ever mention that to you?" The question was addressed as much to himself as to his wife.

"Because you're such a big-mouth. You've got to talk about everything. How much you paid for this, how much you made on that. The biggest deal here, the biggest deal there. You're just a money-mad baby."

* * * *

As soon as the Corbetts had been waved off Mignon romped back into the house unable, unwilling, to hide her joy. "Now we can have another coffee in peace. And some lovely chat. Muvvy kills me." She took Norah's arm and led her towards the kitchen. "Muvvy and I haven't got on for years ever since the time that she and Ashley began quarrelling. I think we acted rather well, don't you?" Everyone laughed. They relaxed. They were at home with one another. "Lovely to have you here again," said Mignon pinching Edward's full, warm cheek. "Awfully nice to be back," he answered looking pleased.

The fresh coffee and cigarettes brought them back to Nesta. Mignon said she half-dreaded her return. "As a daughter and a woman she's been a disappointment. Just when you need her most she's lost in some world of her own, or she's finding fault, judging your poor efforts. A sort of professional wet blanket."

"You used to be so close," Edward said.

"The trouble began at the time of Arthur's friendship with Mrs. Benjamin. Nesta wanted me to condemn him. I refused. I couldn't destroy the father for the pleasure of the child. She's never forgiven me for this. God knows I found little enough to praise in Arthur's behaviour and no one was more hurt than I was by it; but what was the point of being at war with him? I was his wife and he was my husband; there was never any mention of divorce. He never asked for it. I never offered it. It was never once mentioned. So what was there to do but get along as decently as possible? I think we managed very well. Towards the end there wasn't any real respect left and he had no self-respect. It was bearable. I bore it. And Nesta never forgave me. Nesta wanted me to contest her father's will but I refused and that was another nail in my coffin. Just before she went away to Rhodesia she told me that I'd never cared who I

56

sacrificed so long as Arthur had his head. She actually called him 'your beloved Arthur' as though it had been a crime to like the man. I was shocked. I said, 'But dearest, he's your father.' She replied, 'Worse luck' and I said, 'Don't let's ever mention his name again. To talk like this is humiliating for us both.' And that was that.

"You know, Edward, during all the time since Arthur died she's never once asked us how we manage for money. People have got the impression we're well off, which is far from the truth. Thank God, we've got simple tastes or we'd be lost."

"Everything works out well enough," Freddy put in.

Mignon sighed profoundly—a sigh from the balls of the feet —and looked towards the window.

Eventually, as Rohama had suggested, they went blackberry-ing and, walking towards the quarry, Mignon and Edward gossiped about Muvvy. Edward reported on the party— "Chamber of Trade bores twirling glasses while waiting for a conversation to start—" and the odd, tense atmosphere in the Corbett household—"I distinctly heard Muvvy call Ashley a 'shit'—"; and Mignon expressed her devotion to Ashley who had 'no home life and goes around looking for somewhere to attach himself. He comes here like an orphan and I mother him.' "

They touched on the house which Edward was looking for; it was clear he had lost his illusions about the cheapness of Caerifor properties. "I thought Ashley was deliberately putting the prices up."

"Never," Mignon said. "He'd never do that." How the "sordid business arrangement" had come unstuck!

"Every minute we're talking about property," Edward said grumpily, forgetting he had raised the matter. "I'm sick of estate agent's babble. People talk about houses these days as though they were a new invention."

They stopped at a gate for Mignon to catch her breath and looked down at the green county—towards Caerifor and the sea—golden and peaceful under the afternoon light.

"It's the sheer absence of poetry in such people," Edward said mysteriously. They walked on in silence, arm in arm.

In contrast to Edward's disgruntlement was his wife's radiance. She was enchanted by the old people and by the self-contained, uncluttered elegance of their county. As she picked the blackberries—itself a reposing occupation—she stopped to stare over the land with its herds of black cattle, its square church towers, pink-washed farmhouses, red tractors and people at work. There was a quality of wellbeing and generosity in it which she liked.

Returning homewards with their laden baskets, Mignon and Edward got on to families (the re-establishment of roots was in the air ever since the visit started) and Mignon said the great advantage of Welsh society was that the Welsh aristocracy of the fifteenth century went into England as carpetbaggers with Henry the Seventh and left the people to their own devices.

Edward thought this unlikely to be true because the Tudors were from North Wales and had little following in the south and also because some counties, notably Merioneth and Montgomery, had been represented in Parliament for hundreds of years by two families, as of divine right.

"The landlords were never so powerful in this county, but they were still oppressive and in 1868 there were nearly three hundred evictions by Tory landlords of tenants they suspected of voting Liberal. But the landlords met their doom only twenty-one years later when every county but one went Liberal. Your father was called 'the People's Friend' because he effectively broke the power of the landowners on the Caerifor County Council."

"Those were good fights," Mignon said. "Real fights—not the sham battles we have today. I'm sorry for people who don't know what a real battle of principles is like—and also what passionately-held beliefs were like, either."

"When I think now how his generation used to believe in the people, in ordinary folk, it's something of another dimension to anything we have today. Time and time again this absolute confidence in the genius and essential sanity of the ordinary man used to find expression. Every child who went to the new intermediate school in Caerifor was a soul saved for the new world. Education was everything ... and that unswerving ideal of truly democratic institutions!"

"Of course," Edward said, "your father's vision was simplified by the fact that until the middle of the last century there was no middle class in Wales worth talking about. They hadn't turned into Ashleys and Muvvies who feel they've got to spend money to prove their existence."

"Ah, dearest, what it is to have someone around who can put things into perspective." She pinched his cheek and, turning to Norah, said, "Isn't history wonderful? And isn't a sense of history even better?"

Amid general amusement, Norah said to herself, "What a character and personality. Everything she says has its own ring."

After tea, Norah asked whether she might see over the house and, as Mignon led the way upstairs, Edward marvelled how little the place had changed. In the little sitting-room Mignon opened the cupboard where all her husband's papers were kept. Edward was surprised that no one had used them. "Memoirs sell like the proverbial hot cakes now. People get more historically minded as they feel they've got less and less future. The results are quite phenomenal. Who would have thought that my little book on the 1906 Liberal Government would have sold nearly 18,000 copies?"

"Bravo!" Mignon cried.

When Freddy said he had found the book deeply interesting, Edward, without thought, offered to sign his copy. Freddy looked stricken, for they had read the County Library copy. "We don't have money to buy books any more." Edward glibly promised to send them a copy as soon as he got home, "after all, our family had some part in helping that Government into office."

He went over to the cupboard where his uncle's diaries and papers were and marvelled that Sir Arthur had never written his memoirs when he retired since he'd been at the centre of things for years.

Mignon shrugged. "He was too tired. Now nobody looks at them but Freddy."

"And I can't read them as much as I'd like to," Freddy put in quickly, "because the fine writing tires my eyes. But they're full of good things. Arthur got everything down."

"Then what are you waiting for?" Edward asked on a rising note of unfelt enthusiasm. "Publishers fall over themselves for that kind of material these days. Try one. If I had the time I'd go through them myself."

Edward had little faith in his uncle's genius as a diarist but had greater faith in the rubbish that publishers would accept. In any case, he had spoken in the general sort of way in which people sometimes tell a friend with an old painting to get it valued and had not really meant the remark to be taken seriously.

"Do you really think someone would publish them?" Mignon asked.

"Now or never," Edward replied glibly. "Cash in on the craze while you can. The diaries might have as much value as a general's memoirs. Try."

"And what publisher do you recommend?"

"Try Heinz. He's my publisher. He's bringing out a rather grandiose prestige series called, 'Twentieth-Century Documents' which has had a surprising success."

Mignon was hardly listening. She had opened her husband's old desk and found paper and pencil. "Write the address down for me, will you? I'll write to Heinz."

This interest alarmed Norah who had realised how little involved her husband was. She knew that had he had the slightest belief in the diaries he would have looked through them himself. As Edward began printing the address he suspected that his aunt might have been thinking of doing something with the diaries even before he spoke.

"I'll write to him directly," she said, placing the paper carefully aside. "Perhaps I could mention your name."

Edward considered and then said he would speak to Heinz himself. He realised that a couple of words on the telephone could do more good than twenty letters from the provinces. Mignon's gratitude abashed him.

Neither Edward nor Norah could say, "Be careful. Don't expect too much", for the incident clarified for them much that was vague about the obscure sadness both had felt since arriving in the house, the pathetic wistfulness of the brother and sister alone in their beautiful and decaying home, the defencelessness of old age.

Mignon's interest in the idea had been born spontaneously out of a quiet desperation; it was the last throw of a person on the edge of despair. In an odd way it galvanised her—she had seemed to droop a little after the walk and the tour of the

60

house—and when they returned, as it were, to base, she suddenly returned upstairs and began searching in the chests and cupboards where the sentimental trophies and relics of generations were stored.

She returned by and by with a baby's dress that had once been Edward's, had been worn by Nesta a few years later and by *her* son a generation after that. It was crumpled and faded but essentially sound and an impressive piece of handiwork with lots of embroidery and crewelling in faded blue silk. Mignon offered it rather doubtfully to Norah as a dress for the coming baby: "Wash it carefully and you'll restore its value." Norah's face flushed with pleasure; such a gift was the secret reason for the whole visit only neither Edward nor his wife had known it: the need to establish themselves as people with roots and origins, people with continuing and echoing lives. Then, Mignon produced her trump card. She opened her cardigan and revealed an old teddy bear, about twelve inches high, which had once belonged to Edward. It was still dressed in a funny little jumper he had himself knitted as a small boy.

Norah fell on it as though it had been a sacred relic. "It's been waiting in a cupboard all these years to be wanted again and loved." She was almost overwrought with sudden pleasure and emotion and Edward was moved to the quick to see this. They thought at first that he was laughing at her as she hugged the bear, but it was quite the reverse: he was shaken, humiliated, overwhelmed by this pathetic piece of flotsam that had survived for years without his knowing it. The idea suddenly came to him: who knew what other relics of his childhood might not be hidden away in one of the rooms upstairs, in the one with the Victorian rose wallpaper, for instance, or the one with the peacock-blue hangings? They had given back something of himself, the lost perspectives which nobody but himself would recognise again. He belonged here; he had been a child and a young man here; it was his home. What remained without answer was why he had stayed away from it for so long.

Mignon and Freddy hovered near them as Edward and his wife prepared to depart. "Ah, my dears, your visit has been one of the nicest things that has happened to us for years, hasn't it, Freddy?" Mignon took Edward's hand. "Don't let such a long

61

time pass before you come back, dearest. This has been a wonderful boost for us. Not only to see you but to see how successful and happy you are. We feel you've done splendidly. You've made something of your life. My one regret is that Arthur isn't here to see how you've got on. You know how he believed in you." She kissed Edward and then hugged Norah. "It's been wonderful having you. I feel I've known you for years and that's a lovely feeling."

* * * *

And so they parted. Before returning to Caerifor Edward called at the station house to see Hughie Phillips, an old poaching crony. The former stationmaster was half-hidden by a floppy straw hat, as he cut back some bushes. He was a strong, energetic man who had recently taken to wearing glasses for close work and they gave him an obsessed, professorial appearance. When Edward called to him across the white wicket gate, he lifted the glasses to his brow and stared at the intruder from under a strong, hairy arm. As soon as he realised who Edward was he invited him and Norah to sit on a green bench under a laden Bramley Seedling.

And how had they found the old people? "Older," said Edward, "like the rest of us."

"Things have changed over there. I see a big change in them in the last year or so. The place is going to rot for sure. To rack and ruin. Nobody bothers, you might say. It's not much pleasure owning property when you're their age and with no one to help. And it must have been a nasty shock when that young Roma, as they call her, came over to take up her share."

"I think they get on quite well though. Don't they?"

"I never said otherwise. But it must have gone against the grain. That's only natural. And the worry of keeping the place going—that's something, too."

Edward said diplomatically that repairing the farm needed more money and energy than the old people had. Hughie fervently agreed but he did not see how anything could happen until the old people died when somebody might take the place over and restore it.

"I'd give a lot to see the old place in its old glory and still in the family."

Hughie's voice had become snug and cosy as voices tend to be when they discuss property, even other people's. It is as though something magical in the brick and timber comes into their souls, as though it were understood in the blood that property is palpable magic and cannot be set aside.

Edward was struck by this undertone and touched, for something in this came from the ordinary people's attachment to the farm, to the tradition it housed, to the family which had created the tradition. What took place in the house concerned the ordinary people. It was extraordinary to find this traditional glow should have lasted so long: two generations removed from the great days, not to speak of the depersonalisation of politics.

He had forgotten or taken for granted this aspect of the life in Caeriforshire and the memory of it, restored by the timbre of Hughie's voice, made him momentarily uncertain of his own judgements. There was pleasure, a magical pleasure, in having this suddenly restored to him, and regret that he had come back in time for its sunset glitter very far down among the branches of a dark wood.

The mood of regret and nostalgia made Edward another person, for the latest emotion was always the most pure and deep.

"It's rather foolish, in a way, to return like this, you know. One is churned up to no avail. One can't do anything. Everything seems so small, defenceless, somehow lost in time and space, like a crumb on a large table."

"The mystery to me is why you cut yourself off from your people for so long. They didn't show half the resentment I'd have done. In fact, they showed no resentment at all."

Edward was absorbed in his driving. "I must do something to show them that we appreciate everything. Do you think Heinz would be interested in those diaries?"

"You know Heinz," she replied.

"And many of those books he publishes in that series are really so remote from what can be considered ordinary source material that I don't have a great deal of faith in his judgement."

"But if it gave your aunt and uncle pleasure?"

"Do you think it would?"

"Immeasurably so."

"Then I must do something. Although I can't hide my own opinion that the publishing of this mound of material can only be justified by the belief that, in the future, people will have so little present to work on that they'll be able to spend years delving into the small debris of the past."

He considered a while.

"It must, of course, be small debris. Could it be anything else?" It was as though he were talking to himself.

"Would you like to look through them?"

"Not really. I would do if I were asked but not of my own free will."

The cynicism of his reply was not lost on his wife who said, "In that case you feel they can't be much good."

"Just an intuition, having known my uncle."

"But, if it would give your aunt a quarter of the pleasure I've had this afternoon, you must do it."

"Good enough. I'll speak to Heinz."

6

SIR ARTHUR FOR THE MASSES

SIGHING like an actress who has brought off a big scene, Mignon reclined at full length on a sofa, her head resting lightly on a small embroidered cushion. After the excitements of the afternoon the house had regained its customary stillness although tremors still remained as, outside the window at Mignon's head, the fresh wind from the sea shook the ash-trees and beeches which guarded the inner entrance to the farm. This was the new feeling of excitement: no more than the slight breeze that fills the sails of a becalmed ship, no more than the sound of a distant trumpet, yet enough to stir the heart—and all because Edward, returned like a ghost from the grave to point to her the household's buried treasure, had given her the idea of exploiting her husband's relics.

These jottings and clippings and amassings of fifty years were to have been the material for Sir Arthur's memoirs and towards the end of his life, when the task was beyond him, he talked of leaving the whole lot to the National Library for the use of scholars. No one had taken this notion seriously for Sir Arthur had enjoyed grandiose visions from time to time, but it had sounded good and Mignon was able to recall (with the dispassionate clarity of most of her memories of her husband) the sententious movement of the lower lip as he made the remark.

Freddy was less impressed by the idea of interesting a publisher in his brother-in-law's papers than by the whole flavour of Edward's return, the mere fact of it, even. It was as though Divine Grace had moved the man's heart. These were not words that sold themselves to Mignon's irreligious humour but she, too, felt the rightness about the way things had gone and the way that, step by step, they had been brought to speak of the diaries. Already, it seemed to her, this was the main reason for the visit. To be sceptical about the providential nature of the whole visit was to limit the possibilities, the endless richness of life itself. Mignon was swept away by the new movement she saw in their lives, as some wave abruptly forms itself in the middle of a still sea and carries all before it towards the shore. No ancient thaumaturgist accepted his vision with greater awe and thankfulness than Mignon as, from her comfortable couch, her face turned towards the windy tops of the trees, she saw their lives transformed by the visit of their nephew. This certainty that Edward was mixed up with the movements of the stars in their courses and Providence was the source of Mignon's strength in later periods of stress and doubt.

They lapsed into happy, fertile silence; Freddy puffing his pipe, Mignon gazing at the trees with radiant eyes, her face still lightened by the miraculous day, her mouth dreamy, wrapt, unexpectedly youthful as though the Lloyd-Ballantynes had carried off a score of years.

"I'll give him a fortnight, Freddy. If we don't hear by that time I'll drop a line to Heinz myself mentioning Edward's name. That would be fair, don't you think?" Freddy agreed.

His sister promptly went on: "Imagine the difference to us, Freddy, if the papers were published. There might even be some money in it."

"Don't count too much on that," he said sagely thinking of his own experience. "One never knows. I've always thought those diaries were good. At the back of my mind when I read them I used to marvel that nothing had been done with them. Edward knew without looking at them that he had made a find."

The "without looking at them" struck a false note and Mignon asked whether Freddy thought Edward had talked emptily. Freddy gulped. "But why should he? We're not children who need fobbing off."

Mignon had risen and was rearranging Norah's roses under a shade of doubt. Edward had always been glib, a bit inclined to say what would please. "But he's promised faithfully to write to Heinz. I'm absolutely sure now we can sell those diaries. The cash will come in damned useful, don't you feel?"

"I think more of the glory."

"Blow the glory for a little hard cash."

"But don't sacrifice everything for material gain."

66

His tone infuriated her. "I'm determined to sell those diaries. That's settled." She brought down her hand on the mahogany table and Freddy nearly jumped out of his seat.

"But I'm agreeable," he cried. "I want them published."

Mignon's eyes were keen, suspicious. Recalling his lush praise of the diaries, she said it was a bit strange that he had never suggested before that they should be published. Freddy's surprise prevented a quick retort. "But, my dear girl, how was I to think of such a thing? Please be reasonable."

"I feel hurt and vexed that you didn't suggest this years ago."

He was aghast at her turn of thought. "Micky, are you suggesting I've deliberately held back my opinion of Arthur's diaries all these years?"

"Not at all. But you might have thought about the matter. They could have been published by now."

"That's entirely unjust. I think that's as hurtful a thing to say as anything you can think of . . ."

"Then we're both hurt. After all, you're the literary person in this household. You ought to have seen their value; you ought to have known that."

"You're hinting that I've been hiding my real opinion. What motive could I have? That's wicked of you, Micky. You're not your usual self."

"That's what I feel, Freddy, and I can't help but express myself clearly. It's really a most amazing thing you never once mentioned having them published, especially as you said you'd thought of this."

"But only in a general sort of way . . . as one does."

"Either you think of these things or you don't. That's my point."

"Well it's no point at all. It's just your nastiness, in my opinion."

The absurd argument went on for some time until Mignon said, "Don't say anything more, please. But also, Freddy, please don't rile me by suggesting that I don't publish the diaries."

At this, he curled back his lips angrily and shouted at the top of his voice, "I have never suggested you stopped publishing those diaries! Do you hear?" He stared at her wide-eyed with rage. "Let me make that point once and for all."

His anger purged her nervous irritation and she laughed at him with a superciliousness that was uncalled for and silly. "But you're not very encouraging, are you, Freddy?"

In a voice only slightly less loud than before he asked her what she expected him to do.

"I don't want you to do anything. But sometimes your lack of generosity chills me. You loved Arthur as much as I did and you must agree that his glory will redound as much on you as on me."

"You're moving ahead too quickly. You're building on sandy foundations. You're making bricks without straw. If you're not more balanced about this you'll end up with a mighty disappointment."

"Agree with me that Arthur's fame will redound on us both!"

"Redound? What do you mean: redound? Is there such a word?" He looked sideways at her. "I doubt it."

It was his way of bringing her to heel—to poke fun at her occasional lapses and grammatical faults (although this was not an occasion).

"Yes, of course there's such a word. Look it up in the Oxford."

He lost faith in himself and scoffed at the idea of looking in a dictionary. Mignon flounced across the room, found the book and handed it to him. Rather sulkily he turned the pages while she looked up at the ceiling and tapped her feet on the brass fender with wicked humour. "It's there, isn't it? Tell me."

When he pushed the book aside Mignon laughed. "How that's put me in a good humour, Freddy! What a silly pair we are. We've got like this because we haven't got anything else to interest us. That's my firm conviction. Aren't we silly to argue the toss like this when we may be both on the edge of something great, something really terrific and good? We mustn't be skunky with one another now, Freddy. I know you're as thrilled as I am by the idea that Arthur's writings will see daylight in a way he could never have dreamed possible." Freddy sniffed scornfully; he was deeply hurt.

After supper he picked up the new wedding hymn he was writing for a grocer's daughter in Caerifor and prepared to ignore his sister and her extraordinary humours, but she said gaily, "I wish Edward's visit could have taken place years ago. It's the nicest thing that's happened to us for years. I can see how dull and countrified our lives had become."

Freddy looked up coolly, not deeply impressed.

"Yes, dearest,"—and as she spoke her eyes glistened with emotion—"the magic had gone out of our lives and now, just today..." she looked around in wonder like a hermit after a vision—"it's returned. Don't you feel it? Don't you feel something wonderful and good is going to happen?" She sighed with excitement. "It's made me feel young and daring. Thank God, that all these miserable years of scrimping and saving will be over. We'll be able to travel a bit. I promise you things are going to be different from now on. As I see it, the future is very bright indeed."

She had walked across to the window and stood looking over the darkening wind-swept fields pensively, rubbing the lobe of her left ear.

"It's something I've always known would happen. I couldn't believe that we had nothing more to look forward to. Edward's visit marks the end of an epoch."

As she spoke she became more and more certain that the whole thing had been pre-ordained while Freddy suddenly realised that even if Edward spoke to Heinz there wasn't any certainty that Heinz would be interested. If there was a disappointment after so sudden a raising of hopes Mignon might never be the same person again: sober thought. So Freddy prayed that something good would happen as she herself hoped.

The next day, as an act of piety, he took the diaries from the cupboard and arranged them, as far as possible, in chronological order. Mignon looked at them calculatingly as though at a promising crop.

*   *   *   *   *

The next time Ashley called, Mignon told him about Edward's suggestion and mentioned the possibility that her husband's papers might have a good market value. Ashley liked the idea of publication, but was unsure that it could earn much money. He knew nothing about publishing and even less about editing political diaries but his common sense told him that bringing out an edition based on masses of unrelated papers would involve an enormous amount of sifting, pruning and research taking at least four or five years. That also assumed that the publishers liked the material and, more basic, that Edward would use his good offices in getting Heinz interested. He was disillusioned about Edward and had no faith in his bright ideas.

Although he had doubts, Ashley himself added fuel to Mignon's flames by suggesting that *The Sunday Age*, the newspaper which specialised in generals' memoirs, might be interested in serialising the diaries.

Since Edward's visit, Mignon had developed all sorts of modern nervous gestures and at this point she clicked her fingers impulsively like a village schoolmistress. "You've got it, dearest. If Heinz doesn't turn up trumps I'll write to the *Age*. It's the sort of paper Arthur's old cronies will read regularly."

Then Ashley had doubts about his own suggestion and threw up another idea: what about letting his old friend Willy Thomas of the *Caerifor Journal* look at them?

"Oh," said Mignon, having another of her moments of doubt about Ashley. "Oh."

"He's a very competent journalist."

"I'm willing to try anything, dearest; but is Willy Thomas quite the man for the job? I mean, his experience hasn't been very wide, has it? And the leaders in his paper are so awful, so ungrammatical, that I've often asked myself whether he really knows what's what."

"He's no great shakes as a writer but he's no fool."

"Would his recommendation carry any weight?"

"Where?"

"With London newspaper editors. You didn't think the *Journal* would publish the papers ... or did you?"

"They would create a lot of interest locally," Freddy said, hating to see Ashley's idea crushed. "Arthur was well thought of around here."

"My point is—" Mignon spoke carefully—"is that Arthur's papers belong to the whole nation. He was a public servant, highly-placed, well thought of. His experience of men and affairs puts him rather outside the range of local newspapers."

Impasse. Ashley fell silent. Freddy put forward his idea for a solid three-volume edition in demi-calf with an introduction by the Prime Minister: *The Journals and Papers of Sir Arthur Benson-Williams.*

"That would take ten years to produce," Ashley said. "Dear people, you must be sensible." He was more than slightly irritated by both of them. "Wait until you hear from Edward. He may have forgotten all about the matter. Have you heard from him since he returned?" He thought the frenzy about publication a sign of old age.

When Freddy had gone out, Mignon produced a little note from Norah, thanking them for their welcome. Ashley returned it with the sour comment that it was almost identical to the one they had had.

"I don't think you and Muvvy got much out of Edward and his wife, did you?"

"They're an odd pair," he said slowly, "I hadn't expected them to be like that. I think he's a communist."

Mignon burst out laughing. "A Marxist-Leninist? Dearest, what a ridiculous idea." She stopped laughing abruptly; Ashley had been serious.

He held to his point of view; he insisted that Edward had "very funny ideas".

"Oh, but never a communist. He'd be the plumpest *sans-culotte* in the business."

"Well, if he's not a communist he's something very similar. His opinions were so cranky. You couldn't make a remark about the weather, but he'd take you up. Really. It was utterly boring."

"What did you do with them?"

"They didn't go out much. We had a walk around Caerifor one evening. Frankly I was a bit embarrassed by them. They looked so odd—much more like father and daughter than husband and wife and Norah used to carry her stomach before her like a little football."

"Well, she can't help that."

"God knows, I know that. Having children's not an illness but what finished us off was the way they kept talking about it. I hope I'm not a prude, but I think there are certain things best left unsaid."

71

"Such as?"

"Well, Edward said it was a pity we'd not had a couple of children. All right. I agree. It's a pity. But he said it twice, three times. He'd made his point the first go. Then they were most critical of Caerifor and kept saying patronising things. 'All these little towns have got the same appearance nowadays,' he said, 'I'm sorry to see that even Caerifor has got the department store look. Every town in Britain looks the same now.' I asked him what he expected from a town of twenty thousand people and he said, 'Ah, but Caerifor had such great charm. I remember it as a place of some distinction.'" Ashley waved his hand in disgust. "I could quote his opinions for ever and you'd still not hear anything interesting or original. He was too wordy, altogether too literary and academic." But he went on: "Then the last evening we had a few people in for drinks— Ward-Finch, the Robertsons, you know. And Norah began to show off in the most ludicrous way. She suddenly said to Mrs. Ward-Finch, 'Teddy tells me I look terribly pregnant, is that true?' Well, what could the woman say? She said she never noticed such things. But Norah had to insist."

If Ashley had not been so taken up by his sense of outrage he would have noticed the curious glitter of humour in Mignon's eyes.

"And Norah had to go one better by saying, 'There you are, Teddy, I'm not so noticeable after all.' And then she gave us a demonstration of some new American skirt—it may not be new —which cuts away to allow the stomach to kind of stick out freely. Everybody was most embarrassed to see this woman pushing her stomach around the room like a feather bed falling out of a window. They seemed to be sex-mad. One evening she was sitting in a chair, leaning back with a book, and he suddenly put his hand on her stomach and said, 'How's Charley?' and she said, 'Better for the change of air.' Well, I'm not a prude, but I think there are certain things that aren't said."

"I don't suppose they meant any harm," Mignon replied with a bigness of vision which only her amusement allowed her. "What happened about the house sale?"

He pretended not to understand. "What sale?"

"I thought Edward wanted a house."

"Oh, that's fallen through. They lost interest when they knew the prices. They seemed to think they'd get something for nothing."

"So the visit wasn't a great success. One wonders why they came."

"I don't know."

"I thought they were enjoying themselves fine."

"Yes, but what did *we* get out of it?"

"Were we supposed to get something out of it, dearest?"

Ashley's voice rose to a whine. "Well, he neglects us for years then writes out of the blue and before you know where you are he's arrived and was rather patronising, rather apart, unwilling to admit that anything could have happened while he'd been away. Infuriating attitude. Didn't you find him infuriating? After all, you didn't hear from him properly for years and you were as good as a mother to him."

"No. I wasn't infuriated. I didn't expect anything, I suppose. Edward is amiable, amusing and can be very, very close to you while he's here—like Aneurin Bevan or Lloyd George. When you're with them you alone count; but out of sight, out of mind. And that's how his father was."

"The whole thing was disappointing."

"People *are* disappointing. There'll be more disappointments for us when Nesta returns. But I shan't be taken in. I expected nothing from Edward's return and I got a great deal in pure happiness. I expect nothing from Nesta's visit; but perhaps there'll be something nice to remember."

She laughed happily, feeling invulnerable again. The fact was unpleasant, but the signs of Ashley's weakness had done her good.

When he said with a note of final contempt, "The only thing that seems to have really thrilled him was getting his old teddy bear," Mignon laughed with real gaiety. "But that proves he's human after all even if he is a communist under the skin."

Ashley had never seemed so second-rate to her. She coolly, accurately, assessed the undercurrent of sexual jealousy in Ashley's account of the Lloyd-Ballantyne visit, as though, she said to herself, he envied Edward the young flesh of his wife. Young flesh was what Ashley wanted more than anything else;

his money, his local offices, his buying and selling were absorbing (and he would relinquish them with pain) but he could not enjoy them as much as he might because his flesh was starved of its own kind. Mignon came to what she called "these terrible truths" intuitively, with the observation of a lifetime to feed her senses; but she would put the truth away quickly as into a black handbag; these were the things she kept to herself. One of the reasons for her slight contempt of Ashley was his inability to create some sort of sensual truth for himself. The little nugget of truth in the black bag was held against him.

Discussing Ashley's visit with Freddy later she said, "He's rather a surprising sort of person, isn't he? He came here and complained about Edward in almost the same words I'd used before he came. He didn't seem to think it was ironic. He's naïve, isn't he? So easily hurt, so wet in so many ways."

Freddy could not accept this vicious cut at their best friend.

"He's a darling, of course," Mignon said gaily, "and I'm utterly devoted to him. But he can be a wet and I always think when a fundamentally nice person's a wet it's always more upsetting, don't you feel?"

"If it's a sign of a wet to have been our very good friend for years then I thank God that Ashley is what he is. It's an odious way to talk. You've got a good heart, my girl, but there are times when you've got a wicked tongue. Like a snake."

Even that did not upset her. She looked amused. "I see things clearly, that's all."

"Only a wicked tongue says everything it knows."

"Believe me, I don't say everything I know. I keep lots of dark things to myself. Anyway, you'll pray for me, I daresay: and now the question is: do you want something to eat?"

Her good humour sent her humming tunelessly into the kitchen.

She returned to the matter of the diaries: "Listen to me. I've had a naughty idea. Could we play off the *Sunday Age* against the publisher? If one knows the other is interested there's hope of a better price."

"Does that follow?"

"Surely."

"Better get a letter from Heinz first," he said sepulchrally.

"Do you think it's wrong to play one off against the other?"

74

In her amateur businesswoman way Mignon had thought this a master stroke.

"There's no harm in getting the best price you can but you can't play around with Heinz when Edward is recommending us to him. Wait until we hear something. We've got to think about Edward. We can't let him down in front of his publisher. I'm sure Edward is one of his best authors and we've got to be on our best behaviour." Mignon saw that he was right.

*   *   *   *

The letter from Heinz compensated them for their prudence. Sir Ragismund Heinz, it appeared, had known Sir Arthur; they had served on some obscure committee together. Sir Ragismund had greatly admired the dead man and his capacity for work and constructive action, but had never suspected that he had been a diarist. As he was sure that nothing Sir Arthur wrote could be without interest he thought that a preliminary investigation was called for and with this end in view he would be sending down a young assistant editor who would spend a week or ten days looking over the material. The young man, Mr. Charles Milford, would be writing himself and would be anxious to know whether he could be accommodated locally.

In her reply to Sir Ragismund, Mignon's excitement overflowed in a flood of furious underlinings and exclamation marks. Of course, she underlined, Mr. Milford was at liberty to see the papers and she would be hurt if he were to stay anywhere but in her home. She awaited with the very greatest possible pleasure and interest the young man's arrival.

Charles Milford. Charles Milford? Where had she heard the name before? Freddy could not place it and consulted a *Who's Who* in the library without finding any sort of clue.

In a few days Milford himself wrote to thank her for the offer of hospitality and gave the date and time of his arrival. He looked forward to making their acquaintance and reading the writings of Sir Arthur. The word 'writings' suggested overselling on the part of Edward, but this was less important to the old people than trying to build up a portrait of Milford from his letter. The writing was elaborately italic; the address 'Imperial Mansions, Victoria Place, South Kensington' suggested a

75

certain social security; and there was a furtive crest, too small for Mignon to decipher, at the head of the paper. "An interesting person," both she and Freddy agreed.

Mignon's intimations of glory were henceforth only equalled by her energy. She cleaned out a spare bedroom and hung everything that could be hung out in the wind, while Freddy cut back the creeper which had begun to enter the window. In the midst of all this preparation and expense of energy a letter from Nesta and Patrick was an irrelevance. Mignon promptly mislaid it and could not recall whether they were to arrive the next Wednesday or the Wednesday after that. Ashley, mournfully attendant as usual, offered to meet Milford in Caerifor and tried to suggest that the project might not succeed. It was useless. He had never seen Mignon so obsessed by an idea, so certain of her success—and with so little to build on.

Rohama, of course, noticed the new activity, the beatings, the shakings, the dippings and swabbings, and at first imagined all this was for Nesta and had a mood of wistful longing for someone to welcome home after a long absence.

She met Freddy just outside the farm one day and he, forgetting his sister's warnings, told Rohama that a young man was expected to look at—he paused—"my brother-in-law's papers."

"You mean my father's papers?"

Freddy nodded foolishly, caught offside.

"I see." Impossible to say what was moving in Rohama's clear-cut eyes. What were the papers about? Thoroughly alarmed by his indiscretion, Freddy said vaguely, "Mostly historical documents."

"Didn't you give all that old junk to some library?"

"How did you get that idea? The papers are all indoors."

Rohama turned her face sideways to disengage herself from the strand of hair that had blown across it: her expression was jealous and angry. "I suppose they didn't want the rubbish."

"You're quite wrong, my girl. They didn't go to the library for different reasons."

"Anyway, it's a lot of showing off."

"Roma, you can think what you like."

"Well it is." She flashed her eyes at her baby in its push chair. "There's more in his head than there ever was in my father's. If

76

there'd been anything in the papers they'd have become interested in them before now. Isn't it odd they've taken so long?"

Freddy would say no more; he was thoroughly put out by her manner.

"Maybe I should have some rights in the matter if they're my father's papers. I'll have to consult our solicitor."

She regretted her remark as soon as she had made it. The impulse to retaliate in some way had been stronger than her good sense. She pushed the baby away hurriedly and left Freddy caught in his own trap. It spoiled his walk.

Rohama's peace of mind was also destroyed. She told her husband, of course, and decided that if anything came out of the publication, any fame, any notoriety, she would get in on the act, if only to spite Mignon. As a regular newspaper reader and television viewer she knew something of the workings of modern publicists and she had seen the profitable and brutal honesty of great men's children when faced by the television cameras. She was prepared to sit before them herself and tell everything she knew—the way she was brought up, the way she had been treated, the way she was ignored. She wouldn't spare feelings or reputations. With the cold calm she knew so well how to command she would sum everything up in one phrase, "After all the pain and trouble my father caused, it would have been better had he been forgotten."

She saw Freddy returning from his walk and made some excuse to accost him, and practised on him the jewelled turn of phrase she would use on television. She knew he would never dare to repeat it to his sister; to have done so would have been to confess to his own foolish babblings.

His uneasiness, his sense that he had betrayed his sister's secret made him more lush in his praise of the late Sir Arthur. History, he said, was mainly written by people on the sidelines who had the power of the pen, while the great men who were at play, had neither the talent nor the objectivity to write up their own times.

Mignon was not greatly impressed by this intuition for she herself had come to believe in the papers and their destiny. "I've always known in my heart that Arthur's work would see the light one day and be recognised for what it was."

This was so untrue that Freddy gasped and he caught himself watching her say these things with such lugubrious faithfulness to the movement of the lip and hand that it might have seemed he wanted to paint her. It was, however, merely his way of trying to absorb conviction from the sight and sound of the one convinced. He could not forget that Arthur had never shown any talent as a letter-writer and his judgements, divorced from the weighty way in which they were offered, were triteness itself.

But he played up to his sister's new devotion without a hint of doubt. "There can be no doubt," he said slowly, as though weighing up every syllable, "there can be no doubt, not the slightest, that Arthur was one of the key figures of the first half of this century. Even we can hardly visualise how valuable his work will be to historians."

Mignon was pleased by this remark, in the same way that Royalty are gratified by tributes of loyalty: but their absence would have made a deeper impression. In a sense, both were play-acting, both were pretending to have been converted to the virtues of Sir Arthur. That neither found the other's conversion convincing seemed to show that neither was convinced.

Still impelled by his guilt at having spilled the beans to Rohama, Freddy decided to compose a few lines in English on the subject of the diaries. Normally, he wrote in Welsh, a language in which he had a real lyric gift, where the results were satisfying because his simple, honest sentiments were clothed in a language for which his ear was accurate, his command masterly. The elegance of the expression concealed the simplicity, the naïvety of the thought. His writings in English lacked this mastery and inevitability and his decision to write in English was taken because he hoped that room would be found in some future edition of Sir Arthur's work for the little poem as epigraph.

That evening he sketched out his ideas and slept badly that night so much did composition in English make him nervous. In the morning he tried again and although having inspirations was his major activity there were no real sentiments to express, so the work went badly. In the usual way, Freddy could write a sonnet or an ode for publication in the local press on all

78

sorts of public occasions—Winston Churchill's eightieth birthday, a Royal Progress through the county, the death of an alderman—but usually his absence of real feeling was balanced by his absence of reservations, so that his pen could flow harmlessly on. On a lower level, he readily accepted commissions to fill in forms and would contribute humorous verses for local weddings and concerts and solemn elegies for funeral cards. Often these commissions were paid for in kind: a dozen eggs, a piece of bacon, a sack of potatoes. This was as pleasant a form of patronage as anyone could expect in this age and place and neither Freddy nor his sister felt it was in any way demeaning to receive a fowl at Christmas or a piece of pork at the pig-killing for something written a time before. But on the subject of the diaries neither sentiment nor self-interest aroused the Muse to strum the lyre! So he decided about half-past eleven to go for a walk and try to get his ideas into shape.

The wind that blew that noon was dusty and tiresome, a wind that filled the sky with dun-coloured clouds and sprinkled the farmworkers' soup with grit. The warm, capricious wind sent poultry into the shelter of haystacks, disturbed the cockerels' tails and blew pieces of hay, straw and leaf in little defiles along the lanes near Swanquarter. Such a warm, September wind was not unknown but it severely put out Freddy's constitutional, irritated his eyes and mouth and made him lose his breath. It tugged at his lichened coat, flapped the brim of his battered trilby and treated him with the same lack of respect that it showed to an old scarecrow. It knocked the energy out of him and he was obliged to sit down in a hedgebank near a flock of fat cross-Cheviot sheep who were scavenging a harvested field. Looking at the sheep and thinking of Charles Milford's coming visit his inspiration returned and when he got home he was able to write down with one élan his

Lines on Hearing that the Diaries of Sir Arthur Benson-Williams are to be edited and published.

> I never thought to see the day
> When editors would quarrel
> To publish my dear sister's
> Husband's diaries and squabble

79

For the honour of discovery
A new Hervey or a Creevey.
These diaries wherein are kept
The secrets of a nation
Will soon be read by every man
Of every generation
To learn how England saw it through
From nineteen ten to forty-two.
There'll be something there to interest
Each person in the land;
But most of all those who hold dear
And Christian virtues understand.

Unhappily for him, Mignon had no feeling for poetry and all her brother's efforts were usually 'jolly good'. The last two lines of the verse needed some exegesis: what did they mean? Freddy hated to unpack his tighter lines and by the time he had explained that the diaries would interest all those who understood and held dear Christian virtues—not necessarily complementary feelings—he was no longer sure the lines were true for the simple reason that Sir Arthur had been an agnostic or a waffly-mystical rationalist who used to irritate Freddy by saying, "My God is over there"—looking towards the mountains. Sir Arthur had been unexpectedly mystical, unexpectedly sceptical, and both in terms alien to Freddy. Mignon lost interest in the poem and Freddy's doubts. "Dearest, it's impossible to say the truth all the time, don't you feel?" She was enjoying her boiled bacon and beans too much to have any energy for Freddy's verses.

"To be honest with you, I keep thinking about the *Sunday Age*. I think serialisation would give pleasure to a lot of Arthur's old cronies and we'd get some cash quicker. Publication in permanent form could follow."

"Don't lose sight of the bigger thing for the cash in hand."

"You've said that before."

"But it's true."

"It's also true that some cash in hand would have been useful with Nesta and Patrick coming." She chewed on silently and then said at a tangent, "Of course, what Edward said is true. People have never had such a sense of history as at the moment. Arthur was so sure his work would be appreciated. I remember well when we were living at Rutland Gate how he used to put down the day's impressions no matter what the hour. I often used to cook bacon and eggs or warm soup at one o'clock in the morning. I suppose it was all part of the excitement of the times."

She actually began to reminisce sentimentally about Sir Arthur to Freddy's embarrassment. This was unfair; if she chose to forget certain things he could not. "Yes," she wound up, "his devotion was beyond praise. The only time he let up was when he came down here or we spent the summer holidays together in Scotland. He had an idea those papers would be interesting. 'Perhaps,' he said, 'they'll help people to understand what it was like.'"

"That's the whole point," Freddy cried, anxious to return to a safer region. "That's the whole point: what it was all about. Most history is false. Something always escapes."

Mignon went away to make coffee and as she was setting down their cups they heard Rohama climbing the stone steps outside. Mignon had time to hiss, "Not a word, Freddy! Remember!" before the young woman came in with a broad shaft of sunlight which fell on the red tiles of the kitchen and extended well into the doorway.

"A lovely smell," she announced, scrabbling in the skip she was carrying. She threw a handful or so of runner beans on the table and looked around her inquisitively, as she usually did. "The beans are pretty well over now and these"—she threw out a couple of beetroot—"are for your dinner tomorrow. Shall I boil them with mine or do you want to bake them?"

Mignon consulted Freddy and it was decided to boil them. Would Rohama like something to drink? She shook her head; she had already eaten. She sat down on a chair and sighed like an old man. "I don't mind telling you I'm tired. I think it's the wind and now the sun's come out it's taken the life out of my legs."

"You do too much," Mignon said casually.

"I know." Rohama went on to talk of her health as though, in bringing up such a personal subject, she got closer to them. There was a self-importance about them during those days which she found intolerable. Although she knew they were

81

hiding many things she knew better than to tackle such a subject in Mignon's presence. There was a regal pause while Mignon blew on her coffee. The aroma reached Rohama who said, "Gosh, I love the smell of coffee but I can't drink the stuff for love nor money."

Mignon smiled sweetly. "You're missing a real pleasure."

But Rohama's pleasure was to sit watching the old people eat and drink; their pleasure in eating was so child-like and constant. She liked their table manners, too; they had a certain dispassion in the way they squared up to a meal and used their knives and forks which seemed to Rohama the height of breeding. "And what's new?" Mignon asked between sips.

"Anne Lewis and her mother have come back and so I'll be able to go out one of these evenings."

"Ah, yes, she babysits for you." Mignon was vague. She had never offered to babysit herself and did not intend to.

"She's bought herself a Jaguar," said Rohama, sharing in the triumph. "They've got money for everything."

"They must be extremely well-to-do," said Mignon.

"Oh, they are. Mrs. Lewis owns streets in Liverpool."

Mignon sipped her coffee.

"And she's such a simple girl with all her money," Rohama went on. "I never feel she thinks we're below her because we're not as rich as she is."

"That's nice," Mignon said without enthusiasm.

There was a pause. At last, Rohama said she would have to go. She stood up and looked over herself. "Don't I look a sight? I had to put these wellingtons on to get the beetroots."

The brother and sister considered her without comment. She looked to them as she usually did: strong body dressed in a flowered overall, head tied up in a piece of colourless voile, sturdy legs bare inside their wellingtons: a general impression of a person older than she was; but dissatisfied. When she went away she left the ripples of this dissatisfaction behind her. "I know Roma longs to know what's going on here but I've never said a word. It's best that she shouldn't know." Freddy said nothing.

Mignon set down her empty cup. "All the same, if we get some money one day I'd like to give her a real good present—just as a gesture of thanks for all she does for us. She really is kind." She thought a while. "I'll get her a basket of those Bramleys that came down in the night and you can take them over."

So, that afternoon, Mignon went out into the garden to pick up the windfalls, humming to herself like a very old bee in a very small bottle and enjoying the warmish, south-east wind and the sensation of things on the move.

While she was there a car drove up to the front of the house. The horn was blown three or four times. Picking up her basket, Mignon hurried forward under the low trees towards the gate into the lane and there saw her daughter and grandson looking up at the house and waiting for some response. She called. Nesta and Patrick hurried towards her and they hugged one another. Patrick took the basket and, linking arms, with Mignon in the middle, they turned back towards the house and Freddy.

There was some reserve, some hesitation, some doubt as to what was exactly the right thing to say but everyone admired the car which Nesta and Patrick had picked up second-hand in London. Patrick was struck by the old people's countrified air: the lined, brown faces, the uneven teeth, the uneven smiles, the rather large noses and ears, the knobby hands and wrists—and the bright, shrewd eyes.

They went indoors, were shown up to their rooms, talked about their European journey and Nesta, who lacked interest in museums and cathedrals, said she had seen enough things to last her for the rest of her life.

"You mean you haven't enjoyed your trip?" Mignon asked.

"Those places are all so much alike," was the reply.

Mignon looked costive. "Humph," she said to herself, "it's the same Nesta."

"And what's happening here?" Nesta asked aggressively.

Mignon laughed happily. "There's going to be some excitement shortly, dearest..." and she told them about the diaries and the coming visit of Charles Milford, the emissary of Heinz.

Nesta's face dropped. "You mean someone's going to publish Father?"

"His diaries and papers. Yes." The smile faded.

"Are they any use? He was the driest letter writer since the long drought."

"But historically they're of immense significance. It seems

83

we've been sitting on what may prove to be a goldmine."

"Is that what Edward told you?"

"Well..." Mignon found herself on the defensive ... "not in so many words."

Nesta looked at her son and at Freddy. "I wouldn't have thought Father's writings had much value, would you?"

"That remains to be seen. But don't you think it's exciting?"

"Well, it all depends." Nesta could not hide her implacable hostility and Mignon understood that despite all her years abroad Nesta had not changed but was still encapsulated in the past with her frustrations and resentments, insulated against time, place and changes of climate.

"Did Edward come here especially to look at the papers?"

"I told you, dearest, he's married again and he wanted to introduce his wife to us. He was most charming. Mellow and pleasant."

"But he must have wanted something. It isn't Edward not to want to cash in on whatever's going."

"He wanted to see us."

"That's hard to believe." Nesta sniffed. "He was always so calculating."

Mignon tried to paint a cosy picture of the new bride and did not mean to mention the house-buying episode, but Freddy brought it in.

"I thought he was after something," Nesta said drily. "Did he make an offer for this place?"

"Do you think he'd want this place?"

"I shouldn't be surprised. I can think of a lot of people who'd like it. He probably just wanted to spy out the land. Did he realise I'd be around so shortly?"

"He was very sorry to miss you; and you can go to stay with them any time you like."

"No thank you. I've seen enough of Edward to last me all my life."

Mignon protested. After all, Edward had interested Heinz in the papers. Nesta was not impressed. "If there had been any real value in them Edward would have kept them for himself. There must be a catch in it somewhere. He's bound to be getting something out of it: a commission. There's something for him in the affair."

84

"Oh, dearest, how can you say such things? If you feel *that*, there's nothing more I can say."

"Mother ... please don't forget I know Edward as well as you do. I was brought up with him. I know what he's capable of. He's just out for himself all the time. It's all most fishy."

"Edward has treated us as badly as anyone, I agree. But on this occasion you're wrong. I've only my instinct in this matter and my instinct was to accept Edward's little act of kindness."

"All right. But don't sign anything away. Be very careful. That's my advice to you."

Patrick asked, "Well, what would Edward want?"

"That's what we'll find out. This place probably. He thinks I've lost interest being away and he's looking ahead to his retirement ... he's got the whole thing worked out."

"I can't help but say what I feel: and I disagree!"

Mignon had grown soft in the matter of arguments (having had too long with the weak-willed Freddy as sparring partner) and she found her daughter's sharp attacks uncomfortable. She flushed with vexation, jumped up and hurried out to the kitchen. Nesta knew well enough that she had angered her mother, but made no apology. She was bitter and hard against her mother's unreal enthusiasm about digging up her father's rubbish for sale. To Freddy, who asked her to be more encouraging, she said:

"It's more than I can bear. If Mother wants to fool herself she's free to do so; but don't try to fool me. They must be scraping the barrel if they want to publish Father's ramblings. He was such a bore always. Searching for hours for the predictable thing to say."

Freddy tut-tutted furiously. "It's made a big difference to our lives, I can assure you. It's given us something to live for."

"That I don't doubt. What flabbergasts me is the way you killed the fatted calf for Edward and allowed him to bamboozle you. It's a big confidence trick. What could Father have to say after all these years that's of the slightest value? For God's sake, Freddy, let's keep our heads clear! Father's sense of values was cockeyed. He had a good brain, I grant you: a

85

brilliant brain; but no heart. He was a lopsided person and as I've always said, the biggest bore you could meet. For me, even as a girl, he was utter, absolute boredom. Whenever we went somewhere he killed all interest by his manner. He knew the secrets behind everything; he had to try to keep his mouth buttoned up to prevent state secrets dropping out—and he knew nothing much more than the next man. You must have felt the same about him."

Freddy's voice was high with irritation. "Never. Never."

"Then you forget your own feelings. He used often to irritate you to death."

"What feelings? I always respected your father. To say otherwise is to be untrue to me. Your father mixed with some of the greatest names of his time and you don't reach such a position unless you've got something in your belly."

"The more I see politicians and so-called great men the less I agree with you, I'm afraid."

"Then we must disagree."

Freddy hurried away to tell his sister that Nesta was being brutal and disloyal. Mignon cried aloud in impatience. "Oh, that girl's become intolerable. She's such a drear, isn't she? She makes me feel young, young, young. She's been here only a few hours and she puts our backs up and in a few more we'll all be spitting like cats. As far as I'm concerned she can go away whenever she likes—and damned good riddance."

Freddy was abashed. "Oh, but you mustn't say that. However tired you are of her, remember that she hasn't been here for years."

"She's a drear and I don't feel dreary. I don't want her sighings and bitterness. I've pushed the past aside and am looking ahead. There's no time for all that bellyaching. She lives in the past. Let her! I'm looking ahead."

Freddy walked uneasily back and fore.

Mignon went on, "All she's saying now is a new excuse for an old bellyache. When has Nesta ever approved of anything? When has she ever been happy?"

Freddy thought it was unkind to say this within a few hours of the woman's arrival. "Well, it's the truth." Everyone excused rudeness and silliness by claiming they were the truth, Freddy said.

"And so what?" Mignon asked staring at him full in the face, anger in eyes, voice and brow.

After their meal, Mignon had a small revenge. Nesta, who was listlessly leafing through a woman's magazine, asked how Rohama was getting on. Mignon promptly assumed tremendous enthusiasm. "She's a great help to us, do you know."

Nesta was taken aback by the tone but said she was glad to hear it—"things turned out better than one would have thought."

"*We* get on very well. I hope *you* do, too."

"Why shouldn't I?"

"I'm afraid you might have some lingering grudge against her."

Now it was Nesta's turn to be on the defensive. "Me? Why should I?" She sounded as though nothing could have been further from her thoughts. Mignon ignored this and went on, "I'd like you to make some sort of friendly gesture towards her." She noted the carefully hidden surprise and went on: "Go out of your way to be friendly. You'll probably meet her here tomorrow. She's always dropping in."

"I don't mind meeting her, Mother, but don't expect me to weep on her shoulder."

"I never regretted my decision to accept them." This was not as simple as it sounded but the remark was enough to make Nesta abandon her pretence that the magazine interested her more than the conversation. She asked what Rohama's husband was like.

"A first-rate farmer and he adores Rohama." Then, honesty compelled her to add: "He's not up to Rohama's level, really. He's a bit rough."

The idea that Rohama had any level had never struck Nesta and a movement of her mouth showed her doubt.

Mignon retorted quickly: "You'd better not make the mistake of looking down on Rohama. Despite her odd background she's a subtle and perceptive person. She's got far more of your father's spirit than you have."

"She's welcome to Father's spirit, whatever that was."

"Her eyes are exactly like Arthur's. She looks straight at you and she's not taken in. Shrewd's the word and you should know it."

There was a pause. Then Mignon said Rohama wanted to meet Nesta and if the other woman did not call at the farm within the next couple of days it might be a good idea to visit her home.

Nesta was not for or against the idea. She merely said, "Uh-huh" but this provoked her mother into saying, "Please don't have any more dark thoughts about Rohama, Nesta. I'm too old to live with these tensions."

"I shan't have any dark thoughts. Believe me, I have no thoughts of Rohama. I've not thought about her for years and she doesn't enter into my calculations."

"You mustn't be . . ."

Nesta interrupted: "Really, the way you talk anyone would think I had a duty to Rohama. I owe her nothing. She owes me nothing. I don't want to be involved. If she's got Father's spirit I hope it takes her somewhere."

She picked up the magazine again and there was a cold silence while Mignon looked at her daughter and wondered how such a good-looking woman should be so crabby and boneless.

"Where's Patrick?" Mignon asked by and by. Nesta thought he had gone for a walk. She looked around vaguely as though expecting to see him hanging from a curtain rail. Mignon was about to say what a fine person he had become but thought again and said aggressively, "What's he going to do?"

"It's not sure."

"What about the university place?"

"Oh, that! We've just found out that no university will look at him unless he's got three passes—or two, I get confused—at A-level."

"So the university's out?"

"For this year. At least."

Mignon drew in her breath in disapproval and Nesta who knew her mother was longing to get at her through her son refused to be drawn.

"Then what's he going to do?"

Nesta flipped over a page casually. "God knows. You try to get him to make up his mind."

At that moment they heard Patrick in the hall coming in from a walk around the fields. He was subdued, rather perturbed by the farm's isolation and the absence of anything interesting near at hand. He had seen a couple of women driving by in a green Jaguar and that was all.

"That's the girl who baby-sits for Roma," Mignon said.

"A baby-sitter with a green Jaguar?"

"The mother owns property in Liverpool and they sometimes play at farming here. They've become friendly with Rohama."

"The daughter was gorgeous," Patrick said. "She looked about twenty."

"If you want to meet her you must speak to Roma."

"What does she do here?" Although he tried to sound casual he gave away his interest and Mignon laughed.

"I told you, dearest, they play around with a little farm they've got and then when they decide to run off to Liverpool or London they hand over all their stock to Martin and Roma and begin all over again the next time. Freddy knows Mrs. Lewis fairly well. He says she's a well-read person. At least she likes Freddy's things which is what matters. He finds them very much to his taste. He once told me that they reminded him of children playing with cardboard money, entirely lighthearted and unaffected. The big difference is that the money's real."

Patrick had a real respect for money having spent his formative years in a colonialist-imperial society in which money and a good climate were the twin poles of a comfortable and amiable existence. He was inwardly agape at this vision of a mother and daughter in full command of a large private income commuting here and there in between playing at farming. It seemed to him the sort of life he could enjoy.

"I suppose you'd like a life doing nothing," Mignon said, having understood his expression.

Patrick giggled. "Doing what one liked. That's different."

And what did he want to do? Read for the bar?

"Good God," said Nesta. "He'd never do it. I don't think he's ever read a book from cover to cover in his life."

Even Mignon's severe eyes did not abash him. "Well I lose interest after a few pages. Life seems so much more interesting. And there's so much drivel written these days."

Mignon burst out laughing. "I've never met anyone before who boasted about his inability to read. It must be a Rhodesian habit."

89

Patrick took himself seriously even when he was being most absurd and he agreed that he had inherited his aversion to reading from his father who had read *Lady Chatterley* and *Lolita* and other such titles, but for the kicks not the literature. Mignon, rather bemused by this self-satisfied philistinism, looked at her daughter and said with the right note of piety, "If you get the reading habit when you're young it lasts all your life."

Nesta yawned. "He's heard that since he was a tot. I've given up. Patrick hasn't listened to me since he was in short trousers so I've stopped offering advice."

"Can anyone go through life in such a state of ignorance? Doesn't he need some sort of discipline, some diploma or whatever it is that people need these days?"

Patrick agreed such things helped but were not essential. His tone suggested to Mignon that he had never worked at all.

"I had a job. There was a plan to make me a banker. A friend of Dad's offered me a place as a trainee. Somewhere along the line I lost interest."

"Be honest, dear, the bank also lost interest in you."

He looked calmly at his mother. "It was fifty-fifty."

"You mean he was sacked, dearest?"

"Not sacked, Grandma. I just felt the heat rising around me so I left. Probably with about five minutes to spare."

"And where was the bank?"

"In Salisbury."

Patrick waved the whole thing away as he stretched out on the sofa with the corgi on his belly. "How can people take such careers seriously? I only went in for it to please Dad and because I couldn't think of anything else." He noted the strange flicker in Mignon's eyes and turned to the dog. "You wouldn't want me to be a bank clerk, would you, Ianto?"

"He's a lazy charmer," thought Mignon primly. "He gets that from his father. And what would you like to do, dearest, assuming that everything was perfect in a perfect world?"

Patrick looked at his mother before replying. "That's the big question. I'm full of ideas but I don't know whether they'll pay off. I might write."

"His father all over again," Nesta said. Patrick ignored her. There was an attempt at largeness as he added, "I'll find something" although the cross-examination, coming at the end of a dreary walk, tended to deflate. "You know, this is an extraordinary period for people with initiative and intelligence and, of course, imagination. I call it the Age of Wonder, don't you? A couple of generations ago chaps such as myself would have been sent into the church or the navy. Everything would have been laid down but now the whole world lies before me. I've got lots of projects. A friend of mine has just inherited an estate in New Caledonia from his maternal grandfather and I'll probably go out there with him and help him to run the place."

Mignon mentally whizzed a globe round and then had to confess she'd no idea where New Caledonia was. On being enlightened she was filled with disbelief. "The South Sea Islands?"

"Think of it. Gorgeous climate. Gorgeous girls. Fruit and nuts falling off the trees. Moonlight bathing. I'm all in favour, Grandma, aren't you?"

"What will you get off the estate?"

"Coffee. Mostly."

"Coffee? I thought that came from Brazil and Kenya."

"It's a very important crop in New Caledonia, I can assure you."

"Well," Mignon said, unable to think of anything else to say, "it sounds remote. Very remote."

His mother, who had begun to polish her nails, looked up. "And when do you sail, darling boy?" Her irony was not lost on him.

"Who can say? The project may not work out."

"You can say that again, my dear."

Eventually Patrick grew tired of their banter and went to bed. Mignon immediately began to deplore the freedom which he was allowed and Nesta's indifference to his future. She thought her daughter ought to take a stand against his wild talk. The boy needed discipline and his South Sea Islands talk needed discouraging.

"And do you think I take it seriously?" A pause. "Do you?"

"Impossible to tell with you."

"Oh, really. If I go along with him it's because ever since he was about seventeen I've learned not to argue. Whatever I say he does the opposite. He's his father all over again with the madness of youth tacked on. I tell myself it will pass."

Mignon couldn't argue with this, so she said severely: "He's dangerously seductive, you know," as though this was his mother's fault. "He's an easy charmer and that can be fatal."

Nesta found this remark old-fashioned. How could anyone find his charm dangerous? In what way? Everything he did was so easily seen through. "He lives out his little enthusiasms like a good actor and it's all naïve and touching. What possible charm can there be in him?"

Mignon was at pains to get her point of view over exactly and explained that all this was "bad for the boy." In a phrase: he ought not to expect easy pickings in life. He ought to think of a career.

"But why do you say this to me? You speak to him. He may listen to you."

"I suppose he's living on you."

"Who else? He hardly earned anything at the bank."

"Is that good enough, Nesta? At his age?"

"Now tell me what I should do." It was an ultimatum to her mother to shut up. Mignon said she had no wish to interfere. "But, Mother, I want you to interfere if you can make him see sense. He wanted to come to England. It never occurred to me to leave him at home. Besides he's awfully good company and we've thoroughly enjoyed the trip, cathedrals and museums excepted. He's got the most incredible gift of picking up interesting acquaintances. He was awfully popular on the boat and it did me the world of good to meet all the people he teamed up with."

Mignon was fascinated by this aspect of her grandson and wanted to know more.

"What kind of people? All kinds. There was a little Italian engineer and a French couple with whom he spent a lot of time."

"Oh, foreigners," Mignon said.

"Who else? We were on an Italian ship. We were the only British people on the boat."

"Oh, I'm not against foreigners."

They were both aware that they were on the edge of a

quarrel. Nesta was ready to flare up so she said she'd go to bed. Mignon pulled herself together and offered something to drink and they went out into the kitchen together.

"I suppose," Nesta said as she filled the kettle, "that there's hardly anybody left here now of the people I knew."

"Oh, I don't know..." and Mignon promptly rattled off a dozen names of people—not forgetting the Corbetts—who would welcome a visit from Nesta and Patrick.

"Yes, I'd thought about them," Nesta said without conviction. "Although I don't want to see Muvvy very much."

Both mother and daughter agreed that their kinswoman in Caerifor was a bore. On the other hand, Mignon said, if visits were out what were they going to do with their time at home? And late at night, sipping weak tea, the period of the stay at Swanquarter opened out like an enormous ledger that had to be filled.

They were not the only ones who foresaw utter boredom. Patrick looked out for the girl in the Jaguar, failed to see her and wondered whether he should take up woodwork or something. Ashley came and suggested they should go fishing together. Patrick agreed, but when he pressed Ashley for a date, Ashley withdrew into his diary and found that he was booked up for some time.

Ashley was fascinated by the visitors and watched them as though they had been a pair of strange sea creatures washed up by a high tide. Like Mignon, he was deeply impressed by the distinction of Nesta on the threshold of the middle forties and liked her langour, which he found restful and feminine. She promised to visit Muvvy in the same disinterested way she promised Rohama, too, that she would visit her, when they met. But she visited neither immediately for she and Patrick had other things to do. On the third listless day Nesta announced that they had promised to attend the eighty-first birthday party of Nesta's mother-in-law in Dublin and a couple of days later they set off for Holyhead in the second-hand car. After nearly a week of pointless activity they blew out with the same casual charm with which they had blown in. No one seemed to have made much impression on them; they seemed more glad to be going than staying: that was all.

"How restless they are," Freddy said. "Life in Africa seems to

93

make people unfit for the small circumstances here. You felt they were being chafed."

Rohama was astounded. "Those two didn't clutter up the place for long, did they?"

"They'll be returning," Mignon said. She was already preparing the bed for Charles Milford and because Patrick and his car were not available she asked Ashley to meet the young historian at Caerifor. Ashley, faithful to the last, agreed.

7

THE FIRST SUITOR

ASHLEY CORBETT had no idea what the young assistant editor of a prestige historical series would look like. He expected youth, certainly, but a youth already pledged to early decreptitude and, even, a premature hobble. He found himself, among the familiar red-faced crowds returning from the autumn horse fair, shaking hands with a tallish young man who seemed hardly out of his teens. A modishly striped shirt and a rolled umbrella were undergraduate effects; the cascades of palely auburn hair which almost hid the hazel eyes, the pink, unlined face, were effects associated with pop singers. The hair straggled over the face like a well-grown conservatory plant; behind it were the human features, including a bright, un-involved smile. This juvenile figure carried two antique pieces of hand-luggage: a valise that might have gone honeymoon-ing in 1910 and a briefcase, bulging with books, held together by string. Although the conventional Corbett strained forward in order to get a glimpse of the whites of the young man's eyes, he was considerably taken aback; to send so young a person on such a mission diminished its importance, its possible scope. It was clear to Ashley that the publishers did not expect a great deal from the papers.

Ah, the young man said, leaning forward to peer out through his curls, how he had been looking forward to seeing Caerifor! How he enjoyed visiting such country towns! How much he appreciated—especially after London—their organic life, their intimacy! Ashley, struggling to fit the large case into the car boot, agreed but without quite understanding what Milford found so marvellous. "The sense of belonging must be so strong, Mr. Crockett."

Ashley let the first misnaming pass without correction; but when, as they were driving through Station Road up to the town, Milford said, "It must be possible to have a deeply satisfying life here, Mr. Crockett!" he felt he had to put the record straight.

The young person was abashed in an unfelt sort of way. "How silly of me. Corbett. I shall remember that." He smiled wildly and without focus and went on making his elderly remarks about small-town life.

"It gets a bit tedious at times, you know." Ashley felt he had to be honest. "You see the same faces week after week; you almost do the same things."

"That's where we differ, Mr. Crock—" he lurched in mid-syllable—"Corbett. I've never been bitten by the metropolitan bug myself. In fact, I try to spend every weekend with my aunts in Sussex."

"That must be agreeable."

"Essential for my sanity. Without the country I'd wither at the roots."

These flat statements coming on top of the pre-Raphaelite presence puzzled and baffled Ashley, who was trying to make out what Mignon and Milford would make of one another. They drove towards Ashley's office in silence for Milford noticed that his companion did not greatly enjoy his conversation and shut up. They parted temporarily outside the offices while Milford went uptown to buy toothpaste and writing paper and Ashley signed the day's mail and got over his astonishment.

* * * *

Milford loved new towns; he opened himself to them like a medium picking up impressions and essences. He fed on Caeri-for—the stones of the houses, the faces of the people—like a ghost drinking wine on All Souls Eve. His new perceptions awoke the poetic and literary echoes in his memory—he had an essentially Victorian cargo of allusions, quotations and anecdotes—and the first name that stirred was Kilvert. For fifty paces, maybe, he saw the town as a backcloth for the *Diaries;* later, while standing at a street corner waiting for a bus to pass, he heard two women talking in a way that suggested Dylan Thomas to him; but when he looked up at the sky beyond the roofs his mood changed and he was reminded of the Flintshire poems of Gerard Manley Hopkins. In fact, despite their differences, all three men seemed near to the spirit of the town.

Walking down the High Street, along the crown of the whale-backed hill that, even before the Romans, had provided the ancient Britons with a natural defensive position, Milford was able to appreciate the double views of the town. On one side, narrow, shadowy streets opened towards wide perspectives of a tidal river; on the other, the streets dipped towards the Victorian folly of the railway station and the quiet stretches of fields and woods, brilliantly green in the September evening light, which lay beyond.

Having made his purchases, Milford went towards the river where the tide brimmed the quay. Deep golden leaves fell from the horse chestnut trees lining the river walk. One of the leaves had settled on the open paint-box of an elderly artist, a dewdrop at the end of her nose, who dabbed spiritedly at a small canvas. Behind her, through the arches of Grimshaw's bridge, the slanting sunlight made a wash of gold.

Milford walked on towards the bridge and then began to cross it. Halfway over, he stopped and turned back to get the famous view of the town rising against a lemon-gold sky like Nazareth in a Byzantine mosaic. The sharp roofs, the church steeples were simplified by the clear autumnal air into the basic outline of a nineteenth-century provincial capital; and all this was made more beguiling by hundreds of rooks flying overhead at that moment from the pastures beyond the river to their rookery in the castle grounds. For a long time Milford let the sights and sounds create their own mood in him before walking slowly backwards towards the town.

By climbing some steps off the quay and by following a rising path under ancient, windowless walls, he came out in one of the town's small squares where the elm trees had gathered the autumn evening light about them and the people who passed seemed to him like characters in Firbank's *Caprice,* the sort of antiquated snobs who might refer to actresses as 'abandoned women on the boards'. He walked on through a shady street lined on one side with substantial houses (a *c.* 1830? formed in his mind) which he stopped to admire. While appreciating the detail of their fanlights and their balconies he noticed, with a start, the wall immediately at his side (it was as though it had

nudged him) and he recognised the stonework of an ancient
bastion which had, in the course of time, acquired its own
green cover of valerian, toadflax, stonecrop and geraniums, and
had become a summing up of every piece of ancient Roman
wall he had ever seen. He lost a breath with pleasure.

As he stood by the wall, savouring his discovery, a light went
on in one of the (c. 1830?) houses nearby and the red-shaded
lamp picked out the books and silver of a room that had been
lived in by the same family for generations. He walked on
slowly, divided between the ancient wall and the comfortably-
furnished room, turned the corner and with an unerring instinct found his way back to Ashley's office.

* * * *

On the way out to Swanquarter, over Grimshaw's bridge, up
the steep hill opposite, and along the rolling tableland beyond,
Ashley wondered whether it would be wise to warn Milford
against promising Mignon too much.

He touched on the subject of publication carefully, found
Milford ready to talk, and, with a certain deliberation, said,
"The family at Swanquarter are hoping there's a lot of money
in this for them."

"Are they?" Milford tossed a couple of curls back. "Who
gave them the impression they would make any money? Professor Lloyd-Ballantyne? Or is it just supposition?"

Ashley did not know. He thought Milford might like to be
warned so that he was not led into unconsidered speech that
might be misinterpreted.

"I'm most grateful to you for your hint. I'm a small fish in
the Heinz organisation without power to promise anything. In
fact, I'm here mainly to assess the material available and take a
cursory glance at some of it. So I can't say whether it will be
published or not. I merely offer a first opinion. You understand,
of course, that Professor Lloyd-Ballantyne has interested Sir
Ragismund Heinz in the papers, but I don't hide from you that
most of us in Heinz feel that if the papers had had any value
the Professor would have wanted to have some say in editing
them himself. After all, he's a modern historian. These diaries
cover his period."

98

Ashley nodded silently, impressed by the young man's candour.

"So, you see, Mr. Corbett, so far as I am concerned

a. I can't even say whether the diaries will be published and

b. I can't promise that they'll bring in any money even if they are. Unless they have quite exceptional interest the chances of their hitting the jackpot (as they say) are dim indeed."

"It's all very dodgy, then?"

"I should say so. At the worst, their interest would be limited to specialists and historians."

Ashley wondered whether it was worthwhile bringing out a book for such a small public.

"Ah," said Milford, "the smallness is relative. With the fifteen hundred American universities and colleges as a basic market we might expect to move about 3,000 copies over the first five years: the usual figure for this documents series."

"And would there be much money in this?"

"Highly unlikely. Bringing out such works is a labour of love. Can I explain?"

Milford said the editing of a mass of material of this kind was expensive and long: the full-time work of one or more scholars, involving the full-time services of a secretary for transcribing manuscripts, work in libraries and research centres fitting in the background; long, painful days of reading proofs and checking notes. The whole thing would take years. Even if everything went smoothly there were all kinds of problems, and the firm would be involved in enormous outlay before they had sold a single copy.

And did he feel that the diaries might contain good material?

Milford thought a moment. "Put it this way: I should be astonished if they were good. I keep remembering that the Professor has shown no interest in them all these years. It's too much to expect that they should be good. On the other hand they may contain new facts of value to the historian."

Ashley winced for Mignon.

"Indeed, Mr. Corbett, there's almost certain to be nothing of value. Every civil servant is keeping notebooks these days and the field is much better documented than it used to be. And, then, politicians are only too anxious to sell their memoirs and cash in on their names before they're forgotten. There just isn't much left to say. I must also confess that I'm prejudiced against the period covered by these papers. I hate every one of the main figures—Lloyd George, Ramsay MacDonald, Baldwin, J. H. Thomas, the Duke of Windsor, Mrs. Simpson. That inter-war period was sordid."

"You think ours is any better?"

"It's worse. I tell you: I'm prejudiced. I don't like my own times. I'm a late Victorian. I'd have been at home in Great Malvern about 1889, say, in a big solid house on the hillside made for a large family. I even like Victorian painting."

"Victorian things are all the rage. They fetch good prices in the sale-room."

"Yes, the period corresponded to the age of Maximum Security, everyone's happy childhood, and the furniture reflects this. Whereas modern furniture is made for households where the women have to go out to work to keep the car on the road."

Ashley laughed. "That's well thought out." This is a very lively chap, he said to himself, and one who's not going to be easily taken in despite his girlish face. He suddenly became interested in him as in some old clock that appears to work by waterdrops or camphor crystals.

And would Milford be excited if the papers were good?

"If they were good and I was asked to edit them and did a first-rate job it would make me as a historian and completely alter my prospects. It's no good thinking of that, I'm afraid."

Ashley began again: Did Milford know Lloyd-Ballantyne personally?

"I've met him."

"Is he well thought of?"

"He's a popular author," he said, which was ambiguous.

"You disapprove of popular authors?"

For the first time Milford looked less than candid. "Ah, in order to answer that question one wants to know

a. What the subject is.

b. Why the author is popularising it, and

c. The effects of the popularisations. I think it's true to say that no specialist likes his subject vulgarised. By this rather rough standard Professor Lloyd-Ballantyne just passes muster."

"He's my wife's cousin, you know."

"So you told me at the station."

"So I did. Well, I can't stand him."

"You mean as a man."

"As a man."

"I know nothing about him, Mr. Corbett. One tends to distrust intellectuals who try to vulgarise their subjects. It's a question of integrity. That's all."

"He put all these wild ideas into the old people's heads."

"That's rather a pity. They can only be disappointed. We couldn't possibly promise early wealth. He should have known that."

"He makes a lot of money from his books?"

"Quite nicely; he sells well and then he gets all sorts of well-paid commissions. He does very well, I should say."

"Anyway, be that as it may. All I ask you, if you'd be a good chap, is not to overplay your hand. Don't build up hopes that can never be fulfilled."

"I shan't promise them anything. I can't."

"That understood, it remains for me to say how much they are looking forward to seeing you."

They had reached a piece of open common land, without hedges or trees, offering a wide panorama of the country, of the estuary narrowing towards Caerifor, of the smoking chimneys of Port Rydal, made almost poetic by distance, further along the coast, and, near at hand, clearly defined against the illuminated sky, the pinewood on a hilltop near Swanquarter. Ashley stopped and they left the car in order to enjoy the clear view. At that time of day there was little traffic (most of the Port Rydal traffic took another road, in any case) and all they could hear was the seawind trilling in the telegraph wires and curlews calling to one another over the common. This was the sort of country that, in the last century, had heard the train whistles and the ships' sirens, the sort of country common to parts of Wales and Ireland, which seem haunted by the presences of those who went away into exile.

More recent times had brought prosperity and freedom from anger but the wind still shook out the ashfruits over places of broken stone and the curlews created their own presence in this heartbreak country at the edge of Europe. The melancholy of the place, the sheer poetry of it, intoxicated Milford who knew that such a scene, such an evening light slanting over hills and sea, such a notion of a vanished peasantry, were things he most loved. He knew he had been right to come, if only for this. "God!" he said to himself, "it's heaven!"

They resumed their journey, winding out of the common in a slow curve into a wide, sedgy valley where black cattle grazed.

A little further on were the beechtrees, the milkstand and the twangy iron gates that marked the entrance to Swanquarter. Milford was slightly disappointed by this simple entrance and was pleased to notice, so far as the failing light permitted him, that the house was more interesting than its approach. The pinetrees nearby provided the sunset scenery, their branches and jagged outlines involved with the lemons and golds of the sky.

They blew the horn in front of the house and then everything happened at once: Mignon and Freddy bounced out of the front door like cuckoos out of a Swiss clock; Milford's briefcase burst open and shed its contents on the path; Mignon cried, "Your beautiful books!" Milford did not stop to pick them up. He dropped what remained of the case as an item of no consequence and advanced with outstretched hands towards his hostess (Freddy, meanwhile, tripped over Ianto and only saved himself from falling by grabbing the doorpost). Ashley began to gather up the fallen goods and Milford did likewise (his angelic curls tumbling over his face) laughing and reassuring everyone that such a catastrophe had threatened for months. He had been let down by his string.

It was only when they were indoors that Ashley saw that Mignon had daubed on a little lipstick in a haphazard fashion and Freddy wore full canonical fig, with a clean alpaca coat hanging lugubriously around his fleshless thighs. It was all in Milford's honour! And what charm! What wild lopsided smiles! Milford hardly knew how to be sweet enough in response as he was borne forward on a wave of smiles and charm into the large sitting-room where, on a low table before one of the first fires of the autumn, a late tea had been laid.

Nothing could have been more sincere or charming than

Milford's welcome; and he rose to it. He was grateful and affable. He thanked them for sending someone to meet him; they thanked him for coming such a long way to see them; he said it was all most interesting; they said they were sure he wouldn't feel he had wasted his time; Milford bowed; Mignon curtsied; both sides were charmed with the other.

Milford's extreme youth did not upset Mignon, who was used to precocious brilliance and was sure that young Milford was, in the old cliché, 'a coming man'. Freddy, too, warmed to his youth partly because he liked young people, partly because youth was a rare commodity in their lives, a missing principle. For Milford, the old people, that first evening, had the charm of forgotten childhoods. Everyone, he thought, carries residual memories of such people within the soul: the people who had smiled at one's cradle, the remote generations that had passed on at the period of one's birth or extreme infancy, but were subconsciously remembered and regretted.

When they had taken tea they went up to Milford's room. By this time, the house was quite dark so they went aloft with a blue hand lamp, carried by Mignon, and an electric torch for the stairs, carried by the young man. They entered the carefully arranged bedroom and the first object that Milford saw was a white china jerry, its edges garlanded with roses, sitting like a sacred vessel in a little cupboard of its own. Mignon set the lamp on a chest of drawers and began opening cupboards to show Milford where he could keep his things. She drew close to him and "Incidentally," she said, "incidentally, you don't mind using a *pot de chambre*, I hope." Milford shook his head. "I was sure you'd understand that country life is still behind the towns in many ways. We have a water closet but it's such a long way if—" and she tittered deliciously—"you're taken short." She felt she was overwhelming him with refined charm and was about to leave him alone when a new thought struck her. "There's one thing I'd like to point out to you, Mr. Milford, which may not have occurred to you. It's this: my brother and I would be most grateful if you could keep the reason for your visit to yourself. For instance if you meet any of the local people, don't tell them why you've come. Do I need to say more? I want to mention especially the people who live in the farm up the hill behind us. They're relations of a kind but not really our sort and we've found it's best not to let them know our affairs. People's interest is often merely destructive, don't you feel? Keep them at arm's length, Mr. Milford! They're quite capable of writing off to some other publisher to let the cat out of the bag."

She saw the uncertainty in his face, the hint of disbelief, so she went on hastily, "Relations, Mr. Milford, can be very funny at times—almost your worst enemies. They would do things no non-relative would do. I've told them you've come down here to read some family papers. That will do for them." She spoke loftily, as of the dogs and their meals. "That will satisfy them. That's all they need to know."

The lamplight, the old lady's vehemence, the note of intrigue, caught Milford's imagination. He stood as though bewitched, saying nothing.

"Of course, dearest, be polite and that kind of thing ... but a word to the wise ... ? We understand one another ... ?" She turned to go and then asked him in a husky voice whether she had mentioned the *pot de chambre*? He nodded, smiling.

"Good. I forgot whether I'd mentioned it." Another fugitive smile and she was gone.

Milford had been promised some hot water for washing and he partly undressed, waiting for Mignon to return. He unpacked, arranged his books on a small table by the window, raised the wick of his lamp and got out his notebook which, as a budding poet, he carried everywhere with him.

On the last used page was a quotation from Stephen Spender's *World within a World*: "But Greece seen through the eyes of the Greek landscape suggests a different conclusion; that great art and great thought can go together with austerity. More than that, they can result from a consensus of enlightened opinion in a democracy; and a shared social vision of justice, tolerance, and truth can have as complements principles of beauty, sculpted in marble, rhythmed in verse."

He read this quickly and then, his imagination on fire, jotted down hastily in his clerical hand: Suggested Encomium of Caeriforshire: A mystical openness; cromlechs; ruined castles among a few trees; druidic circles; poets' houses; a distant prospect of mountains; hermits' cells; saxifrage-covered springs; Celtic crosses at the empty cross-roads; square-towered churches; rhythm of outcrop of rock and quarry edges; islands off the coast; low, sandy shores flanked with pinetrees; little chapels at the far ends of fields away from the main roads; tumuli; ancient tombs; a sacred land; every displaced stone somehow numinous. Its open light; its sea-born illuminated quality; its primitive Italian gold soil; its peat bogs, peat-ditches and workings flooded with autumn rain.

"Among the moorlands and open fields, cultivated valleys, rather shallow and unsatisfactory as valleys without producing more than a certain bogginess at the edge of a meandering brook. Here a selection of white-washed farms and pink-washed cottages whose inhabitants stand and stare at passing cars with Robert Colquhoun faces, unflinching in sunlight or rain. A mountain ash covered with red fruit; a gorse bush in flower among the rocks, the clouds rolling over Caeriforshire and mingling with the belfries of Caerifor. A land of ancient warriors, first of all; a land of poets and divines; a land where an heroic fullness of being might be possible. Heroic friendships (??); heroic lovers (??)".

At this point his inspiration failed him and, the hot water not having arrived, he went on to write a letter to the three aunts who brooded over his destiny. His aunts expected Letters; he did his best to oblige:

"Meanwhile, the traveller bound for Port Rydal yawns out the last stages of a tedious journey. He takes the landscape as read, too bored to enjoy the subtleties of the two lights meeting above him, too blunted to see any charm in the patient dip and rise of the pastures under their shawl of twilit clouds. As light flickers from distant windows he asks himself what sort of people can live in such places and what kind of life they have. Surely such places must be dull, so far from the centre of things, in the original back of beyond. No, those lonely lights amidst the sparse woodlands give no sense of return, as after a long absence, but only a sort of fear—largely the fear of being forgotten.

"Eight miles west of Caerifor and still twenty-three miles short of Port Rydal the railway skirts the lands belonging to the old home of Daniel Samuel Roberts, for over forty years the M.P. for Caerifor and known there as the 'People's Friend'. The farmhouse, built of purple-blue stone stands on a small bluff. It looks vaguely like a Burgundian fortified house with high out-flanking walls topped with pigeon lofts, now empty, and its roof pierced with mansard windows.

"Inside the house there is the atmosphere of a museum. Things have not changed much for forty years. The good furniture has lost its lustre, the books on the shelves echo the controversies of the last century and the first years of this—disestablishmentarianism, the abolition of tithes, the limitations of the powers of landlords. Nothing is so far away from us as the immediate past; even the Corn Laws and Waterloo seem more instantly in focus. The reputation of such a house, such a family, would live on in the memory of the people; one feels instinctively that in local mythology this strange farmhouse, rather enchanting despite its decay, stands for something. The stone walls and the chimneys mean little; but the people they housed do. The old people are in keeping with the place, utterly out of this world in way of speech, in manner. They live here surrounded by the past, with the faded sepia photographs of the dead, in a variety of frames, lined up on the walls. A house, in short, that feeds the sad nerve and might stifle the young."

The gong sounded below. Suddenly he realised that dinner was late, that he'd not washed, that he'd not changed. He thrust his letter aside and began stripping. It took him a surprisingly short time to change but he was still long enough to cause Mignon and Freddy to wonder where their erudite young guest could be. They wandered into the hall and peered wonderingly towards the darkness at the top of the stairs. While they stood there, Charles Milford appeared at the stairhead carrying his lamp and sporting a splendid dinner-jacket and bow-tie.

The brother and sister gaped at him as he came slowly down. With a curious half-turn of deference like old retainers they stood back at the door and Milford entered the dining-room. He was still so preoccupied by the letter he had left upstairs half-finished that he only slowly realised what a sensation he had created, that he realised what a hush had fallen on his hosts. Having grasped the situation he laughed without self-consciousness.

"I seem to have overdone things, don't I?"

"We've become so informal," said Mignon. "We've let things go too much. It does us good to be reminded of the way things are still done."

Milford was thrilled. "Oh, you're far too generous, Lady Benson-Williams."

They sat down; Milford lordly in his dress suit, Mignon coy and girlish with a woollen shawl over her shoulders; and Freddy homely in the white apron he always wore to carve a bird because of his tendency to spatter himself with fat. For Milford, that first evening was like being in a charade; his presence was charmed, he had nothing to do but be agreeable and expansive so that when Freddy produced, for examination over the coffee, some ancient monographs on local historical questions, written by their father, Milford showed more than a polite interest.

"The mystery is how a public man could have found time for this sort of research in addition to his political work."

"That's what always strikes me, Mr. Milford. Don't you feel it's partly the energy of the Victorians and partly a sense of mission which would make you do twice the normal stint?"

"It must have been."

"Father felt responsible for people," said Freddy. "He found that the ordinary people didn't know their own history—the children knew all about ancient Rome and had no idea when the union with England had taken place—so he set out to produce this little series. It's in simple Welsh which everyone could understand. Before being published in booklet form they were printed in a weekly newspaper."

Milford said it was hard to imagine a modern Member of Parliament doing as much.

"There isn't the need. People are autonomous these days, don't you feel? They need neither religion nor politics. It's the consequence of affluence: the best so far as I can see."

The old people were too enthralled to notice the slight tremor of disapproval in Milford's face and the cool way he turned the conversation; had either of them, he asked, inherited their father's literary ability?

"My brother is the only one. He's forever scratching away."

"But trifles," Freddy said modestly. "What I write is simple: from the heart to the heart."

"I can assure you, Mr. Milford, he is very well thought of by people whose opinions count."

This compliment was about the best that Freddy had ever received from his sister and he glowed from within; he fell into a silent ecstasy to savour it while his sister discussed their father. Suddenly he chipped in: "Both my sister and I are a great man's children, Mr. Milford. Do you know what that means? It means we're small extinct volcanoes—all the heat and fire gone up the main chimney! Brought up in the shadow of a really powerful personality we've never seemed, even to ourselves, anything but pale echoes of that genius for living, for serving, for being of use as a friend and a leader."

Mignon nodded fervently. "Do you know, dearest—" in her excitement she confused Milford with Ashley—"our father has been a standard of measurement all our lives. And the miracle was that it all sprang from nothing. All the family were perfectly ordinary, remarkable in nothing, neither renowned for brains nor beauty, and suddenly there was this man who could speak for the ordinary people, embody their aspirations as no one else in this part of the world has ever done. You understand what I mean? And then taught himself so that *he* could teach *them*. That was devotion of a kind you no longer see in public men."

Because it was his first evening at Swanquarter and because he felt warm towards his host and hostess, Milford discussed the career of Samuel Roberts, M.P., for a long time and never once showed that he had stood for almost all the things Milford abhorred. He was touched by the enthusiasm of the brother and sister but the thought struck him that he had really come to examine the works of the husband not the father. Mignon divined his thought and, with a click of her thumb and fingers, snapped off the talk and offered to show Milford the diaries, late in the day though it was.

Milford had a strong professional curiosity and was willing to see a sample at once, since it would be another hour or so before he felt ready to go to bed. He moved into an arm-chair and Mignon laid a huge tome, almost every page interleaved with additional papers, on his knee. She brought a lamp closer to him and then, as though she feared Rohama's baleful eye might be watching them from an apple tree, she drew the curtains. Milford opened the volume carefully and a slight smell of mustiness was let out.

Freddy and Mignon took up books, too, but could hardly concentrate on their own reading; they watched Milford with an intense interest and hope. Both were fascinated by the young man who looked, despite his silly hair, distinguished in a juvenile kind of way with the heavy tome on his narrow knees, his white cuffs gleaming from the sleeve of his dark jacket, his high forehead, between the strands of his hair, gleaming with the strength and virtue of the untried. From the bow-tie to the well-polished shoes he was cared for, polished up by many hands, brooded on, doted on, thought about, depended on, calculated over. He had begun to read without glasses but suddenly, to their surprise, he shook out a heavy pair with the aplomb of a man of forty and murmuring something about fine handwriting, returned to his reading. He turned over the pages carefully, replacing exactly such loose leaves as fell out. Mignon explained how her husband had worked: the pocket diary for engagements and notes, the odd leaves for jottings in inconvenient places, the main diary for writing up the body of the narrative, as it were. Because of Sir Arthur's good memory a couple of words were often enough to tell him everything he wanted to know about an event, a thought, a speculation. Often he appended material to an entry if later he remembered something he had overlooked at the time or had only realised its importance later.

Milford thanked her and returned self-consciously to his reading, aware of the four eyes watching him from time to time: he felt he was playing in amateur theatricals. To ease himself he moved once or twice but the fine script, the heavy volume and the unfamiliar though restful lamplight troubled him; he had not chosen the best conditions for a preliminary skirmish with Sir Arthur. In addition, the writer had used a variety of abbreviations and initials, as though he had clearly intended working up the material himself. Milford sighed, for the whole thing made wearisome reading at the end of a long day, and he eventually sat back, removed his glasses and sat staring into the fire while the brother and sister looked at one another but said nothing; and then, almost before their eyes, he went off into a doze—abandoning Mignon and Freddy to their stupefaction. He awoke after barely two minutes, started in guilt, and began to read again, hardly daring to look at Mignon for fear she had noticed his lapse. For what seemed a small eternity he ploughed on through the book longing for someone to say a word which would break the spell and lead to a departure for bed. No one spoke and he was eventually obliged to put away his reading glasses and call a day a day. Mignon was waiting for an opinion about the diaries. It was not clear what she had expected Milford to do but she had never foreseen anything quite as untouched as his reaction. "We must see," he said. "Tomorrow I'll make soundings at certain points which ought to provide meaty stuff, so until I've begun that I can't really say anything."

"And the style?" Mignon leaned forward archly. "Is it saleable?"

Milford laughed drily. "That's asking too much, Lady Benson-Williams. It seems adequate."

"Adequate" wasn't the word either of them had had in mind. It seemed a trifle patronising but it was too soon to take offence or lose nerve.

After Milford had gone upstairs Mignon forgot her doubts. The young man, she told Freddy, was a joy—"utterly unlike what she had expected; a dear young fellow". Freddy approved, too, and called him an accomplished and informed young person. They both said they had met a friend; then stopped, worn out. Of course, they were all emotion, all wild impulses and hopes which bred from day to day and could not be restrained but they were exhausted by the day and slept like children.

*   *   *   *

Mignon rose first in the morning and made morning tea for Milford. When she tapped on his door he was still asleep and she bustled into his room, crying, "It's half past eight and a fine morning." Milford was less than thrilled. He apologised for oversleeping. She waved the matter away. "You needed the rest, dearest. Young people burn themselves up. Freddy and I are so old that we seem to need hardly any sleep and, in any case, we don't get any pleasure from lying in bed; so we're stravaging around the house from the peep of day." She stood over him with a black tray and he was obliged to rouse himself and open half an eye lugubriously.

"Yes, when you get to our age you feel it's a waste of time to sleep and loll around because your days are numbered whichever way you look at the matter. Believe me there's nothing like your seventieth birthday for giving you a sense of urgency."

Very gallantly, Milford doubted whether she could have passed seventy. Mignon laughed happily, "Well past it, I assure you. There are times when I feel like a survival from another age; something that's been saved from the Ark."

Milford laughed and choked on a piece of biscuit.

"Oh believe me," she said, banging him on the back, "that's the truth. And there can't possibly have been an age more unwelcoming to survivals than the present. You've got to keep abreast or you lose your human status. Believe me, it's awkward to be old in this century and it will get worse. And for people of our generation it's so confusing! You see, there's no link between my memories of my youth and those of a fifteen-year-old today. The ideals and ambitions one grew up with—took for granted—have become entirely irrelevant. It's weird."

He thought every age had felt that and although she didn't doubt this for a moment, she wondered whether any age had had to adjust quite so much as hers.

"A point is reached—I was only saying the same thing to my brother recently—where one just doesn't understand the way things are going any more. It's deeply disconcerting, I assure you. There's only one source of comfort. As you get older the small things of life mean more and more : a good night's rest, a well-cooked meal, a happy visit. The rest has to take care of itself. But, believe me, Mr. Milford, to be over seventy in this age and place is to be in a very awkward age."

Milford would have liked to be left alone with his tea and his thoughts but Mignon had to engulf him with facts and figures. She began a potted family history, told him that the Family Bible contained entries from 1670 "in the original handwriting". She repeated this detail as though it were vital. "You must see it. As a historian you'll love to see how the handwriting evolved across the generations and how the families, after a certain date, grew smaller but longer-living. Now there are only two of my generation left, only three of the next generation, and so far those three have only produced one child with another on the way. That's Professor Lloyd-Ballantyne's wife..."

Milford was plainly indifferent to the professor. To test him, Mignon said, "He seems to be one of Sir Ragismund Heinz's favourite chicks, doesn't he?" Milford agreed but without enthusiasm.

"We read all Edward's books," she said grandly, observing the effect. "He gets some quite splendid reviews. One in the *Age* praised him to the skies. To the skies. I suppose you read his books."

Milford said Lloyd-Ballantyne had a 'certain influence' but with so much bleakness that he appeared to equate it with a pain in the behind. Mignon mentioned the highly successful book on the 1906 Liberal Government. Milford had reviewed this rather cruelly and entirely anonymously in a small historical review and so his enthusiasm was a trifle false. This did not escape Mignon who said to herself, "We'll have to watch this young man. He's not on our side." She had caught the flavour of his little act: the carefully suspended judgement, the smiling indifference, the discreetly concealed disapproval. She had sniffed out something in the smiling, two-faced Englishman which she was later to call 'the supercilious Tory' and 'the milk-fed Jingoist'.

What she had surprised in Milford was his coming to his senses after his hopeless misjudgement of the family's social position the night before which meant that, like a good English snob, he could not quite forgive Mignon for not being the Lady Mignon Benson-Williams of his dreams. Everything had seemed so right: the address, the circumstances, even the huge, authoritative handwriting of Mignon's letter—about ten lines to a page—and the autumnal beauty of the household had itself contributed to the mystique; but ... they were not at all what Milford had imagined them to be and Mignon's opinions were loathsome into the bargain.

When he went downstairs for breakfast Mignon showed him the room where he was to work, with everything arranged and a fire burning in a jolly little grate. Milford said he was delighted by the arrangements and sat down cosily in front of his bacon and egg. The meal went well until Mignon insisted on bringing up the subject of the diaries. Some seemingly innocent question about copyright led to her supposing that as the holder (of the copyright) she would be entitled to a certain percentage on all sales.

"Naturally," Milford said, "but I don't think we should discuss that yet, do you?"

The question was mild, reasonable, but Mignon hated him for it.

"You can't see people queueing up to buy a work of this kind, can you?" The coldness of the young voice startled Freddy as much as his sister. She pointed out that there were 'enormous numbers' of people who would find the work interesting.

"I'm quite prepared to believe that the diaries will be absorbing, but for specialists only. At least, that's what I think." Mignon's face stiffened with hostility and Milford, who felt this was the time to bring the untethered balloon of her pretentions down to earth, asked with smooth brutality how many people could pay fifty shillings or three pounds for a volume of memoirs. Freddy agreed there would be very few, adding, "I haven't got fifty shillings for a book."

"Everyone's so discouraging," Mignon said, half-defiant, half-petulant.

"Not at all, Lady Benson-Williams. Only you must not expect to get rich quickly by means of these papers."

The brother and sister finished their breakfast quietly. They were thoroughly put out by the young man, who only the night before had embodied all the virtues.

Milford went away into his work room and sat down. He knew he had disillusioned his hostess and that the cosy conditions of the first evening could never be repeated; but he could not pretend. It this respect he was strong; he refused to peddle illusions for the sake of popularity and he refused to think of the editing of the papers as anything but a scholarly task demanding integrity and sound judgement. He would do his best by the memorialist; he would work carefully and methodically.

He had already drawn up his method of work. He had taken

certain periods on which he expected the diaries to throw new light and he would only later consider whether the material had any entertainment value. This, he believed, was justified by the Benson-Williams style which seemed to him as bad as anything he had ever encountered: bathetic and sententious, the product of a club bore, the man who uses three words when one would do.

The early pages were the jottings of a minor civil servant with socialist leanings who wrote out long quotations from Ruskin, Blatchford and William Morris. Later, as the diaries got under way, there were difficulties because of the writer's habit of referring to people by their initials. It would have been a primary task to establish a check list of these hidden persons and he mentioned this to Mignon when she came in with a cup of coffee. She was delighted to help him and showed an astonishing memory, being able to place about a third of the initials at once.

In doing so she put on her best elegist's voice, using all the clichés that thrive daily in *The Times*'s obituary page. "Ah, how well I remember her in those days..." "...later she was renowned for her gracious dinner parties" ... "a witty and accomplished hostess..." "The few who could appreciate his work..." It was as though she had been learning a part for years: the terms, the tone of voice, the act, had all been waiting for the seminal word. Although he distrusted her, Milford was impressed both by her memory and by her witty and acute observations about people.

The second part of the morning dragged. Although it was understood that the early diaries would be small stuff and that the real excitements would only begin after the move to London and the friendship with Lloyd George, there was an aching inadequacy in the style and the thinking that presaged ill. Much of the material was badly presented and Milford idly drew up a circular letter to all civil servants doing a Benson-Williams act, asking them to compile their notes in triple spacing.

His first morning over, only one impression remained: how had it been possible that anyone could have thought of making money out of such material?

He worked on doggedly through the afternoon, switching

his sampling to the fuller diaries on the 1914–18 War period
and emerged dazed and confused, which was hardly surprising
because, it should be made clear, Milford was a medievalist,
who was ignorant of most of the twentieth century.

Mignon brought him tea about three thirty and asked
whether he wouldn't be wise to take a little walk. Freddy was
going out for his constitutional and would be pleased to have
his company. Milford was delighted and sauntered out with
Freddy, swinging a stick and feeling all his pent-up energies
released.

As a companion Freddy could hardly have been bettered.
He could answer all Milford's questions and provide potted
biographies of all the families whose farms and houses they
passed and was able to present each story in such a way that
Milford was never made to feel that Freddy was gossiping idly;
he could feel the old gentleman's human concern for these dim
lives; he could see that every detail was dear to him. The windows of the solid Caeriforshire farmhouses beat back the long
September sunset indifferently as the two men plodded along
the fallow end of ploughed fields, along cart tracks, through
little woods which were no more than windbreaks and down
the hill towards home again. This was Milford's first walk for
days and he enjoyed its period flavour as much as he enjoyed
the sunset glitter lightly strewn with clouds: a mingling of
green and old gold, touched with pinkish sunset light, rather
like a background by Poussin. Across the rolling fields, the
dark-green expanses of the peat bogs, were the bright lines of
the open drains, running towards some unseen river. The air
which sprang into life around the hedges was fresh and heroic
bringing to them the special scents and sounds of the early
evening in Caeriforshire. Then, most impressive of all, was the
emergence out of this emptiness and silence of the evening
express on its way to Port Rydal. It seemed to announce itself
miles away and they watched it move towards them and then
away, at an angle, towards the west, outpacing the thin belts of
trees, the pinewoods and the outcrops of rock. At this point
they abandoned the view of the country to the falling evening
and the autumnal freshness of the air.

*   *   *   *

Not to know what people think of you (within certain limits, of course) is one thing: to misjudge utterly the impression you are making is another; and that evening Mignon made a misjudgement. For some reason, she asked Milford whether he was married. The question was rash enough since the young scholar had all the marks of the virgin boy and nothing to suggest the widening of exasperation and the narrowing of experience which marriage usually brings to young men.

"Choose wisely when the time comes," said Mignon. "Marriage makes or mars your life. Marriage to Arthur Benson-Williams was the turning point in my own life. It was a fairy tale and I still feel something of its magic."

Freddy removed his glasses as though he mistrusted not only his ears but his eyes.

"I was twenty-five when we met—dangerously late for a girl of my generation; people already thought of me as an old maid. Arthur was an acquaintance of my father's and while staying with some distant relations in Port Rydal he came over for the day. My brother, who was staying with us, went down to Caerifor to fetch him with the pony and trap. I was not very well that day. I suffered a lot as a young woman from headaches and nerves, all marks and signs of frustration—I couldn't make anything of my life—and I came downstairs to meet the guest and the cousin who'd come over with him. He was chatting to my father and as I came downstairs I heard him say, 'That may well be true'. And I knew as soon as I heard the voice that the man was going to mean something to my life. It just struck home like that. Arthur had the same certainty as soon as he saw me. We met and that was that; we were made for the other."

("Oh," said Freddy to himself, "Oh, dear, she shouldn't talk like this.")

"We had a marvellously happy life. Then, of course, we were lucky, because we were placed in what I call the main, broad stream of normality. There was no madness or sickness or drunkenness in the family; we weren't terribly clever or eccentric or that kind of thing and, what is even more fortunate, we never wanted anything outside the scope of our means and talents."

She smiled lopsidedly again, shielding her eyes from the lamplight, every inch the actress.

At first Milford was puzzled by this tone and then faintly sceptical. He knew that if she continued in this palpably false way he would say something undiplomatic and offend her. "If only," he thought, "I could get on with my reading without being obliged to listen to this nonsense."

He was in a most awkward position. He had no wish to offend her but he certainly had no wish to spend the rest of his time listening to her fantasies.

Freddy could not understand why his sister had to talk like this. It was unlike her and it was embarrassing. What was so astounding was the failure of her instinct. Didn't she see how her false-toned reminiscences and the affected memorialising irritated Milford? And (Freddy thought) if she once suspects that Milford is against her she'll make his life a misery even though to do so would be against her own interest.

Milford ploughed on with his reading and on the fourth day of his stay they nearly came to a showdown over the midday meal. The tension cracked after Mignon made a sweeping statement about the origins and purpose of the Church of England. Milford thought she was unfair. Freddy was able to hold the antagonists apart and then Ashley came to see how things were going. Mignon went into a council of war with him in the kitchen.

"Ashley, I can feel it in my bones that Charles Milford is not going to report favourably on the diaries. He's the wrong person to assess them. Heinz should have sent an older person, someone who had lived during part of the period covered in the entries."

"Surely, Milford is a specialist."

"In what? All he does is make silly little notes, take walks by himself and write letters to his maiden aunts."

Ashley laughed.

"I'm serious, dearest. I'm going to complain to Sir Ragismund."

Ashley began to shake his head.

"Yes, I'm going to," she said.

"Oh, no, Aunty Micky. Never. You want to get him into trouble, or what?"

"I want to protest against his attitude."

"What attitude?"

"Everything. He's not the man for the job."

"I wouldn't. You'll regret it afterwards, I assure you."

She spoke scornfully of the young man, of his opinions, his outlook, his approach to his work and his ignorance. She despaired of him. What she wanted to do was this: write to the *Age* or go up to London to see the editor.

"Oh, write," he said hastily.

"I'm a great believer in personal contacts."

"What would you say to the editor? And since you take these 'contacts' so much to heart what will happen if you find you don't get on with the editor? Your personal contact might be disastrous. You're not prepared to give anyone a chance; everybody's got to see eye to eye with you or they're villains. You're a hard woman in your judgements, you know."

She outlined a plan of campaign. He looked glum, unable to accept that she should do anything behind Milford's back, especially while he was her guest. "Look, Aunty Micky, you don't know what this young fellow's going to say. Agreed? You haven't heard him give a definite opinion. Agreed? Your fears are based on instincts and intuitions. Is that also agreed? Well, I don't think they're enough to work on. My instinct, for what it's worth, is to trust the young chap. I don't think he'd deliberately act against you. Whatever his faults he's straight."

"We do so want some money, Ashley!" It was a cry from the depths. "Those diaries have got to be published."

"Very well, but you've also got to behave responsibly. You can't go around in circles."

"This is a business deal, isn't it?"

"Not if it involves plotting against your guest."

"Who's plotting against a guest?"

"But you are, Aunty Micky."

"Is that quite fair, dearest?"

"That's the truth." Only a few months before, Ashley would never have dared to speak to the old lady in this way. Impatience had made him callous. He watched her wipe her mouth with a small handkerchief, take a deep breath and try to begin again; he saw she was beaten for the time being.

"Has young Milford said anything to you which proves that he can't do anything about the papers?"

She shook her head.

"Then for Edward's sake, let the matter work itself out. If he puts in a nasty, unfavourable report you're free to act as you like. Otherwise you've got no right to offend him. He may be a friend in disguise."

Mignon had never heard anything that was less likely. Still, she agreed with him and waited.

8

MISUNDERSTANDINGS

MIGNON had soon realised that Milford would never open any avenue to glory; because of him her plan to sell her husband's papers would fail and the brief period of invigoration would be succeeded by doubts and hesitations, even by a return to the mood of last summer, the sense of living entombment, the harsh despair. The threat of this was enough to make her act; so that almost in the same second as she perceived that Milford and Heinz were no longer serious prospects, she moved ahead to the next possibility, serialisation in the *Age*. The effort needed to drum up optimism in the face of major disappointment aged her and, the next day, when she went into Caerifor, this effort made her oblivious to the way she walked and held herself so that people who knew her remarked to themselves that she had aged but how, on the other hand, she kept up her attack, her independence. When people saw Mignon's savage expression, the shut-away eyes, they said to themselves "She doesn't spare herself"; and although this severity with oneself seemed very 'old school' and 'gamey' to the shopkeepers in Caerifor, who had seen Mignon on her regular shopping jaunts for more years than they could name, it was dreadful to witness.

While Mignon was walking about the town in a daze of determination, her daughter and grandson arrived back from Ireland and heard from Freddy of Milford's visit, the progress of his researches and the difficulties that had cropped up. Nesta made a sour mouth and said nothing; but she waited with eyes as cold as a hawk's for the young man to return from his daily walk.

That was a hard day for Milford. He was wrestling with a draft report for the eyes of Sir Ragismund and did not know what to say. He had rushed out of the house earlier than usual and was caught by a heavy, spiteful rainstorm on an open hilltop and by another one when he was nearer home. By this time he was too wet and despairing to bother to take shelter and trudged painfully on. Whatever there had been between himself and the Caeriforshire landscape on that first walk with Freddy had gone; communication had broken down under the sheer exasperation of his thoughts and the violence of the rain. Wet, dejected and alone, his curls hanging in bedraggled lines across his brow, his heart grumpy and unsociable, he was as happy to meet Nesta and her son as they were to meet him. In short, their mutual antipathy flashed like sheet lightning, but force of circumstances and his need for a warming cup of tea brought them together in the large sitting-room.

Milford, having changed his clothes and wiped his face, sat fidgeting with his watch strap. Pink, rainwashed cheeks and flattened hair gave him the air of an adolescent as he stared at his teacup in dejection, chewed cake mechanically and wondered how, in God's name, he would get out of the house without offending everybody. Nesta thought his silence rude and asked him briskly whether he had found anything worth publishing among her father's papers.

Milford's instincts began crying "Help! Help!" but there was no one to help him and, gulping and hesitating, he said it was hard to say. Nesta found this an extraordinary answer. Wasn't it his job to give an accurate and authoritative assessment? Milford smiled greenly, trying to look amused and superior, trying to command a superior tone.

There were, he said, ('evidently') good things; there were also lots of bad things in the diaries; but mostly there were long passages which contained nothing very much. People kept diaries in the way that people built houses and there was no more reason why they should be published any more than every house should be listed as being of architectural interest, unless, of course, one subscribed to the view that anything that had been committed to paper deserved publication. He did not.

Patrick said they had almost taken publication for granted and what really interested them at that point was whether "there was any lolly in the project".

"Oh, no. I should say none at all." The rainstorms had

purified Milford's soul and he had the strength to tell them the truth as he saw it.

"You were to have been the saviour of the family," Patrick said to him with a hint of mockery.

"I'm not surprised," Nesta said grandly, as though an expert on such matters. "I thought there wasn't much of interest in those diaries."

Milford refused to go all the way with her. "For the specialist there is interest in every document in the sense that it's an individual witness, an individual point of view; I'm not sure that there's much of general interest."

"The way this thing has been exaggerated has surprised me more than anything. I'm amazed that my mother agreed to making these papers public, in any case." She watched the effect of her words on him and as her mother was absent went on waving her wet blankets. "The cupboard was arranged and locked up when my father died and we regarded that part of our lives as finished. We even thought of burning them." Nesta smiled in a hard way. "My mother has been completely changed by the idea of publication. She gives the impression she would do a deal with the devil to get these things into print. I can't think why. I hope you don't think we're so desperately short of money that we've got to sell our personal integrity."

"I can't discuss money. The question has not arisen ... but ... your son ..." he looked towards Patrick diffidently, "did ask me whether there was any money in the affair. I've got the impression that people here hoped for some."

Nesta, it seemed, had misheard. "I thought you'd come down to fix the sale."

Milford was beside himself with embarrassment. "Not at all. I can't. I've no authority."

Despite her earlier aggressiveness, Nesta accepted this coolly. "There's no doubt my mother is madly keen to get rid of the diaries for some reason known only to herself. She's a brave woman and she's making the gesture, I suppose, from some mistaken notion of family loyalty. Why she should lose her head I can't see." She went on: "Had we been establishing something big, *that* would have been different. To try to sell private papers for money is another thing and rather distasteful, in my opinion. I know that Britain is far less staid than it used to be but there still seem to me things that one doesn't do."

Milford said, "But there's a difference surely, between private papers and those kept by a semi-public figure with publication in view."

"If publication is called for, the best and most fitting way is to have a scholarly edition with notes and that kind of thing."

"I couldn't agree more."

"If one was compiled, Father's papers could make a contribution to historical research. Perhaps *any* form of money-making sensationalism is out of the question. It would be abhorrent to our side of the family and to the Civil Service. As you must know, Daddy was sworn to secrecy. I don't even know whether we have the right to publish these papers and whether we might not be infringing the Official Secrets Act."

Milford did not at once appreciate that this would offer him a possible excuse for backing out of the whole undertaking, but he was keen to defend his honour. "I shall be most careful on that point. I had not realised that the diaries were covered by the Official Secrets Act."

"They must be. Didn't my mother tell you?"

"We didn't mention it."

"It's common practice in that section of the Civil Service—and Father was a civil servant, he drew a government pension until the day he died. It's only reasonable that we couldn't have our top public servants selling their secrets to the first bidder. I've never read the diaries—I don't want to—but I'm sure there are lots of things in them that might still be on the sealed list. The Foreign Office takes years before it publishes its papers and even then some are still held back as state secrets."

"A lot of rubbish," Patrick put in, "when everyone knows the Foreign Office is filled with spies. There *are* no real secrets."

"All the same, a publisher like Heinz wouldn't want to get involved in a court case, would he?"

Milford hastily assured Nesta that legal opinions would be obtained before the diaries were published. Nesta's manner became warmer as she saw that the young man was impressed by her words; for the very same reason Patrick thought he must be rather stupid. All the same, he was fascinated by the man's background and as soon as they were alone he asked him whether it would be difficult to get a job in a publishing house.

"You want to work in publishing? Why?"

"Might be interesting." As Patrick had only thought of the matter at that moment he had no other ideas. "I suppose you want all sorts of degrees and so forth."

"Not necessarily." Milford's eyes were wary. "You need some sort of educational background, naturally. You went to a good school, I suppose."

"St. Andrew's College in Salisbury. Is that considered a good school or not? It had a certain snob value over there. I thought talk about good schools went out with the ark."

"Oh, it still counts for something, believe me."

"I've got to be honest with you: I learned nothing at school. I've not even got a school certificate. I just didn't pass exams and I'm sorry but I can't see why I should."

"It depends what you want to be, of course."

"Well, looking round you see that the people who get on are mostly without any qualifications or culture for that matter. The prizes go to people who speak a secret language."

Milford looked perturbed and asked for elucidation. This was more than Patrick could give him since he had imperfectly understood the phrase himself. He had heard someone use it and it had sounded good. Milford, who was impressed by his own qualifications, expected such things to be taken seriously by others.

"In publishing, you've got to know what's going on. Good academic qualifications count for a lot."

"All publishers aren't looking for historical documents. I'm sure romantic novels don't get prepared for the printers by doctors of literature."

Milford was all prim pride. "You didn't tell me you wanted to work in a house printing trash. That's another matter."

Patrick laughed. "I'd work where the lolly is. I bet the romantic stuff brings in more money than history. I bet there's a fortune to be made in romantic novels."

Thin-voiced, Milford said he didn't know.

"What sort of work do you do?" Patrick asked.

124

Milford outlined the duties of an assistant editor in a large publishing house and the only duty which registered in Patrick's mind was that of proof-reading. Surely, he asked, this was a mechanical sort of job not demanding great qualities or initiative. "I don't think I'd want to be *only* a proof-reader."

"The fact that I'm here proves that I'm not only a proof-reader," said Milford, flushing. Patrick showed no mercy: "And how much are you earning now?"

As his salary was less than a thousand pounds a year Milford did not feel he could give it.

"Well, will you be earning two thousand a year by the time you're thirty?"

"That depends," Milford replied.

"On what?"

"Oh, lots of things."

"It doesn't sound promising. Why don't you try trash novels?"

"I couldn't think of anything I'd hate more."

"But if they bring in the money..."

"*You* said they'd bring in money. I don't know if they do."

Patrick ignored this. "For me, living means two thousand a year plus expenses by the time you're thirty. The rest is romantic nonsense."

"You realise that many professional people don't touch that kind of money at the end of a life of hard work. It's arrogance to assume everyone does."

"It's that attitude which depresses me so much about this country. People seem to expect so little from life. They don't set their sights very high, do they?"

Milford thought it depended on what people were aiming at.

"You agree that living means money?" Patrick insisted.

"A certain kind of living—not necessarily mine. Some of us have simple tastes."

"You've *got* to have simple tastes if you don't get two thousand a year by the time you're thirty."

"I don't agree."

At this point Milford refused to pretend that the conversation was a friendly exchange of opinions and rose abruptly. "I've got too much to do to waste my time here," he said haughtily and went back into the little sitting-room. His heart pounded with hatred for the whole family. He could not concentrate on his report for nervous tensions and he stood looking out of the window and cracking his academic knuckles in anger and agitation. "These dreadful people! These perfectly awful people! Dishonest! Arrogant! Pretentious! Rubbishy! And their sacred Sir Arthur! I hate them."

He was muttering to himself at the window when another shower of rain came riding across the open fields. Far away in the gloaming he saw a Caerifor bus stop at the end of the farm lane and a bowed figure, that could only have been his hostess, begin the hard push against the storm towards the house. She walked slowly, laboriously, weighed down by shopping, buffeted by the gusts of rain; she seemed to age the nearer she came to the house. Milford made no move to go out to meet her with an umbrella but sat back in a position where he could just see out without being seen. From this mean vantage point he watched the old lady struggle slowly homewards against the rain, a baffled, tragic figure divided in herself and her thinking, unable to disentangle all her worries. He heard her come in. He heard her walk slowly towards the kitchen, sighing as she went. She did not call out as though she expected no great welcome and the way the kitchen door closed she did not want to see anyone.

A little while later, after she had taken off her wet clothes and had begun to rally, Patrick went into the kitchen to speak to her and ask why Charles Milford was so touchy.

"Right-wing Tories are always touchy," Mignon replied without thinking.

Patrick blinked at her in the lamplight. "Is he a right-wing Tory?"

Mignon stopped blowing on her tea and looked at him in surprise as though such a question was entirely unnecessary. "It sticks out a mile, dearest. He's unusually right-wing for one so young. That's one of the reasons why he doesn't like the diaries and why he's going to give Sir Ragismund Heinz an unfavourable report about them."

"Is this so?"

"Of course! They say too much about people in high places. He doesn't like that kind of history. He likes the smooth front

126

and the lie." Her vehemence made Patrick say, "Ooooooh!" as
though hearing something shocking. "You don't half let him
have it."

"He's a silly little prig, dearest."

Patrick sat down opposite her and helped himself to a biscuit. What, he asked, did right-wing Tories believe in? Mignon
poured herself some more tea. "They don't believe in anything; they never have done. They have certain stock re-
sponses, not beliefs. They're what Arthur used to call
Pavlovisms."

"Pavlovisms?"

"Dearest, you mean you've never heard of Pavlov?"

Patrick nodded without shame.

Mignon, who was touchy and *vieille fille* that afternoon, said,
"It's rather like having to name the Prime Minister. I thought
everyone knew about Pavlov—or had heard of him."

Patrick did not grudge her this moment of asperity and
simply said, "I'm extremely ignorant. I don't know anything
really."

She shook her head and scolded him like a village schoolmistress about the error of his ways.

"All the same, I'll get on. You see."

His manner was disarming as though he were sharing a
secret with her. "I hope you're right, dearest. Would you like a
lot of money?"

"It's very, very nice. Don't you agree?"

Caught off guard, Mignon said hastily, "Don't make a fetish
of it. That's the danger." Had she not been so involved (and
was seen and known to be involved) in trying to sell the diaries
for money she would have lectured him on the values of social
purpose and the dangers of worshipping money. This was one
of the pleasures she forfeited when she became imbrangled in
business affairs.

"What would you like to be?"

"There are so many things."

"Then what does your father say?"

"He thinks I'm a born waster. He used to get exasperated
because I never seemed to know what was going on. For instance, he used to say I was the only person in Africa who
wasn't interested in politics. He didn't realise that I understood

very well what was going on and didn't say anything because I couldn't deceive myself like the others."

"In what way?"

"Oh, people were always talking about the wonderful civilisation the whites had built up in Rhodesia but it seemed to me that the first rule of life there, as in every other place, was 'Feather your own nest first', which I could not accept as evidence of a particularly high civilisation."

Mignon approved of this remark and said, "There's something of us in you, after all."

"Well, you didn't need to be a genius to get the hang of the life there. People were always talking about the dreadful things that would happen if the Africans took control but in many respects I prefer the Africans to the white Rhodesians."

"Do you now! Why was that?"

"Nothing special. They just seemed better-hearted."

"You had lots of African friends?"

"Not especially. I didn't have many friends at all. I don't seem to see eye to eye with many people for long. Acquaintances, yes, I had hundreds of them, but friends..." he thought a while ... "three or four. But they're not the sort I'd cry about if I never were to see them again. Does that shock you?" he asked, seeing a strange movement in her eyes.

"I was thinking that you've got your mother's flat, debunking spirit. You make everything seem savourless in some way. There's no excitement or enthusiasm anywhere."

"I think you're right. I don't think I could ever get excited about people."

"When I was your age I was deeply involved in my friends."

"Ah, but then you're a woman. That's natural."

He laughed. "Now tell me who Pavlov is."

Mignon laughed, too. "He was a famous Russian scientist..." and she tried to fill the gap in his knowledge.

"A Pavlovism," he said. "That's good."

With that he mooched off into the large sitting-room where his mother was writing a bread-and-butter letter to the family-in-law in Ireland. Without her permission he looked over her shoulder and read what she had written. He made no comment.

"Will it do?" Nesta asked.

"Why not? They'll be so staggered to get a letter from you they won't open it. They'll think you're after money."

"You *are* dreadful. You say the most insulting things."

"That's a Pavlovism."

"A what?" Nesta looked up.

"A Pavlovism. It means that each time you see me you get a fixed reaction: in this case a critical feeling. You're a mass of Pavlovisms, I believe."

"Mass of Pavlovisms yourself!"

"But you are, Mother. If anyone mentions 'Diaries' you foam at the mouth with rage and if anyone mentions me you sigh. Isn't that right?"

She brushed his witticisms aside. "What a lot of nonsense you talk, darling. Haven't you got something to do?"

"I've been talking to Grandma. Before that I was tweaking Charles Milford's back hairs. I formed the impression he's only a glorified proof-reader, hardly the sort of person who could help us really."

"Shall I tell you what he is?" Nesta looked furtively at the door before adding, "He's just a bloody little spy for Edward. It stands out a mile. It's all a plot by our darling cousin Edward to get the papers into his hands. It's the real reason why he came down and the real reason why those publishers have sent that dim young person down here. What this person with curls is trying to do is also quite clear: to play down the value of the diaries and then make us think that Heinz is doing us a tremendous favour in taking them out of our hands. It's transparent. It wouldn't deceive a child."

"You mean Milford's nothing more nor less than a shark?"

"He's in on the racket, you bet."

"Milford's so dim he couldn't even invent the amount of money he's earning. He's too slow for any sort of trick. Had he been in on the racket, as you say, he'd have let the cat out of the bag before now."

"He's not so innocent as he looks."

"He's not innocent; he's stupid. The way he lapped up all your eyewash about the Official Secrets Act."

"What I said was true."

"You put it on a bit, I thought. *I* wouldn't have believed you."

"What I said was true."

"You exaggerated, though."

Nesta lost her patience. "Oh, get a book to read for heaven's sake and don't bother me. Try reading for a change."

* * * *

Left to her own devices in the kitchen, Mignon had begun to draft a letter to the *Age*, having decided to play off the newspaper against Heinz, even if it meant overselling in the first place to get the newspaper interested. In order to get the right note of expertise into the letter she used words like 'significant', 'deeply felt', 'key witness': the whole thing of a splendid ambiguity. She could not say that Heinz would publish the diaries and papers since this was untrue; she did suggest that a big editorial project was under way. That night, as soon as all the others had gone to bed, she rewrote the letter and carried it down to the postbox on the main road. She had learned that if you have to act, act with conviction.

In the morning she told Nesta what she had done. Nesta was horrified—or affected to be horrified—at what she took to be her mother's duplicity and by the mere notion of trying to foist her father's writings on a newspaper. There were, she said, certain unwritten rules in these matters which Mignon might well have observed.

"No undertakings of any kind have been given, no agreements entered into. The diaries are my property and if *I* believe in them I must have the courage of my beliefs. The diaries are going to the highest bidder. It's a game of poker."

"Standards in Britain have really declined if you think this is normal behaviour. I think Milford's a prig but I don't think he should be stabbed in the back while he's our guest."

"We're doing very well by Mr. Milford, dearest!" Mignon indicated the morning tea prepared for the young man. "He's all right."

In fact, Milford was not 'all right'; he had taken cold and was lying in his bed with streaming eyes and sneezing every third minute. Mignon came down from his room and began to prepare a hot-water bottle. It was clear that he would have to spend that day in bed. Later, when he realised that he would be expected to stay in his room, Milford felt immeasurably better. He got out his own books and prepared not only to ignore the grey autumnal day outside but the family as well. Freddy went upstairs to see him and thought he'd never seen such a happy invalid, surrounded by his books and papers with a jug of lemon water on his bedside table.

* * * *

With the guest safely hidden away in a bedroom Mignon and Nesta had a pitched battle on the subject of the diaries.

"Now look here, Nesta. Let's get this matter into perspective before I lose my temper—" trembling with anger—"let's say certain things which you seem to have forgotten. I've been left this barracks of a place and no one gives me a penny towards keeping it in repair or proper order. I'm left here with Freddy who's not a damned bit of use—more like a child than a grown man—and full of his own whims and fancies. I can't turn to him for help or advice and I've got to make my own decisions. You're here for a short visit and one fine day you'll sail off again and leave me with all my basic problems unsolved. Please leave me to manage my own affairs. I've got too much on my plate just now to be bothered with you. I've got to get on with the catering."

Patrick came in and asked, "Who for?"

Mignon snapped at him, "Who do you think?" and his mother cried, "Go away. Don't bother us."

"Oh well, if you want to keep your fights private..." he shrugged and mooched off feeling crestfallen. There must be something he could do—but what? He looked out of the windows and saw the uniformly grey sky, the stone-coloured light which foretold downpours of rain, the rooks flying low; everything dim, subfusc, uninteresting, *old*. For the first time since they'd left home he was homesick for the colour and vividness of his usual surroundings. His mother, who had the same thoughts, went upstairs to make the beds. She had just finished when the first rain began to fall and Ashley Corbett called.

By this time Mignon had become so cross thinking over the conversations with her daughter, that she had shut herself in the kitchen and refused to come out. Nesta shook her head.

"How mother has changed, Ashley! How she's grown old. Both she and Freddy are just bundles of mannerisms and manias. They make me feel desperate. I've been home just a couple of days and I feel I want to run away."

He simply said, "Oh?" with a note of inquiry which suggested "What had you expected? We're all growing older."

"It's the disfigurements of old age which are so dreadful. The small things that count as mountains, the want of balance. Mother's become a complete egocentric. We've not had a single, decent conversation. We don't ever seem to have sat down and Mother's said, 'Well, how are you? Tell me about yourself.' It's just as though she's either too bored with us to ask or she's too involved in her own affairs and couldn't be bothered. Then, when we have a conversation it disintegrates into a squabble."

"You've had one tiff and that's put you off," he said soothingly. Patrick chipped in: "They're always tiffing. I've not seen them agree yet."

"Don't interfere. You don't help. Mother disapproves of the way Patrick goes on. She thinks he's a waster in the making and I tend to agree with her."

"Steady on. I'm supposed to be on holiday."

To try to remove the sting from the situation, Ashley laughed and said, "There are no rules when a woman wants to criticise you, old chap. She'll find the right formula."

Patrick took himself seriously; he hated being slighted in front of an outsider. "You make me sick. Just because you and your mother can't agree you've got to make yourself unpleasant to everyone. I don't want to be your whipping boy. I'll go away tomorrow if you want me to. It's deadly dull here. Nothing happening; no one to see; nothing to do. I don't know why we came here. We're not particularly welcome and we don't get anything out of it ourselves."

"Now you're going to extremes," said Nesta, embarrassed.

"I'm not."

"Don't blow your head off." Nesta spoke too late for Patrick had built up a splendid head of steam and needed to release it. He left the room, slamming the door, and ignored his mother's pleas from the other side. She was left to shrug in a way which equated the very young with the very old as though people such as herself and Ashley, the solid people in the vital twenty years from thirty-five to fifty-five, were the backbones and stabilisers of society.

The question hovered in Ashley's mind as to whether Nesta thought, in her indulgent way, this behaviour was, despite the noise and the rudeness, becoming. "What can he find to do here?" he asked.

"Exactly. In such weather what is there anyone can do?"

"I feel a bit guilty because I promised we'd go out fishing. . . . You know how it is—something always turns up."

"Oh, no," she replied hastily, "you can't be expected to take Patrick off our hands as well as do your job." The idea that they expected him as the only man available to the family to entertain Patrick embarrassed her. She was sufficiently her mother's daughter to believe that not to be self-sufficient, not to be able to live without continual outside stimulus, was a confession of failure.

Nesta and Ashley were mutually fascinated. Both had relied on Mignon to a great degree for the picture which each had of the other. Mignon's opinions and impressions were imposed on long acquaintance dating back to the period before either of them had married, and taking in a time when it had been rumoured, in the way of small communities where the professional class is limited, that they would marry. They themselves had always laughed at these rumours, even enjoyed them together; they had never imagined the rumours being likely.

It was mostly because they seemed to have grown up together, like cousins or brother and sister, and the possibility of anything further was taboo. Nesta had had many boy-friends before her marriage but Ashley was the only one who knew her loathing of her father, her irritation with her mother, in short, the two most powerfully-shaping emotions she had. It was Nesta who had first told Ashley that her cousin was in love with him and had suggested he should marry her. Ashley had forgotten this; Nesta had not and could never be sure that her action had not been mischievous when she saw, through her mother's eyes, the withering and warping of Muvvy, seven years nearer the end of youth than her husband.

Complexities there might be in their understanding of one

133

another going back into the past, taking in all kinds of scenes and confidences, and it was because of this that Ashley could ask her, with his customary gentleness, whether Nesta and her mother were always at cross-purposes.

"We hardly seem to see eye to eye about anything, I'm afraid. Now there's the question of these diaries and I'm furious at the way Edward has been able to take them both in. He's not interested in helping Mother at all. I'm positive he's trying to get his hands on them himself. Positive."

Ashley did not agree. Although he had been ruffled by Edward's visit he was sure that his motives were disinterested. "He thought he could do your mother a good turn."

"What good has it done her? Have you seen her recently? The excitement, the worry have reduced her to skin and bone. She lives on her nerves. She's worn out. She thinks of nothing else and what's equally bad she's getting poor Freddy into the same state."

And where was Milford? Ashley inquired. Nesta pointed upstairs. "He caught a chill while out walking yesterday. I should think he's relieved to be out of our way."

"It must be awkward for him if he can't give you the answers you want."

"That Mother wants," she insisted. "It's Mother he's afraid of. She knows he's not keen on the diaries and he knows she knows. She's now trying to interest the *Age*."

"I warned her against that."

"Well, she's written. She's behaving abominably. And what for? To revive a myth! It's only because she can conveniently forget the past that she's able to do this. Even now she's building Father up into some sort of folk-hero. Such a person never existed and she knows it well."

"Does it matter? Really?"

"I dislike it. I can't tell you how intensely I dislike it. I hate people deluding themselves. I suppose Mother feels she must hold on to something."

"I thought she wanted the money."

"Oh," with a splendid airiness, "that's incidental. Mother wants something to hold on to."

"You're wrong, Nesta. Your mother's interest is purely financial."

Ashley's tone of voice made the daughter take in her breath. It suggested an interest in financial matters bordering on depravity. As though the image of Sir Arthur were only being built up in order to sell it the more easily.

"Does she want money so desperately?" Nesta thought for a moment that Ashley knew more about her mother's affairs than she did.

"I wouldn't say desperately. She wanted the place done up for your return."

"That may be, but now the matter is more than financial. She wants to create a new myth in order to vindicate herself. It's dangerous at Mother's age trying to believe in Santa Claus. Mother's lost her head and that's why there's no peace any more."

Ashley was sorry for this. Freddy and Mignon had been so happy.

"I can hardly believe it. I look at them and feel they can never have been happy in their lives."

"You couldn't be further from the truth, Nesta. It's usually a pleasure to call here. They were always the same, always pleased to see one." Irritation at her gesture of scepticism made him add rather loudly, "I mean this."

"How can Mother be happy when she's given her life to a shadow? What happiness can she get from looking back at her time with Father? I feel so sorry for her. A life wasted. All the lovely things wasted!" She burst out, "I'd do anything to stop this publishing nonsense. I hate the memory of my father so much. I wouldn't want to have him brought to life again— even in print. The older I get the more I resent the way he behaved and the things he did to our lives! Dreadful selfishness! The last thing I ever expected was to come home here and find him set up in a niche like a holy statue. I suppose I ought to indulge Mother and her whims. I wish I could. The truth is: I've got out of the way of old people and coming among them again is like entering another country where you don't speak the language. As soon as I can see some shape in Patrick's affairs I'll hop off home again—and won't I be glad to go!"

Ashley seemed to have heard vague talk of arranging Patrick's future before and having seen no proof that anything was afoot he was obliged to ask what the boy wished to do. He tried to keep a certain coldness out of his voice, but failed. Nesta's reply was as vague as she herself was and he commented, "I've got the impression Patrick is perfectly happy so long as he can fall back on you."

Nesta was uncomfortable. To balance the impression created by her son she reminded Ashley that he was on holiday. "He's by no means a sponger, if that's what you fear."

Like most self-made men, Ashley distrusted and secretly despised the children of rich parents whose path in life appeared already smoothed out by money, influence and the inbred assumption that the gods were on their side. Ashley resented Patrick's self-assurance which assumed that everything he did would be a success and that, in fact, success depended entirely on the moment he made his choice. Patrick's confidence in himself affected his mother who, at heart, refused to be concerned about him even though she joined her mother in nagging. To this mixture of facile grumbling and complacency was added a certain infatuation with Patrick which came out in remarks such as, "He has all the charm of his father's side"; or "Patrick's got all the good looks of his Irish family".

"What would you do if he were your boy?" Nesta asked. She never got her reply because Mignon put her head into the room at this point and glared towards them with jealous, resentful eyes.

"I wish you'd come here to talk to me," Ashley said in a voice which tried to make up in fullness of tone for the earlier disloyalty. "Another time," Mignon said brusquely.

"Come along, Aunty Micky, come and say a few words to me."

Mignon closed the door. "I've got far too much to do." She was thoroughly put out by the sight of Nesta and Ashley chatting together.

Then the door opened again and Patrick came back in. He, too, felt vaguely threatened by the intimacy between his mother and Ashley.

"Are you still talking about those diaries? The whole thing's absurd. I call it 'Uncle Arthur for the Masses'."

This essentially adolescent tone of voice pained them both.

"Don't," his mother said briefly.

"Why not? You always used to say that your father was the biggest conniver and rogue one could meet."

Ashley took out his cigarettes. "Have one, Patrick, and don't say brash things about difficult subjects."

To change the conversation, Nesta asked what Charles Milford was doing.

"He's writing to his aunts," Patrick replied, blowing out smoke.

"Again?"

"Yes. He's in love with them."

"What's this?" asked Ashley.

"His aunts. Charles Milford lives with three aunts in Sussex," Nesta said by way of explanation.

"I asked him about his family," Patrick said. "He says his aunts are the daughters of a bishop. They think St. Paul's is Low Church. At least that's what I gather." Patrick laughed heartlessly. "He's rather secretive so I have to rely on their postcards to him for the real truth."

"Patrick!!" His mother was scandalised.

"I copied them," Patrick said shamelessly, "I thought I'd never seen anything like them. The first one—" he drew out a piece of paper—"went: 'So happy you are enjoying your stay in Wales, darling boy. The book you want is J. Wickham Legg's *English Church Life from the Restoration to the Tractarian Movement, Considered in Some of its Neglected or Forgotten Features* (1914). Shall I ask the L.L. if they've got it and ask them to send it to you urgently for your return? Bea.'"

Nesta, not sure of Ashley's reaction, held her breath until he burst out laughing.

"You made it up," he said.

"Would I have the wit to make up something like that? Then here's another, 'Basingstoke: Divine drive with Ellie to Silchester. Nothing but ploughed fields and a couple of houses. Then on to Basing House and here to see the Chapel of the Holy Ghost (ruins all very Gothic and 18th century, as you know). Ellie loving it all. Rhoda.'"

"He's obviously in a bad way," Patrick said. "And he doesn't like me. He's very careful what he says."

"He knows you're making fun of him, you cruel boy."

137

"Well, he's such a prissy object of pity with his carefully-arranged lovelocks and his striped shirts."

"This much can be said for him: he's got a career that interests him. Which is more than I can say for you."

The young man drifted round the room self-consciously, sure that both were finding him irresistible. He was also sure that he had solved everything except how to fill in his time at Swanquarter. Playing the squire to his mother through three continents had given him a tremendous amount of confidence in himself and his place in the world. Despite Ashley's ideas of him, he had no money, no training, no immediate prospect of a university place or even work, no inherited privilege, but he knew he would succeed. He had never once thought otherwise. He went out as brusquely as he had come in and Ashley found his mother's indulgent laughter rather foolish.

He said, "He seems to have such a good flow of words and a quick eye for a document, you ought to make him a lawyer."

"He'd never apply himself."

"*You* never made the most of your training, you know."

"I? With my fourth-class degree?" She laughed briefly.

"Was it a fourth?"

"A fourth. Father nearly died of shame. But he insisted I went. That's why I never insist on anything with Patrick. He must be allowed to make his own choice in his own time."

"I don't think I've ever had a single person to help me," Ashley said, "and, in some ways, since I married your cousin I think I've had someone working against me."

"As bad as that?"

"Pretty well, believe me. I don't say much about it to anyone: there's no point. No one is interested in other people's troubles."

Ashley liked to think that he kept his family troubles to himself and that each time he began complaining about his wife he was breaking a long period of stoic silence; he liked to give an atmosphere of catharsis to his conversation. In truth, discussing his wife's faults had become as common a subject for conversation as the weather. Nesta determined to show the firmness that he could not. "Whatever the state of my marriage—and I'm pleased to say it's extremely happy—I couldn't ever discuss it with anyone. That's one thing I admired about Mother. Even when Father was doing his worst she never mentioned it to anyone."

"Don't I know it." A suggestion of resentment in his voice did not escape her. "I've been put in my place more than once."

"By whom?"

"Your mother, of course. Once, when Muvvy was being more than usually trying—I've forgotten why—I was at the end of my resources, morally speaking, and I went to your mother for advice. She listened carefully and, as I thought, with complete sympathy until I'd finished and she looked at me straight in the face and said, 'I'm a moralist of the old school. You've married Muvvy and you've no right to discuss her with anyone, even with me.' Smack!! Right between the eyes."

Nesta raised her shoulders as much as to say, "Typical."

"What's more, the next day she wrote me a note and said something to the effect that although she understood only too well what it was like to suffer hurt at the hands of those one loved, she had also learned that no good ever came of expecting other people to interest themselves in the matter."

His eyes reflected once again the amazement of the day he had received the letter.

"I thought it was hard, hard. In those situations one doesn't really want advice; one wants sympathy. I got neither—beautifully."

"Oh," said Nesta, with her own brand of glibness, "other people's emotional problems have no reality for her. She's not interested in people and hasn't got much curiosity in the ordinary way. Mother even once told me she didn't attach much importance to the life of the emotions or the senses."

Recognising the Mignon-esque brusqueness, Ashley gave a short laugh, but Nesta was not amused. "What are these hard words, in the end? Merely an excuse not to listen to other people's troubles. It's a form of washing your hands of your friends. I suppose if you're like Mother and have no time for emotions or the senses, it's true enough. I wouldn't want to live in such a world."

"Do you think they're important?"

139

Her eyes were lucid, suddenly lit up with a university girl's enthusiasm for a newly discovered truth. "Fancy asking such a question at your age. Of course, they're important.

"People develop theories against the emotions and the senses in self-defence," she said rapidly, her words falling out impulsively. "Emotion and sensuality are human life. Deprive the human being of these and he's a machine."

He did not recognise such a mental trick in Mignon. He thought she was merely old-fashioned in her attitudes. He recalled the time when Muvvy left him and went to London.

"About three weeks afterwards, your mother came into the office. We had the usual tea and gossip; time went on. I didn't mention the subject, neither did your mother. Then, just as she was putting on her gloves, I said: 'You know that Muvvy's gone off to London. Walked out.' She looked embarrassed and then said, 'Heavens, dearest, what a damned silly thing to do. How unsporting of her.' Just as though Muvvy was a cook who'd walked out before a big party."

Nesta was fascinated. "And then?"

"That was it. She sat there pretending it was all a breach of contract and that's all there was to it. I wanted just one word of feeling, of sympathy, if you like, but it never came."

"What did happen eventually?"

"She came back because she couldn't bear herself in London any more than she could bear herself here."

"And how are things now?"

"How could they be anything but miserable? Everything's an excuse for a scene. We don't have a single thought in common." Without thinking what he was saying, he went on, "We haven't slept together for years."

He at once became scarlet with embarrassment but Nesta was not her mother and said matter-of-factly, "I hope you've found someone else."

"There have been others. They meant a good deal to me. For a time. There's never been anyone who might have moved me to try a divorce."

"Does Muvvy know about these friendships?"

"I hope not. I'd loathe hurting her."

"She must know. How could you do anything in Caerifor without everyone knowing?"

He sighed. "How indeed?" He cleared his throat awkwardly. "I've always been as careful—as discreet—as possible. A decent hypocrisy has always seemed essential in these matters. And sometimes you get a bad name for no reason at all. I had an awkward time not so long ago when someone told me that I was about to run away with the wife of our County Planning Officer. It was completely untrue. But how are you to scotch such rumours?"

"Had you been a Frenchman you'd have been delighted to have your name coupled with the County Planning Officer's wife. If she's pretty, that is."

Stirring uncomfortably in his chair, he merely said, "It would have been awkward for both of us."

"Naturally."

"I see marriage exactly as people are supposed to see it: a sacred bond. You *should* try to honour your promises and flouting convention isn't my line of country. Not unless I had something else to put in its place."

"Is that why you and Muvvy stay together?"

"I suppose so. What could we do if we separated?"

"Oh," airily, "you might marry again."

He considered the matter gravely. "You might well be right."

Everything he had said was unexceptionable. To Nesta, it had the stale smell of unfelt emotions. What can one expect? she asked herself. He's never left Caerifor. The conversation had gone as far as she wanted it to go. Her woman's curiosity about the way a man like Ashley ticked had been satisfied. She had been looking for more spunk in him. It was not enough to be the well-liked, well-dressed local business leader who has made good at an early age. How to admire a tamed domestic creature who cannot make a success of domesticity?

She despised him. What he took for discretion and right-thinking she saw as little-mindedness. He was all moderation, all weak-kneed decency, all careful calculation as though engaged in building up a reserve of credit in some bank of respectability for use on a future public occasion. It was the worst kind of provincialism.

Ashley never realised how Nesta despised him for he believed that to be totally understood is to be admired.

"Well—" Mignon burst in, determined to break up the flaccid conversation that had gone on too long—"Well, who are you tearing to pieces now?"

"Me," Ashley replied without thinking.

"I might have guessed, dearest. Nesta is always able to manoeuvre you into the dock. She's got a genius for that." She poked the fire aggressively. It was teatime and she wanted everyone to take tea upstairs with "poor Mr. Milford who's been by himself all day".

They went upstairs, of course, and arranged themselves around the invalid's bed while Mignon poured tea at a table set up near the fireplace. Her gesture touched Milford to the heart. It was the kind of cosy touch he was used to; and sipping tea from a big cup he felt ready to forgive the family for all their crassness and their irritating ways. The conversation turned on painting and Milford said he liked pictures more if they had literary associations. It followed that his favourite painters included the pre-Raphaelites, Piero di Cosimo, Samuel Palmer and those landscapes—Wilson could do them, so could Claude, so could Poussin—where everything was grouped together for enjoyment and sensual pleasure: water for bathing and reflection, mountains for fine prospects, trees for shade, classical ruins for gorgeous effects against vast, clear skies.

Mignon liked pre-Raphaelites, too, and Millais's 'Autumn Leaves' was her favourite picture. A reproduction hung on her bedroom wall because the children in the painting had haunted her all her life ever since she first saw them in some exhibition or gallery.

"They are *haunting* children," Milford exclaimed with engaging enthusiasm. "Unforgettable." Seeing him at that moment, his eyes flashing the pure enthusiasm of which only the young and untried and people of genius are capable, it was hard to believe he was the right-wing reactionary who might blight Mignon's hopes or the stool pigeon for some dark stratagem by Professor Lloyd-Ballantyne. Mignon and Nesta caught a glimpse of the Milford they could not allow to exist, if their own ideas and passions were to survive, and were uncomfortable. Of course, they knew he wasn't a bad person or a dishonest one but, in the manner of women, they had taken against him.

The talk turned to modern painting and here Ashley showed the tolerance of the uninvolved. When Nesta said this painting was all rubbish he said, "Quite well-informed people don't think so," which raised the tone of the argument so greatly that no one heard Patrick come in. He was furious at having been left out of such a gathering.

"But where were you, dearest? I looked everywhere for you."

"I've taken the car into one of the barns and I was cleaning out the what-do-you-call-it but the light failed and I had to come in."

"I thought you'd gone for a walk."

"In this rain?" He sulked. Tea grouped around the bed of someone suffering from a mild chill was hardly a star day in the social calendar, but Patrick was a sociable animal and missed contacts with people more than anything.

Outside the comfortable room lay the empty county, sad, withdrawn under the rainy early evening with only an occasional car splashing by along the high road, a flash of light here and there where doors, opened on lighted interiors, were hastily shut against the gloom. No one could want to turn out into such an evening, least of all Ashley, who went away because he could not leave his wife alone all the evening. Back in his office he kept thinking of Nesta and their conversation and when he remembered how she had said 'I hope you've found someone else' he began to drum his fingers in agitation on the top of his desk. Impulsively he picked up the telephone and rang Swanquarter. Nesta answered.

"I hoped it would be you," he said. "I just wanted to say how much I enjoyed our talk this afternoon. It was like old times."

Her voice appeared to warm. "Wasn't it?"

"It makes a real red-letter day in my life when I find someone to whom one can talk."

Her voice was edged with surprise. "Oh, thank you."

He said impulsively, "Sometimes, I think we were really made for one another."

"Oh, what makes you say that?"

He said, rather tremulously, committed to the unknown, "I've always admired you no end, you know."

"But how nice of you, Ashley." She was still only just containing her surprise.

"Yes, I've always admired you."

She made no reply.

"Are you there?"

"Yes, I'm still here." Her voice now sounded as though she were hundreds, even thousands, of miles apart, on steamers bound for opposite ends of the earth.

"I thought you'd gone."

"No, I'm listening."

Then, it struck him that he had gone too far, something doubtful and unprepared sounded in her voice. He had said the wrong thing. What had he been trying to say? Whatever it was the thread was broken before it had left the spool. There was nothing more to do but hang up and go home.

His mistake throbbed within him like a knife-wound. He knew he had, in some way, disgusted her, and he had only meant to be warmhearted, grateful. It was all due to the inferiority of his modes of expression, not so much sparseness of vocabulary and thinness of tone : too much or too little. It was the gaucheness and naïvety of the incident of Edward's letter all over again.

As he went home, his inner ear reheard the gradual replacement of warmth by coolness in Nesta's voice, the ebbing away of her contact with him over the telephone : a summing up of all the dropped bricks and false steps of his life.

* * * *

"Why did Ashley ring?" Mignon asked.

"He wanted to say how much he had enjoyed his visit."

"Nice of him?"

"You know, he talked to me a lot about him and Muvvy."

"Not again!"

"Does he talk about her so often?"

"He'd talk of nothing else if you'd let him, dearest. It's his worst feature. Ashley is a dear person, as good-natured as they come, but so immature in so many ways. Don't you feel, too?"

"He always gave me the impression of, I don't know quite what to say: a kind of weakness. A man like that would drive me round the bend. Something silly keeps peeping out all the time."

"Exactly, dearest, that's what I've always found. I forget it because there's so much good."

All that night it rained. When they opened the curtains in the morning they saw that the fields between the house and the railway were flooded as a river beyond the railway, usually hidden by trees and bushes, had burst its banks; they imagined they could hear the murmur of its waves as it swept all before it.

Milford felt better, but when he looked out of his window he thought the world had been washed away. He could not ever recall, except during fogs, such a complete cutting off of the near horizon. This was not fog but black rain that seemed to fall in blackish smoke, like a volcanic eruption: fog with grey rods in it. The morning light was not the golden-soupy fog haze but a prehistoric, antediluvian light, as grey as a rhinoceros, imbued with awareness of spiritual suffering. A black bird or two flew by the window wheezing hoarsely, an occasional car sped by on the road below the house, a van went down to the next farm bumping through dips and hollows filled with water; the whole world was melting and oozing.

After dressing, and before breakfast, Milford glanced hastily and without pleasure at the opening phrases of his draft report to Sir Ragismund Heinz.

"Perhaps," he had written primly, "too little has been written by the professional civil servant about his work, the relationship between the initiators and the executives. A collection of papers which cover the major part of a senior civil servant's working life must satisfy us on one or two main points:

"*A*. Is it a work that fills in gaps about what we already know of the period? or

"*B*. Is it a work that has a life and style of its own that would deserve to be considered as a creative work, as much say, as Kilvert's Diaries?

"Having decided what answer to give to these two questions there remain two other questions.

"*A*. Does one think there's anything original about this? or

"*B*. Is it particularly well done of its sort?"

The lofty academic tone was suddenly interrupted by a paragraph that belonged to a place further down the report: "Sir Arthur Benson-Williams *was* a prominent civil servant over a long period of time and while one respects his public service one is not at all sure of: *A*, his scholarship, when he attempts to rationalise what has happened and put it into perspective, and *B*, his objectivity in describing events which concerned himself or his protectors."

Mignon had not been wrong in her instinct about his report: Milford was preparing a statement that would praise with the adjectives and damn with the verbs.

That afternoon, despite Mignon's warning that he would do himself no good, Milford went into Caerifor to get a 'trim' (he said) and ended up in a hairdresser's shop where the village youths went on Saturday afternoon and were sheared to last three months. Milford emerged like a ram in June; all his Victorian, pre-Raphaelite luxuriance of curl had been removed, leaving an even more youthful but considerably more worried face to emerge, all poppy eyes and bulbous mouth, like a poet on the bottle. Little wonder that Ashley hardly recognised him when he entered his office and flopped down in an arm-chair.

"Can I be frank, Mr. Corbett?" A pause. "I feel really gloomy. I can't help feeling that Lady Benson-Williams is going to be upset."

"You mean the stuff's no use?"

Milford nodded. "Of course, they knew it in their hearts, too. They know by my manner that there's nothing I can do for them but they don't understand my position at all. They're behaving so oddly. They no longer listen to me. If only someone had been able to put them right in the first place they wouldn't have built up such extravagant hopes. They'll be utterly crushed by the whole thing and I worry for them because I can't possibly say what I don't feel."

It was no more than Ashley had feared. He tried to assure this shorn young person that no one would hold him responsible.

"It's not so easy as that, really. You see, I've suddenly realised that all the time I may be being unfair to the papers because I loathe the personality of Sir Arthur so much."

His anguish, his wrinkled brow, made Ashley thoughtful. It seemed years since he had cared about anything so much.

"He's so mean, so self-righteous, so unclean: a sort of François Mauriac of Whitehall. Every night he went home to put down some nasty little thought. Hindsight is his speciality. A phrase that sums him up, 'As I had foreseen'—and usually when he'd done nothing of the kind. I can't be fair to such a man!"

"Pity to have got so involved all the same."

Ashley abruptly held up the flow of Milford's miseries to warn him that he would have to cut short the conversation since he was obliged to visit a property outside Caerifor. If Milford would like to accompany him—the whole thing would take about an hour—he was welcome. Milford accepted and trailed down the stairs after Ashley like a mournful calf-boy.

Ashley was not at his best with bulbous-faced late adolescents wallowing in the shallows of their own integrity and often said "Yes, yes!" when he should have said something more understanding. Milford knew he had begun to bore his listener so, steering the conversation away from dangerous ground, asked Ashley what the late Sir Arthur Benson-Williams had been like as a man.

The change of theme brought Ashley back to the conversation. He thought Sir Arthur had been a difficult man to describe and know. "He gave such an impression of secrecy, of things bottled up. Everybody thought he must be such a profound, well-informed man. I suppose he was in a small way."

Milford said he had seen photographs of him and thought he had had an interesting face.

"Or," he asked, "was it just a face that photographed well?"

Ashley said Sir Arthur had looked like a Greek police chief or customs official. This was the last thing Milford had expected. "Are you serious?"

Ashley tried to recall the man: the sallow, swarthy complexion, for one thing; the dark, hard eyes, the powerful nose, the two gold-filled teeth, the largish expanse of hard belly which had seemed to carry an imaginary ammunition belt around it.

"He looked somebody ... but exactly what you couldn't quite place. He had an air of power and purpose, but devoted to small ends, like a customs official walking up and down the quay of a Mediterranean port. There was a kind of meanness in the face, a streak of cunning and bitterness."

"But was he what you'd call a clever man?"

"He must have been. He had a position to hold. He may, as they used to say, have got the job through influence but he must have held it by something else."

Milford agreed reluctantly that this must be so.

"Of course, to me he's more the local great man than the eminent civil servant: the man they once held the London express up for at Caerifor. I saw a lot of him and was always struck by his watchfulness. It seemed that he was always watching, waiting, judging, assessing, seeking out the weak points. In his old age he had a dreadful expression of bottled-up rage. He was a truly terrible old man, in appearance, like a fallen angel who'd retired to a spa. Yet I should be the last one to criticise him. He was awfully good to me. I've been close to the family for years."

Ashley thought again. "In old age, he was not at all pleasant. His hands—they were small and narrow—became heavily mottled and so did his neck. He became more and more difficult to approach or understand. It took me a long time to realise people might find something extraordinary in his writings. Tell me, honestly, what exactly do you find so awful in them?"

"Essentially, Mr. Corbett—" he had got the name at last— "Essentially, I'm not a modern-minded person. I don't want to know everything about everybody and that's exactly what the modern mind wants: it roots after truth like a truffle-hound and respects nothing, loves nothing, reveres nothing." Milford made a gesture of abhorrence. "Protect me from such minds. I like a distance kept. Do you understand? Nowadays, I know people love having their gods debunked: who drank, who drugged, who was homosexual; you know? It's a strange phenomenon. We're always telling ourselves fairy stories and then longing to have them disproved."

"Oh," Ashley said contemptuously, "people can be made to believe anything. You've only got to try selling houses to see that. People begin with one fixed thing in view and end up buying something entirely different because the salesman has convinced them. In a small way, it's happened in the case of Lady Benson-Williams. I really think she believes her husband was a great man now."

"You mean she didn't used to?"

"He was never mentioned. He treated his wife too badly. No

148

woman likes a man who's always having flirtations, spiritual and otherwise, with other women."

At this point Milford could no longer keep back the dreadful truth that he had discovered from reading the diaries. "His papers are full of filth about people, you know. He's always naming lovers like an old brothel-keeper."

For the first time, Ashley was more interested in the talk than the winding lanes. "Surely that's the sort of stuff people love these days!"

"They won't if I have my way. There's nothing for public reading."

"But what is it?" Ashley asked.

"Hints about people, about the Royal Family; things that would compromise the reputations of people who are still alive." The young calf-man made a gesture of disgust that passed through his body from his elastic-sided shoes to his shorn head. "Nothing that any normal person wants to know. Do you," he asked aggressively, "want to read anything more about the Duke of Windsor and his friends? Do you?"

"Not especially. Other people might. Isn't this the sort of stuff you're looking for? Wouldn't it appeal to the public?"

"Not to Heinz."

What a stupid prig, Ashley thought; and said aloud, "Then you want to censor history, in effect?"

Milford denied this but was unable to put over a convincing reason. Ashley found him weird and said so; Milford's discomfort was plain. He wanted to know how much weight they could give to Sir Arthur's evidence.

Ashley had stopped the car to open the locked gates of the property. He looked at Milford coolly. "As much as you want to, I suppose."

"But all that stuff goes against the grain, doesn't it?"

"They are the opinions and evidence of one man, I suppose. They're *his* opinions, because they're *his* diaries, based on *his* experiences; you can't expect him to write with someone else's eyes. I don't understand your attitude."

The truth was that Milford didn't understand himself and he said more than he realised when, slamming the car door and preparing to follow Ashley into the garden, he said, "I just hate the man and his loathsome opinions."

Ashley walked briskly towards the front door trying to put a little space between himself and the young man who seemed to be making a basic mistake.

Milford stopped a moment, knowing that he cut a poor figure, and was confused. He looked up at the strange, empty house, a sort of dwelling for a hermit that would be sold as a week-end retreat for jaded Birmingham professional people, and then ran after Ashley. The door was pushed open and they went inside into a strange, tiled hall that looked as though it had been transplanted from a Manchester suburb—coloured glass in the windows, an over-elaborate stair-rail, an air of having once been over-furnished in abominable taste. They went into the back quarters where the assistant had made a mess of the plan and Ashley handed Milford the end of the measuring tape. They moved over the house quickly, Milford trotting about with the tape-end in his hand while Ashley made quick calculations and scribbled little notes.

The art of selling a house, he said, was to find the right formula. A house with a view of the gasworks was labelled 'convenient for industry', while a house with a bathroom big enough for two rabbits was described as having 'luxurious tiling effects'. The present property would, in basic estate-agentese, be a 'place of character but suitable for conversion'. Once the tour of the house was over, the whole problem of it dropped away and Ashley was left with the young man who seemed to loathe what Ashley himself called 'bedroom stuff'. He wondered why a person of that age should be so puritan, so revolted by the flesh. Something of his doubt and perplexity about Milford touched the young man because, on the way back, he said half-apologetically, "I know it sounds bad to fall down on one's first job. But to praise what I loathe would be to set aside everything I've ever been taught. After all, I must keep my integrity."

People talked about their integrity as Victorian girls talked about their honour, Ashley thought. He had withdrawn from Milford and, for the first time, saw the justice of Mignon's opinion of him. How could anyone have patience with such a man? "You don't think," he asked him on the way back to town, "that you're cheating? Aren't you, in effect, suppressing evidence?"

Milford looked even more dejected and deflated.

"I feel I'm holding down the cork on a bottle that's got a nasty smell inside."

"That's going a bit too far. They can't be as bad as that. You're exaggerating."

From a long way away, Milford raised his voice in anguish, "Well, knowing what I feel and believe, what would you do in my position?"

Earlier that afternoon, Ashley would have tried to find a comforting phrase, the sort of soothing remark he knew so well how to make, but at that hour, driving recklessly through the narrow lanes with small branches swishing against the side of the car, he could only advise Milford "to follow his nose". He went on briskly, "What you've hinted at sounds saleable, sounds interesting, the very marrow of people's interest in the past. You hate all that, so you can't speak well of it. If I were your employer this is the very stuff I'd want you to point out to me; and I'm speaking now as the ordinary man. The ordinary man is very much touched by anything that savours of bedroom stuff."

"But not in this documents series!"

"Then you know your own mind; you don't need my opinion."

"Sir Ragismund would hate this stuff as much as I do."

"Then why are you uncertain? If you and your boss see eye to eye, good for you."

Ashley abandoned the effort to persuade or understand "Look, it's clearing up," he said. He felt he had heard enough about the diaries and seen too much of Milford's conscience in turmoil. The young man's duty was to his employer, to Mignon and to the interests of history; it was not for him to protect society from Sir Arthur. When they parted it was for the last time for Milford had only two more days in Swanquarter.

He left Ashley's office and crossed the town to visit the County Museum. This took about half an hour and when he came out he found the town changed by the theatrical reappearance of the sun, with large expanses of blue sky over the flooded reaches of the Maddau and an autumnal light, as clear as varnish, over everything; the essence of reconciliation. He hurried down the street to the river bank and there, to his astonishment, facing the bastions of Grimshaw's bridge, was the same lady artist with, it might be thought, the same dew-drop at the end of her nose. It seemed she had sat there through the horrendous storms into the clear, illuminated weather. The blue sky, the shimmering light of the sun, the new softness of the air were like bells, like paeans of praise for the lifting of the cloudbank, the end of the long darkness, almost as though it had been the turn of the year and not a brilliant pause in the destruction of the autumn.

Once again, but with little of the ecstatic tread of his first visit, Milford walked out towards the middle of the bridge. He looked down at the swirling waters littered with the small debris of the flood, green branches, pieces of wood, bottles and tins from village dumps, a strange shape like a half-smashed chair. The skies have cleared, he thought, trying to recall a verse he half-remembered, "The skies have cleared, the day is calm and still..." and looked back at the town on its whale-back hill, every window half-open to the soft, damp, autumnal air, the roofs glittering with the released shimmering of the light. These were the moments when he lived most freely and deeply when, from some vantage point, he could explore a townscape or a panorama at his will. He still found the mass of Caerifor, although all its parts had a provincial smallness, satisfying against the diamond-clear sky, which seemed the background of a saint's illumination or vision. Even a pigeon, in flight from one cornice to the next, seemed a creation of art, not chance. For that moment, all his preoccupations fell away. Whether he had misjudged, whether he had been unfair or cowardly hardly mattered at all, about his own joy he was quite sure.

His moment of ecstasy was short-lived for at that moment the dreadful thought came into his head, "Didn't I leave a half-finished letter on the table in my bedroom?"

In the normal way, leaving a half-finished manuscript open to prying eyes is not a fatal error, but this letter, with a résumé of his difficulties to his aunts, contained numerous remarks about his hosts which were the essence of venom, not at all the things he would want them to see; not at all the products of a man of integrity.

"My God!" He stood still, riven by horror. "I'm sunk. Someone is sure to read it. Someone's always fiddling about in my papers the moment I'm out. I'm sunk."

It was the final cut. It was the ultimate humiliation. It was all very well for *him* to find the family lacking in elementary decency and courtesy and to say so with a great show of righteous indignation to his aunts; it was another thing to be found out as a viperish guest. He cursed his own absent-mindedness which had led him into such a position.

This turmoil of guilt and regret was intertwined with his own lack of judgement. Perhaps, after all, the diaries had immense public appeal? Perhaps, who knew? Corbett, the ordinary man, knew what ordinary people liked? Perhaps he had a blind spot? He remembered famous cases where the value of works had been ignored ... André Gide rejecting the first book of *A la Recherche du Temps Perdu* as a fashionable novel; *The Edinburgh Review* quoting the whole of the great Wordsworthian *Ode* to prove that it was meaningless ... George Meredith, when a reader for a publisher, rejecting *East Lynne* and, as if that was not enough for one lifetime, also rejecting *Erewhon*. Waiting in the bus station he had only one loophole: the Official Secrets Act; he would play this up to the full.

He was sitting gloomily in the bus waiting for it to leave when he saw Mignon. She had also seen him and sat down next to him, mysterious and jovial in the way he had grown to suspect.

"I had to pop into town," she said. "There's always something to be done when you've got a bit of property." This was pure invention; she had been into town to see Ashley and had been waiting for him when he returned from his expedition with Milford. Her first words set him once again in the middle of the problem: "Ashley, I've written to the *Age*." He said nothing. "And they've written back. They're sending along a journalist to look things over."

"And will you introduce him to Milford?"

Unsuspecting any irony, Mignon said, "Of course not. I'm going to play one against the other." She pulled down her hat. "I've got no feeling left for Milford. The trouble is: he's a Tory."

"Well, so am I in a mild sort of way."

"Well, he's an extremist. A right-wing idealist and a jingoist."

"Oh, Aunt Micky ... young Mr. Milford a Tory reactionary ... how can you think such a thing? Whatever his opinions are they're the opinions of a young person, hardly worth bothering about except that they're rather quaint. Goodness, there are so few people like Milford these days, interested in the things of the mind." Ashley was teasing her, suspending paper clips from pieces of string as he talked.

"Yes, but he's such a prissy. So fuddy-duddy for a young man. Such a drip, as Patrick would say."

There had to be a reason for this opinion and it came out: "Now you remember Arthur. He used to get to know things in a most amazing way. I remember there were lots of things he knew about the Duke of Windsor and Mrs. Simpson years before they were general knowledge. He knew all the secrets of that decadent set around the Duke and of course it's all there in the diaries."

"How do you know?"

"I've been looking at the diaries myself and something that Milford himself said put me on my guard. What emerges is that Milford is offended by Arthur's remarks. He feels we ought not to gossip about the great. That's the root of the matter."

Mignon was not far off the scent but Ashley pretended complete ignorance. What could have given offence to the young man?

"They're spicy, Ashley. That's what they are. They're spicy. It's the stuff of living history and poor, simpering, curly-headed Charles Milford can't see it. Not only is he a real little academic, he's also a bigot. He feels the Old Boy Front has got to be maintained. As you know that's nothing to me at all. As far as I'm concerned that was a rotten, evil period in British history and as radicals we were always opposed to the whole set-up."

She went on for some time on this theme and it became clear that she had renounced Milford; she expected nothing more from him and that she was not so much playing the *Age* against Heinz as seeking a substitute.

Her new eagerness to get rid of Milford and get in touch

with the newspaper made him laugh. "You want me to meet the man from the *Age*, too?"

"He'll be coming by road. He'll have a car." This seemed to imply an improvement on the Heinz-Milford set-up. The radical liked her men well-heeled.

"Milford's departure isn't fixed, or is it?"

"It must be," Mignon said airily. "He can't go on as he is, pretending to read while all his time is spent writing letters to his blessed aunts. There's that lack of enthusiasm, that subtle air of not being on your side. You know, dearest? I feel it. I'm not deceived. The boy's a Tory with implicit faith in the powers that be and cannot bear to have a Prime Minister or a general criticised. In a way he's being true to his conscience but I couldn't care a jot about Mr. Charles Milford's conscience. We've got our way to make with the diaries, don't you agree? Those diaries are dynamite in their way and I'm going to see that they reach the light of day. Unknown to himself, Charles Milford has convinced me where their market lies."

"Which is ... ?"

"Serialisation in the *Age*. After that, I'll be able to choose my publishers. Once their appetites are whetted there's no knowing where we'll end."

Ashley realised that he was now suffering from a splitting headache which reduced everything Mignon said to a sort of gabble. "If the man needs me to get him to the farm I'm ready. You know that."

"Oh, but he's got his own car," she said and hurried away to catch the bus, where she met Milford.

All the way home they had a carefully innocuous conversation but Milford's heart was moving through his knees to his boots as he thought of his indiscreet letter open on his table, a sitting prey for the curiosity of whoever chose to enter his room. The first thing he did on reaching the house was to run up and try to make amends by putting the indiscreet pages away. Even as he bundled the papers together he caught glimpses of his handiwork ... "As I told you my hostess is a Problem, a wild Celtic lady, like the Irish Morigan, a goddess appearing in battle in changing, horrid guises. I never know what guise will be her next. One moment she is the fey, land-owning lady, hinting at mysteries and secrets—très celtisante;

155

the next she is the brisk radical virago, the ideal daughter of an agricultural populist; the next she is Mother Nature herself and forming with her lifeless, enervating daughter a sort of cut down triad of fertility goddesses. But, whatever her guise, always a bore, always not to be entirely trusted."

He smacked his brow with the flat of his hand at the thought of his own carelessness in leaving such damaging statements uncovered; he was sure someone must have seen them. He would know by their eyes when he went down to the living-room; he would be reported to Professor Lloyd-Ballantyne, who would protest to Sir Ragismund Heinz, who would send for him and ask him with his cold authority whether it was possible that he, Charles Milford, had had the effrontery, the sheer bad taste, to write such a letter while a guest in the home of such a distinguished person etc. etc. What were the possibilities? "Milford, you can never expect to be quite as *persona grata* here as you were." Or "I think there's only one thing that we can now ask of you, young man, your resignation." Milford's imagination produced foul fiends with several faces, each equally bad. What was worse, he could not present himself in a very interesting or virtuous light. He had merely been indiscreet and silly.

He went downstairs. He was sure he would be met by scowls and hatred. He was sure he would be asked to leave the next day; he found himself trembling like a deposed royal baring his neck, in spite of himself. Yet there were no scowls waiting for him—only complete silence. Mignon and her daughter had quarrelled furiously about redecorating the house and Patrick was suffering from boredom. Milford did not know this and interpreted the dark brows and taciturn faces as a reaction to his piece about Mignon-Morigan. He crept away after supper and lay on his bed wondering and worrying. In the morning he told the family that he had finished his report and would return to London the next day. No one, as the saying is, turned a hair. It was as though he had said nothing at all. Thoroughly unnerved, he began to talk about the weather, a subject which he regarded as the hallmark of all true bores.

"The autumns can be mild here," Mignon said enigmatically, "and they can be very wet and blustery. Pass the marmalade, dearest," she said to Patrick.

"I think I'll drive over to Port Rydal today," Patrick observed.

"Whatever for?" asked his mother.

"It will give me something to do."

Another silence.

"That's an idea," Nesta said. "We might all go over there to look at wallpapers in Harbins."

Freddy said, "I've got a meeting in Caerifor this afternoon."

"Then you and Mr. Milford can have lunch here together," Mignon replied.

"We'll manage," Milford said gaily.

"For once you can make do," Mignon replied in her most neutral tones. She tried to smile at the young man but failed to achieve anything more positive than a sort of simper, as though she had been removing a crumb from the corner of her mouth.

Their joyless preparations for their trip to Port Rydal terrified Milford. He could do nothing at all when they left but gather his papers together. At lunch alone with Freddy the talk never warmed up; nothing stirred outside the house and once Freddy had set off to catch his bus Milford felt entirely abandoned; and so, in the minor key, his visit to Swanquarter ended, with doubt, relief, dissatisfaction and sheer social fright.

As a final pill, no one offered to run him into Caerifor and he was obliged to use the bus. The only things he seemed to have got out of his visit were a basin-bowl haircut and a rather more substantial piece of string with which to tie up his brief-case.

9

THE SECOND SUITOR ARRIVES

ONCE Milford had gone, everyone expected Mignon to show by sigh or pucker of mouth that she knew the most reputable way of interesting a publisher in the Benson-Williams' papers had failed. Everyone understood that Milford's reports would not be favourable and the matter would hang fire for ever.

All this was food and drink to Nesta, who waited for a suitable moment to hope piously that Mr. Jack Cappland, the roving correspondent of the *Age*, would not give a repeat performance. Mignon asked why Cappland should behave like Milford? Why should she assume he would reject the papers?

Nesta did not answer directly. "Young Charles Milford went away with a poor impression of us. You realise that, I suppose. He was sure we were all crooks."

"Then you and Patrick were responsible. You treated him odiously: patronising and silly."

"You weren't much better, either. You went sniffing through his papers to see what he was saying."

"Look here, Nesta, who are you to talk of integrity? Who are you to interfere? If you don't like what I'm doing, you can go away. No one asks you to stay. You talk like this because you're jealous."

"Of course I'm not."

"Yes you are. You're jealous of me."

"Why jealous of you?"

"Because I believe in something," Mignon said with an old lady's snarl. "You, you're dead. You've no faith in anything, not even your own son."

"What have beliefs to do with Father's scribblings? And what has Patrick to do with it?"

Mignon knew Patrick was Nesta's vulnerable point and pursued her advantage meanly with the thrusts and jibes only long hatred could have forged. "You criticise everything about your father and yet you tolerate far worse things in Patrick. He just sponges off you. He's got the instincts and the cool eye of a regular little ponce."

Nesta was knocked sideways. She groped for her mother's real meaning.

"I mean he prefers living off people to hard work."

A pause. "I never imagined I should live to hear you call your own grandson such a name. If you feel like that we'd better go."

"Yes," Mignon retorted defiantly. "Go."

But Nesta stayed on. She would not, could not, abandon the field of negotiations to her mother. She would stay on to spite her and, if possible, upset her schemes. Wild horses could not have dragged her from the house in view of Cappland's arrival.

Both women complained of the other to Ashley so that a three-cornered chat became a dangerous undertaking with both women making mean grimaces at him behind the other's back. Everything was loaded with ironic double meanings and meaningful, ambiguous glances. Ashley was astonished by them both; he was disappointed that they could both be so childish.

In addition, he was a little afraid of Nesta and was unable to see how he could ever have taken her for a fellow spirit. Those things which he had at first taken for signs of distinction—the clear, patrician skin, slightly patined by the African climate, the blue, nobly-formed eyes, the strong, straight nose, even the well-formed mouth, seemed created over a void. She was null, with neither warmth nor generosity. There were positive defects: the hair, tinted a clever shade of ash-grey gold, ended in a commonplace way at the nape of the neck and, final departure from grace, she wore moccasins in the house. Ashley hated women in sloppy, flat shoes and felt Nesta's moccasins reduced him to the level of a cousin or elder brother; he felt deprived, cheated of some homage due to him as a man.

He resented, too, the way she kept fobbing off his wife's invitations—always finding some glib excuse for not coming to see her. All was vagueness, flabbiness and indulgence towards her son. The final exasperation was to be asked to meet

Cappland at Caerifor station because his car had broken down and Mignon did not trust Patrick. "Why not?" he asked. "Because he may be as rude to him as he was to Milford. Besides, it's my way of being independent of them," Mignon said.

*　　*　　*　　*

Ashley's first moments with Cappland were not reassuring. In the first place, Ashley was late, the train was to time and Cappland was sitting on a bench smoking and reading. He held a cigarette holder with a dandy's precious gesture as though it were part of his act to impress even the porters.

Then, when Ashley introduced himself, there came the shock of the incongruity between the sharp style of dressing—the immaculate, family solicitor get-up, bowler hat, cuff-links and black overcoat with velvet collar—and the brutal, common face, pale-cheeked, sharp-eyed: a vile face (Ashley thought) with a pugilist's coarse smile. He swaggered out to the car in his suède half-boots and, as he took his place next to Ashley, said, "I don't mind telling you I'm cheesed off. I've been on the go pursuing small business for a fortnight. And now I think I've got a cold coming on."

On their way to the farm, both dismissed the other. Cappland considered Ashley a poor thing, a small-town somebody who was essentially a nobody; Ashley thought Cappland one of the hardest, least attractive people he had ever met.

Passing through Caerifor, Cappland wanted to know what the people "did". Ashley, sensing the contempt behind the question, made some vague reply to which Cappland retorted, "I bet these little streets are full of scandals. My experience has been that people in small towns go in for vice because there's nothing else to do."

Ashley gave a light answer deliberately; there was no point in getting involved with the pug-ugly at his side. "Perhaps you've got a flair for sniffing these things out."

"Human nature being what it is," Cappland replied, offering Ashley a menthol cigarette. Ashley refused. Cappland lit up alone. "And this Lady Benson-Williams: is she as gaga as she sounds in her letters?"

"She's far from gaga, believe me, old boy."

"Rich?"

"Who can say? She's a widow; her brother is retired."

"They have a farm?"

"But they don't work it any longer; they're too old."

"It's a big place?"

"You'll see."

"Well, it looks damned interesting country," Cappland said. "There seems an air of mystery about it. What always interests me is the story behind the story. There's no art in reporting the obvious. The hidden facts are the ones to try for. I won't really get the edge about this diaries business until I know a bit about the family."

Ashley did not understand this.

"Well, she's after money, isn't she? I've got to go carefully to make sure I'm not taken in."

This was a devastating comment on Mignon's letters to the *Age*. All Ashley could do was to assure Cappland that Lady Benson-Williams was not the sort of person to deceive anyone. Cappland was unabashed; he merely blew out blue smoke and looked knowing. When the farm came in sight, its interesting outline made Cappland wonder if the place was haunted.

"Not so far as I know," Ashley replied.

"Pity. I'd like to think it had a live ghost, preferably female. I like women who wander at night."

"We all do," Ashley replied drily.

Mignon knew at once by the expression on Ashley's face that Cappland had failed to please and she was rather cautious in her welcome. "Nice place, you've got," Cappland said, removing his bowler. For a moment, Mignon had nothing to say; it might almost have been that she was intimidated by the velvet collar and the hat and the suède shoes, or she had lost faith in her mission; at all events compared with the welcome which Milford received this was a muted, minor performance, gauche and ill-at-ease.

From the first moment, Cappland refused to accept the family as they were. To him they were more crooked, more eccentric, more extraordinary, more old-fashioned, more out-of-this-world, more faded, more snobbish, more false, more secretive, more hobbledehoy, more pretentious, more falsely romantic, than they could possibly be. Although Cappland was

161

used to all shapes and sizes of human life he had never seen anything quite like the farmhouse or the brother and sister, whose unfashionable and rustic appearance made it seem impossible that either had ever had any connection with the seats of power. By the time he had reached his room he was muttering under his breath, "Quaint as hell and not to be missed."

He manipulated the washstand fittings as best he could and then went downstairs to ask for a "barth". The boiler was being overhauled—at Nesta's instigation—and the water would have to be heated in a copper and carried upstairs in buckets. It seemed a tremendous undertaking so he did not insist. "A pity," he said, "I've got a stinker of a cold coming on and barths are the best thing, really."

Nesta and Mignon began pressing cough syrups and aspirins on him but he waved them aside. He had his own pills—mostly French ones. He went back to his room for some nose-drops and then came back for hot water. Nesta and Mignon stood before him in perplexity. "You mean you're going to drop hot water down your nostrils?"

"NO! no! I want to rinse the dropper."

"Rinse the dropper?"

"But, indeed, one must. After inserting it into an infected area I don't want to replace it in the otherwise uninfected liquid."

"I never heard of that before," Nesta said.

"But, indeed, how could one do otherwise?"

Hot water was produced and he rinsed the dropper carefully.

"Will you have to do this every time, Mr. Cappland? It might be better to keep the hot water beside you."

"But one should never use the drops too often."

Nesta shrugged and turned her back on him; but Cappland had not finished his requests. He asked if he could telephone London. It was suggested that he wait until the cheap calls began at six o'clock but he replied mysteriously that the person he wanted to speak to would have gone home by that time. He then made his call with the door of the room shut and made no effort to pay for it; and never did. Mignon was shocked. "Of course, I wouldn't have accepted his money, but he might have asked. It seemed the decent thing to do." Nesta looked evilly at her mother as the person responsible for getting Cappland into the house; she said nothing.

Patrick was trying to edge up to the new arrival but without much success. Cappland was taking his approaching cold seriously and said he thought he'd better go to bed early with a hot-water bottle and one of his special French aspirins, which looked like a model of a flying saucer in rice paper. He waved the oblong, green box in front of the family and declared they were the "only possible analgesic" he could use. He added casually, "I discovered them when I lived in Paris."

"All these medicinal preparations are the same," Nesta said scornfully.

He looked away; he did not deign to reply. He then took the most comfortable chair before the fire and after some small talk began to resume his reading. He sneezed often and pressed an enormous white handkerchief soaked in menthol to his nose. Just before supper he went upstairs and they heard him gargling and spitting in the bathroom. Freddy looked up in surprise. "Do I hear horses?"

"It's Mother's Mr. Cappland," Nesta replied viciously. "Oh, my God, it's vile," she cried, as the Wagnerian trumpetings continued.

Mignon put her hand to her head. "Please, Nesta, please."

When Cappland came down again he had a newly-drenched handkerchief and a small smile. He had taken his temperature again and it was only 'marginally' above normal.

"Do you catch cold easily?" asked Patrick.

"I suppose it's the change of climate. This part of the world is much fresher than London."

"For the time of year it's hardly cold, Mr. Cappland. You must live in a centrally-heated flat. I feel quite at ease and I've come from Rhodesia."

Again Cappland ignored Nesta's remark and returned to his chair with a theatrical shudder to show how cold he was. Freddy was embarrassed by such rudeness and Nesta flounced out of the room just as Patrick came in with more coal. "Mother's off her head to have asked such a person to stay," she hissed as she passed her son. "She must be going simple."

The evening meal followed. Cappland ate enormously and was appreciative of Mignon's efforts. He told them about some

163

of the "classical meals" he had eaten in his life, dropping well-known names and vintages. No one was particularly interested but as he liked the sound of his own voice this hardly mattered.

Towards bedtime he was given a hot-water bottle and Freddy, hoping to be of help, asked whether he rubbed his chest with anything and suggested goose grease. Cappland's eyes rolled to heaven, as he pulled a wry mouth. "Animal fat. No thank you. I couldn't bear it on my body."

Freddy goggled at him: "But that's nature's own cure. It's most efficacious."

"It may well be—for geese! The mere touch of the thing would make me sick or ill, or both."

"It's a good, old-fashioned, well-tried, country remedy," Freddy said stoutly. "I've got great faith in these old remedies. Medical science hasn't taught us much our old fathers didn't know."

"But, indeed! All the same, I'd sooner not try."

He asked abruptly whether he could have a rum, milk and honey in bed. Mignon agreed and with that Cappland went upstairs. As soon as he had gone, Nesta began wondering aloud whether he would stay in bed as Milford had done. "We seem to get all the old crocks here, don't we? And that chucker-out upstairs had better watch his step or I'll go up this minute and throw cold water over him. Did you ever see such ill manners: to ask for rum and milk just like that! I grudge every drop of our rum for that vulgar brute."

Mignon put her hands to her head and begged her daughter to be quiet. "Please. Please. Please."

"He hasn't done anything but moan since he came here. I've never met such a babyish oaf."

Mignon did not know how to defend the genie she had let out of the bottle; she left the room downcast, perplexed. Freddy hurried after her and found his sister standing by the window with her forehead on the cold pane. Could he do anything? She shook her head. Could he go to speak to Cappland? She shook her head sadly: it was the first low-water mark of her faith in her schemes.

Freddy watched her with a screwed up face. He knew that the diaries had become an obsession; he knew that she was within a knife's blade's distance of serious moral defeat. He watched her as she prepared the hot drink for Cappland and knew how her courage had ebbed away under the shock of Cappland's crassness and her daughter's hostility. After all, she was old; the mere effort of being courageous was more than most people could have borne at her age. With a little gesture of retreat she thrust the tray at Freddy. "You take it to him," she whispered. Freddy took it willingly enough but Nesta way-laid him and snatched the tray. She intended to speak briskly to Cappland. He was lying in bed wrapped in a bright-blue Paisley dressing-gown, reading Simenon and sucking black-currant pastilles. At his side, the little night-table was covered with linctuses and syrups like a chemist's stall. Nesta could not help saying that it looked as though Cappland had come down to be ill.

"But, indeed, I'm always prepared, if that's what you mean. You've got to be on this job."

Did he want anything more?

"Not this evening, thank you. I'm very comfortable here with my Florence Nightingale lamp. But no visitors, please."

The cool cheek flattened Nesta and she went downstairs with only her eyes ablaze with anger. Well? they said to her mother. Well? We hope you're satisfied this time! Mignon turned away and nothing was said. It needed a single mis-placed word to precipitate an avalanche.

Of course, Mignon was horrified by the man. She could see at once that this was not the sort of person to whom the diaries could ever be seriously commended. The man was a roaming sensationalist who had picked up the commission almost casu-ally from the *Age*, having telephoned the news editor on the same day as Mignon's first letter arrived. He knew nothing about politics or history; he didn't pretend to. "Between our-selves," Mignon said hoarsely to Freddy, "I don't know who sends my heart to my boots the quickest, Nesta, Patrick or Cappland."

"Oh," Freddy said, in a hurt voice, "what has Patrick done?"

"He's just the same as ever: a cynical little charmer but you can see he's deeply taken with this ruffian upstairs."

"He's looking for company."

"But both are preferable to Nesta. I swear to you that she'll drive me into the arms of a mental specialist. She treats us as though we were delinquents or worse, doesn't she? She's got to be told that this is my house and will continue to be until I'm gone. She can't come here bullying us."

"I agree, Micky, I agree."

"She's terrible. Dreadful. Nothing we do pleases her. She goes about the house patronising everything, patronising you. Me. Ashley. Everybody. Everything. Why in God's name doesn't she go back to her glorious life in Rhodesia? Nobody asked her to come home!"

That night Freddy found it difficult to sleep and heard his sister walking down the corridor twice. How threatened all their happiness was! The night, for years a familiar country presence, was full of menace, full of the cries of hostile people, the jargon of different values which could not allow people like Freddy and Mignon to live. They were threatened in every way and by an enemy to whom they had opened the door.

Freddy could not imagine the flowering of dread and fear in his sister's mind as she watched the ceiling in her room and waited for the time when she could get up and put some household task between her conscience and her thoughts. They both dreaded seeing Cappland again; they dreaded seeing his common face, his vulgar, showy manners, his contempt for them. As so often happens their fears were proved groundless, for after a good night's sleep Cappland, although still streaming from every pore, felt better and sat down happily before them reeking of menthol and after-shave lotion. He also carried a box of tissue handkerchiefs. His cough and his sneeze did not prevent his wolfing vast quantities of toast which Freddy had himself prepared at the kitchen range.

"You can tell this is genuine toast," Cappland said happily. "There's that indescribable something which sets it apart from toast cooked on an electric machine. Somehow, the fire has really entered the bread. Gorgeous. It's a thing of the past in London, of course, because of this smokeless zone business." He took liberal portions of butter and went on, "The last time I had toast like this was at Lord Cavington's place in Hereford-shire. I'd gone down there to write up a feature on the mansion for *Ideal Homes* and Lord Cavington—it was about this time of the year—had a fire prepared in his room where he cooked the toast for himself and his wife. They are the most devoted couple I've ever seen. Every day they had breakfast in their room, Lady Cavington in bed and Lord Cavington seated at a tiny table between her and the fire arranging the toast. An elderly butler served tea and coffee from a kind of marble-topped sideboard and any guest they particularly liked sat opposite Lord Cavington. A fascinating atmosphere."

"You mean," Mignon said, "that you've had breakfast at Lady Cavington's bedside?"

"But indeed. That's one of the pleasures of being a freelance journalist."

"I don't think," Mignon said, "I'd like comparative strangers in my room first thing in the morning."

"Ah, but it wasn't first thing in the morning for them. Lord Cavington had been reading Ruskin to his wife since just after six o'clock."

"The dear man!" Mignon cried. "Reading Ruskin to his wife so early in the morning."

Cappland smiled with real warmth. "I told you they were devoted; they shared everything: even a passion for Ruskin."

Freddy was thrilled by this and said happily: "My goodness! There's a lot of good stuff in Ruskin."

"I wouldn't know," Cappland said indifferently, taking another piece of toast.

He suddenly began thinking aloud about the possibility of using the farm as a subject for a television series called *Hearth to Hearth*.

"Don't you work for the *Sunday Age?*"

"Yes and no. I'm a freelance. I'm open for any offers and I happened to tell the producer of this *Hearth to Hearth* series—who is a friend of mine—that I was coming down here on a commission for the *Sunday Age* and he told me to keep a look out for something interesting." Cappland nodded briefly to Nesta who took her place opposite him.

"But why should this place be of any interest to your friend?" Mignon asked.

"It's got atmosphere; it would make a good subject."

"That's all nonsense about using this house for a programme," Nesta said promptly. "It's not at all interesting and it's looking very shabby just at present."

167

"That wouldn't matter," Cappland replied easily. "It's different. The kitchen is perfect, with that big open chimney and the bacon hanging up."

Mignon could not believe her ears. "The kitchen? Have you seen the kitchen?"

"I had to get up for some water in the night and found my way down."

"Who wants to film kitchens?" Nesta asked. "People nowadays like new ones with gadgets and electric fittings."

"For themselves, I agree. But they love reading and hearing of the other kind. To see a household where you've still got to pump water and where you've got those old iron things hanging over the fire."

"All that gives me a pain in the neck," Nesta said promptly. "I never heard such rubbish."

Cappland, too happy at his own idea of a feature, said they'd be surprised how people love things which are old and quaint.

This irritated Nesta even more: "That may well be, but those of us who live in such places hate to be considered old and quaint. In any case, this place isn't old or quaint—it's simply old-fashioned and in need of repair. For various reasons, which wouldn't interest you, the place hasn't been kept up; but only twenty years ago, when it was in full production, things were different."

Mignon did not like this at all. "Mr. Milford thought the place had great charm and atmosphere!"

"The less Milford is quoted the better." Nesta's eyes were all menace.

Cappland was curious to know more about Milford but Nesta snapped: "No, he doesn't want to buy the place: he's just an old friend." This made Cappland stare long and hard at Nesta, saying to himself: "I don't like you very much, beautiful"; and in order to spite her he went on to say how much the film company paid for being allowed to use private houses in its series.

The bait was taken by Mignon and the sum of £250 was mentioned.

"Some friends of mine living in a Cotswold manor house got that amount and some other friends living in a converted oast-house made somewhat more because the BBC used their place as the setting of a serial they put on last winter. Since then, advertising companies have used the place as a background for prestige adverts."

Nesta wondered what her grandfather would have said at the use of his old home for glossy magazine adverts. "You may not be aware of it, Mr. Cappland, but my grandfather was a Liberal M.P. for over forty years—and very radical! To use this place for pushing the ideal of gracious living—whatever that means—would be like using Shakespeare's birthplace to advertise a correspondence college."

The idea had gone to Mignon's head like wine. "Two hundred and fifty pounds are two hundred and fifty pounds, dearest, don't you feel?"

"To me it's like selling the past."

"What an outrageous thing to say."

"It's what I feel, Mother. I'm sorry." Mignon felt she was staring into the heart of her daughter's perversity, that joyless centre where even the clearest ideas turned into something corrupt. "Then I'm sorry for you if you think that."

Cappland knew they were both outraged to find themselves, despite themselves, arguing about money and principles in public, that is, before him, and was delighted. To squash Nesta further he pretended to play the arbitrator.

"It may never happen, you know. After all, the idea has got to be sold."

"I can't see anyone ever being keen on coming down here. Mother may deceive herself but the farm is essentially too ordinary."

Deliberately prolonging the argument, Cappland said: "You never know these days." He smiled mockingly: "People are crazy for new things. If this place suits them they'd use it and pay good money for doing so."

Mignon eventually got Cappland to herself. "You know, that was a most intriguing idea of yours ... about using this house for a series. I can assure you it has a very interesting history and there are lots of curious features about it—almost unique."

Cappland nodded neutrally.

"Without a doubt, it's one of the most interesting houses in this county. It's not large but it's got atmosphere."

"Exactly," Cappland said, blowing into a square of tissue.

When it was time for his ten o'clock pill, Mignon said, "I wonder if you'd like to see over it?"

"That would be nice."

So they set off through the bedrooms and up to the top floor where one of the rooms was used to hold lumber. Cappland held a tissue against his nose, for the dust was making him want to sneeze. "Is that a harp?"

"It's mine. I used to play."

"You ought to have that in your drawing-room for atmosphere. That would be a wonderful touch, you know, if you could sit at the harp and play a Welsh folk-song."

Mignon tittered. "I'm afraid my voice is past its best."

"We could get a professional in for that," Cappland said. "You could sing and pluck the strings and we'd get some shots of you through the strings and then we'd get the Kensingtonian harpist, Gwyneth Greenbaum, to dub the whole thing. That would be splendid. Do you ever play the harp now?"

"Well—" lying gallantly—"I sometimes come up here on wet afternoons and play for my own pleasure."

"Glorious and spooky," Cappland said appreciatively.

"Not often, of course."

"But you still come. That's all part of the atmosphere."

Mignon was watching him craftily and he was assessing her calmly, without involvement. In some way, he wanted to capitalise his introduction into this curious little pocket, this limbo where the old folk had such sweet, crooked smiles. Despite herself, Mignon was taken in by his note of authority, his range of reference and his air of a successful intermediary; already she counted on him more than Milford, who was no longer a seller. She did not realise that, already, he knew she was crazy for a little ready cash.

On the way downstairs they paused for a moment before a window where they could look down into the deep, slated courtyard where the fig tree spread its broad leaves over the water-spout. The surplus water fell out of the stone basin on to an iron grating, which sounded pleasantly in the quiet place.

"Gorgeous sound," Cappland said. "For me a real country sound."

"I've grown up with it," Mignon replied, looking down thoughtfully. "I've never known it to fail."

"There's nothing like flowing water for giving an atmosphere."

"It's supposed to be haunted, too."

"In what way?"

"It's what people say. I'm not the sort to put too much faith in old superstitions. Although they're often charming."

"But indeed, Lady Benson-Williams. Especially if it's haunted by a beautiful lady—all in white and trailing water weed."

"She's a water sprite: a white lady. She's supposed to appear on the eve of a marriage or a betrothal." (She deliberately chose this word)—"But as we're all beyond the marrying age here, the poor darling hasn't had much opportunity to leave her spring for years."

"She *has* been seen, though?"

"Plenty of times. My mother often used to talk of her." She paused and the water sounded in the still day—"but it's so long since she appeared it might be she's gone away. Do you think she's done that?"

"We'd have to have a love affair to see."

"She doesn't appear for a love affair, Mr. Cappland ... I don't think you got me correctly. I said for a marriage or a betrothal."

"A very moral phantom ..."

She laughed uncertainly, caught in the absurdities of her own inventions.

"Of course, you must realise I don't believe in such things ... all these old stories are pretty and all that but you can't put any real faith in them. All the same, they do add a certain mystery—and charm—to life—don't you feel?"

"I firmly believe in the spirit world, I've had too many experiences not to."

"Experiences?"

He blew into a tissue. "I must tell you some time."

They were now carrying on into the little sitting-room and it was time for him to look at the diaries. When she came to show them to him there was a slight lessening of her faith ... "Perhaps you won't find them very interesting, perhaps you will." Then shamelessly adding what she had read in Milford's notes—"The most vital thing there is the account of the 1916 Munition Scandal ... some big names are involved."

"Oh? What scandal was that?"

"Oh," she waved a vague hand—"you know, there were people who got munition orders and didn't fulfil them."

"Sounds as though someone was remiss. But that was in 1916."

"Then there were the entries for 1934 and 1935 leading to the Abdication Crisis of the autumn of 1936: many things about the Duke of Windsor and his clique."

Cappland wrinkled his nose. He felt that there was little new to be wrung out of *that* old dirty washing. Mignon's hooded look as she said there *was* did not impress him. He was not really listening to what was being said. He was trying to catch the background music, trying to work out exactly what the old lady was moving towards.

There was little doubt but that his chunky, confident manner intimidated Mignon. At the same time, she was sure that he was a practical man who knew where to pick up a bargain and where to find the right market. She still had hopes of his doing things although she knew that the values he represented were untouched by any contact with scholars or historians. In brief, she knew he was an ignorant man who had no interest in or feeling for history, the 'how it really was'.

She slowly laid out some of the diaries from the closet and saw that they still held Milford's pieces of white paper, with which he had marked key dates, and a couple of sheets of his notes were there, too.

Cappland was quick to seize on these. "Ah, I see you've marked the juicy passages. That's fine. I'll skim through these in no time. I hope you've done the others, as well. That will considerably help me. You see, I've got to get enough material for about six weeks. Nothing can hold the public interest after six weeks. But all this depends on the publication angle. Who's going to bring these out? Heinz, you say?"

Mignon nodded, uncertainly.

"He's a phoney. I'd watch him."

"A phoney? You mean he's not honest?"

"I wouldn't trust him with my lame cat."

172

Mignon was so agitated by this that she fished her funny old glasses out of her bodice and plonked them on her nose. "Are you sure you're speaking about the same man? He was knighted only three years ago, my brother says. He went to look him up in *Who's Who* in the Public Library!"

"But indeed! Remember though, that a rogue isn't altered because he's got a handle to his name."

"Mr. Cappland! One expects a certain amount of probity from a man in that position, doesn't one? I mean, I can't see the queen offering him a knighthood if he was a palpable rogue. I mean, can you?"

"They have very little say in the matter in Buck House. Those are political awards. Nothing else. Heinz publishes the political vapourings of Lord somebody or other—you bet your hat."

"Well, of course, you probably know Sir Ragismund better than I do, Mr. Cappland; but I must say it's sadly disillusioning to hear even a whisper against such a man. After all, who is one to look up to or trust in these times?"

He blew out his menthol smoke softly and looked amazed. "But what people in their position do has nothing to do with me. I don't want to look to them for an example. Does anybody?"

"The ordinary man-in-the-street does, Mr. Cappland. Why, a little woman—who's lived here for many years—refused to have her baby inoculated against polio until she saw whether the queen did the same thing. People still look up for a lead."

"But Sir Ragismund is hardly on a level with the queen. He's a beetle-browed little Hungarian Jew with a dash of Russian on his mother's side. A very sinister little man."

"You're making my eyes pop out of my head. I can feel them opening very wide, Mr. Cappland. I hope, indeed, that you're not just scandalmongering."

"You think what you like, Lady Benson-Williams, I'm only saying what I've heard. And I repeat: I wouldn't trust my lame cat with the man."

'A lame cat' was such a strange image to use. She took off and replaced her glasses, stared at him wildly but said nothing. He turned over the 1935 diary casually—riffled through the

173

leaves was how Mignon later described the action to Freddy.

She entered Freddy's room as though she had a liaison with him and closed the door softly.

She stood before him and said: "I feel sure those diaries are dynamite. That young man wants to publish them, I can see. We must play our cards carefully."

Freddy was thrilled. Why did she think this?

She half-turned to the door to make sure no one was entering. "It's like this ... you see, he's said some very curious things to me ... I don't know whether they're true or not and if they're not true I want to know why he should have said them."

Freddy was shaken to hear that Cappland would not trust Sir Ragismund with a lame cat.

"A lame cat, Micky? You're sure you heard correctly?"

"He repeated it."

"Why a lame cat?"

"It's just a phrase, maybe. As one normally says 'I wouldn't trust him any further than I can throw him'."

"Yes, but there's a world of difference between that and a 'lame cat'. I don't know what you think ... the whole thing raises such sinister possibilities. I mean: do you think he was referring to something *sexual*?"

"Perish the thought."

Their eyes rolled in their heads. "Well, it was a very strange thing to say. I can't get over it."

"Perhaps you shouldn't take him so literally, Micky. After all, he's a very glib young man. He throws out his phrases as most people shake dusters out of a window. He's got what they call the golden gift." He tapped his mouth.

"Why don't you go in to have a word with him? He might tell you something more—I mean, you're a man."

"I'll go willingly enough," Freddy replied stoutly. "But I can't promise to repeat everything to you."

"Don't be absurd. It can't be as bad as that."

Freddy went to see Cappland and found the door of the little sitting-room was locked. He rattled the knob, stupefied, and after a time it was opened and Cappland, with a strange smile, invited him inside. "Can I sit down?"

Uneasy glances and movements before Freddy said: "Do

174

you think Heinz is the sort of firm that ought to be bringing out my brother-in-law's diaries?"

"Not for my money."

"You prefer any other firm?"

"No. I just don't like Heinz."

"You feel it's a frivolous firm?"

Cappland had no special feeling against Heinz; his warning had more melodrama in it than facts, so he made some vague movement of the head. "My sister," Freddy went on, "was deeply perturbed by what you told her; she's already thinking of breaking off the business with the firm."

"Oh, I wouldn't let her do that, you know. After all, Heinz has a big name and he may treat you well. But my experience is otherwise. Of course, there's nothing really wicked he could do. These diaries are hardly best-selling material."

Freddy was agape. "You don't think anything of them?"

"Oh, they're all right, I suppose. I've no doubt they'll help to fill up the *Age* for six weeks but there's no real value in old documents, as far as I can see. Ever since the *Age* decided to produce an American-sized newspaper it's been clamouring for this kind of material—people read it like a drug hoping they'll get to know what's really going on in this democracy of ours; but that's all hazing: for the simple reason that nothing's going on. After all, what happens in Britain doesn't amount to a brass farthing. Britain doesn't really count any more, so her politicians don't have much more than footnote value."

All this was more than Freddy could understand; he had been born into a period of absolutes and one of these was Britain's role in the world. It hovered behind all his thinking like an old and friendly sheepdog. He had never questioned it. And as usual with Freddy, when he didn't understand he shut up: he never challenged; he just shut up. Then he noticed that Cappland had opened one of the packages of papers first tied together when Sir Arthur had died. Cappland lit another menthol cigarette and said he'd opened one out of curiosity to see if there was anything there that might add to the diaries. He added casually: "There wasn't much there—they're mostly personal letters which I've replaced. Some of them are quite interesting—from famous names. But they have no interest for me."

Freddy did not know whether to be cross or not. Cappland said grandly, "Your sister told me to browse where I liked; I thought these were included. I've seen all I want to see." He could tell that Freddy was aflutter at this action of his, so he smiled craftily and asked Freddy whether he himself did much writing. He had seen a letter from Freddy in one package which referred to his verses.

Freddy was at once charmed by this interest in himself and asked whether Cappland would like to see his work. "Later," was the answer.

"I'm known to a limited audience so far. Perhaps, one day, a collection of my sermons or of my poetry will put me on the map."

"You want to publish?"

"It would be something to have in one's hand. There's a Welsh saying which goes: 'Every old hen likes to see her eggs'. It may be rather late now. I've got masses of poetry upstairs. I've been writing since I was in my teens. I've not destroyed a thing." Freddy's breathless sentences betrayed his excitement.

Cappland, never at a loss for the right bait, said, "Perhaps I know someone who could advise you. There's a big market for poetry these days. I never read it myself but thousands do."

Freddy added, "I ought to warn you: I'm not a fashionable poet, you know. I write simple things—of praise and celebration."

"People are crying out for simple things," Cappland answered suavely. "People go watching birds because they say birds are the last mysterious things left on earth. They haven't been docketed. People's minds are very queer these days."

"They're looking for a faith," Freddy cried with conviction.

"But indeed! That may *very* well be true," Cappland nodded wisely, as though he, too, had sought the answer to the riddle of the universe. "I believe you've *really* got something there." He was dangling the old man like a fish merely to test his own powers of persuasion. Then, when he saw the old boy gasping on the bank, he said abruptly: "Let's leave the matter there for the time being, shall we? And if there's time before I go back to town we'll go through your poems and I'll take them to this friend of mine."

"That would be really wonderful," Freddy said.

"But keep this to ourselves. Yes?" He spoke as though the old boy had a faulty command of English.

"Well, there's no harm in letting my sister know, is there? After all, she'll be very interested."

Cappland made a musician's movement with his open hand. "Perhaps better to keep quiet at this stage."

But Freddy didn't do so and he went at once to tell Mignon that it might be possible for Cappland to arrange for the publication of his poetry.

To Freddy's surprise, Mignon was furiously jealous.

"I won't have you bothering him with your trifles," she cried.

"They may be trifles to you, Micky, but they're very important to me—and you mustn't speak like that."

"Rubbish. That stuff of yours is good enough for the local papers but it's not good enough to publish in London—and you ought to know it."

Freddy cried. He sat down at the kitchen table and sobbed like a grampus—to have been on the summits of poetry for only as long as it took to walk from the little sitting-room to the kitchen and then to be kicked off by a jealous woman! He looked ashamed of himself and even Mignon was dreadfully shocked at his complete collapse.

"Oh well, Freddy, it's not as bad as that ... but you must know that I'll be all on edge until this matter of the diaries is settled and you mustn't start crossing me now."

"But I want to push my own affairs if I can. Micky, you've become very worldly recently. You're not a bit as you used to be. I don't think business suits you."

"My nerves have gone to pieces, that's true." And without warning she, too, sat down and shed a few hard tears. Between sniffs she said, "I thought this thing was going to be so simple ... but people keep putting up so many hurdles ... difficulties ... doubts ... I'm beginning to doubt myself ... I sometimes wish Edward had never visited us. What have we had since, except worry and strain? And I know I'm getting mean-minded. I've been mean-minded with you and I can't forgive myself."

"Can I do anything for you?" asked Freddy. He was trembly and lost. He felt that his own selfish interest in his poetry had

177

driven his sister to tears. Mignon jumped up abruptly. "We mustn't let Nesta see us like this or she'd give us another lecture. She's dead-set against Cappland."

Freddy asked wanly: "Do you think that all he says is really meant?"

"He's glib, certainly, but he knows the markets. After all,"—and here Mignon showed how quickly she was learning—"with these matters you've got to be brisk haven't you? It's no good our trying to sell the diaries to people who don't want them. We can save ourselves lots of trouble by knowing the right person."

Mignon had also had doubts about Cappland and was obliged to admit that Charles Milford was a person much to be preferred—if only, she sighed to herself, Milford had had more *GO*. She would much have preferred Milford to have the sole interest in the affair of the diary. But she also wanted money. Yet when she was with Cappland, she forgot her reservations in her desire to please him and to further her own ends. He vampirised her; his large, cold blue eyes held on to her like a vacuum cleaner and seemed to suck all sorts of absurdities out of her innermost soul—as though he was the conductor to her absurd fantasy life and the more she talked the more *involved* she became until she felt that if she stopped talking all interest in her and her case would drop out of his mind like a setting sun. Cappland knew this and smiled to himself as he thought: "Metaphorically speaking, the old girl's already in her shift; there's only bra and panties left."

There was a strange mixture of bargaining and whining in these conversations. On their decline in status she said: "I suppose one will go on, as most people must do in our position these days, realising assets here and there in order to meet the demands of the present. It's very difficult, Mr. Cappland, believe me, when you're two elderly persons in the modern world. You really are up against it. And financial burdens get ever greater and this and that and all one's savings for six months go if you have the builders in for a day and a half. It's really frightful. Other people manage better, I think, because they aren't held back psychologically—do you understand what I mean? Psychologically, we just aren't equipped for survival. All our standards are those of another age. We were brought

178

up to believe in the simple virtues—hard living, plain living and a decent day's work—but all that has gone by the board now. You know this is a very old established family. My forbears go back to one Marchudd ap Cynan, a ninth-century prince of Caerifor. We're one of the oldest families in Wales and they, of course, trace their lineage back to before the Norman conquest. We had poets and singers attached to the family when the heads of family still helped their servants to skin sheep and spin the wool. There wasn't any place for drones in those days. At one time, I believe, we had rights over 15,000 acres and the family fortunes were at their height in the eighteenth century when people had a genius for suitable matches bringing in large territories. Now, it's nothing but a glorified smallholding."

"There's another tradition that we are one of Catherine of Berain's descendants. That's nothing really: she was known as the Mother of Wales. She was a ward of Queen Elizabeth and had four husbands—the first a Catholic, the second a recusant, the third an Anglican and the fourth a Puritan. So, as Freddy often says, she ran the whole gamut of the Reformation. And through this remarkable old girl a great number of Welsh families are related."

Cappland nodded wisely; although he had long since stopped listening he felt resentful: just what the hell did she think she was doing? Whom was she deceiving? They were nobodies and they ought to know it and all those small ancestors bored him to grief; they were nothing; all that rubbish was dead; it had died on the world years ago.

His first instinct about the family had not been correct. He no longer thought of them as a source of material; he no longer took very seriously the question of the publication of the diaries; reading between the lines he had seen that Heinz was not too keen; he no longer took very seriously the possibility of getting the house into the *Hearth to Hearth* series— unless they wanted some exclusive shots of the old couple in their antique bathroom; but he had realised that some of the letters wrapped up in the little sitting-room closet had value for collectors. And as soon as he had got the old lady out of the room he began sorting out some of the likelier ones—letters from Lloyd George, from Winston Churchill, from Dukes and

M.P.s. None of them had great intrinsic value but some collector would probably pass out a few guineas for them. Without hesitation he popped them in his briefcase and felt he'd done a good thing. Then he sought out Patrick and asked him if he'd like to go out for a drink.

10

BACK TO THE LAND

LIKE his mother, Patrick considered Cappland a smooth rogue but found him amusing and well-breeched, two great virtues in Patrick's world. After his period at Swanquarter unfashionable penury was the virtue he could least easily forgive. He accepted Cappland's invitation at once and then cadged a couple of pounds off his mother since he had no money left of his own. The two then decided to set out across the fields to the square inn at the crossroads, which was the local Soho.

For his first sortie into the rural underworld Cappland was aggressively turned out with a loud check coat and a woollen weave tie. To complete the arrogantly rustic effects he had set aside his cigarette-holder and his menthol cigarettes and attached a pendulous cherrywood pipe to his lower lip, like an unsuccessful author seeking an image. "There's nothing I like more than a brisk walk across country and some genuine draught beer, cheese and pickles afterwards," Cappland said, striding manfully in his chunky suède boots, the last link with his old urban self. He continued enthusing about beer and pickles as though he had been a disciple of Belloc. He went on to talk about a visit to France earlier that year. There was one place which they had discovered where they'd had a bang up meal with unlimited vino for "just under three pounds a head. I mean, you couldn't get that kind of meal in London if you wanted to."

"But how many restaurants would dare to ask you just under three pounds a head?" Patrick's normal scepticism asserted itself. "It strikes me that you Britishers prefer to spend your money on cigs."

"That's a matter of class. The middle-class person realises now that if you've once got into the habit of eating well you've got to learn to pay, as well."

Patrick listened to a good deal more of Cappland's memories

of good meals, and thought the way he talked was a send-up of every gracious living column ever published.

Then, Cappland, who had never said whether he was married or not, asked whether there would be any women in the pub. Patrick thought this unlikely since the local women, for the most part, did not go out drinking with their husbands. Cappland had not been thinking of married women; he had been imaging some local talent "hot for it in hedges and ditches".

Patrick laughed and Cappland said that in Paris he had seen a brothel where one of the rooms was arranged like a barn.

"Why a barn?" Patrick asked.

"For *amour rustique*," Cappland answered in between drawing on his pipe. "You know, there are piles of straw and hay instead of beds and the girls used to put buckets of fresh cow-shit in a corner to give the right ambience."

"Good God. Whatever for?"

"For this *amour rustique* atmosphere. Actually, because there aren't any cows in Paris they had to send a taxi out twice a week to Ste. Marie des Vaches to get fresh shit. This put up the price of the room. Overheads and all that."

At the next stile Cappland stopped to fill his pipe. "Come to think of it, you know, I could do with a little bit of *amour rustique* myself. Nothing too coarse, nothing too classy, something hard and warm, a well-fleshed dairymaid, say, or a bright-eyed young horsewoman."

He smacked his lips at the thought. "I might as well shut up. The prospects of finding any talent in an out-of-the-way place like this are so remote. In these kinds of places a man's best friend is his hand."

This was the sort of remark that Patrick had not yet learned to take. He reacted sharply with a flash of displeasure and amazement. Cappland looked at him askance; the idea that a young person could feel there were limits was unknown to him. "Well, isn't that the truth?"

They crossed the road to the inn in silence. Cappland, who was only taking up Patrick for lack of someone more his kind, thought his remark had probably been too near the truth for Patrick's taste.

They barged into the pub and Cappland banged a half-crown on the counter. "And what will you have?" But Patrick had left his side to go over to a woman sitting on a secluded settle: it was Rohama, drinking a gin-and-orange while her husband Martin played darts nearby.

As soon as she realised that neither of the men thought any the less of her for being found in a bar she made room for them on the settle and was delighted to have someone to talk to. Martin came up, nodded curtly towards Cappland and took hold of Patrick by the shoulder. "We don't see much of you. Won't your grandmother let you come down to see us?"

Patrick tried to disengage his shoulder from the hard grip. "Why should she stop me?"

"I get the feeling we're not good enough for the rest of you."

"He's putting it on," Rohama said hastily, making gestures of annoyance at her husband. He turned towards her with a certain menace. "You shut up."

She tried to laugh gaily. "Martin's got a funny sense of humour," she said to Cappland, who was watching her, fascinated.

"Ah, you're all the same over there," Martin was saying, "none of you dares to cross the old girl. You're all as afraid of her as that poor old bugger Freddy is."

"I think there are other ways of looking at our relationship," Patrick said stiffly.

Martin made a great show of contempt. "I can't see you crossing the old girl. You're dead scared of her."

Patrick had thrown off the vice-like hand. "Why should I be scared of her? Why? Tell me."

"God knows. That's the mystery to me."

"Oh, come, she's not as bad as all that. I assure you we do exactly as we please."

Martin suddenly changed his position and laughed. "Drink up. What will you have?"

"A little less aggressiveness," Patrick said, still half-angered.

"Oh, he's got some spirit," Martin cried, turning to his wife. He took notice, at last, of Cappland. "Are you from Africa, too?"

Cappland, who disliked Martin's manner, gave nothing away. "I'd have thought you'd have recognised a fellow savage without asking any questions."

No one knew how to take the remark, so Martin said, "You're a testy bugger. Damned if I care whether you're from Africa or Jamaica. It's all the bloody same to me."

Martin turned back to Patrick. "She must have poisoned you against us. She does it with everyone."

"Never. Never."

"Who are you talking about?" Rohama asked anxiously.

"The old girl," her husband replied tersely.

"Well," said Rohama virtuously, as though to wind up the conversation, "I get on with her very well. We understand one another perfectly. No one could be nicer than she is."

Cappland couldn't be sure what was involved; he could see that the husband was as much spoiling for a fight as the wife was anxious to smooth things over. Were these some of the relations mentioned to him by his hostess? Had she been referring to this countrified couple? Then Cappland looked at Rohama again and could see that she had some unused quality that was out of the ordinary: something that might look well given better taste and better clothes. He summed up her defects—the messy hair-style, the wan taste in cardigans, the insipid necklace—and looked at her again. Something still remained. "Um," he thought, "she's got a splendid body and a brilliant skin."

Work in the potato field had given Rohama a deep brown complexion which modified into golden-rose on the cheekbones. Her hands, well-shaped and well cared for, showed no sign of the hard work she might do, the scrabbling in the earth, the rubbing against the rougher textures of things.

Both she and her husband shared a sort of purposefulness which Cappland found attractive even though, at that moment, Rohama was suffering because her husband was calling Lady Mignon "a bloody old battle-axe". It was the half-defiant, half-contemptuous suffering of the woman who has married beneath her, who hated the lack of finesse, the inability to imagine the impression being created, the wilful refusal to drop a subject when it had already been pursued too far.

"Oh, Martin, let the matter drop," she cried impatiently. "You won't let a thing alone once you start."

"We understand one another, don't we, Patrick?"

184

"I've convinced him," Patrick said to Rohama, "that he's misjudged my grandmother completely."

"I'm not convinced about anything," Martin replied, "but as you're a nice young chap I won't argue. There's no side about him," he said to his wife, at the same time smiling in the softened way of semi-tipsy men at Patrick, as though he had found a new toy.

Patrick took out one of his mother's pound notes and bought them some more drinks while Cappland looked curiously at Martin. How was it possible, he asked himself, for a woman of any real intelligence to marry anything as hobbledehoy as that? The man was probably a good farmer but as a human being he was a silly clown; and the only way to teach clowns, thought Cappland, was to kick them in the crotch. Martin took Patrick away with him to show him to his cronies at the other end of the room. Cappland and Rohama were left alone.

Cappland said no one had told him exactly what relationship there was between herself and Lady Benson-Williams.

Rohama was about to say, "I think you'd better not ask the question" when she thought again and said, "I'm really no relation to Lady Benson-Williams; but I am a half-sister to her daughter."

"That makes you Patrick's semi-aunt."

Rohama twirled her glass nervously. "I suppose you could call me that. Patrick never thinks of me as that, ever. Oh, they're complicated, these family relationships."

She sipped her gin nervously.

"I still don't get how you can be a relation to Patrick and not to his grandmother."

"My position is rather difficult. I'm the daughter of Sir Arthur Benson-Williams ... but he never married my mother ... well, he could not since he was already married."

Cappland's regret was almost feminine in its intensity. "Forgive me. Please forgive me. What must you think of me probing all the time?" His face was contorted with contrition.

Rohama was without rancour. "You didn't know; and how were you to guess?"

"It couldn't make any difference in any case."

"To some people it might; less than it used to. Just every so often I have to go through the whole thing although it's not so bad for me as for some: after all, I was recognised by my father. And in a little community like this everyone accepts you without question after a certain time. Just recently, since the birth of the baby I've thought it might be nicer to go away—and give the child an ordinary background. Do you understand?"

"Well, I ought to," Cappland said softly, "seeing that I'm illegitimate myself."

"Fancy that!" she was greatly touched by his confession.

"My mother married later. I've got five half-brothers and sisters: all in Glasgow."

"Fancy that, now. I've only got Patrick's mother and she's been away for years. We have nothing at all in common. In fact, there's a lot of resentment, really. I suppose I'd be the same if I were in her position."

"They're cold with you."

"Well, I can't honestly say they are. I know the old people quite love me. Their eyes don't lie, do you know what I mean...? Yet, there's something between us, despite everything we do. I must say, it's not on my side."

"They're a very intellectual family. Books, papers, radio, politics, discussions etc., etc. Intellectual people don't know how to give themselves very easily."

"Why do you talk of intellectuals like that when you're one yourself?"

"Me an intellectual? Don't make me laugh."

"Well, that's how you appear to me."

"I'm not. Believe me, I get too much out of life to be an intellectual. I never think, except when I have to. It's bad for the health."

"Well, you should know." The gin had warmed Rohama's innocent blood and she smiled happily at Cappland—she couldn't stop herself smiling—and as she was smiling Cappland was reminded of a girl he had once been in love with.

Somehow, it was implicit in the tone of their voices, the way they felt consideration for the other, that had Martin not been present they would have held hands. Cappland bought her another drink and as he was standing at the counter there flowed from him the social ease, the self-confidence of the man of the world who appealed to the unexpressed side of Rohama.

186

She loved her husband—their marriage was passionate, successful—but she was nostalgic for something else, which was summed up in Cappland's paying for the drinks affably and speaking to the woman behind the bar without any sense of reserve or condescension; and, of course, Cappland was charming to Rohama herself. He showed her none of the casual insolence he ladled out so liberally to Mignon and Nesta. In fact, he might have been another person.

Martin and Patrick came over with cheese and pickles.

"This is the life," Cappland said, popping an onion into his mouth. "And just as I like them: not too harsh and vinegary."

"I can't stand them," Rohama said. "Pickled onions and coffee are two things I can't take."

"You don't know what you're missing!" And Cappland picked up a small onion and held it to her nose.

After chomping cheese and pickles, Cappland was ready to do anything and when Martin asked him whether he'd like to try his hand at potato-lifting the next day, he promptly agreed.

"You will? Or is it the beer and pickles talking?"

"We'll go, won't we, Patrick?"

"Why not? I'm bored to tears doing nothing."

"What's the old battle-axe going to say?" Martin asked.

"Oh Christ, what does it matter what she says? You know, Mr. Martin Lloyd, you've got a bundle of wrong ideas in your head!"

Martin was completely won over and offered to buy both Patrick and Cappland double whiskies. He would have bought them another and another had they let him. They saw that, despite his rough manner, he was a good, if silly, man. Once he felt they accepted him he couldn't hold himself back. They had to have everything he possessed; they had to share everything.

So, when ten o'clock came and the pub closed, the young men had to return to his home for supper and Rohama promised them bacon and eggs.

Martin drove them home and while Rohama and the baby-sitter prepared a meal Martin searched out some old rubber boots which fitted Cappland.

"Now you've no excuse not to come tomorrow."

After supper, Cappland and Patrick took themselves off hastily, a little anxious about Mignon's reaction. Walking along the rough lane, Cappland told Patrick of his gaffe, of his blundering intrusion into Rohama's relationship with the others. He stopped and held up his hand. "I'd rather have this cut off than hurt her. She's a wonderful person."

"But was she hurt? I thought I'd rarely seen her look so happy."

"Really?" Cappland's voice lifted and he was aflame with happiness, thankfulness.

"I've not seen her often, but she was quite different tonight. I feel sure she's a good sort and so's her husband. Our bloody family doesn't play fair with them."

"Be careful, old boy. It's not an easy position for anyone. What bothers me is why everyone has to live so close."

"My grandfather's will."

"He divided the property, you mean?"

"Exactly. And no one can afford to buy the other out. Well, that's a simplification, I suppose. I've never been very interested in the matter."

"She doesn't really look your side of the family. Rohama, I mean."

"She's supposed to be the image of my grandfather."

"She must get those remarkable eyes from him. Have you noticed them? Really deep, sexy eyes. They could smoulder."

"You think so?" Patrick's surprise caught his voice unprepared.

"God, at first you don't think much of her. You think, yes, that's O.K. but a bit too countrified for my liking and then suddenly you see that underneath the bad taste and the obsolete trimmings, she's a real woman with real distinction."

"She'd never impressed me in that way," Patrick said, "but then she wouldn't. Well, I suppose not. But I agree that she's a wonderful person and I want my family to love her and her husband and that cross-eyed woman who was frying the bacon. If we loved them they'd be real friends—more than just relations you've got to watch and be suspicious of all the time. That was why Rohama looked so happy tonight: it was because she knew we liked her, that we were happy to be in her company."

"You've drunk too much beer and whisky, young Patrick," Cappland said. "Breathe in deeply and let's get moving."

They were standing in the open part of the lane. It was a clear, fresh night, a sheet of brilliant stars overhead while twenty or so miles across country they could see, as rarely before, the lights of Port Rydal. The distant twinkling of the lights and the stars gave the impression that they were surrounded by November-the-Fifth sparklers. It was as much as Cappland could do to prevent himself saying to his companion, "I'm glad I'm not you. I'm glad that I've gone through all that adolescent half-light and can see with the eyes and desires of a man." Yet Cappland's happiness overflowed even towards Patrick and his colonial naïvety and they trotted home together in good fettle.

The lights were still burning at Swanquarter. Mignon and her daughter were sitting on each side of the dying hearth stiff-backed with disapproval because a brief evening's outing had extended until bedtime. They blinked at their sociable faces without enthusiasm. "You've been having supper with Rohama and her husband? Whatever next?"

"Well, we were invited."

"And what did she give you?" Mignon asked coldly.

Cappland, stimulated in every way by his evening, spoke lyrically of the home-cured ham and the orange-yolked eggs. Mignon sniffed. "Eating home-cured ham at this time of night? Of course, Martin's got an appetite like a horse, but how he and Rohama can sleep after stuffing themselves before bedtime I don't know."

The men wanted to go to bed. The mother and daughter looked at one another carefully. "Aren't you going to tell us a bit more about your evening?"

So Cappland explained how they'd met and about the plan to pick potatoes the next day. Dead silence.

"You ... you often pick potatoes, Mr. Cappland?"

"All the Capplands were tenant farmers in Northumberland until they went north to Glasgow," he replied robustly, even getting a kind of northern accent into his voice.

"And Patrick?"

"I was thinking that Rohama and Martin feel very left out of our lives. They've got big chips on their shoulders where we're concerned. I don't understand why they're not invited over one evening." Another dead silence. "I suppose it's because you feel they're beneath you."

"Do we feel we're above them?" Nesta asked her mother.

"I've never felt above them. They've their own life and Rohama calls here whenever she feels like a little chat. She's always having cups of tea and pieces of cake. I can't do more."

"I think we ought to be more friendly."

"There's no need to be so aggressive, dearest."

But Patrick was not to be silenced. "Maybe not ... but there's a certain barrier between us isn't there? They're not really part of our lives at all, are they?"

"Well, since you ask," Mignon said, "I have to be honest and say I've nothing in common with Martin ... and Rohama is devoted to him and that's that."

"You think Martin is common, I suppose."

"Well, am I wrong?"

"But, Grandma, don't you ever try to see people as they are? Just because he doesn't want to read *The Times* or because he doesn't go around the farm pretending he's a gentleman and really gets down to work, can't you find anything to like in him?"

"Oh Patrick, what rubbish you're talking," his mother said briskly. "You can't throw your arms around everyone because they don't have any polish any more than one falls for the first person with a little glib finish. You either like people or you don't. Leave your grandmother alone. She's lived here for some time with Rohama and Martin; if they don't like it they can leave. Don't forget they've got their land for nothing."

"But they give quite a lot in return," Patrick said.

Mignon was shocked. "Has Rohama been talking to you?"

"She hasn't said a word; I only look at things for myself. It's a pity we keep that couple at a distance, that's all."

Ah, Nesta yawned. "It's so late and there's so much one could say..."

Mignon was disturbed by this hobnobbing with Rohama and Martin and by their going potato picking. The position had been eased out of her hands; she was lost; and Cappland seemed to have forgotten all about the diaries. Nesta, on the other hand, thought a bit of honest manual work would not harm either of them.

"But he isn't here on holiday, you know."

"Who isn't?"

"That Cappland man. He ought to read the diaries."

"He's been reading all day."

"I don't think so. Freddy doesn't think so, either."

"Then what is he doing?"

"Daydreaming."

Meanwhile, Patrick and Cappland had taken chairs near the fire and were reviving the embers of their earlier conversation in low voices.

"What I feel so strongly," Patrick was saying with an unusual note of aggressiveness in his voice, "is that all this business fanned up by my distinguished second cousin Edward Lloyd-Ballantyne and aided by yourself is all a form of Father Christmas making. It doesn't really mean anything."

Cappland, too benign, too tolerant, at that moment to take offence, defended the interest which the *Sunday Age* was taking in the Benson-Williams papers. It was, he said, a case of keeping their eyes on the horizon and understanding what might be the talking point in six months' or a year's time. If the publishers, Heinz, were to bring out the papers, the newspaper would like to cream off the sensations and run extracts for about six weeks. If Heinz decided not to bring out the diary, the interest would be considerably lessened.

Patrick failed to grasp the distinction, real enough to Cappland, between papers that were to be published and papers that would only be published in the *Sunday Age*. Wouldn't the papers stir up interest without being published in book form? Cappland gave some long explanation which Patrick didn't believe and his face showed it.

"You've got to realise," Cappland said at last, in some exasperation, "that the average reader will have forgotten all about your grandfather and we'll have to get little paragraphs into papers to remind people that your grandmother is still alive: that sort of thing."

"What it really means," Patrick said, "is that the *Sunday Age* has so little faith in its own judgement that it won't publish a thing like the Benson-Williams diary unless some reputable firm such as Heinz has shown an interest in it."

For the first time Cappland was at a loss for words and bit his lower lip awkwardly.

Patrick's contempt knew no limits. He had shared his mother's belief that the diaries were phoney documents and his grandmother's plan to sell them a phoney project; it might have been expected that such material, such a scheme, should attract a phoney like Cappland to put them before the public. He was sure that Cappland would go away—as Milford had gone away—and nothing more would be heard of him. He looked at the strange creature from another world and without haste, but without relenting, Patrick dismissed him from the scheme of things as a person who had 'no class at all'. The only thing that puzzled him was why he didn't ring true.

* * * *

It was, as might have been expected after such a starlit night, a dry, clear morning; the distant hills in the autumnal morning brightness looked very old; very old and very far away.

Mignon went out to cut some dahlias and came back looking old and troubled. "Will you be back for lunch?"

"I doubt it," Patrick replied. "So far as we gathered we'll be eating with the rest of the gang."

Their departure took away the brightness from the morning for Mignon.

At the sound of their footsteps, Rohama rushed across the room to the window. She had been on edge with expectation ever since rising for, as she explained to them, she had not thought they would fulfil their promise. She was peeling onions, and already dressed for work in the fields with a head-scarf and rubber boots. A few minutes later, while Cappland was putting on wellingtons, the first woman helper arrived, carrying a coarse apron in a roll under her arm. A little later, a couple more rode up on bicycles and were amused to hear that they had two amateurs to help them. One of the women—Fay Evans—warned them that once Martin got them into the field he'd drive them to death. "He's a right bugger on that tractor," she said casually, throwing aside the core of the apple she'd been chomping with a noise like a horse.

"Oh yes," the other woman agreed, "he don't give you no time to straighten your back before he's round again."

"Oh, but they'll be rising lovely," the woman with the coarse apron put in. "There hasn't been rain for days, you might say."

Without any doubt, it was a good year for potatoes. Fay Evans knew of a farmer who had never had such a crop: he was short of storage space and the last fifteen hundredweights were stored in the house. Everyone was sure Martin's potatoes would be the same.

They went outside into the yard among the poultry to wait for Martin to drive them up to the field. A slight breeze ruffled the plumage of a splendid cockerel, which looked at them sideways before giving out a tremendous clarion call.

"That's right," said Cappland laughing, "it's the foreman's whistle."

Somehow, the free call of the cockerel in the bright, clear air set the seal on the day; in its own strange way it would be perfect.

Martin arrived with two farmboys from neighbouring places and noticed the red woollen cap which Patrick was wearing. "I bet that's Freddy's night-cap," he said.

"Be careful what you say about him," Patrick replied, "he's promised to come over here later on."

"To lift potatoes?"

"To watch us, I suppose."

"Good old Freddy," Martin said. "He does that well. As sure as God's in heaven, he's the laziest bag of bones ever stitched together."

All the workers, village women, hands from nearby farms, had assembled and Martin had thrown an assortment of sacks and skips into the trailer; two of the other men had lifted up a weighing machine. Then everyone else climbed aboard and the tractor pulled up out of the farmyard into the lane towards the potato field.

The rutted lane made the trailer sway and bounce and the women shouted and cursed as their breasts swung about in motion with the wheels. Martin turned the tractor sharply through a gate and under the lee of a high hawthorn hedge and everyone lurched to one side of the trailer. Everyone knew it was his idea of a joke but no one was amused; as so often with Martin's jokes, the result was irritation. The tractor stopped with a lurch so that those who had just picked themselves up from their first tumble were thrown forward. Cappland was furious and asked Martin whether he'd rather spend his time carrying them to hospital than have them in one piece to work in the field. Martin laughed, half-expecting him to walk off, but Cappland didn't. "You're nuts," he said cheerfully. It was the sort of language Martin might understand but he rarely had the opportunity to hear it, since people tended to be afraid of him. It made an odd beginning to the day and the village women, not certain of the footing on which Cappland stood, waited for another flare-up. It never came.

Martin began pacing out the stints and marking them with short sticks. Bags and skips were set out at regular intervals and, in due course, Martin opened up the first row. As the woman had foretold, the potatoes rose beautifully and lay on the fine earth like large, round pebbles. Gathering them was not difficult and the work advanced rapidly with hardly a respite. The women had the energy to talk but Cappland and Patrick, new to the job, had all their work cut out to keep pace with the tractor which seemed to return at alarmingly close intervals. Cappland said, "After the first hour you get used to it; it becomes almost natural to rush forward scrabbling up potatoes with your head ducked forward like an ostrich looking for a pile of sand." He seemed astonished that he was there at all.

About half past twelve the gang returned to the farmhouse where they ate roast beef, fried onions and potatoes, followed by rice pudding and tea: a typical potato gatherers' meal. Rohama, although helped by the cross-eyed baby-sitter, served at table herself so that Cappland, while eating an enormous meal, could enjoy the sight of her good, round hips and her strong legs. The conversation of the evening before hovered between them and when they looked at one another it was like the recognition of a reflection.

The meal was followed by a short rest for a smoke and a chat in the yard. They then continued working until sunset, when the women packed up and the men went around the field weighing the bags and loading them on the trailer. As they

walked over the harvested field, strewn with dry haulms, and
swung up the bags with a strong, clean movement, Cappland
and Patrick felt satisfied and elated; they had succeeded in
doing something that was unfamiliar.

"Ah," said Martin to Patrick, "you ought to go in for farming. It's in your blood."

They were the last to return to the farm. As they rode down
the lane from the field the air was coldish, as though building
up for a frost, the first of the autumn, and the distant hills had
a new purplish tone. Overhead, the darkening sky, empty of
clouds, brimmed with its own deep-blue emptiness, like the
high, still tides along the coast and up the estuary towards
Caerifor; and into this high, still air the smoke from the farmhouse chimneys rose in thin, perfect columns. It was almost as
though they could hear every sound from the valley below, so
great was the stillness of the horizons and the sky that joined
them.

The news that Patrick and Cappland were going back to
help again the next day gave Mignon and Nesta a further
shock. One day, they had thought, would be enough; one day
away from his duties would have been all that Cappland could
have spared. Shortly after the two set out again the next morning Ashley, on his way to a council meeting, called with a box
of pears.

"Guess what," Mignon said to him when he asked how
Cappland was getting on, "he and Patrick have gone all agricultural. They met Rohama and Martin in a pub and now
they're spending all their time picking potatoes. They're having a fine old time with the village women." The spirit of
comedy was twinkling very far away.

"What about the diaries?"

"Oh he was far too tired to look at them last night."

"How long will he stop here ... picking potatoes?"

Mignon shrugged. "Another thing, dearest: Patrick has become very pro-Martin. He thinks we ought to make more of
him. He's the sort of man who's the backbone of the country:
capable, practical, honest in every way."

Ashley whistled and laughed. The whole thing intrigued
him—so much so that he called back again in the middle
afternoon and suggested they should all go up to the potato

field. Freddy and Nesta had already set out like pilgrims, trekking uphill to see a wonder, but when they saw Mignon and Ashley following they stopped.

"You see," Freddy called, "we've all gone back to the land." The way he spoke and the mere fact that the whole household found itself walking up the hill to look at people lifting potatoes showed up the quality of their sequestered lives, where every little thing had to have its moral price put upon it.

Rohama was the first to see the quartet approaching. "Wonders never cease!" she called out. Everyone stood up to watch the visitors walk slowly round the edge of the field to the nearest point of the workline. There were only about a dozen rows left to be gathered and everybody hoped to finish the task before dark.

"Well, Mr. Roberts," Fay Evans said, "it's a long time since I saw you with mud on your boots."

"You can't go into the pulpit looking like a tramp," he replied briskly, a little taken aback by the familiarity of the woman's tone.

"Well, your Patrick will make a proper farmer," Rohama said to Nesta. Nesta smiled wanly but not without kindness. She felt, as did Freddy and Mignon, that they had made a tactical mistake in coming. Among the dark-handed workers in Martin's field they had the air of intruders, of people who were, in any case, not useful and close to a sort of social rubbish heap.

"We'll have to send Patrick to Aberystwyth to get a degree in agriculture," Freddy suggested. "I believe some of the old urge to return to the soil is driving him."

"And we must find a nice local girl for him and his friend Jack," said Martin.

"He's a married man," Fay Evans cried pointing at Cappland.

He laughed. "Can you tell?"

"Well, I could tell you how I know, but I won't. There's refined people around."

"Well, there's one thing, Fay Evans," said Freddy, "that we can leave Mr. Cappland's reputation safe in your hands."

"I don't know about *his* reputation. But I tell you what, Mr.

Roberts, I'll find a nice young thing for you. They say there's nothing like young love in old shoes."

How Freddy laughed. "I wouldn't be ungentlemanly enough to say you're making fun of me."

"Mr. Roberts, dear, I've always said you were a good man wasted. You ought to stop all that writing. It's very bad for the head. Get a nice little woman, Mr. Roberts, and leave those old books alone."

Freddy was delighted to be the centre of attraction. "Ah, there's some truth in what you say but I'm sure of one thing: it's cheaper to keep a shelf full of books than one woman."

"That may well be," said Fay Evans, "but there's more fun in one woman—if she's properly handled—than in all them books put together."

Freddy was stumped for an answer and wondered aloud what Fay Evans's mother would have said had she been alive.

Fay continued to rib him about his unmarried state and his sermonettes in the weekly paper but without spite and with a certain gallantry, as though humouring a child. Cappland and Patrick listened to the old-fashioned chit-chat while Mignon, looking aquiline and imperious, waited silently, at a loss to know what to say to such people. The brutal, familiar way the young woman spoke to Freddy irritated her; she could not think of anything to say which would have put the young woman in her place without causing offence; so she moved away, supported by Ashley's arm.

It hurt her to see the field that had once been theirs invaded by the people Rohama and Martin found useful; she wished that Patrick had not been involved and yet, as he joked with the women, she saw that he was not out of place.

Freddy moved away, too, and disappeared into the bushes at the side of the field. "Why," Fay Evans said to her neighbour, "Freddy have gone for a pee." Mignon heard her and turned away, as though in pain.

Yet, out of this discomfort Rohama and Martin made something good. Ashley praised the crop and Martin gave him a sack of potatoes on the spot while Rohama begged Nesta to walk down to the farm with her to have tea.

"Do you hear that, Mother?" Nesta asked. "Rohama wants us to have tea with her."

"Oh, you've got your hands full," Mignon said briskly. "Another time. Another time."

Rohama insisted and Ashley said, "I would very much like to come." The mother and daughter had no reason not to follow him. Rohama at once abandoned her stint and hurried down to the farm and by the time the visitors had reached the door she was waiting for them with a bright fire, a set table and herself bright in a clean overall. The cross-eyed woman prepared the tea for the fieldworkers in the outer kitchen while Rohama, nervous and excited at the thought of having her half-sister in the house, did all she could to make her feel at home. Her uncertainty made her more attractive and ingénue; her mouth half-parted with apprehension and pleasure, her eyes alive with happiness and affection as though receiving them on her own terms. Happily, Nesta was in a good mood and her first words on entering the farmhouse kitchen gave immense pleasure. "My goodness, Rohama, how you've been busy here. I don't recognise the place."

Rohama stood, as it were, aside from her handiwork and smiled happily. "You think it's improved? I did it all myself."

"Out of recognition." Nesta pointed to the window. "But that's entirely new, isn't it?"

How happy Rohama was to recall her heroic efforts to restore the kitchen; how she had scraped at old paint with a knife, how she had refilled holes in the wall with plaster, how she had covered old boards with hardboard ... At this point the woman helper came in with the baby; Nesta held out her arms and took the child on her knee. In a short time, he was laughing and trying to grab Nesta's necklace. He was a splendid child, with a face that was a minor version of his father's. Mignon and Nesta played with him until the tea was ready while through the big new window behind them the clear, frosty evening sky began to take on the first autumnal shade of gold and the first load of potatoes was stored away in a barn.

At the teatable, Rohama insisted that Nesta should sit next to her so that she could admire her clothes and defer to her opinions at close quarters. Rohama's role was to avoid appearing too ingratiating or pushing, Nesta's to avoid, at all costs, the appearance of patronage. Mignon noticed the calm way her daughter sat in her chair within the heat of the log-fire and seemed to have no feeling for her either way; she was just there.

When the potato-pickers came in from the field, Rohama withdrew a little to help feed them but returned to introduce to her guests a brilliant-eyed young woman who had dropped in. This was Anne Lewis, the girl who sometimes would baby-sit for Rohama, a girl of twenty-two living with her widowed mother in a house across the fields.

Freddy knew her fairly well, Mignon a little, Ashley and Nesta not at all. They all smiled encouragingly at her and she smiled back tentatively and sat down near the baby, who turned to her, as to an old friend.

"It's been a most lovely day," she said politely. "I had to spend most of it in Caerifor with my mother. Otherwise I'd have come over to help."

"We managed very well, dear," Rohama said breathlessly. "We had Patrick and a friend here and we finished the field in two days."

"It's a fine crop, too," Ashley said.

While they were talking, Nesta tried to place the girl. She seemed a surprising sort of person to find in Rohama's kitchen and it was only later, on the way home, that she found out how she came to be in their circle of acquaintances at all. Freddy knew the mother well—what was more, admired her greatly—and described the way she and her daughter moved about together, now in London, now in Caerifor, now in Chester, living on the rents brought in by 'terraces of houses' in Liverpool. It was a strange life which seemed to suit the mother and daughter well enough. Anne had no wish to earn her living, her mother had no wish to force her and, as they were free to move around as they wished, they did so. Their visits to their Caeriforshire home had grown progressively longer and, at one time, had lasted over a year, the time when Anne set herself up as a poultry farmer with hundreds of hens on deep litter. Martin estimated that this venture, which folded up before it ever got under way, had cost the mother about £500. The latest venture was a Jersey cow called Juliet and a sow in farrow called Queenie. Those not in the know grasped enough of the essential facts when Martin came in and asked her about the young litter of Landraces: would she be having the young males cut?

"Oh, must I?" she asked with a nervous glance at the other people around the table.

"Of course," Martin replied. "You can't get rid of them as boars."

Anne looked put out and ran her hand nervously through her hair. "That means I'll have to get the vet?"

Martin made a scornful noise. "Of course you won't. I can do that for you in less than thirty minutes. I'll come over this evening."

"I can't help you," she said hastily, wishing the ground would swallow her up rather than discuss the castration of the pigs in such company. "Can you do it by yourself?"

"Not by myself. I'll get young Patrick here—" the young man and Cappland came in at that moment—"to help me. Just to hold their legs."

"Oh, poor little things!" Anne said.

"Poor little things or not, it's something that's got to be done."

"It seems so awful."

"It's no good being sentimental about your stock or you might as well turn the whole lot into pets."

"How's Juliet?" Rohama asked.

Anne laughed with relief. "She's taken a fancy to cake."

"Cow cake?"

"No, Dundee."

"How did that happen?"

"I was eating a piece of cake the other morning—I know it's wrong, but I like to walk around eating something—and she came up to me and more or less grabbed the piece out of my hand and then followed me around for ever and ever and kept putting her head into my pocket. I went indoors and cut her another slice, which she ate with the greatest of pleasure. You know, you could see her eyes rolling in ecstasy. Honestly, you've got to see her to believe it; she's the craziest cow I've ever seen."

They asked her whether she yielded more milk on a cake diet.

"Not noticeably, but it's got a fruit flavour—like a milk-shake."

"That cow," said Martin, "that cow is the rummest animal I've ever seen. It hangs around the house like a dog. Never seen anything like it. I'm often in my doubles because of its tricks."

"Your mother was telling me," Freddy said, "that it's never been the same since it fell down the well."

Nesta clapped her hands in astonishment.

"They put a piece about it in the paper," Martin said. " 'Ding, Dong Bell, Pussy's in the well', or the cow's in the well, or something."

"How did they get it out?"

Anne said she had never quite understood what happened, but the firemen had pumped water from a nearby brook into the well and the cow had floated to the surface none the worse for wear. "She wasn't very far down and we got her out quite easily. There had been some boards and zinc over an old well and she got through the fence. The roadman saw her disappear with a crack and a splash and then people came from nowhere—women and children I'd never seen before—and gathered round waiting for the fire engine to come."

"Yes," said Martin, "it was just like a pit disaster. A pit disaster. And poor Mrs. Lewis—Anne's mother—was on the verge of tears and Anne was trying to be brave about this blessed Juliet and as soon as she was out Mrs. Lewis drenched her with a bottle of whisky. In my opinion that whisky was the animal's downfall. It's spoiled for ever."

"You mean," said Ashley, "it wants more."

"Of course it does. It got the taste."

Martin had to leave to milk the cows. He completed his arrangement to come over that evening to cut the piglets. Patrick, it was understood, would come with him.

"Won't it upset you?" Anne asked, looking at him for the first time.

He shook his head.

"You're sure you won't faint or something? It's not very nice."

"If he faints," Martin said, "I'll get him round with a bucket of pigswill."

At this point Nesta said, "I don't think you've met my son, Miss Lewis." They shook hands. Cappland also shook hands. He was introduced as "Someone who's staying with us" and by the bleak way Mignon looked at him Anne might have thought him the black sheep of the family just home from prison.

"I thought I recognised you from the car outside ... I've seen you around," Patrick said. "That *is* your Jaguar, isn't it?"

Anne nodded. Patrick looked at her with eyes so bright with appreciation and admiration that they might have been newly made; he hardly knew which he liked the more, the girl or her gleaming car.

11

PATRICK FINDS A HOME

At the end of their visit there was no good reason why Freddy, Mignon and Nesta should not return as often as they pleased and Rohama said as much as she accompanied them to the gate. Mignon agreed, although the visit had been a humiliation.

By an irony of timing, they had called at a period when Mignon was busy creating, even for herself, a favourable image of her husband as the great public servant and the confidant of statesmen; and there, in the person of Rohama, was the evidence of the other side of the man. Everything recalled the injustice which he had brought about in dividing the family lands. It was hardly surprising that the life in motion in Rohama's household, the new arrangements and the new relationships she had brought into being reopened an old sorrow. All these things were something more, too. They were a hint of what it would be like after Mignon's death once this new, purposeful life had covered over the traces of the old family. The dispossession which hurt them in life would be nothing in comparison with the sack of their works which would follow their deaths. Mignon and Freddy were figures slowly subsiding into the night and there was nothing they could do about it. The new life was waiting for them to die so that it might flower.

Even on the paltry, human scale Mignon felt humiliated. She and Freddy had been treated with the half-derisive disrespect shown to village idiots or representatives of a vanishing order, whereas Rohama and her husband belonged. They were more surely a part of the community now than were Mignon and Freddy who, in comparison, held a fringe position bolstered by a fading prestige. Rohama's success diminished them and they were frail enough to resent this.

All this underlying tension Nesta perfectly understood. Ah, her malicious eyes told her mother, you *would* go over and you

got what you deserved. There's no retreat from such a con-
frontation with flags flying or with elegance of carriage. Still,
she offered her mother her arm and they walked home in an
enigmatic silence. They might have been aristocrats, over-
thrown in a revolution, going into exile.

Nesta's self-satisfaction began to get on Mignon's nerves and
gradually the humiliation of the afternoon turned into anger
against her daughter. "She's a bitch," she thought. "Laughing
up her sleeve at everything." She restrained herself all the way
home but once indoors it was less easy to keep quiet. Nesta
could not stop herself goading her mother and she began to
criticise Ashley whom (she said) she found more and more
empty as a personality. It was doubly vexing to plumb the
depths of a man one had always admired, she said; and her
mother agreed with her: "You must take him as he comes.
He's been such a dear to us."

Nesta jabbed again. She said she disliked men who were
always hanging around other women. She thought Ashley
ought to spend more time with his wife. The notion that anyone should be concerned about Muvvy was new to Mignon,
who had always assumed Ashley visited them to get away from
his wife.

The daughter lit a cigarette. "Ashley's a blood brother to
Jack Cappland. They're both men on the prowl—" Mignon
raised a worried, dishevelled head—"and I often wonder what
would've happened had you taken that £250 he offered."

"The question doesn't arise."

"But supposing you *had* taken the money?"

"There was no question of accepting. Friendship is such a
perilous thing. The loan or the gift would have spoiled it."

"On the contrary you'd have fallen further into his grasp."

Mignon's reactions became confused. "I don't think I quite
understand you."

"I mean," and here Nesta drew on her cigarette in the ugly,
mannish way she affected. "I mean, he looks further than the
end of his nose. It seems clear to me he wanted an opening to
get his hands on the property."

"What property?"

"Well, here, of course. Where else?"

"To get his hands on our property? You must be mad.

Never! No one has been more disinterested than Ashley. Quite beyond praise."

"Oh—" an explosion of contempt—"Oh, really, Mother! You're too gullible for words."

"I beg your pardon!"

"You let people take you in. You've got no sense of self-preservation. You've never had it."

"You ask me to develop a sense of self-preservation against Ashley? Oh, Nesta! Ashley's our best friend."

"But you *do*," Nesta retorted, trying to get back to some shaky general principle, "you allow situations to build up around you that become really intolerable—even when you're warned."

"You're most unfair."

"You never react with any energy." Nesta was thinking of Mrs. Benjamin (and Mignon knew this). "If you were more aware of what people around you were doing you wouldn't be taken in so often—as you were in the past."

"Forget the past, dearest. What's this dreadful suggestion you're making against Ashley?" She adopted her best memorialist manner. "I trust Ashley implicitly. I know exactly what made him offer us the money. It was a form of self-importance. He's done well and he wants everyone to know it. At the same time, he wants us to share it. That's a lovable quality, don't you feel? My refusal cut him to the quick. I regret I had to do it ... but there it is ... I can't go back. Freddy would have preferred me to accept and at one point I nearly did. But Ashley did not press the offer. I regretted this at the time. Now I'm sure I'd have regretted accepting more. I don't see how you can misinterpret what he's done."

Nesta crossed her legs. "I still say he's got his eyes on the place."

"He can't have. He knows perfectly well it's tied up."

"You bet he's thought up an answer to that one."

The sneer, the clear accusation of dishonesty brought Mignon to her feet. She clenched her fists and shook them under her daughter's nose. "Dare to say such a thing about Ashley! Dare to suggest such monstrous things! Who are you to talk? What have *you* done for us? Or your bally husband? Since the day you married until this moment he's never once put pen to paper—never even at Christmas time. And you, you soft jelly-belly woman, cloying and spineless wonder, who are you to throw doubts on other people? Who do you think you are to come here like a damned health visitor, walking about in your damned pearl earrings and holding your crocodile hand-bag as though you thought we'd run off with it? 'You bet he's thought up a reply to that one'! You village gossip. What the devil's gone wrong with you? Life doesn't flow through you any more. It's all dead inside you."

Mignon withdrew her fists and her face enough for Nesta to protest: "Please don't shout at me, Mother, or spit in my face."

"You damned bitch of a woman, I'll say what I like to you. And if you say another word against Ashley I'll drive you out of the house with a stick. You and your worthless, patronising son. I'll have you driven out of the country."

"Please, Mother, at your age!"

"At my age, you jeering hen! It's you who ought to act your age. You say these damnable things you can never prove in order to shake my confidence. You said poor young Charles Milford was Edward's creature come here to spy on us; you've said so many things about Jack Cappland that I feel I ought to lock up the cutlery. What more evil can you do? And now you want me and Freddy to be on guard against the only real friend we've had all these years. You're a vile person. A really vile person."

Mignon flopped down on a chair. "You have this terrible effect on me ... your cruel tongue ... your indifference ... your implacable hostility to everything I do and say. I can't breathe in your presence. Go away and leave us alone. Things are twice as bad when you're around."

Nesta tried to apologise for her remark (which, she saw, had exceeded good sense or good taste) but Mignon refused to accept her excuses. "In your heart you aren't sorry. You need to say these wicked, cruel things because you aren't happy in yourself. Saying these poisonous things seems to relieve you. God knows why you don't seem to have any nice thoughts, nice, ordinary, family thoughts. Ever since you've been home you've been poisonous and the truth is, hard though it is to say so, I look forward to your going away. You're nothing to me any more and you can go away when you like."

Nesta's eyes reflected her distress at her mother's words. "You don't mean that."

"I regret to say so, dearest, but I do. We've nothing more in common and that's flat!"

"You really want me to go away?"

"It's not for me to say when. This is your home, after all. On the other hand, it would be best for both of us if you fixed a date for your return so that *I* for one know I've only got to put up with you for so long. I'm sorry, dearest, but that's how I feel."

Nesta smoked her cigarette ruefully.

"And Patrick," Mignon resumed. "I try to be fair to him. He's a fine-looking young man, well set up and self-assured, but he's got the equipment for life of a child of twelve. It's going to be hard for him later on. You do nothing to help him at all and I can't. What you and his father are thinking about I'll never know—but that's your problem. All I want to know is when you're going away. It strikes me that if you were to go away tomorrow we needn't ever bother to write to one another again. You can forget about us and I'll get the solicitor to tell you when we're dead."

"How can you ask me to do that? You know I can't do that. You don't seem to realise that I love you."

"Well, you show it in a funny way, dearest. You make me as miserable as hell—and then say it's because you love me."

"I get angry for you. You let other people take you in."

"Rot. I'm never taken in. I may seem to be but only because it suits my purpose. I'm never duped, believe me. And it's no good wiping your eye because that won't cure anything. I'm sorry if you're hurt but the truth is this has been boiling up inside me for weeks. And you've been damned subversive over your father's papers. Please let me do what I think is best. That's all I ask."

"I try to save you from yourself—and your own stupid behaviour."

"The truth is: Freddy and I get on your nerves, don't we? You feel we've let the place go to pot. You think we're full of manias. You'd really like to have us put away in a home, wouldn't you?"

Nesta stirred uncomfortably. "I never said such a thing."

"Ah, not to me. But you said as much to Effie Johns the last time you were in town, didn't you?"

"Not in that way..."

"In what way?"

"I said—I admit I said—'Mother and Uncle Freddy might be better if they gave up the house and went to live in an old people's home where they could be looked after properly.'"

"Thank you, dearest, but both Freddy and I are capable of looking after ourselves and would hate nothing more than going to an old people's home—just because you think Freddy and I would be 'looked after' and get our heads washed more often—as though we can't still look after ourselves."

"It was an idea," Nesta said feebly.

"Well, please don't bother with it. I don't want to sit around in an old people's home like well-fed battery hens or loaves on a conveyor belt—and with only one destination ... everything stuffed in a tiny locker. I visited one. And do you know what shocked me most? Just before I left a nurse came round to collect people's teeth. Even before the people left. I hoped to God the teeth weren't communal, too, like the knickers and the nightclothes. It gave me heartache for weeks, I assure you."

Nesta was flattened and Mignon knew it. With a suggestion of good humour, Mignon left for the kitchen to make supper and as she worked among her disorder she hummed tunelessly.

Looked at with a painter's eye the kitchen was that of an old person and had the confusion and unexpected zones of order which reflected its owner. There were piles of carefully folded paper bags, little screws of string stored in jugs and bowls, left-over items saved on saucers and plates indiscriminately—and every item in the hoard had its purpose; nothing could be thrown away or burned. Everything had to be held in readiness for some alarming situation which would call for acres of brown paper, hundreds of neatly-folded grocery bags and scores of small hanks of string.

The old corgi Ianto accompanied Mignon into the kitchen and flopped down before the stove. She rubbed her foot on his belly and as she smiled at the old dog there was, in her face and spirit, the same wonderful absence of rancour that she had known in the far-away dream when Edward Lloyd-Ballantyne had visited her and asked for forgiveness. She had told Nesta, absent for years, the truth about their present relationship and once this had been purged it was not impossible that something new and good could grow, because Mignon was without resentment once it had been adequately expressed.

When Nesta came disconsolately into the kitchen to see if she could help, Mignon, all passion spent, was mellow and amiable.

"You know," Nesta said, "I think you overstepped the mark. You completely misunderstood me."

"I understood you very well, dearest. And what you don't say I know from your face. You're transparent. In your heart, you think of Freddy and me as people who've reached some position outside the human race and quite clearly ought to be put away."

"Rubbish!" Nesta said firmly.

"You say so but I understand you better than you do yourself. Don't you see, dearest, that when you accuse Ashley of being a carpetbagger you not only undermine the basis of our old friendship but you imply that there's nothing to love in us because we're old and the only things worth bothering about are our material possessions. You plainly infer it's impossible to love us, because we're old."

"That's not true."

"Well, it's what *I* take to be the logic of your attitude. And you may be right, dearest, but you can't expect Freddy and me to act on your assumptions. If we did we'd have to live behind permanently locked doors."

"You misunderstood me entirely."

"No, dearest, I don't think so." Mignon adopted the tone of a mother speaking to a wilful adolescent. "What you said suggests that there isn't a single disinterested emotion left. So you leave Freddy and me nothing but our infirmities and our poor old chattels. You've taken away all human value from us. That's what I meant when I said you made us feel we'd wandered outside the human race."

Nesta sullenly began laying the table while Mignon recalled how, as a young woman, the daughter of a famous father, she had suffered because she was plain and imagined that people were only interested in her because of her family connections.

Then, with marriage and increasing self-confidence, she had outgrown this phase and had known what it was like to be loved and admired for herself. "Now, in extreme old age, I've come full circle apparently and am being courted and cosseted not for my distinguished father but for these dowdy old rooms and the few acres left to us. Luckily I'm old enough to know you're talking rubbish. So no more of your warnings! They hurt me more than the people I'm supposed to be protected from."

There was an unholy frizzling as Mignon dropped some potatoes into the chip-pan. "The shocking thing about you, dearest, is that you're obsessed by the past. Twice as much as I am. You can't escape it. Yes, dearest, you may well open your eyes. I've been amazed to see how the past lives on in you. You go away for years, you travel thousands of miles, and as soon as you come back here all the bitterness of the past comes over you again. You sit about here filing your nails, turning all these old things over in your mind. It's mad. And then you criticise and when we ask you what you would do or would have done you can't say anything. And when you try to help Freddy and me it's like having help from a charity commissioner. We're grateful to you for taking over the household bills while you're here; we wished you didn't feel obliged to. I never feel you do anything spontaneously or from the heart. It's all served up with reproaches or done in order to shame us or make us feel inadequate—"

"Oh, Mother!"

"Yes, you don't help at all. When I see you here in the kitchen trying to help me I want to cry out: 'For God's sake, leave me alone. Leave me in my muddle.' You've got your own problems. As for ourselves we'll soldier on here as long as we can and afterwards if Rohama and Martin want the place it's theirs."

Only the perfect good humour of Mignon's tone prevented another pitched battle. Mignon appeared to be busy frizzling chips but she was enjoying the discomfort of her daughter. She had become mistress of her own house again.

* * * *

While Mignon and Nesta squared their accounts Patrick and

Cappland accompanied Martin to the Lewis house. Just as they left, Rohama placed two buckets of boiled potatoes on the back of the Landrover as a gift for Anne's sow, hardly the most romantic of presents to be carrying to a young woman's house on a brilliantly moonlit evening with dogs barking their heads off at the large beechen-coloured moon and not a breath of wind stirring in the hedges.

Pain and suffering fascinated Cappland and he looked forward to the coming castration. This was at the back of everyone's mind because Martin mentioned an uncle of his who had had a leg amputated at the thigh without ether. Cappland asked how they cut the thighbone.

Martin was splendidly casual, driving the Landrover into the main road: "They sawed through it with a little meat saw. They said the noise was enough to turn you over."

"And the pain?"

"They dosed my old uncle with whisky, put cottonwool in his ears so that he couldn't hear the noise and gave him a piece of old rubber to bite on."

"For Christ's sake," said Cappland, "don't you have modern surgery in this part of the world?"

"Sure enough but my old uncle was afraid that once he went into the sleep he'd never wake up."

And what happened to him, they asked.

"Lived to be eighty-seven and was the most cantankerous and opinionated old man you'd ever meet. Very witty in his way. Get him to tell you a story—some little incident, something he'd seen, and he'd have you in your doubles."

"My flesh curls with horror," Cappland said.

"You've got a soft stomach," Martin said with the affability of the completely insensitive. He was vaguely amused by Jack Cappland (whom he thought of as a bladder of lard) and promised he'd teach him to be an expert knacker.

"No bloody fear," said Cappland.

"Somebody's got to do the dirty jobs," was Martin's reasonable enough reply. "When I was at school and learned all about Ancient Britons I used to wonder how I'd have got on hunting with sticks and stones and stripping the skins with those little flints they used." He sniffed. "I think I'd have managed."

When they reached the Lewises they were received by the mother and daughter, who had made themselves presentable. "Come in," they both cried, delighted to be having visitors. Their smiles were those of women who had just left their looking-glasses. They were also almost identical in appearance so that, at a first glance, they might have been sisters: the same shaped faces, the same shaped teeth, the same full breasts and the same uncomplicated manner.

They had prepared drinks and sandwiches but Martin said he must press on with the task. "We won't say no afterwards," he cried taking up the storm lantern and leading the other two down to the sty. Anne watched them swing away and would have accompanied them but her mother said it was hardly ladylike to be present on such an occasion.

As soon as he heard the pigs squealing, Cappland lost interest and remained outside the sty, leaving Patrick to hold the little legs while Martin expertly performed the operations with the matter-of-factness of a man pipping an orange.

"That's what's so horrid about having animals," Mrs. Lewis said when they returned. "One always seems to be depriving them of their natural lives for some reason or another."

"Well you only rear them to kill 'em and eat 'em," Martin retorted briskly, washing his hands. "People with soft hearts shouldn't go in for the business. That's the long and short of it."

"We're incorrigible amateurs," Mrs. Lewis said happily and led them into the sitting-room.

"I don't know how it is," she said to Patrick (handing him a whisky) "but I hardly ever see your Grandmother although we're so near. I see your great-uncle Freddy often enough. We think he's a dear person and more than gifted with his pen."

Patrick was sure Freddy would like to hear that.

"He knows my feelings, Patrick. I've told him often. I can always recognise his style in the local papers. I know at once whether Mr. Roberts has written an article before I reach the initials."

She smiled at him radiantly. "Mr. Roberts understands the life of the villages, the people, so well. He gets the flavour of their lives. Don't you agree, Martin?"

"No one can say otherwise. He ought to have gone further."

Martin's respect was genuine enough although his tone reduced Freddy to a brilliant scholarship boy who had taken to drink.

For Mrs. Lewis, Freddy embodied his world. When he ceased writing there would be no one to take his place. "Yes, I wish him well. He has all the unfashionable qualities I admire."

"I wish someone would speak of my work like that," said Cappland.

Mrs. Lewis looked at him speculatively. "Perhaps they will one day."

"Not much chance I'm afraid."

"Why?"

"Well, I ask you, what is there to embody in London?"

A little later, Mrs. Lewis sat next to Patrick and again raised the question of Freddy's writings. Had he read the essay he had written that week? It was a little piece called *Cymylau* (Clouds) "one of those subtle things that catch everything there is to say about certain subjects."

The conversation ought to have ended there—since Patrick could never read Freddy's essays—but the young man wanted to impress his hostess (partly because she was Anne's mother and partly because he liked her) and asked to hear more.

"Oh dear. Now you've caught me." Mrs. Lewis set down her drink and put her elegant, beringed hands together. She thought a moment. "Well, he begins by describing the clouds passing over in autumn, passing over the empty fields. He thinks of all the autumns he has known and the fatalistic way we watch for the first signs of winter and, as we get older, the thought comes to us that this might well be our last autumn and that, maybe, before the next one, we will have moved on like the clouds. That's all it is, but it's full of the sort of phrases only Mr. Roberts can make. Full of the observations only he knows how to put down. It's the summing up of a lifetime's thinking and feeling as a human being and a countryman. It's about being old and close to death."

Patrick had no idea what to say so twirled his glass awkwardly. Mrs. Lewis, carried away by recollected emotion, hardly noticed. "It's a long time," she said, "since anything has so moved me. He's the last of the old kind of writer; the last of the old kind. He's got the deep, inborn feeling for the old life, the old ways, and people trust him because he always sees the best in people, never the worst. It's a great pity you can't really appreciate his work."

The glass continued to twirl and Patrick began to look longingly towards Anne laughing and talking with Martin and Cappland.

Mrs. Lewis realised she had lost his interest so said briskly, "What will you do eventually?" At this Patrick launched out into an account, rather less self-deprecating than usual, of his plans. He made the rash statement that he had "hundreds of irons in the fire" and they might all grow hot at once. He was also "seriously wondering whether I ought to try my hand at farming".

Mrs. Lewis liked the youthful assurance in his voice and the sense that it might be a good thing for the farming community if he decided to become a member. "What a splendid idea," she said, although there was a hint in her voice that she might have said the same thing had he said he was going to be a witch doctor.

At this point Patrick did not care. Mrs. Lewis's voice was musical and feminine and, after the sharp denunciations of his mother and grandmother, the very sound of approval, the voice of the woman encouraging the man, not the flat voices that destroyed and undermined. He was renewed by this simple note of conviction and although he had never seriously thought of taking up farming until that moment the idea took shape in his head and Mrs. Lewis, hardly knowing how great a fire she was creating from so small a flame, asked him whether he wanted to farm locally.

Thereupon he grew cautious. He said he didn't know.

"At all events, Patrick, you like living in the country."

He had been hating it, yet he found himself saying with a cockiness unusual even for himself, "I love it. I'm no city slicker."

She laughed as though she had never heard the phrase before—all part of her capacity to build him up as a man and a human being—and her eyes sparkled with the sort of appreciation which goes to a man's self-esteem like wine. She knew the effect she was having and was even slightly amazed that she was managing it so effortlessly, sitting back in her elegant

Victorian arm-chair twirling her sherry glass while a big, marmalade cat slept on her lap. Some good came of their talk and afterwards Patrick was to say that this ten-minute conversation did more for his future life than all the barracking of his mother and grandmother together. He would have done almost anything Mrs. Lewis suggested. Her eyes told him, "You are young enough to be my son, but you are a man and you'll be an even better one by and by".

When Patrick asked her if she preferred the town to the country she said she was happy anywhere so long as she had a telephone. Her favourite diversion could be carried on anywhere: it was making money.

"You know, Patrick, it's not intelligent to be poor nowadays. You've got to wake up to the fact that money just *does* grow on trees. Every morning I wake up with a sense of excitement and wonder how the markets are going to do. Every evening I listen to the closing prices and I play by ear accordingly."

Patrick was dumb with admiration; this was the sort of diversion he could understand and appreciate. He asked her with bated breath whether it was dangerous "playing the markets".

Mrs. Lewis fondled her cat before replying. "I don't really play them in a big way but I keep an eye on things and see what's happening in the world. It's all a question of trends. If women took to wearing black feathers in their hair you'd invest in rookeries, you understand? It's as simple as that!"

Patrick tried to show by his smile that he realised this was a simplification.

"No, seriously. I have what my husband used to call my Fundamentals: things which have been paying well for years and will continue to do so so far as one can foresee. Then I have my experimental cash and my flutter cash. People get absolutely furious with me because they say I'm so lucky. It's not luck at all. It's having a nose for the wind. I *do* draw the line. I decided South Africa was paying out dividends in terms of blood so I sold my Limpopo Consolidated years ago. So far as I'm concerned there's something tainted about most money coming out of Africa. It *is* a moral issue, as *The Times* said."

Such a remark from Mignon would have made Patrick redden and gulp with anger; he took the remark from Mrs.

Lewis like the proverbial lamb even though he did not agree. All he said, quite mildly, was, "In Rhodesia and in South Africa the Africans get exceptionally good money."

"I daresay, Patrick, but they should really be having much more. Co-operate as equals is my policy and it gets results. One day I'll take you to Liverpool to show you my home-from-home for business girls. Two big houses converted into self-contained flatlets. I'm very proud of that. They all choose their own decorations and in four years only one girl has left for a reason other than marriage."

Patrick was open-mouthed with admiration; his head was whirling with notions of the Lewis income. Why, he almost gasped to himself, it couldn't be less than about £200 a month! Maybe even three hundred—or, more!

Anne took Patrick's empty glass and gave him another whisky. "I hope Mummy isn't boasting about her investments; she's like a child with a chemistry set."

Mrs. Lewis twinkled at both of them. "Patrick and I are getting on very well. We understand one another perfectly, don't we, Patrick?"

At this point Martin winked again at Cappland. They were both amused to see how Patrick had fallen for the mother and the daughter and how coolly the two women had landed him.

In fact, they had both had the same instinct about Patrick summed up by Mrs. Lewis's remark after the men had gone away. "He's the sort of type I thought had gone out of fashion years ago: the young colonial boy with a lot of bluff but an excellent heart. He thinks he knows a lot which he doesn't; but he can be made into something with careful handling."

Mrs. Lewis had decided to cultivate the young man and as he went away she told him to come back whenever he wanted to. Although Mrs. Lewis did not carry Cappland in her heart, as the French say, she also included him in the invitation.

"I shan't be here very much longer," he replied. "If I do stay I'll be happy to come over."

Cappland gushing socially was a strange sight but both he and Martin were united in praising the Lewis whisky. "That label's the best," Cappland said knowledgeably. "There's nothing to touch it and I'm speaking as a Scotsman." He punched

Patrick's arm. "I'd go over there as often as I could if I were you. You've made a hit all right."

"He'll be going, don't you worry," Martin replied. "He and Anne are very taken with one another."

"Anne thinks you're fucking marvellous."

Patrick attempted to remain unconcerned. "Oh? Does she?"

"Don't be so bloody public school," Cappland retorted. "She had her eyes on you all the time you were talking to her mother. She's out to get you. And you could do worse."

"Hear, hear," said Martin.

"Good taste, plenty of money, lots of goodwill. It's all handed to you on a plate."

Martin agreed that they had a good life and could "fettle themselves like prize poultry."

Cappland had decided that the women were so attractive because they had money, good taste, no affectations and couldn't seriously imagine that there were people in the world who had not organised their lives to their own satisfaction, or who were prevented from leading the life they preferred because of shortage of money or opportunities. Their own happiness overflowed into their relations with other people and it was this goodwill which had so charmed Patrick. The women were happy and without envy; they were eager to create an atmosphere of confidence and appreciation and at that moment he could not have said which of the two women he liked the more, the mother with her elegant hands and her subtle appraisal of him as a man or the daughter with her feeling eyes and her expensive Italian cardigan in fuchsia and white. He had not felt so well or happy for weeks.

* * * *

Rohama was waiting for their return. "And how was Anne?"

"She thanks you for the potatoes," Patrick said.

"And thanks you for introducing her to Patrick," Cappland added.

"Oh?"

Cappland rubbed his hands. "She was looking superb in an eight-guinea cardigan and she and her mother gave us some of the best whisky I've had for months and," he insisted, "I'm speaking as a Scotsman. And when we were all merry and bright it was quite clear that Patrick can't take his eyes off her and she's in the same position."

"Rubbish," Patrick said.

"Anne's my best friend," Rohama said loyally. "She'd do anything for me."

"She's a really sweet girl," Martin said slowly as he began removing his boots. They waited for him to finish what he had to say but he began examining the soles mournfully.

"Finish what you're saying," his wife urged.

"There's only one thing: marry the girl and you marry the mother. I can't see them ever separating. Can you?" He turned to his wife.

Rohama agreed that the mother and daughter were close but was sure that an attractive woman such as Mrs. Lewis would be able to marry again "once she'd got Anne off her hands".

"Why not before?"

Rohama admitted that there was no reason why not. "If I look as young as Mrs. Lewis does when I'm her age I'll be happy."

Martin had padded across to a cupboard and brought out a bottle of whisky. "We'll have one more before you get along home. I want an opinion from a Scotsman about this bottle I won in a raffle. It ought to taste good; it was free."

Rohama, like the good, devoted wife she was, set out four tumblers and produced water. Cappland sniffed carefully before taking a sip, before pronouncing the whisky first class. Martin looked gratified. "Wales is a good country," he said, "but we don't produce a spirit to touch *that*."

"Can you imagine Welsh whisky?" Cappland asked. "I can't."

"We've got lots of potatoes," Martin replied. "What we lack is up here." He touched his head two or three times. "In the old days people were afraid of being comfortable and happy. Well, I'm not like that." And with a gulp he finished off the glass. To Cappland's regret he recorked the bottle—which was half-full—and put it back in the cupboard. "Ah well," he said and it was quite clear he wanted to go to bed and expected them to want the same thing, too.

Walking home, Cappland decided there were times he could

not believe the people he met really existed. "It's uncanny. There we are in London caught up as though drugged, our minds all in pieces, and here things are just great—just like it used to be with time to talk, time to get to know people properly. It's just great. Like everybody's childhood. If I had an income of £2,000 a year I'd leave all that fucking southern English nightmare behind and strike out somewhere with a gun and a good dog. Take up fishing. Do things. What the hell, it's the sort of life that's still possible if you look for it. People relaxed. Not bothered about things. No teenager values to pander to. Just fucking great. People are getting full value for money, too. Look at Rohama and her husband. Couldn't you feel the sex in the air? He wanted us out of the way. I knew how he felt with three or four whiskies in him and a gorgeous woman wanting and waiting for it. Think of it. He must be just undoing her bra and lifting up two lovely big tits for closer inspection. You bet he's in his pants already."

"You're a nutcase!"

Patrick's shock disgusted Cappland. "Don't you ever want a girl? You must do. It's maddening. There must be talent here but we don't know where to lay our hands on it. There's talent everywhere these days; it's the great discovery of the twentieth century."

"What is?"

"Why, cunt, of course. People can see it for themselves everywhere waiting and warm—and mostly for free. In London, all those beefy girls at the bus stops standing four-square with 'Fuck me!' written across their arses. It's enough to make you go off your top. And people are getting it, too, as they've never had it before. Look at Rohama. The way she walks you can tell she gets enough for three."

"They're a perfectly ordinary couple. You make them sound like sex maniacs."

"We're all sex maniacs. Don't you know that? I am. I've no shame about it. I like it whenever I can get it. If I thought that I could get hold of Rohama this evening I wouldn't hesitate— not even if her husband was snoring in the next room."

"You're just talking for the sake of talking."

"If you can't do it, describe it." Cappland was indifferent and changed the subject: would it be a good thing if he offered to pay something towards his keep. "I'm fartarsing around here. Can't make up my mind whether there's anything in this diaries business or not. I don't think so. I've got to think in terms of a couple of million readers. Who's interested?"

"Then why stay on?"

"The place gets me. I like it. It's so different from anything I've known before."

Patrick could not see his grandmother accepting money but saw no reason why Cappland should not ask her.

"I will," he replied. "The real story may be elsewhere."

"Such as?"

"It could be Rohama's. The great man's illegitimate daughter tells all."

"She doesn't know anything worth telling."

"You get an instinct in these matters. I know there's some way this story can be approached." He remembered what he had said to Ashley Corbett. "I won't really get the edge about this diaries business until I know a bit about the family." He had been right.

The house was in darkness when they returned but no one was asleep as a result of the scenes earlier in the day. Nesta got out of bed to ask her son where he had been so late. "You seem to get on well with Cappland," she said grudgingly.

"He's not all there. He says such extraordinary things. At first I thought he was trying to be funny in a stupid sort of way and then I thought he's just a clown. You can't make contact with him. He's got a wall of invisible glass around him. He sees nothing except as he wants to see it. I think," he said, with the moral righteousness of the young, "that's he's an unscrupulous and immoral man."

"Yet when I warned Mother about him she threw the dictionary at me."

"You been quarrelling again?"

"The worst so far. Tell me, shall we go away?"

"Oh no. I don't want to go."

"I thought you were bored."

"Yes, when it rained it was boring. But I like it here now. I think I'd like to stay somewhere here and take up farming."

"You mean you'd like to stay here with Mother and Freddy?"

He rose on one elbow. "Not necessarily. But I wouldn't mind for the time being. I don't want to go. And don't go away yet. We said we'd be here until after Christmas."

"You've got to do something," she said aggressively. "You've got to work at something. Your father's been awfully patient but in a couple more weeks he'll want to know what we've been up to. It's no good being vague about these things."

"I'm not against work. I'd like something to do."

Despite this she had to unwind her thoughts about not being a dilettante and about not taking things for granted and she played the heavy mother with an abstracted air as though she were listening to herself. She appeared to approve of what she was saying for she repeated certain phrases wearily and with an actress's delicious sense of timing.

Patrick, inflated by Mrs. Lewis, resented this.

"You're picking on me because you've been arguing with your mother again about Arthur's papers. Why don't you agree? Don't drag me into your squabbles. Think of yourself. I'm going to be all right."

Nesta made some feeble protest to which he did not pretend to listen. At one splendid leap Patrick had moved out beyond them all into the safe, hospitable arms of the Lewises. Intuitively, he had decided to let his mother and her mother quarrel between themselves while he cultivated the women who lived over the hill.

12

STRATAGEMS

As he walked towards Rohama's house the next morning (and knowing that Martin had gone over to Port Rydal "to talk business" with his brother) Cappland was sure that he was attracted by Rohama because she was a creature after his own style with the special nervous system of an inhabitant of two worlds. "We're the odd men out," he thought.

Rohama was standing near her kitchen window rolling out pastry for a tart as Cappland arrived in the yard and all trustingly, like the bewitched princess in the fairy story, she opened the door to him.

In her first few remarks Rohama gave him the chance he was looking for to discuss the other part of the family; she asked about Patrick and was told meaningfully that he had arranged to visit the Lewises. Cappland paused a moment. "Can't say I blame him for preferring Anne and her mother to his own lot of women."

Rohama tried to brush away a drift of white flour on her cheek. "Why do you say that?"

"Because they're so dreary. Muttering among themselves and only poor old Freddy keeping them in check."

Rohama considered his words a moment but said nothing. She made no comment either when he said, "I'll be going off shortly. There's nothing in all that rubbish about the diaries for me. I'll have to tell the old girl. She's bound to be disappointed. Do you mind if I smoke?"

For answer she threw him a box of matches.

"Have *you* ever read those diaries?" he asked.

She shook her head. She had not, she explained, even known of their existence until a short time before. He breathed heavily down his nose. "They should have been burned years ago."

"I thought they were valuable."

"That's what they like to make you believe." He breathed heavily again. "All this rubbish is kept because it might be useful for historians. That's the excuse for keeping every silly piece of paper that falls into your hands." He looked at the end of his cigarette pensively. "I'll have to go, of course. I asked Lady Benson-Williams whether I could stay on a few more days—offered to contribute something for my keep—and she didn't seem unwilling; but her ladyship's daughter keeps giving me dirty looks and tells me as plainly as she can that it's time I went."

"You mean she doesn't like you?"

"I don't like her, either. She's a beautiful dried up old bag, if you'll excuse my language. She'd torture her grandmother for kicks."

Rohama, holding her astonishment in check, asked him why he should say that.

"Because I keep my eyes open and I can see her there day after day niggling her mother, prodding at her directly or through Freddy. Sighing. Throwing up her eyes. Complaining about the food. The egg's not cooked as she'd like it. The bread's stale. The old girl isn't exactly my favourite historical character but I'd walk round the world with her rather than walk a mile with her daughter."

He flicked some ash towards the stove and Rohama handed him an ashtray. "You've got all that nervousness that goes with smokers. Why don't you give it up?"

"It's better than picking my nose, isn't it?"

"Is that the choice?"

Her retort's briskness amused him. "You're quick," he said. "Dead quick. You're wasted here. Do you ever want to travel?"

Rohama rarely thought of such things. She liked her new life although she'd like to be able to go away if she wanted to. As she and her husband were running the farm without help it was impossible for them both to go out. "We're stuck here, more or less. Perhaps one day we'll be able to get on a better footing. At present it's a fourteen-hour day seven days a week."

"You'd be bored anywhere else," Cappland said enjoying the view of the back of her legs as she stooped to open the oven.

"I never said I wanted to leave. What I'd like is a little help

223

now and again. If we didn't have Anne Lewis or a woman from nearby to sit here in the evenings we couldn't even go to the cinema."

"It would do them good over there to have your work to do. That's what they all need."

"They're too old now."

"Do you have much to do with them?"

"Oh, yes, I see them regularly."

He looked at her eye to eye. "Why do you bother with them?"

"The old people have come to depend on me. Less, of course, now that Nesta's home."

He shook his head and flicked some more ash. "You know, if you were my wife I'd forbid you to go there. You'd make me really furious. You live here waiting for them to smile at you and let you into their potty little world and what is there once you've got in? Pretension and more pretension. That's all. None of them can face up to the truth. There's Lady Benson-Williams trying to flog their old papers and trying to believe herself when she's inventing a lot of rubbish about Sir Arthur and our Family—" he tried to imitate Mignon's voice—"and there's poor old Freddy who lives in some dream world of his own and imagines that I can get some publisher interested in his works; and then there's the daughter trying to cover up. 'Don't think they're doing this for the money,' she told me. The whole lot of them don't amount to a penny ha'penny and yet you seem to live in awe of them. I tell you they're typical nobodies with a great sense of their own importance. But they really are nobodies."

"That's not really true, Jack. And they don't throw their weight around. Lady Benson-Williams hardly goes out."

"Oh, but she's so full of fine phrases and a sort of old-fashioned Roedean grandeur. Her voice always breaking on a rising wave of excitement rather like old Edwardian recordings you can hear on the radio. She'd like to give the impression she's a great intellectual, so above-it-all, but she'd do anything for money. Anything. And that applies to them all despite all their talk about 'integrity'. Integrity! It means cheating in a ladylike way."

Rohama did not agree and, in any case, did not understand

224

why it was a fault to want money since he himself made no bones of his liking for it.

"I don't pretend. I'm bought," Cappland said, tapping himself on the chest. "I'm in the game for the spoils whatever they are and everybody knows it. If people don't recognise themselves in me then they can avoid me."

"You say you don't pretend but you do—in other ways."

"How?"

"Well, in your own way you like to create an impression that you're somebody."

His bluster ended immediately and he wanted to know how he gave such an impression.

"The way you dress. The way you hold yourself. Even the way you smoke a cigarette. The way you talk and stand. Everything. You're a natural dandy. Like a little bantam cock."

Cappland hated references to his height and was mortified. "I don't think I'd like the person you say you see."

Rohama laughed; it was the nearest she could come to tenderness for the man at the moment. "Even I can see through you, Jack. You like playing a role like a child. You like to give the impression you can have all the women after you, that you get invited to all the right places, even if you hate them or despite the people, and you like to think you know everything about food and drink and clothes—even women's clothes—because, I suppose, you've lived with a lot of women and seen them at close quarters. It's you. That's all that can be said. Lots of the things you say about Micky and Freddy could be said about you but I don't need to. It's not important enough; you're a dandy and that's all there is to it."

"I like good things. I suppose it's because we never had them when we were young."

"Then why be ashamed of showing that you like them or of showing that you still can't believe that you've got all these things?"

He was appalled. "Do I show it?"

"Of course you do. Why worry? You haven't got that real polish that comes from years of easy living. You've got to sell yourself too much. Well, that's what I think. And you think that Micky and Freddy are patronising you and this isn't true because they're not snobs in that silly, obvious way. You can make fun of Micky if you like but you can't get away from it that for years she was at the centre of things. She knew what was going on; she met people of all ranks and she learned to appreciate the genuine from the false. She's not taken in by you when you talk of the marvellous meals you've eaten. She was probably laughing at you to herself."

Cappland still could not understand why a proper pride in his appearance and a love of good living should seem vulgar in him.

"Because you make such a thing about it," Rohama said and not without kindness.

"I hate dirty, unpressed clothes. I like good food. (He pronounced the word 'fud'.) Am I never supposed to appreciate them because I wasn't born to them?"

Rohama smiled patiently. "Not at all. But because you speak of these things so much we know you didn't always have them."

The telephone rang and she went away for a short time. When she returned he was wandering around the kitchen chewing a piece of apple he had picked up from the table.

"You know, Jack, I'd like you to see the wife of a farmer about three miles from here. She's a Cambridge woman and she wears a filthy old duffel coat all the year round and a filthy pair of wellington boots and a big diamond ring on her hand all among the filth. Yet there's something about her, the diamond, the way she talks and her Harrods' hat, which tells you she's from a good family."

"For an intelligent woman you're bloody reactionary, you know. You'll be saying next that the Tories should always be in office because they have the right accents."

"Well, perhaps I do."

He looked her up and down professionally. "I meant to ask you: why do you wear your hair like that? Why don't you try it a new way? Your style make you look older than you are."

"It's easy like this. It takes no time first thing in the morning."

"Surely there are other ways just as simple. After all, you aren't thirty yet. You could look twenty-two."

"Flatterer!"

"But indeed you could. Get a new style. You'd be surprised how much difference it would make."

By and by she asked him whether he liked the way Nesta did her hair.

"Sure. She's got taste. Her hair isn't half as good as yours, all the same."

Rohama did not disagree. "She's got breeding. Everything she has is good."

"You've got a real thing about her, haven't you?"

"Well, she's my half-sister, isn't she? I used to hope we'd become very close one day. I don't think we will but it doesn't stop me admiring her. She's one of those women who doesn't have to try. Whatever she does is right. I mean in dress and appearance."

Cappland began breathing heavily again. "You *are* smitten. Pity it's not true. Trouble is she looks grumpy half the time."

"I suppose she's unhappy."

"What about?"

Rohama thought a while. She had her own theories. She supposed she was depressed by the way her mother had grown old, the way the farm had fallen into neglect and by the renewed acquaintance with Ashley Corbett, the man she was supposed to have married. Predictably, Cappland dismissed this as romantic tosh.

"That's the reason why Ashley Corbett is so devoted to the old people. He's still in love with Nesta, really."

Cappland began to mimic Rohama. "Ashley," he said mockingly, "Ashley. What a name for a local estate agent. Ashley. Ashley Corbett. What a *Gone with the Wind* woman's noveletish name. How can anyone take a person with such a name seriously!"

"Don't be so silly," she replied.

"I'm sure he's been cut out of cardboard, for some Do-it-yourself-write-your-own-novel kit. Imagine him like an ex-John Buchan character. With his understatements and his dullness. His carefully understated clichés. 'We did pretty well in the war, old chap. The war against the unspeakable Huns was certainly no picnic with some ugly bits of scrapping here and there and Brother Boche sending over all he could. It orften struck me as the Howitzers were smoking us out: Not

227

much fun to die among these continental types. A rotten sort of ending.'"

Carried away by his own imitation Cappland swaggered as he imagined an officer might carrying a stick. Rohama laughed against her nature. "He's not a bit like that. Anyway, I think Ashley's a very aristocratic name."

"You would. Honestly. I really marvel at the extent of your devotion to these nobodies."

"They're not nobodies to me. What's more, I prefer Ashley as a name to Jack."

"Fair enough." He sat down again wondering whether he had ever heard before of an illegitimate child in love with its half-family. "I wonder if I could have a drink of water."

She pointed out the glasses. As he leaned across to take the water from the tap he lost his balance and put his arm around her waist to steady himself. "That's a comfortable place," he said and she giggled. Despite herself she giggled and he thought to himself, "Had she not giggled she'd have given me the brush-off. But she giggled and that's the next step."

Continuing what he took to be their cosy, intimate conversation, Cappland asked whether she had any relations on her mother's side. Rohama shook her head; her mother's family were even less interested in her than her father's. "They thought my mother was a scandalous woman."

"How do you judge your mother?"

"I'm sorry for her. What could she have hoped to get out of her friendship with such a man?" Rohama said that when she and her mother were living alone together they had discussed their position openly. These discussions had made Rohama feel grown-up and important and they had bred the nostalgia for her half-family which Cappland found so remarkable.

"Yet they're nobodies," he said. "Nobodies. They haven't half your warmth or your courage."

Rohama said simply: "They're different. Aunty Micky's not without courage. Believe me. I'm full of admiration for the way she's behaved all these years. And I'm the only one who really cares about her. The others are only interested in their own lives."

He had been looking for signs of revolt or resentment but

there were none. He was trying to lead up to the point where he could make some sort of hint—even an offer—about the story she might write about her father; the bastard's history of the distinguished political family. He was about to mention the subject, then thought better and asked her what sort of relationship had existed between her and her father.

His interest in her life had long since passed the bounds of normal curiosity but as she could not quite understand what it would lead towards she did not, at that point, object. After all, this is the twentieth century; people ask one another brutal questions without apparently ulterior motive. And, then, when all was said and done, how well had she known her father? Brought up to regard him as both a kind of Prince Charming and Monster (depending on her mother's moods) Rohama had never learned to focus him properly. What was much more important to Rohama, in looking back at her childhood, was to recall the child's dreams.

"I used to imagine that one day I'd be very close to the family. I had a dream I was always going through in which my mother died and they came to fetch me in a big car and adopted me and we went away to live in a castle. After my father died and I came here I realised that the sweet feelings were all on my side and they seemed to think that my upbringing, my marriage and everything had made me unfit to mix with them. Despite that I still like them. Something of my old feeling still remains. I'd do anything for them."

Anybody else but Cappland would have rejoiced at this triumph of good nature over experience; Cappland was furious with her for this was hardly the sharp, acid story he would have been able to sell. She saw he was not listening and thought it was because he disbelieved her. "Oh, I believe you all right. I'm trying to make out what makes you tick."

"You think it's stupid for me to like them? I can't help it. It's the truth."

"Doesn't all this ever make you bitter?" he asked.

"I shall bear everything I'm supposed to," she replied. "There's no point in being bitter. The worst is over. I'm safe now and Martin and I are happy. We get our ups and downs but nothing really serious. We're here and that's all there is to it."

"You see..." and here Cappland dawdled deliberately. He spoke as though half to himself and sketched in the idea of his writing the story of her life based on facts she would give him so that it could be published simultaneously with the diaries.

"There's nothing to say," Rohama said innocently. "I thought at one time that if anyone told a lot of lies about my father I'd go on television and tell the truth. Now I know I wouldn't ever do such a thing."

"Not put the record straight?" Cappland asked the question as though this were a cardinal sin.

"There's nothing to put straight. Everyone knows."

This Cappland denied.

"You were never treated properly, were you? Your mother and yourself never got your fair crack of the whip, did you?"

Rohama considered. At one time, certainly, she had longed for the mysterious power of sophisticated people and was nostalgic for some beautiful world from which it seemed she had been excluded. That phase had passed with time leaving her only the longing for a family, for parents, for a sister, and even this longing would pass. What was central in Rohama was her capacity for work and generous emotion.

She looked at the clock. How the time had flown talking to Cappland and how bored she had become with him. At their first meeting she had been intrigued, even a little impressed, but closer knowledge had disabused her. She found his capacity to reduce everything to his own level shocking; all part of his colossal cheek.

He was planning to go into Caerifor to cash a cheque, and asked about times of buses. He had missed one by a few minutes and as Rohama had no car she suggested he hitchhike. This was a suggestion lightly thrown off as a way of getting rid of him and she was astonished to see him set off for the main road and take up his position looking towards the oncoming traffic. She watched him as she rocked the baby in her arms and wondered what the man had been trying to get. She was left with an impression of someone improvising and wondering what to do next, which in Cappland's case, meant how to improve his own position. She saw him wave to a halt the first car that came along—his manner was superb—and she was sure that he would be able to give his benefactor a sense of having done a favour to a most important person.

* * * *

Cappland rode in great style into town and anyone seeing him in his adopted car would have taken him for the owner.

Caerifor was not a place to impress him. Whereas Milford had been all enthusiasm, all a-tingle with poetic echoes, Cappland felt only a vague ill-will. Such towns always had one effect: why didn't everyone drop dead from boredom? He drew the money waiting for him; he wrote a couple of cards in the Post Office; he stared hopelessly out of the Post Office window for four or five minutes; he then decided to take his lunch at the Golden Pheasant; the only inn or hotel in Caeriforshire recommended by the *Good Food Guide.*

Waiting to cross the street he noticed Anne Lewis's green Jaguar. He looked again and saw that Master Patrick was at the wheel. "Quick work," he thought. "No more satisfactory way of being friendly with a girl than driving her around in her own Jag—especially if she's also paying for the petrol."

He waved but neither Patrick nor Anne saw him—or so he thought. In fact Patrick had seen him, groaned and ordered Anne to ignore him. "He's a nutcase," he said for the fourth time.

Once they were beyond the traffic lights Anne said: "Is he so bad? I'd have thought he was the sort of man it would pay to butter up."

"Whatever for?" Patrick was aghast at the idea that he should in any way try to fawn on Cappland although, as she pointed out, they hoped he would help get the diaries published.

"That's my grandmother's crazy scheme," Patrick said. "We don't approve."

Anne and her mother approved of Mignon's project and were hostile to Patrick's attempts to laugh at the matter. Why ignore Cappland when so much was at stake, when it meant so little to be agreeable to him, she asked. She suggested that as he'd almost certainly be in the Golden Pheasant they ought to go back there to stand him a lunch and a couple of beers.

231

"I'd rather have fish and chips than be with him and his dirty stories."

"He's not as bad as all that and it's such a small thing for your grandmother's sake. If we chat him up and buy him lots of drink he might buy the papers for his editor."

Patrick saw that Anne and her mother had the publishing virus and began to sulk.

"It's for your own good, Patrick. An hour. An hour and a half and who knows what will result? Come on. For your grandmother's sake."

Patrick wanted Anne for himself but decided to give in because he liked the way she was talking to him (as though they were already married or engaged) and this gave him a rare pleasure: one of the small, nourishing experiences which contribute to maturity. He smiled sheepishly because he was being organised, was being told politely that he could not recognise his own interests; but by the woman he adored, and therein lay the difference.

"And say if he's not there?"

"Then we have our meal together, as arranged. Come on—" and she took his hand, squeezed it and walked towards the hotel. Of course, she put him in a good humour and they burst into the saloon bar hand in hand and laughing like two people intoxicated by the other. Cappland took off his glasses to wave at them; he was delighted to have company. He could not have been more flattered by their invitation to lunch with them and they went into the dining-room towards half past one having ordered roast pigeons which were particularly plentiful (and succulent) in Caerifor that season.

As they sat down Anne said: "This place is such fun. There's always hairs in the soup or something and if you complain they compensate by giving you whacking great portions of cheese."

Cappland looked at her lugubriously with his dead, cod-grey eyes. "This place is in the Gud Fud Guide, you know."

"Oh, but the hairs are always scrupulously clean," Anne said irreverently. "That's my experience, at any rate."

Cappland laughed although he thought 'gud fud' was far too important not to take seriously. He was impressed by Anne and asked her if she liked Caerifor.

"It's fun in a way," she returned to the conversation from a long appraisal of the menu. "One couldn't live here, of course. But it's nice. People enjoy themselves. All the same, I'm looking forward to going up to London soon for our Christmas shopping."

Cappland was immediately all ears, all gallantry. If Anne and her mother came they were to be his guests at lunch at the Hilton! Anne thanked him bleakly. She didn't believe in his invitation and she did not want to see him in London. Cappland, who had forgotten that Christmas was just over the horizon, said it bored him more and more every year. It had become just another part of the fantasy act which made the twentieth century different from every other.

"What fun," said Anne. "I like that idea." Everything was 'fun' that day, even entertaining Cappland.

"It's a fact. Once you get through to the idea that nothing's real any more, everything's fantasy, you've got hold of the secret of the modern world. Of course, that doesn't mean to say you'll understand it because no one does."

"I adore Ionesco," said Anne brightly. "I think *The Bald Prima Donna* is my favourite play."

Cappland saw no connection so, after saying, "Oh, yes," politely went on. "The danger as I see it is this : once you've picked your favourite fantasy you must keep a thin line of communication between it and the facts of life. So, for instance, you can dream all night you're a pop star—but don't forget to go to work by nine o'clock and draw your pay before two o'clock on Friday."

"Marvellous," said Anne squeezing Patrick's hand under the tablecloth. "I love that idea. It's very modern."

"It *is* the modern psyche," Cappland said. "You've got to have a fantasy life to be modern. Haven't you got fantasies?"

"Heaps," said Anne thinking to herself that Patrick had been right in calling Cappland a nutcase.

"A solemn warning," he was saying, putting his glasses away as the pigeons came into sight. "A solemn warning. Very few people can bear other people's fantasy lives. The clash in the dream world has been proved to be worse than the clash in the real world."

Anne sighed and fluttered her eyelashes at Patrick (all in one

233

movement) and said: "Will I ever be able to get through all this?"

"What you can't eat," said Cappland, "you pass over to me."

So there they were, standing Cappland a roast pigeon lunch in the Golden Pheasant and obliged to listen to him eulogising a meal he had prepared for some guests a month or so before. Even as he talked he devoured the small pigeon bones and his crum-crums and cracks interspersed his phrases.

"I had some Connecticut wild rice—crum-crum—which costs £1 a pound in London although its cheaper Stateside—crum-crum. And you know how you cook it? You fry it with a little onion—crum-crack—a few bits of tomatoes and some prawns—"

"Prawns!" Anne cried as a convenient form of exclamation at the extraordinary way Cappland was gobbling up his bird.

"Yes, prawns. Nothing better—crum-crum—and then have a white wine with it of a decided character—slup-up-crum—something that neither overpowered nor was overpowered by the dish. And—crum-crum—you know what I hit on? A Châteauneuf du Pape 1960!"

At this point, Cappland helped himself to more chipped potatoes and brussels sprouts.

"That began the meal. Then—" here he burped carefully and poured out some more wine—"with the meat I served a wine I had picked up from a merchant in Beaujolais. They said the wine had lain in a corner of the man's cellars throughout the war—forgotten. It was just labelled Beaujolais 1941 and the Tastevin experts labelled it and gave it their accolade.—crum-crum-crack—It was—crum-crack-crum—full and fragrant. Dignified. Not faded at all. A tremendous success for anyone who loves gud fud but looking back I know I made a mistake—" He paused dramatically.

"What was it?" asked Patrick agoggle.

"Simply that I didn't treat the wine with the infinite tenderness so old a wine deserved. In my haste—crum-crum—the cork snapped!"

He made it sound so tragic that Anne burst out laughing.

"I assure you, it nearly ruined the whole thing."

Patrick's eyes dilated with the inexpressible. Anne tried to control herself.

"You remind me—crum-crum—of a girl I knew who never knew when to laugh or cry. She'd say 'My best friend has died' and laugh—crum-crum—and laugh. Yes, laugh. Then she'd say: 'I'm going to sit in Trafalgar Square until they arrest me' and you'd think she was going to cry."

Cappland was finishing well ahead of the other two and spoiled the meal for them by smoking. "She was an extraordinary girl. That Trafalgar Square experience changed her life. Until then she'd been a virgin (there are more of them than you think) and only because she'd never been really attracted by anyone. Well she got arrested in Trafalgar Square and was lifted bodily into a van and got a blissful sensation, she said. It changed her whole outlook."

"Oh?" Patrick looked up doubtfully.

"Oh now she's way out. Half-dead. Buying perverted books. Fiddling about with muck. Making everything sinful and dirty. Morbid. Morbid as hell. Horrible." Cappland shuddered and repeated the word as though spelling it out. "H-o-r-r-i-b-l-e!" And sucked his teeth meditatively.

"You know some extraordinary people," Anne could not help saying. Cappland accepted this complacently. "And as for that girl there's a lot more about her story I can't tell you." He looked speculatively at Anne's plate. "If you can't finish that I will."

"Oh, please. Please do." He leaned across and swept the half-eaten pigeon on to his plate. "You've left the best bits of meat here. You need a good lesson in how to eat a pigeon."

A few moments' silence as he amputated the carcase and then he was off again. "Yes—slup-crum-crum—that girl got herself a change of destiny protesting the bomb in Trafalgar Square. She told me that she'd fallen in love with the policeman who'd lifted her up—crump-crump—into the van. And now she says she can only have sex successfully with men over thirty-five and over fifteen stones and preferably in uniform. Crum-crum."

Cappland took their blank faces for respect and interest. "Yes, she said—" he tossed away a bone—"she said it would be like having sex with God the Father. Oh, she'll end up in an asylum of course. That's what I keep asking myself. How perverted can you get?" He did not answer his own question but

235

gave all his attention to stripping the pigeon which he held in both hands.

* * * *

"And so your pigeon had no effect on him at all," Mrs. Lewis said when they got home.

"Not at all," Patrick replied.

Anne laughed.

"He's definitely not all there," she told her mother. "Poor Patrick, I forced him into his position and we're no better off than before."

Patrick twirled the car keys happily. "He's got no intention of publishing the papers. God knows why he's hanging on."

Mrs. Lewis was sure he was up to no good. She begged Patrick to warn his grandmother not to be taken in by such a man and suggested they write to the *Sunday Age* to check up on his credentials. "He's a very ambiguous sort of person," she said. "You don't know what he wants. I've never heard of a reporter behaving as he does. He may be a freelance, as you say, but he's by no means a normal freelance. Be very careful, Patrick."

The china and the silver tinkled merrily and Mrs. Lewis invited Patrick to supper so that it was gone ten o'clock before he returned home mightily impressed by his reception. Rather like a child home from his first tea-party he told his family how he and Anne had met Cappland in Caerifor and given him lunch. He and Anne had returned home alone to the Lewis house. He'd stayed on for supper and Mrs. Lewis had opened a bottle of champagne saying, 'Anything's an excuse to drink champagne' and had insisted that he finish the bottle when she and Anne retired from the task after taking very little. "I had practically half a bottle to myself," he said.

"They really must have quite a lot of money," Nesta said with a certain note of wonder and envy.

Mignon replied briskly, "They're not short."

"They're very rich," Patrick added valiantly.

Nesta asked where it came from.

"They have lots of property in Liverpool," Patrick answered, as though he had been their agent, "and Mrs. Lewis invests well."

They asked him how he knew. "Because she told me," was the reply.

"You *are* in," was all Mignon could say.

Nesta asked whether Anne was the only child.

"The only one," Patrick replied.

"Patrick must be thinking of marriage," Freddy exclaimed in his joking voice. "He's been into the matter thoroughly. He doesn't want a pig in a poke."

"If he marries Anne he'll be able to go with her and her mother to Liverpool to brood on their property," Mignon said coldly, hating her grandson and his bright, calculating eyes. Patrick went red. "If I marry I hope I marry for love."

"But even nicer to court a solid bank balance," Mignon said with the same flat voice.

"Oh, mother, what a thing to say," Nesta protested.

Yet she admitted to herself that Mignon appeared to have hit the truth of Patrick's mood as though he had been hugging himself all the way home because he had found a girl who was attractive, attracted to him and rich to boot. The three of them looked at Patrick curiously. Their eyes suspended judgement but in truth they did not expect romantic love to flower in Patrick. They all knew he had too much of his father and maternal grandfather in him.

"Cappland says you're driving Anne's Jaguar. Is it true?"

"I drove it into Caerifor and back and I can have it any time I like."

There was some special, glazed effect in their eyes which Patrick resented. He could not be sure whether *they* had changed towards him or whether his time in the company of the Lewises had changed *him* and made him resentful of their assumption that they had a right to keep tabs on his movements.

"So after all your rich living you won't want anything to eat now." Mignon's cold voice carried all her resentment against Patrick's behaviour, his monstrous selfishness (in Mignon's view) and his having talked about family affairs to the Lewises. Patrick shook his head. Fortunately he was not deeply sensitive to atmosphere and had little idea of the impression he created.

He decided to go to bed because he had nothing interesting to say and was sure no one else had.

Nesta's complacency before Patrick's opportunism irritated, appalled Mignon for she was in the nervous condition where the thoughtlessness and the certainty about small things common to youth was intolerable. There were moments when Nesta and Patrick seemed to have been weighed down around her neck for years and the idea that they would be gone, possibly for ever, in a few weeks' time seemed almost impossible.

"If only," she said to herself as she undressed in her wintry bedroom, "if only Heinz would write to me saying he wanted the diaries despite little Mr. Milford. I could throw Cappland out straight away. Or if only Edward would show some sign of life."

She lay in bed and regretted Milford, so desperate had she become. Had she known then what she knew now she would have played Milford differently. Regrets, she sighed, only regrets, and here I am abandoned between Cappland and Nesta and it's damned hard to say who is the worse.

Freddy tapped on the door and wished her good-night. "I thought I heard conversation," he said.

Mignon in confusion admitted that she was alone and blushed for a long time afterwards to realise she had been talking loudly to herself.

13

MOVEMENTS

ALL the time the sky was moody and changing, the river rose and fell with the rains, the carpets rose and fell with the draughts. At night, the windows of the house were lashed with leaves and small twigs. Hailstorms dislodged soot in the chimneys sending it in a ceaseless trickle down into the fireplaces below. Wild, windy sunsets found themselves reflected briefly at the end of the short afternoons in the house windows, and as often as not there was already a lamp lit inside.

On such a day of wind from the north-west and hail, Freddy went out to a funeral. While he was away, Mignon, for the first time, missed him. In the normal way she busied herself with her own affairs and waited without concern for his return. With the house filled with people, none of them people to whom she could really talk, Mignon suffered a sort of homesickness and nostalgia for her brother and she often went to the windows to look for him and to observe the cold blue zones in the clouds, the frantic movement of leaves and showers over the near fields and the distant hills. Everything was on the wing.

Eventually he arrived with his ancient coat spotted with rain, his eyes watering from the wind and his venerable but battered hat crammed on his head in the careless, uncertain manner of the very old or the sick. Mignon opened the door for him and caught hold of his hands as though to warm them. She had no need to. Despite his outward dishevelment, Freddy was dry and warm inside his coat and as he smiled at his sister, charmed by her attentions, all the happiness in him came into his eyes and created a warmth, a well-being which no north-western wind could take away.

"Dearest, I can't tell you why ... but I was so lonely without you among all these people who belong to another world, another age."

She attempted to sound humorous but the remark hurt and saddened; it would mark a milestone. Seated together before the fire drinking tea and making toast, Mignon began to sound Freddy's opinions on Jack Cappland. That day, to her complete surprise, Cappland had gone off to Port Rydal with Nesta, Patrick and Anne Lewis—in Anne's car and although Mignon had been asked to accompany them she had not gone.

Freddy chewed a while, trying to guess what his sister wanted him to say.

"Of course, during all these days he hasn't once looked at the diaries."

Freddy offered to speak to him, so that they could know what he was proposing to do. Mignon was agreeable. The uncertainty had gone on too long.

"As I see it, dearest, he's simply here for a rest and now that he and Patrick have palled up with the Lewises and have the freedom of their whisky and their Jaguar we hardly see them."

Freddy shook his head slowly from side to side.

"It's going to be rather difficult. Mr. Jack is a smart little man..."

"But he has to tell us what he proposes to do. Otherwise he'll be here for Christmas."

Freddy was thinking of Cappland's promise to get some publisher interested in publishing a volume of his verse and wondered whether he would dare raise the matter again.

As it happened, when he approached Cappland, the first thing the man said: "You probably think I've forgotten all about my promise" made Freddy forget at once the question of the diaries. He fell, with an ecstatic smile, into Cappland's falsehoods.

"Now, where had we got to?" Cappland asked. "Have I seen some of your stuff?"

"I haven't shown you any."

"Are you sure you didn't give me a manuscript the other evening. Refresh my memory."

"I've never shown you anything."

Cappland looked gratified, like an editor who has remembered the name of a contributor. "My mistake."

His cunning eyes and smile were not apparent to Freddy, who was in a haze.

"What shall I do, Mr. Cappland? Shall I copy out a selection for you or shall I bring some for you to see now?"

"It might be better if you copied some out carefully." Again Freddy did not notice that he was being treated like a schoolchild and went on happily, "Of course, you understand, Mr. Cappland, that I'm not making any pre-pós-ter-ous claim to genius. I am what they call one of the *Beirdd gwlad*. In English that makes you think of Wordsworth and all that worship of Nature; here it simply means a poet in his own region, a poet in and of his country and it means that we have a social function, if you understand what I mean. I write from the heart to the heart; everything is simple and straightforward and on the human level."

Christ, said Cappland to himself.

"*Beirdd gwlad* vary enormously, of course. Some are very good; some are really very bad; but for the most part they have one thing in common. That is, they believe it is as natural and agreeable for people to communicate civilly in verse as it is for me to speak to you like this and share a compliment, or an elegy or share one another's griefs. A serviceable thing, Mr. Cappland, and a lovely, natural, free expression of one heart speaking to the other."

Cappland's mind had wandered away and he wandered long enough not to grasp what Freddy meant when he said he was going away to fetch some examples of his work from his room. "Good idea," Cappland said and, before he knew what was happening, Freddy had thrust a sheaf of paper into his hands.

It had never been quite clear how Freddy thought Cappland was to interest English publishers in a series of Welsh verses or whether he had thought Cappland would have sold his English verses, which were rubbish, to Christmas card or cracker people. At all events, he came back with a sheaf of his Welsh inspirations and pressed them—marvellous things that they were, all written out in faultless italic—into Cappland's stubby hands.

"I can't do anything with these."

"Oh?"

"They're no good to me."

"Why, Mr. Cappland?"

241

"They're in Welsh."

"I thought you understood that I wrote in Welsh as well as in English." The ambiguity of Freddy's reply reflected the ambiguity of his intentions, which had never been clear to himself.

"Well these are in Welsh and I can't do anything about them." Cappland's impatience with the old man and his relief at finding a way out of his false position, created a sort of explosion of derisive irritation. "Who do you think would want to publish these? Why, I can't even read them. How can I recommend them to a publisher?"

Freddy's first reaction was one of apology. He was about to say something placatory for having taken up Cappland's valuable time when a second wave of shock, a tremor of rage, passed through him and he woke up from his vague dreams and saw himself being treated with contempt by a person who looked fit to be a chucker-out in some low dive.

"Very well, Mr. Cappland. Please give them back to me. Thank you. Thank you very much." With agitated hands Freddy began to stuff the immaculate manuscripts back into the large brown envelope in which they were kept. "And now tell me something: when are you going back to London? We all think it's time you stopped playing about here and went away. My sister, my niece and myself, we all think it's time you left."

"As it happens—" Cappland tried to sound pontifical—"as it so happens I'm considering leaving this week-end."

"Ah," said Freddy, still stuffing the manuscripts into the envelope and creasing them in his excitement. "I'm afraid that's not good enough for my sister. She wants a definite date. She thinks you've been bluffing us long enough."

"She never said so," Cappland said, reasonably enough.

"My sister is one of the old school; she has to be protected from herself and from people such as you. You're almost a disreputable person, Cappland."

Cappland recovered some sort of composure and smirked heavily imagining that once the old man had shot his rage he would be left defenceless. He did not know Freddy, who said, "We've been extremely patient. There comes a time when people are entitled to ask whether they're not being duped."

242

"Why didn't you mention this to me before? No one said a word, yet you seem to have been praying for me to go."

"Praying is too strong a word, Cappland. Hoping will do. We've been hoping for a long time that you'd have the decency to go once you'd made up your mind about the papers."

"Then I must apologise to everyone."

"That's up to you, my man."

"Are you so cross because I can't help you with a publisher? There must be some reason for this astonishing change of attitude. But, indeed, there must be some other reason."

"We're no longer young people, Cappland, and we can only hide our feelings for so long. You've simply overstayed your welcome."

"Then I'm extremely sorry," Cappland said. He was most concerned and wanted to go to speak to Mignon at once. Freddy again said it was up to Cappland. The younger man breathed in deeply trying to fathom the disastrous situation in which he found himself, trying to look back over his time in the house with his new knowledge. There was nothing he could do to hide the shock and displeasure which Freddy's plain speaking had caused him and still he would never guess the real reason for the gentle Freddy's outburst. Cappland had spoken brutally about the verses—that was his way—but how was he to know that in Freddy's mind this tone of voice was associated (from long experience) with a certain tone of voice often used by English people in discussing anything involving the Welsh. "Oh, that," it implied contemptuously. "Oh, *that*. It's bound to be rotten: it's Welsh." Centuries of this attitude had given Freddy a long race memory which stirred at Cappland's voice and that was all. Freddy showed no sign of regretting his outburst for he went on, "I have to speak to you like this because my sister is a widow. I have to protect her. I'm not so sure that you're not an impostor!"

With that Freddy walked out.

Ashley Corbett had called and was present to hear Freddy's report of his exchange with the intolerable guest.

"Yes," he told them, "as soon as I heard that man's insufferable voice—almost shouting at me with such a note of contempt and arrogance in his voice—I felt everything we stood

243

for was at stake." This was a typically Freddyish phrase and he repeated it on a higher note like a preacher. "Everything we stood for was at stake. I simply asked him, none too courteously, if the truth be told, when he was going and he says he thinks he'll go this week-end. That's what he said."

"Hallelujah!" Nesta and her mother shared an immense relief. "Hallelujah."

"It seems the whole thing's got out of hand?"

Mignon shook her head. "Oh, Ashley dearest, if you knew what I've been through..." her voice trailed away, her head started shaking.

"Dearest," she turned to Freddy, "I'm more grateful than you'll ever know. This man presses on me like an incubus. At first I put up with him because I was really sure something good would come despite his evident unsuitability. I played up to him shamelessly; I tried to do everything I could to interest and humour him. The whole thing got out of hand. I went too far. He thought I was trying to take him in. I know it. He lost faith in me. I didn't mind that. God knows I'm not proud and anything was worthwhile so long as the paper took the stuff. And then it hit me in the eyes that in playing up to him I had sold everything short. Everything we stood for, as Freddy says, had been cheapened in order to humour this vile man. I shall never be able to forgive myself for that."

"Oh dear!" This was all Freddy could say at the sight of his sister breaking down and apparently admitting that all her plans had failed and come to nothing.

"At first I thought that the man was stupid, that he couldn't see what I was getting at. Then I realised that he knew very well what was at stake but couldn't be bothered to hide his contempt for it. We had never existed for him as people. We were only poor old things to be used to make a story. We'd lost our human values; we were just things. It was the worst aspect of the whole thing. The bitterest. It seemed I'd never really understood the horror of the modern world until then or the pathetic position we find ourselves in. How could we interest such a man? We didn't even speak the same language. We didn't belong to the same age, even the same world. I saw that he was laughing at me; leading me on, playing me off against my own silliness."

In the difficult silence which followed Ashley suggested it might be possible to try someone else. Mignon shook her head. "There isn't anyone else. There's nothing we can do. It's failed. Our little plan has failed and I'm worse off than I was before."

Nesta denied this. "You're not a penny worse off."

Mignon crumpled up her face at disgust at the idea that she had been talking about money. "I mean something else: it's like losing one's innocence for the second time."

Freddy tried to assure his sister that the situation was not so bad as she made it out. She stared straight ahead, her face crumpled and disgusted and said nothing until she suddenly said, "I didn't know it was possible to be so miserable. Misery from top to toe. Of course, there's no one to blame but myself, in the end. I started the whole thing after listening to that fool Edward with his suave empty speeches. Well, that's that. As soon as Cappland goes away I don't want a single person to mention these diaries. The matter has finished."

She gave an immense sigh and tried to compose her features. The others watched her sadly, wondering what they could do.

"It must be awfully disappointing," Ashley began.

"Don't let's mention the matter again, dearest. All I want to do is thank you for your patience. You were more than good to me. We set out together in hope. Pity that everything ended so sourly."

Mignon's sudden capitulation took everyone by surprise so that something of Freddy's heroic stand against Cappland went by the board. In the morning, Cappland had recovered his phlegm and asked with a certain amount of ill will whether he had done anything that made the family want to get rid of him.

Nesta said the matter was one between himself and her mother.

"Of course," he said, "I suppose she's disappointed that I couldn't recommend the diaries for publication. It's such small stuff when you look at it closely. It wouldn't be of interest to the general reader."

Nesta poured herself some more tea. "None of us imagined it would and I don't know where you got that impression. We weren't so sure either that you were the best person to examine the papers. I think you'll agree that they call for specialised knowledge which I doubt you have. In the end your ignorance saved you from disappointment. I wasn't going to allow the papers to leave the family and was even prepared to go against my mother to see that they weren't. These are family papers and if I have anything to do with it they'll remain just that."

Brave words, thought Cappland, smirking. Braver were to come: "If you feel you've been brought down here under false pretences I'll be happy to pay your fare back and fore to London."

This left Cappland at a loss for the right reply. "I don't need money," he said.

"To be honest with you, we had reached the conclusion that you were waiting for some money before you could go away. We were wondering whether we ought to have offered to pay your fare back to London."

Cappland recognised a master of insulting patronage and replied, "You shouldn't worry yourself. I can manage."

The odds against Cappland were too great. He tried to see Rohama before he went away but she refused to answer the door. In his last hours he did not seem to know what to say to be the most vexing and insulting. He tried to see Mignon, too, for a last settling of old scores but she was unable to leave her room, she said.

* * * *

The day Cappland went away Patrick went over to visit his beautiful farmeress as usual and found her in bed nursing a slight chill. Patrick did the few tasks necessary on the farmlet and then took the Jaguar into Caerifor to fetch a list of things which Mrs. Lewis wanted. When he was in the grocery store he bought a box of Anne's favourite thin chocolate creams and presented it to her with the newspapers when he returned. It was 11.30 and time for Anne to have a glass of port with an egg beaten in it.

No one could have looked more fetching as she sat up in bed sipping her tonic. Her abundant black-gold hair was held back by a broad, yellow Alice band; another great yellow bow held her bed jacket together at her throat. Of course, she was supposed to be unwell and her voice was rather husky, but essentially she was a blooming, nubile virgin who looked about seventeen and a quarter. She had the special freshness of young girls in the clear brow, the rounded cheeks, the bright eyes, brilliant, clear, tawny-coloured. When she moved to reach a paper handkerchief from a box at the side of the bed her jacket opened and Patrick enjoyed a glimpse of the tops of her deeply cleft breasts.

She was agog to hear about Cappland's departure. "Your grandmother must be so sad at the way things have turned out. But, believe me, I think she's got away lightly. Do you know what Rohama told me?" And to Patrick's immense surprise she told him of Cappland's offer to Rohama as reported to her by Rohama herself.

"Did Rohama accept?"

"Of course not. She's too loyal for that. What a question!"

"What a sod of a fellow!"

"So much for our pigeon, darling. I laugh all to myself when I think of the way he crumped his way through two birds. I can't make out which was the more amusing, his silly conversation about the wild rice and the prawns or your face as you listened and watched him. I'm sure there must be a word to sum up your expression but it escapes me for the moment."

Patrick still kept shaking his head at this hint of Cappland's duplicity. "So that's why he was so interested in Rohama. To be honest I thought he wanted to get off with her."

"He tried to do that, too," Anne answered gaily. "You bet. He's what they call a sexy little stoat. Rohama got the measure of him, don't you worry. Besides he'd never get anywhere with her, she's far too fond of Martin. She worships him."

She sipped her tonic and held out her hand to him. "You know that Rohama and Martin have become very, very fond of you. Roma told me she thought of you as a younger brother. Wasn't that nice? She's very warm-hearted."

Patrick agreed, still wondering how much Anne knew about Cappland from Rohama and not wishing to appear gossipy or curious. "It's a pity our family's split down the middle. I think we ought to make more of Rohama and Martin."

Anne looked at him meaningfully (understanding perfectly what he was getting at, but pretended not to know what he meant.

"Don't you think it's a pity?" he asked.

"Oh, families are families wherever you are."

"It's some sort of silly snobbery," Patrick went on earnestly. "We all say we're not snobs but we are. That's what's so funny about Britain, people say they're not snobs and they are but don't know it—or won't admit it. Martin's a rough, straightforward sort of bloke but because of all this we don't get the best out of him."

Anne said she had the impression that something more than snobbery was involved. "I go to Rohama's often and she's really my closest friend here but I can understand why there should be reserve. You can't *make* people like one another. Oh, I don't know what the answer is but I know it's more difficult than we can understand. Anyway, it's not for us to make judgements, is it? I like your grandmother and I like Rohama. Your grandmother's a remarkable woman, the last of her kind. That upper-class, countrywoman's complexion and those large lids to her eyes and the long, rather off-centre face like Virginia Woolf, only older and greyer. She's had a difficult time."

"I shouldn't really tell you . . ." Patrick came closer as though letting Anne into an enormous secret . . . "My grandmother has given up trying to sell the papers. Cappland's disgusted her with the whole idea. She's said so."

Anne's brow darkened. "I'm really sorry. She'd put so much into the idea."

"Too much. Cappland let her down really badly."

When they had got tired of discussing the failure of the project to sell Sir Arthur to the Masses, Anne picked up the newspaper and asked Patrick to read her something. She loved being read to. He read the headlines and then found an odd item which amused him: "Family's conventional attitude drove youth to suicide" and "Plum Pudding Asphyxiates Old People." Anne said he'd made the whole thing up so he leaned over and cheek to cheek they read the item together. "From our special correspondent: Three old people aged from 78 to 92 living together at Ronces-sur-Gauffre in the Pas de Calais were found asphyxiated in their home yesterday. The old people, it was stated, had been given a Christmas pudding in the English style and, being curious to taste it, had decided to eat it before Christmas. They put it in a saucepan and, according to the examining magistrate appointed to look into the circumstances of their deaths, the pudding gave off noxious fumes which contributed to their deaths."

"So there!"

She said softly, "What a dreadful story."

"Another triumph for English cookery."

She smiled at him tenderly and placed her hand on his hair. "You are funny." And then, despite the cold, he drew her to him and kissed her. The newspaper was crumpled by their sudden, convulsive movement. He pressed her back into the pillow and it was only the fear that Mrs. Lewis would open the door that prevented his jumping into bed with her.

They heard the front-door bell ring and by and by, with the newspaper straightened and her hair back in place, they heard someone coming up the stairs. It was the local vet's wife who had called on some errand and had five minutes to spare to give to Anne. She was a middle-class, well-dressed woman in a dashing leopard-skin coat and a hat with a bird's claw attached to the turned-up brim.

For some reason the mood in the bedroom disturbed and vexed her. She refused to sit down and walked up and down nervously darting hateful glances at Patrick whom she had heard of but had never before met. He sat back in his chair and made no effort to be sociable. As the conversation went on the vet's wife grew shriller, more hysterical as though the atmosphere in the room overwhelmed her starved senses like an intoxicant. The intimacy and tension between Patrick and Anne infuriated her; she felt she wanted to bundle the man away with a bucket of water. She knew that as soon as she went away they would have their tongues in one another's mouths again and the idea made her see red. Anne could see the woman's behaviour was not normal and was vaguely embarrassed for her sake. "I should be so ashamed," she said later, "to let people know I wasn't complete in that way. Wouldn't you?"

"In what way isn't she complete?" Patrick asked.

Anne giggled. He smiled knowingly. "Oh, in *that* way!"

And certainly the two of them felt an immense pity for anyone who couldn't be complete 'in that way' feeling themselves to be absolutely sure of getting the fullest self-expression 'in that way'.

"Normally, she's rather nice," Anne said about the departed caller. "She writes poetry," she added as an afterthought.

"Everybody writes poetry around here. Do you?"

"Sometimes. It's not much good. I write stories for children, too. I was trying my hand at one this morning before you came. It's not much good but it gives me pleasure."

"Can I see it?"

"Oh, no," she said, she never showed her writing to anyone.

"Not even to me?"

"Not even you."

Patrick did not insist. This disappointed her.

"Do you read much?" she asked.

Patrick thought a moment and decided, in view of his grandmother's comments on his illiteracy, to shoot a line. "Biographies, mostly," he said, "or real life adventure."

"You don't like poetry?"

"Bores me to tears, I'm afraid."

"Of course, not everybody likes it." She tried not to make him feel left out in the cold. "I studied English literature by correspondence course one time when everyone was getting at me because I wasn't making anything of my life. It went all right until I started to read *King Lear*. I couldn't bear it. It's the most horrible play ever written."

"Shakespeare also bores me to tears," Patrick confessed happily.

"Not all ..." she suspected that literary conversations bored him and so asked him how long he intended to stay in England. He looked at her archly. "I don't think that depends on me any more. What do you think I ought to do?"

She asked him whether he wanted to do anything especially? She had formed the impression that Patrick was not a person to tolerate an indoor life. She had always assumed he would take up farming. He grasped her hand. "Why not?" he asked and repeated the phrase mechanically as he suddenly thrust his arm behind her shoulder and with the other loosened the bedjacket. "Why not?" he repeated as the bedjacket opened out. "They're marvellous!" The conversation came to an end as he put his mouth to her breast. She gave a tremble of pleasure and placed an arm around his head, pressing him to her. It needed the sound of Mrs. Lewis on the stairs to separate them. Patrick sat back in his chair and pretended to be looking for something in the paper.

Mrs. Lewis brought a call to eat. While Anne put a house-coat on, Patrick and the mother went downstairs and began talking about politics. Politics was a subject that interested Mrs. Lewis every three weeks or so passionately. Weeks would pass without her being greatly involved and then, out of the blue, something would engage her sympathies and politics was in. That morning she had decided that the white settlers in Rhodesia were having a raw deal. A case could be made for them and their complaint that they had been let down by the British.

The conversation about the future of the white race in Africa continued after Anne arrived and Mrs. Lewis asked Patrick whether he would join his father in business eventually. Patrick's father—he explained—was the main Roettinger agent in Central Africa and had a number of subsidiary interests and, Patrick added comfortably, "Makes quite a nice packet." On the other hand, his father feared that his time in Africa was limited and was anxious that his son should not make his life there; it was on this vague basis that Patrick had come home. He was looking round for something. Mrs. Lewis thought he had once told her he would go in for farming. He nodded. He was faintly perplexed why everyone seemed to come round in the end to discussing his future as though the mere sight of this strapping young person apparently happy to do nothing at all caught everyone on his puritan side.

This was not entirely true of Mrs. Lewis, who was sounding out Patrick as an economic proposition as a husband for her daughter. Both women had decided that Patrick was the only man who had ever really moved Anne and, given guidance, the man could be made something. To a certain extent, too, their attitude was American: they were shopping for a husband, someone slightly taller than Anne (who was five feet seven), someone who could 'look the part' (in whatever role Anne had chosen), someone with a natural health and distinction who had enough intelligence to make good use of the openings Mrs. Lewis would make for him.

The Lewis women had charm, money, common sense and a way with men. Time and time again when Patrick was in their home he was grateful to them for merely letting him breathe and shine as a male. After his weeks in his grandmother's company he had almost forgotten the pleasure he used to get laying down the law on small points and gradually he got back his old verve and launched out into one of his thinkpieces about the difficulty of creating things in a world dominated by the machine.

"The only creative pleasure left is making money: the only excuse for being alive in the twentieth century. But money is weird these days—almost like an ectoplasm. It's not meant to keep and anyone who tries to save is going against the mood of the times. That's the Americans' greatest gift to civilisation: they've taken away the taboo from money and reduced it to something that can come out of a tap."

"It has to be worked for," Mrs. Lewis said with a note of caution.

Patrick knew all about that and went into some long rig-marole about the point of work being lost in face of the pro-liferation of goods which Mrs. Lewis did not understand and suspected that Patrick did not either, but she got out of the difficulty by saying with unmixed admiration, "Gracious me, Patrick, you're clever enough for three!" and was pleased to see her flattery so delight him that he forgot the thread of what he was saying and beamed at her vaguely, grateful that after the edgy personalities at home he had come to rest among two such reposeful women, who uncritically accepted the world and its wonders and seemed prepared to accept everyone at his own value.

Patrick also liked to cut a dash as a young man of the world and boasted carefully about his travels in Africa. "I wonder how a young man of your age could have seen so much in such a short time," Mrs. Lewis said and there was no hint of the irony which made conversation with his mother and grandmother so risky.

After the meal, they sat around the fire drinking coffee. Mrs. Lewis took out her knitting and Anne stared at the coals. Patrick was expected to entertain them for, after all, he was their knight from the outside world. Every so often Anne smiled at him or formed her lips into a kiss; and so, in this Arcadian fashion, another afternoon passed.

As Anne was better the next day she and Patrick accompanied Mrs. Lewis into Caerifor where she had an appointment at her hairdresser's. They dropped Mrs. Lewis in the town and then drove down to the riverside which was deserted. The winds of the past week had blown away the artist with the drop at the end of her nose and had filled the Maddau with branches and pieces of wood. At the far end of the quay was an empty car park. Here they stopped and after making sure no one was around, Patrick and Anne got into the back seat to play with one another. They kissed like dynamos and Patrick, with his tongue in her mouth and his hand in her knickers, knew that Anne wanted him to ask her to marry him. "Shall we?" He broke off long enough to ask. She half-opened her eyes.

"Shall we marry?"

"At this rate we'll have to." And she drew his head towards her. "Darling Patrick, I love you so much."

"But you haven't answered me, Annie."

"Of course we will. But not if you call me Annie."

He laughed at her. "Will your mother be willing?"

"She thinks you're smashing. Everyone does." With this Anne gave another of her ecstatic sighs and pulled his head down again. "Tell me you love me, Patrick."

"Of course I do. Of course I love you."

"I'm so glad."

A good deal of water flowed under Grimshaw's bridge before Patrick said, "We mustn't forget your mother."

"God, I'd completely forgotten."

They drove back to the hairdresser's and found Mrs. Lewis reading under the drier. They withdrew to a nearby side street. While they sat there Anne's skirt seemed to edge higher and higher up her legs. "Be careful, darling," she said, "or we'll get ourselves arrested for indecency." So they sat demurely side by side waiting for Mrs. Lewis.

Anne said they would say nothing of their plan to marry for the moment but would give the news at a suitably dramatic moment. Anne said this as Mrs. Lewis came kickling towards them in the wind on her high heels. Her hair covered by a headsquare was "like a golliwog's", she said. "I don't know why I bother."

She complained about her hair all the way home but was sufficiently alert to the others to know they were keeping something from her. She and Anne had hardly been alone together for two minutes when Mrs. Lewis said, "I suppose you said yes when he asked you."

"How did you know?"

"Ah!" Mrs. Lewis showed a complacency which would have qualified her for a place in a radio serial. "It wasn't hard to guess, you know."

"Well he did. But we didn't want to tell anyone for the moment."

"It's what you want, isn't it?"

"You know it is."

"Just one thing..." and Mrs. Lewis warned her daughter about the possible opposition to the marriage from Patrick's family. "There's a really big rift between Lady Benson-Williams and Patrick's mother. It could boil over on to Patrick. They might create some sort of drama just to spite the other. They'd do anything just now to do the other down."

Anne rightly felt that Patrick's marriage was in no way linked with the dislike between Mignon and Nesta.

"I've been in the world longer than you have. People will use any stick to beat an enemy. Be warned."

*   *   *   *

The news of Patrick's coming marriage to Anne Lewis came to Mignon at a bad time and was forever afterwards associated with the general horror of the weeks following Cappland's exit. It was already a period where communication between the members of the household was only half-articulated—resentment, doubt, despair, indifference came between them all—and the bald fact that Patrick, with no career and no prospects, had been accepted by Anne Lewis could not be discussed dispassionately by the older members of the family.

To Mignon, with the reticences and the suppressed knowledge of a far earlier generation, the proposed marriage was almost an obscenity; she would have been no more shocked had she been told that Patrick and Anne had gone to bed together on the day of their meeting. Not knowing the Lewises very well she could not divine the motives of the mother and daughter who, with their eyes open, had taken in this young person, hardly more than an adolescent despite his stature and his man of the world airs—and were prepared to take him up like a cause.

As for the feelings that might exist between Patrick and Anne, Mignon saw only two things: opportunism on Patrick's side and biological attraction on both. To say that the couple had hardly had time to get to know one another seemed wholly inadequate. Mignon had almost forgotten the details of her own awakening to love, and physical love especially, but she remembered enough to know how depressing it had been and how inadequate she herself had been. It made Anne's role all the more difficult for her to understand. "How any woman..." she began to herself and trailed off with her mouth twisted as though after the taste of something bitter.

All Mignon's cantankerousness was directed against her daughter. Nesta, she assumed, was a woman who was of her own cast of thought, a woman who would see things in exactly the same way as herself; so why did she hesitate? Why didn't she denounce this crazy plan, this coming together of sexual and social adventurism? But Nesta was too weak, too irresolute to do anything even if there was something she could do. Because of the mounting tension between herself and her mother —she was being blamed for the breakdown of Mignon's plans to sell the diaries—she had suggested a second time to Patrick that they might as well go back to Salisbury. Patrick refused. He thought his mother was mad to have asked such a question and said so. What did he have in Salisbury now? "My life is here with Anne," he said flatly. And what was he going to do? Patrick thought they might farm.

"You haven't any money, you know," his mother said softly.

"Money! You and your money! That's all you think about. What does that matter if Anne and I are in love?"

"It matters rather a lot. Do try to be reasonable. Where are you going to live?"

Naturally Patrick expected to live with the Lewises and this arrangement did not seem out of place in the context of the

Lewis household; in his mother's eyes he saw that such an arrangement was demeaning, as though he had deliberately set out to create a position for himself in somebody else's comfort. 'Hanging up his hat in the hall' is the euphemism for this behaviour; 'making himself on her money' is the one nearer the truth. So Patrick said, "We haven't yet decided what we'll do. We may buy a farm."

"You mean, Mrs. Lewis will buy a farm for you?"

His silence meant "Yes."

Nesta sighed. It was a question of keeping up the side, of not appearing to want too blatantly to succeed on Anne's money; she could not say what was the best thing.

They had reached the point where neither could look directly at the other; shyness and suppressed anger held them back.

"I wish it hadn't been like this," Nesta exclaimed. "I wish you'd had a job or some prospects of a job or a place at a university. It would look so much better."

"Why look better? What's so wrong?"

Nesta lit a cigarette and played with a loose fold of the chaircover. "It's no good talking. If you don't feel that it's not quite usual ... not quite the everyday arrangement ... then there's nothing I can say. I know you like Anne and I'm prepared to believe she likes you."

"Then you feel it's wrong because of Anne's money?"

"No. Not wrong. Heavens above! Men have married rich women before, but you really have no position at all, no idea what you want to do, and it looks as though you'll just move over into the Lewises and live on their money."

He bridled furiously, his face brick-red. "There's no question of my living off their money. Whatever help Mrs. Lewis gives us will be a loan. We'll pay everything back. And I know I'll succeed. Whatever I do will be a success. All I need is time to find out what suits me best."

"In that case let's not talk about it any more. If you are satisfied and Anne and her mother are satisfied it's not for me to say anything."

Nesta believed she was being reasonable enough and so did Freddy—who seemed often to register events only in the broadest outline so that a marriage between Anne and Patrick

256

seemed good because marriage in itself was good and an occasion for joy; he had no real understanding of his sister's objections. Mignon thought Nesta had been feeble beyond words. "At least you should have insisted that he had some work, even as a cattle food salesman, before you let him go ahead with the marriage. Why, dearest, you always try to suggest that Arthur only married me for what he could get and can't forgive me for not being bitter about it, and here you are countenancing the same thing in your son."

"I've never said that about Father."

"You've often suggested it. Perhaps you don't know just what dark thoughts you do have."

The fat was in the fire; the fur was flying; the claws were out—all the classic old clichés came true—but at the end of it no one had anything positive to say about Patrick's wedding plans or any advice to offer.

They floundered helplessly in this strange situation unable to share with one another their dismay (for Nesta was no more sold on the idea than her mother) or their misgivings. Nesta hesitated a couple of days before she wrote to her husband. It was as though she felt the young couple would change their minds as rapidly as they had formed them.

This misunderstanding of their motives was partly due to the fact that Patrick did not feel free to express himself at home whereas with Anne and Mrs. Lewis he discussed his problems freely as between equals.

Mrs. Lewis was anxious to know what the reaction had been to the wedding proposal and Patrick had been unable to say O.K. because there had been none of the usual reactions from his family. He said flatly, "They think it's crazy for me to marry when I haven't got a job."

Mrs. Lewis looked quickly at Anne and it was understood that the time had come to talk seriously to Patrick about his future. Mrs. Lewis shared Patrick's own opinion of himself. She was sure that whatever he took up he would succeed in because he was an uncomplicated person with a single-mindedness that often appeared mere shallowness because it lacked a matter to absorb it. She had already accepted him as a son-in-law—welcomed him, in fact—but she also accepted the fact that they would have to make him and she saw no reason why she and Patrick's family should not set about the task together. For Mrs. Lewis the problem was simplified by the fact that Anne wanted Patrick and would get him, but it was the mother's duty to see that the young man had his feet on the first steps of some ladder. Mrs. Lewis saw nothing objectionable in making a son-in-law with her money since the final result, the final happiness, would be everyone's; and with this in mind she suggested to Patrick that he might like to go to an agricultural college if he wanted to make farming his career. Patrick was not immediately thrilled by the idea but to say yes did already confer a certain seriousness on him and as (he presumed) there were agricultural colleges and agricultural colleges, a couple of years pursuing a diploma might be agreeable.

Mrs. Lewis even had a cousin who was married to a lecturer at the college at Cirencester and was sure she'd be able to arrange an entrance, if not for the spring term at least for the new academic year in the autumn. Patrick smiled in a wizened kind of way. He wondered whether it might not be better to go as a pupil to some large estate and dispense with the theoretical. This seemed possible to Mrs. Lewis although for social reasons a son-in-law studying at the Royal Agricultural College seemed rather better value than one acting as general slogger on somebody's dairy farm.

"Well, we can work that out," Patrick said grandly, "the important principle established is that Anne and I would like to farm and that's the main thing."

Mrs. Lewis did not disillusion him although she was a little bit surprised by his inability to come down to brass tacks. Either he had superb self-confidence or he was a bluffer and she was determined to find out. She decided to attack in another way and said that it might be a good thing if the two families could get together to discuss when there should be an engagement party and when the marriage. Anne objected to this, not because she had anything against Patrick's relations but because she thought it was time to dispense with engagements and 'all that sort of thing'.

Mrs. Lewis said, "Why are you pretending you're some kind of Bohemian? An engagement need not be long but it seems to me the courteous thing to do."

"Oh, Mummy, courteous to whom?"

"To other people, of course." Mrs. Lewis paused. "At least you must give people time to get their ideas adjusted."

"Oh." It was a measure of protest at the idea that other people were interested or had the right to be interested in their affairs. "Oh, not really."

Patrick had never seen Anne standing out against her mother's opinions before and was amused by the petulant tone she adopted. Her mother was not to be shaken by petulance. "If you and Patrick were a pair of beatniks in leather coats and with hair round your middles no one would expect you to be anything but unconventional but you are you and Patrick is Patrick and all your relations expect you to be straightforward and conventional. I'm sorry, darling, but there it is."

"I hate having to be conventional," Anne said. "I think people should be allowed to go off at any time of the day to marry with whomever they want."

It was Mrs. Lewis's time to say, "Oh." She even looked faintly annoyed. "Don't be a bore, Anne darling. Don't let's have all this sort of adolescent talk. Everybody (Mrs. Lewis meant herself) likes things done properly with a decent period of preparation in which to choose the wedding presents and a decent wedding with something to drink and something you don't get every day to eat and that's it!"

"I know," Anne wailed, "that's what I hate. Think of all the people we'll have to invite and all the dreadful presents I'll get."

Patrick took her hand. "Myself I think all that's a very small price to pay in order to marry you eventually."

Anne stroked his cheek. "What touching things you say. You're right, of course."

And so, with a minimum of resistance, Anne accepted a 'decent period of preparation' and a 'decent wedding' and all the trimmings.

Mignon and Nesta were taken aback by Mrs. Lewis's invitation to dinner for the following Sunday although both agreed that the wedding had to be accepted as a firm arrangement. Mignon thought it was for Nesta to go alone; Nesta thought it was natural for her mother to be invited. And if Mignon went Freddy could hardly be left behind. It was another nail in

Nesta's coffin. Mignon did not want to be involved in Patrick's affairs. She did not like him and found she had nothing to say to him. She had nothing against Anne (whom she hardly knew) but she thought privately that the girl and her mother must be blind or wilful—or both—to go out of their way to cultivate a cold-hearted opportunist like Patrick.

She eventually accepted the invitation with poor grace.

Another extraordinary development had taken place during this time which only came out when Anne went across to Rohama's house—it was her first visit for some time—and, unable to keep back her happiness, made Rohama swear by all her gods that she would not tell anyone what Anne was about to tell her.

"Wait until it's announced officially," she said importantly as though entirely converted to the idea of doing things 'decently' —and told Rohama of her coming marriage to Patrick. To Anne's stupefaction Rohama was not in the least pleased.

"You're very young to think of marriage," she said rather sourly, "and Patrick is younger than you are."

"Not much younger than you were when you married," Anne replied astonished by the grudging tone and the sour face. "And Patrick isn't so much younger than I am. Besides it doesn't matter. At least I don't think so."

"He's two years younger than you are," Rohama said, I couldn't have married a man who was younger than myself."

The baby cried and Rohama went across to soothe it leaving Anne turning over her thoughts. "Well," she thought, "you think you know people and you realise you don't know them at all." Rohama's reaction upset her; she had expected an explosion of good will and happiness. She tried to imagine why Rohama should care, why her happiness should have seemed a threat or diminished Rohama's own peace of mind in some way. Rohama returned from the cot looking sour and said, "I've got some news for you. But keep it to yourself, too. If everything goes according to plan Martin and I are going to Cardiff in the spring."

"Whatever for?"

"My brother-in-law, Jack, has got a haulage business and he wants Martin to go down there to help him run it. We haven't worked everything out yet but we think it will offer us a better chance than here."

"But you're so happy here."

"It's hard work," Rohama said simply. "I could have gone on. I will go on. But Martin can get three times as much money for half the hours. We thought about it a good deal and now we've said Yes."

Anne showed Rohama a great deal more affection than she had been shown. "I'll miss you dreadfully. Both of you. You've been marvellous neighbours and friends."

"You'll have Patrick now, won't you?" Rohama said and there was a suggestion of bitchiness as though Patrick was a sort of liability.

Poor Anne took every unfriendly intonation to heart and was too perplexed to pursue the conversation or the call.

"Aren't people weird?" she said to her mother later. Neither of them could understand why Rohama should have taken up such an attitude.

"But keep the matter to ourselves. Let Rohama tell her relations," Mrs. Lewis said. "If I were you I wouldn't even tell Patrick. It's a delicate matter and we mustn't be seen to have interfered in any way—least of all that we had known about Rohama's move long before Lady Benson-Williams did. It will obviously affect their position a good deal."

14

A PROSPECT OF UNION

NEITHER Rohama nor Martin knew how to tell Mignon that they planned to leave and hoped to sell their part of the Swanquarter lands for the ready cash which would be put into the haulage business. They decided that the best thing would be to ask Ashley Corbett for advice. Ashley was flattered to be so approached and then came the surprise. "You really are leaving?" He stared at them fascinated and his voice implied, "After all the fuss and bother of the will and all the trouble since, you're pulling out for good?"

"But why?"

It was left to Martin to make the explanations. "It's like this. Roma was left her part of the estate and so far as the law goes we can be there for all of our lives. What we see now—and didn't see when we first came—is that it's not possible to work in a place where you're not only watched and clocked in every minute of the day but not wanted. We're not wanted there. That's the truth of the matter."

"But who is watching you all the time?" Ashley asked quickly.

"The others, of course. Who else?"

"I'm sorry you think that. I'm sure it's untrue."

"What Martin wants to say is that we've never really been accepted and we feel we've pushed ourselves in. Just recently I began to see things from a different angle. I began to ask myself why we were here and it seemed to me we were doing so in the hope that one day we'd be somehow more part of the family. That won't ever happen. Looking back, it seems to me we were very young when we came here. Only two simple people could have done what we did. Now we're older we're no longer such innocents and putting one thing and another together we decided the time had come to make a break."

"Now or never," Martin said rubbing his chin with his knuckles.

"But why have you changed? Excuse me asking these questions but I feel all this in a personal way. It means as much to me as though we were related. I thought you and Aunty Micky were getting on better than you ever had."

Rohama and Martin looked at one another.

"I know," Rohama said slowly. "In her own way she's become fond of me. I feel that. Until Nesta came home they depended on me for lots of things. I've changed. I admit that. One day you see things more clearly. You understand people and you see what the situation really is."

"I know all that; how has it changed?"

"I realised that we could live together side by side, almost next door, for a hundred years and never get any closer."

"But Aunty Micky and Freddy won't live another hundred years."

"The family goes on." Rohama shook herself in the way one puts aside an irrelevant but interesting idea. "We'd be better trying our luck elsewhere. Now Martin's brother made this offer and it's a better life for us in every way."

"It's a grand opportunity for me," Martin added. "A bobby's life compared with farming."

Ashley looked from one to the other owlishly still turning over in his mind the possibilities of the present situation. Had there been a quarrel? Had something been said?

"Oh no," Rohama said blithely, not recognising the turning point in her own thinking. "No one's said anything. It's just that we've had this offer and we realised it would be better to make a new start for the child's sake."

"It wouldn't be right to bring the child up in this atmosphere," Martin added.

Ashley accepted their right to do what they pleased; he accepted that Rohama and Martin could have had a sudden change of heart; yet he felt he had to offer them the more cheerful possibilities. Every year that passed saw the reserves melt a little and there was a possibility that one day they might even have all the farm. The idea had often struck him that there was no one else interested and Rohama's position was strong.

Rohama shook her head. "Do you think Nesta is really as uninterested in the place as she likes to pretend? I don't. She obviously thinks ahead and in my opinion that's why she brought Patrick back home with her. It stands to reason that they can't go on in Africa for ever and they're probably looking around for somewhere to bring their money back to."

Ashley said he had never heard such a thing mentioned. "Between ourselves, I think Nesta would get rid of the place like a shot. If they have to pull out of Africa they'll almost certainly go to the husband's place in Ireland."

Neither Rohama nor Martin was convinced. "You know, don't you, that Patrick's going to marry Anne Lewis?" Rohama enjoyed Ashley's surprise. "I introduced them," she added irrationally but with—it had to be seen to be believed— a certain pride.

Without realising it Ashley showed all his secret spite against Patrick: "Then he's following his grandfather's footsteps—latching on to a good thing."

Martin laughed. "That's what I say."

"They're very much in love," Rohama said valiantly.

Martin laughed even louder. "So could we all be with Anne Lewis's money."

Rohama was hurt. "They're not like that at all. I didn't know men could be so catty and mean. Shame on you."

Ashley and Martin still laughed. "You must admit," Martin said, "she wanted him and she got him. That's typical of them. They're all up in the air in two minutes. When they decide they want a thing they've got to have it whatever the cost."

"Master Patrick would soon get their number," Ashley said. "He soon recognised a comfortable berth. I never believed he had the slightest intention of doing anything so long as he had women daft enough to support him. He twirls his mother round his little finger and she thinks it's marvellous. Good luck to him," he added in a voice which contained no hint of good will towards Patrick, "Good luck to him, is all I can say. If he can get away with it lucky for him."

Rohama had never imagined Ashley could have been so malicious about something that was no direct concern of his. Her brief romantic élan disappeared under the men's ribaldries and she shrugged. Why should she defend Patrick? Why bother? Nothing Ashley or Martin said could alter facts. She merely thought less of both men, especially Ashley, who had shown that he was not the free spirit she had thought he was. She was left with her old tattered loyalty to her half-family.

They eventually came back to the matter of their departure and Ashley asked them when they proposed speaking to Mignon. Martin said they had hoped Ashley would speak for them. Ashley promptly shook his head. "My dear people, I'd like to help you in any way I can but not in that way. Aunty Micky is in a most difficult mood these days. She's taking things to heart since her plans to publish the diaries—" Ashley glanced uneasily at Rohama—"have flopped. She'd be more than likely to accuse me of interfering. I'm sorry. You'd be wise to tell her yourself before she gets wind of it from anyone else. Why not speak to Freddy? He's always reasonable and helpful."

"You see," Rohama said, "it's very important for us because we have to get some capital behind us for the new firm."

"Naturally." Ashley had understood that from the beginning. "And you need Aunty Micky's authority to sell."

Martin asked whether there was any good reason why she would refuse. Ashley pointed out to him that good reasons hardly mattered to Mignon in her present cantankerous mood. Martin said hopefully: "She'd probably like to buy it herself."

"With whose money?" Ashley asked.

"Now, don't tell me she couldn't buy us up a couple of times."

"My dear man, you're deceiving yourself if you think Aunty Micky's got any money to buy your place or anyone else's."

Martin scoffed: "She's just dirt mean."

"I won't argue with you but believe me there's very little money lying around unused over there."

"Then where's it gone?" Irritated by Martin's aggressive voice Ashley asked in return: "There never was any—and what made you think there was?"

Convinced by Ashley's tone, Martin changed his line of talk. "Well that's what I'd always thought."

"And it was quite wrong. There's nothing. Nothing."

"And nothing can shake him once he gets an idea in his head," Rohama commented. "Ever since Aunty Micky refused to go halves on installing the electricity he's believed she and Freddy were hiding their money in an old sock."

"You didn't ever say otherwise," Martin retorted. "And there's so much swank you'd think they had a fortune."

Ashley was irritated by Martin's truculent tone. "I've never seen any swank. Aunty Micky *isn't* a common or garden person and there's no point in asking her to be. She is as she is and that's it."

Then, the husband and wife asked, what did Ashley suggest they do?

"Go to her. Tell her your plans. Ask her if she'd like to discuss the future of your part of the estate and tell her that you need to have a fairly quick decision on it because of the new business or whatever you like. The main thing is to tell her and ask her advice. Don't try to do anything behind her back which would upset her in her present mood."

"We'd so much have preferred you to do it," Rohama said.

"For God's sake, Roma, why? It isn't a crime to want to leave, is it? Or to want to sell? You've got the right to do so but it must be done with the old lady's permission. It isn't treason to want to sell out."

"You suggested we should speak to Freddy?"

"On second thoughts I don't think that's so hot an idea. Go straight to Aunty Micky. Rohama, *you* can go. She likes you in spite of her funny ways. She'll be reasonable. I'm sure she'd want to help you."

The advice was difficult to follow and by the next Sunday when Patrick drove the family over to the Lewises Rohama and Martin had still not spoken to Mignon and she was still unaware of their plan.

She had accepted the Lewis invitation unwillingly but as soon as she reached the house was happy she had come. It was, of course, her first visit there and she was unprepared for its elegance and distinction, although, on second thoughts, it might really have been expected. Mrs. Lewis received them charmingly and then sat back in her chair as relaxed as Whistler's mother but more youthful, fresh-complexioned, still able to dimple when she smiled in a cosy, lady-detective-writer sort of way. She buttered up her guests with a leg of pork, stuffing, apple sauce, vegetables dripping in butter and followed this with a chocolate mousse which Freddy enjoyed so much that he had two helpings.

During the meal both Mignon and Nesta noted how Patrick, so unwilling a helper at home, seemed able and willing enough to wait at table and be generally helpful: serving the wine, restocking the bread-basket, fetching this and that. He was utterly at home and relaxed. After all, he was among the inheritance which he would come into after marriage. At first, he was nervous lest the meeting between his mother and Anne was not a success—he wanted both to like the other—but Anne easily charmed Nesta.

After the meal, Anne and Patrick went away to wash up and the three women and Freddy tried to sort out the doubts and hesitations surrounding the proposed marriage. The main difficulty was Patrick's joblessness. Nesta, playing the great lady, said it was against her instincts to approve a marriage when the husband had no career or prospects of a career. Mrs. Lewis, with her marmalade cat on her knees, felt this was unimportant at Patrick's age.

"I agree that a man's self-respect demands that he should have a career, that he cannot drift through a life and into marriage without one. On the other hand young people marry so early these days that it's not uncommon for them even to be university students together."

Was there a suggestion Patrick would go to a university? Freddy asked.

Mrs. Lewis smiled graciously. It depended on what he wanted to do. She dropped a hint—which was at once taken up—about the agricultural training college.

"Is this any more than a whim?" Nesta asked. "Those days picking potatoes seem to have given Patrick ideas."

They all laughed but Mrs. Lewis had the facts:

"Estate management is a good thing, you know. It might be possible for Patrick to be articled to a big firm of estate agents or he could learn the business at a college and get a diploma. Being articled at his age will mean he might get anything from £150 to £300—or just pocket money—but most people of any standards are prepared to accept some financial responsibility for their children until the middle twenties. It's a four-year course."

Nesta, bemused by all these figures, nodded. "Is it what Patrick wants?"

"He says he's very keen," Mrs. Lewis replied brightly.

Mignon smiled sourly. "My dear, you've been able to do things with him we've not been able to. If I were you—" she addressed her daughter—"I'd let Mrs. Lewis carry on with the good work."

"I shan't stop him doing anything he likes," Nesta said.

"When Patrick and Anne come in I'll tell them to fetch the prospectuses I sent for—you've got to keep these love birds on the ground—which set out the sort of things colleges can offer."

"Why he'd be able to get advice from Ashley," Freddy cried with his simple enthusiasm.

"He's supposed to be one of the richest men in Caerifor," Mrs. Lewis added. It was clear to her that Mignon and Nesta were astonished at the progress she had been able to make with Patrick and were both impressed and bewildered by her success.

"Look," she said, "Anne and I are going up to London for a couple of weeks to do our Christmas shopping. I suggest you let Patrick come with us and we'll get the best advice we can. We're cut off here. In London I've got all sorts of contacts who can advise him."

"It will be the making of him," Mignon said fervently. "It sounds a splendid idea."

Put in Mrs. Lewis's terms, the whole question of Patrick's future was resolved; or, at least, and this was equally important, resolvable.

By the end of the afternoon everyone felt happy about the wedding and it was decided to announce the engagement officially on Christmas Day. Mrs. Lewis was able to produce a workable sort of timetable for the young couple which left nothing for Mignon or Nesta to complain about.

Mrs. Lewis went further: if, she said, Patrick's father could not help him train at a school or college, Mrs. Lewis would lend money to tide the young couple over the difficult period of establishment.

Everybody understood that it would be a sophisticated *jeune ménage* with the bride going out shopping in her own Jaguar and the inherited items of two families assembled ready to be hived off into their new home, but there was hardly much point in living with a gas ring and a hired bed when neither family saw any reason to do so; and there was no need to. In a phrase, Patrick had fallen on his feet.

"How lucky for Patrick," Mignon said, as they unbuttoned at home, "that Anne's mother should be a woman in a thousand who is not only genuinely fond of him but believes in him enough to start him off in life."

"You surely don't grudge him his happiness, do you?"

"Oh, no, dearest, I merely marvel how some people get life served up to them on a plate and others have to huddle round the dust bins."

"Perhaps it's not accidental," Nesta snapped. "Some people are born expecting the worst and, of course, it always happens."

At that moment Nesta hated her mother. She appeared to her to be a woman who had always picked up life the wrong way and she was vexed because Mignon had not been particularly well-dressed for the visit.

"Why didn't you let me sew your dress? It looks bad and uncared for with a drooping hemline. An uneven hemline, run-down shoes and all that look positively shocking on an older person."

"Thank you," Mignon said. "Thank you, dearest, you always know how to raise my morale."

She took up her coat and went upstairs—it was already dark —and lay down on her bed, wrapped in her dressing-gown and covered by an eiderdown.

Those days Mignon grieved as though she had lost an only child, the star of her old age. In losing the battle to get her husband's papers published she had lost some of her trust in life, in people, in her own destiny, such as it was in the few years of life left to her. The small joys with which she and Freddy had made their lives pleasant before Edward's visit had lost their lustre, because dimmed by the prospect of far greater things. Worse than this was the accumulated experience of meeting Messrs. Milford and Cappland who had come, made her say and do things she had never said or even thought before, and had gone away leaving her cheapened and bought.

Never, since her teens, had she known such heartache, such grief mornings and evenings, such a continual pressure in the pit of the stomach. She could no longer imagine what it would be like to turn an untroubled eye on herself in the mirror, to get up without feeling old and ill in spirit, without loss of confidence and without despair, without aching in bone, muscle and nerve.

Sometimes, during those dark days there came mornings of an angelic softness when the bright day filling the windows towards ten and eleven o'clock suggested the spring, for just as long as the winter sun lit up the dark emerald fields and the flashes of water in the lanes. The brightness clouded towards noon and a muggy, murky afternoon ended the brief day, the first days in Advent.

With the night came the old regret, the old anxiety and she would slip out in the darkness in order to be by herself and away from the all-seeing eyes of her daughter and Freddy. She would go with her pocket lamp down the lane towards the road but instead of carrying on to the junction would stop at a wooden gate half-way down and look out over the fields.

The strange night-life of the open—some unidentified movement in the dry feg in the hedge, some unknown nightbird shrieking from the copse nearby and the strange movements of the low cloud moving out of the west created (paradoxically) a mood of stillness, if not of rest; but it was on one of these nocturnal excursions that she realised she was at the end of herself, at the brink of the place where she must disintegrate and finish; and when she realised this her longing to live, to succeed, to make something that would round off her life, rose in her like a shriek. Strange, unknown birds, flying over in the darkness, created the sound; and when she heard them she was aware of the silent lane, the empty fields and the alien movements in the damp darkness and her whole being longed to escape with the mysterious birds flying over.

To have debased herself and her family at the end of her long life and to have tried to turn the lives of all those who were most dear to her into a commodity was all that had resulted from her attempts to interest publishers in her hus-

270

band's papers. She knew, too, that to make these commodities more interesting to the buyers she had falsified values, suppressed facts and given prominence to others that had only a small part in the general picture. In trying to turn her own family and its traditions, such as they were, into marketable commodities she had fallen into the worst modern vice which, in a society of consumers, likes to put a price on everything; and, after all this specious selling, what would have been the result: £250? £500? Was this the total value of everything she, her father and her husband had stood for?

It was no comfort to say that it was what people expect: that this, in essence, is what the modern world is all about, for she herself was not of this world and to try to ingratiate its idols was to ask for disaster.

And how would she appear to the outside world? They would think of her as a gallant elderly person trying to exchange her values for the currency of the new world. They might even call her a game old thing refusing to be put down and almost succeeding where more skilful and more informed people had failed; after all, she had interested the publishers and the newspaper. Yet all those half lies, those careful exaggerations, that false family history weighed on her conscience and, like bunting put out for a visitor who never came, they had all fluttered down around the sober facts of the case.

It's a mistake, she thought, for elderly people to try to live in the present on its own terms since they can never be more than actors playing a part, nothing more than hams.

Regret savaged her face. Regret scratched even deeper the lines of old age and loneliness as, later, she sat in her broad-based, high-backed chair staring into the bedroom fire and thinking, "There isn't any sort of fool so pathetic as an old fool."

"But no, dearest," she said to Freddy who came up to see her, "I'm not worried about anything. Did I look worried?"

"You don't look yourself at all these days."

"I've been wishing I could have another inspiration about getting the diaries published. Once I'm dead, Nesta will have them all destroyed."

Freddy winced. He advised her not to think about the diaries.

"It's been such a disappointment. When it seemed we were so close to success. Such a disappointment."

Freddy might have said that he, too, had been disappointed over the publication of his poems, but he had purged the disappointment by speaking roughly to Cappland; he had relieved his feelings. His sister had no outlet.

Of course, they would go on living; somehow they would survive intact and once Patrick had left and Nesta returned home their lives would have their old pattern again. And they had this added interest in watching Mrs. Lewis facing up to the problem faced by a good many women with varying degrees of success: how to make an economically viable social being out of the penniless and undirected Patrick.

"Where is Nesta?" Mignon asked from the depths of her chair. Freddy thought she was writing to her husband.

"Hah! She's glad enough to get her precious Patrick off her hands."

Freddy tut-tutted. Why be so bitterly critical of Patrick and his mother? They were her only descendants.

"They've nothing of me in them," Mignon replied contemptuously. "No, dearest, they don't even look like anyone on *our* side."

"Do you know, I find the boy most engaging? We've nothing at all in common—he's what I call one of nature's technicians, always with his head in a car—but we can get on even though we neither of us know what to say to the other."

"I can't forgive Nesta. The way she worked against me over the diaries. She did nothing to help and all to hinder. Of course, she's glad I failed."

Freddy held back a moment doubtfully. Would his sister never forget her disappointment? Or would it remain in her memory for the rest of her life growing harder and harder to bear? He went away, only to return almost immediately. "Guess who's here to see you?" he asked brightly, with a suggestion of a rare treat in store. "It's Rohama and she wants to see you."

Rohama had never visited them on a Sunday evening before. "What can she want? Tell her I'll be down directly."

But by the time Mignon had rearranged her hair and clothing half an hour passed, long enough for Rohama, using the inspiration of the moment, to lay her business before Freddy and Nesta. More, she suggested that as Patrick seemed to want to farm his family might like to buy Rohama's land and house for him.

The idea that Patrick might farm his family's own estate had never seemed possible to anyone; but with Rohama clearing out, the possibilities were suddenly enormous and her suggestion seemed to Nesta and Freddy to be inspired. Nesta could hardly believe that at last a chance had come to get back the lost land and offer something practical and tangible towards her son's future good. Rohama's offer to sell seemed far more important than the news that she and Martin proposed to leave. Of course, the person whose opinion counted was Mignon. None foresaw that all she cared about was the fact that Rohama was going to leave her.

Mignon stood quite still. "Oh, dearest, you don't mean that? What will we do if you go? How are we going to go on without you?"

Rohama smiled uncomfortably, yet deeply moved by the old lady's genuine regret and dismay. "Why, as you did before we came, Aunty Micky."

"Oh, no, dearest. We can't go back again. Too many things have happened. Why, you're part of the family now. Oh, my dear—" and Mignon paused and with tears in her voice crossed the room to embrace Rohama—"You've been so much to us. Freddy and I couldn't bear to lose you. Could we, Freddy? When you get to our age you can't bear changes."

"Dear me," said Rohama, in her false-tough way. "You're making me all upset."

"But you've already upset us. How can you suggest these things to me so suddenly? You forget I'm an old woman and I have to think carefully. One idea at a time, if you please."

Mignon sat down. "Now tell me, dearest, have you had a very good offer from Cardiff?"

Rohama explained in as much detail as possible, Mignon nodding all the time in approval.

"And when will you go?" Mignon asked. It seemed a long time before she came round to the point which had seemed so important to the others. What would Rohama and Martin do with their place?

At this point, Nesta came in briskly. "That's what Rohama is concerned about. She thinks it would be a good idea if we took it over—bought it, of course."

"We need the money for the business," Rohama said apologetically.

"But I can't buy it, dearest. I've hardly got a bean!" Mignon let her carefully-guarded secret out of the bag with a gaiety that astonished everyone. "If I'd had any money I'd have had this house in better shape, believe me."

Nesta said her husband could probably lend the money for the purchase.

Mignon looked at her daughter coldly. "What for? He's not interested in the place. Never has been."

"But he would be if it helped us."

Mignon looked greatly put out. "No. That wouldn't be a good idea. Let's leave the matter to simmer for a couple of days."

Rohama said: "We thought that with the two places put together it would make a good holding for Patrick and Anne when they marry."

Patrick and Anne! The names exploded in Mignon's face like a bomb. "We've yet to see that Patrick really wants to farm," she replied. "No, I'm sorry. I don't think that's a good idea at all."

Impasse. Freddy and Nesta were embarrassed. Rohama was perplexed. She had come to think that nothing would have been more welcomed than the prospect of reuniting the divided estate. Mignon's behaviour proved quite otherwise. She had given the impression of caring nothing for the estate and everything for Rohama.

"The best thing," said Mignon, "would be to put the whole place up for sale and divide the money equitably." She said this as a final jab at her daughter who immediately said: "That I forbid! You have no right to."

Mignon said, "The property is mine while I'm alive and the other side is Rohama's. If we both agree on a plan of action no one can stop us. That's the law."

Rohama mumbled some remark about not wanting to agree to anything which would offend Nesta.

"It's nothing to do with her. It's nothing to her, either. We're

274

free to do as we like. So what I suggest we do is that we go down to Ashley Corbett and put the place in his hands. Any bank would advance you a couple of thousand on your future share of the sale—the whole place must be worth £15,000—"

"Never!" cried Nesta in a passion. "What are you talking about? This house needs at least £5,000 spent on it."

"£15,000," Mignon insisted more to infuriate her daughter than anything else—"which would be useful to both of us. Whatever happens, Roma, you tell Martin I'm more than glad to help you although for selfish reasons I want you to stay. Next week we'll go down together to see Ashley Corbett and we'll get what we can through him."

"Never!" Nesta cried again.

"It's nothing to do with you," Mignon cried and snapped her fingers under her daughter's nose. She had never been more dotty or self-willed.

15

THE THIRD SUITOR

THAT evening, after Rohama had gone home, Nesta and her mother continued, with all the bitterness of close relationship, the struggle begun while Rohama was present. Mignon lost Freddy's support (he found her behaviour odious) but was beyond shame. She had been pushed into a limbo of disappointment and rage and was out of control; she would do anything to upset her daughter and grandson.

That same evening it began to rain and by the morning the whole of Caeriforshire was again floodbound. Monday was an appalling day: the relentless downpouring turned the morning into evening and the midday into some special sort of twilight. According to the radio, the main line between Caerifor and Port Rydal was washed away by the river Maddau at a point about five miles away. The rain and darkness permeated the house and the people more or less sequestered there.

Patrick walked over to Anne's house and, as usual, stayed there for the rest of the day. Mignon, Nesta and Freddy stayed in the large sitting-room. They all wore dressing-gowns and whoever went to the windows and saw the rain shooting out of the drainpipes, over-brimming the ditches and endlessly dimpling the flood-waters, returned chastened to the fireside. The bedrooms had become cold boxes of air sent in from outside to be heated and the whole farmhouse seemed an indoor running track for draughts.

It was with the same cries of amazement with which the American Indians saw the European ships in full sail approaching their shores that Freddy saw a strange car driving towards the house, its wheels splashing up the flooded lane. They all came to watch and, as the car turned slowly in front of the house, Freddy recognised a Caerifor taximan. His passenger with an odd, brown, lined face, all anxiety, all seriousness, frantically rubbing at the steamed up window, was unknown.

Then, before anyone could retreat to take off the dressing-gowns, the man had jumped out of the taxi and was knocking at the door.

"I thought I'd need a boat," he said as he offered a cold, bony hand to Mignon, who was trying to relive some old pre-cognisance of such a scene—such a wild, wet day, so much cold, so much human warmth in the cold hand of the stranger and in his smile. Despite herself, in the very centre of her despair, something living stirred and from a position at the edge of waking, half-broken dream, she presented Robert Couzens to the family.

They brought him into the room but he said he would have preferred a private chat with Mignon.

"Is it so private? This is the only room where we can talk in comfort."

Mignon was still wide-eyed and vulnerable in the presence of this man who was old enough to be her son, perhaps, the kind of son she might have had in her pre-1914, Elgarian hey-days, the child born of her early enthusiasm and nobility, a couple of generations before, a world of manners and feeling ago.

The two others trooped off to the kitchen, leaving Mignon and the stranger alone.

"I won't keep you long for the sake of the driver—" He eased himself in his chair and took out a packet of cigarettes. "May I smoke? May I offer you one?"

Mignon was so flabbergasted she accepted.

"Now," he said, in his deep impressive voice that hardly ever left the key marked "Highly Confidential", and then only to modify to "subtly ironic" or "gently debunking", "Let me get out my introduction." He opened his small brief-case while Mignon waited—as though for a miracle. Later, she was to discover that he was a fifty-year-old divorcee, but at that moment she found his brown, lined, blue-eyed face, with its full lips and cropped hair, unplaceable. She believed in the eyes; she admired their brilliance and intelligence, the way they momentarily held hers before they turned away to look into the brief-case. The eyes held her, the deep confidential voice bound her, the sheer unplaceableness of the man kept her in suspense.

277

He took out a plastic bag holding a couple of dozen letters He handed them to her. "Let these be my introduction. I'm the buyer."

Couzens expected Mignon to see at once what sort of business was afoot and was puzzled, then shocked, to see that the letters meant nothing to her. She pressed one to her nose—she was still too vain to wear glasses—and only saw that it was addressed to their old Rutland Gate home. "You said you bought them?"

"Yes. They're the ones you recently sent up to Yoxalls."

"Yoxalls?" She was staring straight at him in the fullest incomprehension.

"Yes, Yoxalls of Brompton Road."

"No, sir. I've never sent any of my husband's old correspondence to be sold. I've never heard of Yoxalls."

"Yoxalls the booksellers and antiquarians. They used to be near the British Museum."

"The name means nothing to me."

"They specialise in autograph letters and what have you."

"I've never sent anything to them. These are my husband's letters. How they came to be at Yoxalls, I've no idea."

"You mean, Lady Benson-Williams, that you've never sold any of your husband's old papers?"

"Never. My husband's correspondence remains wrapped up in a cupboard across the hall."

"Well, I give up." He made an odd, swallowing motion, slightly over-dramatic. "This is very, very embarrassing for me. You see, Yoxalls said you'd recently sent a handful of letters up with a friend, acting on your behalf—"

Mignon shook her head. "There have been plans to publish my husband's diaries but there hasn't been any interest in his correspondence. I didn't ever imagine such things had any value."

"You know how much I paid for that little package? Sixty-eight pounds. Who passed them to Yoxalls?"

Mignon laughed. "Well, I would have done—if I'd known their value."

"They're letters from people like Churchill, Lloyd George, Ramsay MacDonald. They've a value for collectors."

"You're a collector yourself?"

"For other people. I'm an intermediary."

"A dealer?"

"Not exactly. I go scouting around for clients looking out for items of interest. The letters are intended for Matthiesen College in Pennsylvania which is building up a tremendous archive of twentieth-century manuscripts. They've got money to burn."

Mignon did not at first see the possibilities before her. "I don't suppose I'd ever have missed them, you know. There are so many wrapped up."

"I understand, then, that in the ordinary course of events you wouldn't have sold the letters."

"I would have done, I don't say otherwise, had I known they had such value." She stumbled forward towards the whole point of the visit: Couzens had come to see if there were any more items for sale.

Mignon rose with a radiant smile. She led him to the closet in the little room.

"Oh my goodness! All those!" Couzens cried in amazement.

Mignon had not endured the last few weeks for nothing.

"The complete, unedited Benson-Williams papers." She had lifted her right arm to complete the flourish in her voice.

"And they're for sale?"

"They belong to the world!"

"Then we must talk."

The dialogue flowed as in a play and Mignon was word perfect. She had promised herself this role a hundred times. At the same time, it was more than a play. It was an apotheosis: a triumphal *pas de deux*. He had stumbled on the lost treasure and the princess; she had found her prince. They revolved, they made gestures. Figuratively speaking, they held hands and twirled and when they bowed to one another—Couzens went out to pay off the driver—Mignon hurried forward like a nineteenth-century heroine in her long trailing dressing-gown into the kitchen, where the other two were distractedly talking.

She closed the door behind her—the massive eight-panelled door—and leaned against it with her hands still on the knob. "An American college is going to buy Arthur's papers!"

Nesta and Freddy jumped up crying "What!?" and Mignon

279

swanned forward swirling her shabby dressing-gown as in a pavane. "Yes and I'll get rid of them for dollars, my children." She held up a warning hand. "Don't let him hear you. He's settling the taximan; he's coming back."

Freddy was unable to grasp what had happened. What good, he asked, would dollars be? Mignon waved him aside.

"When I call, come in!" With a flourish of her skirts she was gone.

As soon as she'd gone Nesta began moving about aimlessly: "I'm sure it's untrue. It can't be right. Mother's counting her chicks again."

"But why does she want dollars?" asked Freddy, petulantly as though Mignon had had a choice of several currencies.

"Dollars can be changed," Nesta retorted.

"If it's true it's marvellous," Freddy replied.

How Nesta raged about her mother's stupidity, her gullibility, her foolish, unpractical hopes. "You've seen how she was after Cappland went away: sick headaches, nerves. She aged twenty years in a week—and now look at her. She never learns. She'll never learn."

Freddy defended his sister as though suddenly sure of what exactly stood between mother and daughter. "Your mother rises above things and you can't forgive her for this. She can forget the past, forgive everything and go on. Your mother's a closed book to you, isn't she? You cannot understand how she can be so effortlessly generous about the past? Ah, yes, I've watched you. I've watched you when your mother's been working—trimming a tart or preparing a meal and completely absorbed in her task—and I've noticed the way you look at her, partly envious, partly irritated, partly—I can't say what! You can't forgive her because, while you are obsessed with the past, she's free, she's moved on to newer things. Your mother is a free woman in every sense and you won't recognise the greatness of this."

Nesta made a gesture of impatience.

"You know, my girl, that although your mother is not a religious person she has more real faith in her little finger than you have in the whole of your body. She knows the pure in heart get their consolations and the wicked get their just rewards."

Nesta glowered. "I'd like to think so."

"You think you'd benefit?" The violence of his question made Freddy cough and cough as though he had swallowed a horsehair sofa. "Because if you do you're wrong!"

Exhausted by his coughing Freddy sat down at the side of the table and blew his nose. "You find an excuse to criticise your mother whenever you can but it's yourself who stands condemned and it's time you knew it. Everything is carp, carp, carp: the worst fault in a human being. In your own way you're damned from your own mouth. Instead of always finding fault with your mother ask yourself the simple question, 'What have I done with my own life that gives me the right to stand in judgement?' When you can answer that to your own satisfaction we'll be getting somewhere."

"I never pretend I've achieved very much," Nesta replied. "I hate myself and my life. It makes me angry—with myself, with everyone—that despite the fact that one goes away thousands of miles—a completely different life, different interests, new friends, everything changed—a couple of weeks here and the old life moves in. Perhaps Mother's one of those lucky people who don't feel anything deeply. It's the best way, perhaps, an excellent method of self-defence. And now for weeks we've heard nothing but the diaries. To add to this we now have the sale of the house. Isn't anything worth saving? No dignity. No sense of pride." Nesta looked at Freddy directly: "Do you think I'm happy about all this? Do you?"

"Of course you're not," Freddy replied. "But is anybody? You have to build on the mistakes of the past and go on."

"Well, I'm not that saintly or strong. It just presses me down." And almost as though she were speaking to herself she asked, "What can I do? What can I do?"

Nesta was still flushed with anger as she and Freddy went into the big sitting-room to talk to Couzens. She listened sceptically as her mother explained what Couzens's visit was all about. She was excited and got her facts back to front so Couzens asked if he might explain. Glancing from one to the other he sketched in briefly the plight of American historical research students with little or no material to work on.

"Of course, it's not as bad as all that. But it is one of the problems of our colleges to find suitable material which can

281

give students the real feeling and appreciation of the past. Great work has been done already and so far as availability and presentation are concerned our top colleges are probably better than any others in the world. They're always on the lookout for material as it becomes available and that's where I come in. I'm on a watching brief for Matthiesen University and as soon as I get back to town I'll be introducing them to Lady Benson-Williams and I'll be 100 per cent sure that you're made for one another. You've got the papers and the documents they need—the ore, if you like, to make the steel—and they've got the students and the money. I suppose you're asking, 'Will it be much?' That's difficult to say at the moment but assuming the collection is as good as I think it is, the lowest figure the college would offer would be fifteen thousand dollars. It may go up as high as twenty-five."

Everyone gasped, even Mignon who had not dared to ask a price. "And in pounds?"

"About five thousand at a rough guess, as a minimum."

They looked at Couzens with satisfaction and awe. He tried to appear casual although he knew the impression he was creating. "Yes," he said, "people like being brought into touch with the right people. That's my justification." He looked at them sideways. "Now wouldn't you call that a vocation?"

"Call it what you like," Mignon said, "I'm delighted that you've come. You've solved everything." Even had he not been waving a bundle of money at them they would have been taken by his manner. It was of an unaccustomed warmth but dry, ironic, as though he were aware of his own limitations and quite prepared, even, for people to find him absurd. So far as Mignon was concerned he convinced by his presence. He offered no credentials but his handshake, yet her instincts accepted him. And after the horrors of Milford and Cappland, their rudeness and untrustworthiness, it was a moral windfall to be treated with respect by a man who was dangling such a prize before them. She could hardly believe that talking to Couzens was so simple; he seemed to encourage truthfulness; she would be able to tell such a person everything. And more: here was this rich, globe-trotting man, this amiable, cosmopolitan student of life, treating them as equals, as people of worth. A real man, Mignon said to herself, a real gentleman, and a democrat who no more knew how to be impressed by blood and social trappings than he knew how to disdain humble origins.

"Now we're all together, let's have something to drink. Let me fetch it while you tell Freddy and Nesta about Yoxalls and the letters."

Mignon hurried into the kitchen and went down on her knees before the cupboard where she kept the whisky and brandy against dark days. She found the bottles but when she came to rise she could not get up and she leaned her head against her arm which gripped the door of the cupboard, as though in prayer. In a sense it was prayer; her whole body trembled with gratitude with its 'Thank you' to whatever forces had shaped her life and brought her to that moment of consummation. People clambering ashore after shipwrecks, people reuniting after a long bombardment, lovers rediscovering one another in spite of lost addresses, tremble with such thankfulness and joy; but only the very old find they cannot rise to their feet and realise that this moment has come just before the final curtain like the end of a tremendous play.

All that autumn, ever since her nephew called, Mignon had been haunted by a vision of hard cash. She had been able to visualize a hundred pounds, but talk of thousands of dollars almost unnerved her. She seemed, in her soul, to be smiling at Mr. Couzens and he, in his youthfully fiftyish way, was smiling back at her and they seemed unable to break the beaming smiles which bound them soul to soul. They liberated one another with difficulty.

Back in the room with the others she found that Nesta had been to the closet where the diaries were kept and had found a bundle recently opened and despoiled. "It was Jack Cappland who took the letters," Nesta said.

"I remember him being in the room with the key turned," Freddy added. "He told me he'd looked in one of the bundles."

"He helped himself," Nesta said calmly. "That's quite clear. He's probably got some more, too. It's clear as daylight. Milford would never have done such a thing. He was far too green."

"Too High Church," Mignon said handing the bottles to Freddy and laughing almost sexily at Couzens. She could hardly care less about Cappland's activities. He, unwittingly, had introduced the papers to Couzens.

"It's serious, Mother," Nesta exclaimed. "He may have taken all the best things in the collection."

Couzens was diffident, ill at ease. "Could I intervene here? I think this is all the man took (assuming he took them) because I've recently made a tour of all the main dealers and there wasn't anything more from this source. And I don't think he'd hold on to anything. People who help themselves don't usually hold on to things."

"He was such a rotter! An absolute rotter—one of the new kind they breed in Welfare State Britain now. Someone who'd pulled himself up from the depths."

"For God's sake, dearest, he wasn't as bad as all that, was he?"

Mignon knew that Nesta was channelling her rage into this denunciation of Cappland and waited for her to finish. They ought to tell the police! It was a disgrace that the *Sunday Age* didn't know and that it allowed such people to work for it!

"Everything you say may be right, dearest, and we can clear everything up in good time, but I still think that this should be a double toast: to the conclusion of a sale agreeable to both sides and to Jack Cappland who brought us all together!"

"Ah, no. Not him. Never," cried Nesta.

"But, dearest—" here Mignon twirled her glass—"you're being unreasonable. He did a wicked thing but it was a good turn for us."

"Quiet, please," said Freddy. "We drink to the author of the diaries—my brother-in-law—and then we drink to whoever it was who stole his correspondence."

"To Sir Arthur," said Couzens piously.

They all drank.

"To the inspired thief," said Couzens with a twinkle.

They laughed and drank.

"To us all."

"Yes," cried Mignon. "Good health and Prosperity and Long Live America."

"You must come over to see us," Couzens said promptly. "The university would probably want you to tape record reminiscences of Sir Arthur."

"Me?" cried Mignon. "Me tape-recording in America?"

"Why not?"

"And why not?" Freddy shouted—the excitement and whisky had gone to his weakest point.

Mignon's laughter was cut short by Freddy who said they ought to send a little whisky to Mr. Jack. "He was God's instrument in helping us," he said earnestly.

"Oh, Freddy *fach*, what rubbish," said Nesta, and added under her breath, "You get sillier every moment."

"Don't worry, I'll find a nice way of thanking him," Mignon said regally. "Christmas is coming and I'll send him a little Christmas box, in a plain white envelope as one does for the coalman and the postman."

Couzens swallowed his whisky the wrong way and moved about the room spluttering. "You're going to be a wow if you come to lecture in the States."

Carried away by her own success, Mignon added, "Yes, and I've decided to sell up here, so I'll probably emigrate." Freddy tittered uncertainly and it was left to Couzens to cry, "That's the spirit. Perhaps you'll all come if there's just the three of you."

"I can't," Nesta said stuffily, as though the emigration plan was a serious one. "I've got a husband in Rhodesia, and a son who's here with me."

"Yes," said Mignon, "he's going to marry to get out of going to university." Nesta, in the same stuffy voice, said this was not the entire truth.

Couzens was ready to confess to any academic inadequacies people cared to mention. "I spent years doing things of no value at all. Not at all. I woke up to the facts of life when I was in Paris and turned to vino and misspent afternoons."

"Ah," Mignon said archly, "I can see your misspent youth gives you some delightful souvenirs."

"Souvenirs is the word, Lady Benson-Williams. The mood of the streets, the sudden recollections of certain rooms and gardens; those are very potent and satisfying."

The reflective, amused light remained in his face as he stared at the fire, rather as the strings of a guitar continue to vibrate until the hand of the player comes down flat across them. Mr. Couzens sipped from his glass.

285

There remained, of course, a great deal to be done to tie up the deal. They had to arrange for Couzens to see the diaries and letters the next day and Mignon, who did not doubt but that this time Couzens was the *deus ex machina*, rang up Patrick to ask him to take Couzens back to his Caerifor hotel.

"And we'll fetch you in the morning," she said grandly. "My grandson's fiancée has a Jag, you know."

"My kind of car," said Couzens and accepted an invitation to stay for a meal.

"You do a lot of buying?" Freddy asked.

Couzens nodded, smiled. "Queer business this buying and selling. The last few weeks I've been round the London auctions buying for a private collector in California."

And what, they asked, had he bought? He reeled off a few titles of things he'd acquired for the collector. Did he never buy things for himself?

"My own collection is of signed editions but I never buy just for the sake of it. If the prices go too high I don't bother. For instance, at the last sale I went to at Christies there was No. 11 of the limited edition of 1,000 copies of *Ulysses* which James Joyce signed himself in 1922. That fetched £320 which was more than I wanted to give. At the same sale, they sold a copy of Lawrence of Arabia's translation of the *Odyssey* which didn't attract me at all and which eventually fetched £120 because a letter from Lawrence was included with the volume. You never can tell what a thing will fetch."

"Everything's got a price today," Mignon said but no longer grudgingly because she was about to profit from the century's materialism and appeared to enjoy being corrupted.

"True enough," Couzens said. "This business of buying and selling goes to the heart of the human being: his longing to settle certain values on things—whether ideas or causes or objects. Certain things such as gold, land, property retain a certain fixed value but there's the enormous hinterland behind these three mountains where everything is more or less fluid and here society itself fixes the values and suffers for them. And these values are continually changing and the objects to which they apply change, too. The most perfectly assimilable examples are household goods and painting. Now, we all know how London dealers have been trying to build up a real market for Victorian junk, largely because there were large amounts available and they'd been buying it up—cheap. So what happens? They start a slow campaign to persuade people that Victorian painting had a certain charm—what will happen with these diaries is the same. I begin from the simple premise: they exist. There, in the closet, is the work of a lifetime but henceforward they have the value which *we* and we alone give to them. Matthiesen University will edit these papers probably and they will arrive here in a beautiful edition with notes and they'll be reviewed and the learned reviews will assess them as scholarly works and eventually students studying that period will just *have* to know the Benson-Williams papers. You see how it is? Everything has been justified."

"But so many politicians write their diaries and memoirs," Nesta said. "I thought they were too numerous to have any value."

Couzens looked unimpressed. "Politicians usually write bad books because they're trying to justify themselves. The political diarist is far more reliable."

"Well that's what my husband was," Mignon said proudly at last discovering Sir Arthur's true category.

"And I hope he's good. The true political diarist is a man near enough to the centre of things to see what is going on and who writes it down at once and fights the temptation to alter much afterwards. He knows he can't always be right or always seize the significant thing."

"How I agree," the widow said piously.

"Curiously enough, although this is a political age we haven't thrown up many political diarists. There was Dr. Thomas Jones, but he seems to have limited himself deliberately in his contacts. Then there was the Clerk to the Privy Council, Sir Almeric Fitzroy. He knew how to record events accurately and perceptively. Sometimes he can be vivid."

"I met him," Mignon put in.

"Then Lord Esher comes to mind. A conceited man and not really reliable despite a wealth of detail."

"What about Beatrice Webb?" Mignon asked.

"Beatrice Webb? Of course, in a class apart. In most ways."

Couzens must have enjoyed his visit because it was well after seven o'clock before Patrick took him down to Caerifor in Anne's car.

"Your grandmother," he said, "is one of the natural actresses of all time. What a character! You must be all very, very proud of her."

"We get on well," Patrick replied. "She's most up-to-date for her age, isn't she?"

"She's just great," Couzens said. "It's been a pleasure meeting with her."

Couzens had left behind a Mignon stirred and grateful. "There's nothing to say is there?" she said to Freddy. "He's just a perfect gentleman. This is how I imagined the whole transaction would be: a gentlemanly transaction—not a battle with the callow odds and ends of the West End!"

The next morning, without affectation, but with the instinctive affection of an old servant or dog, she took up her place in the sunlit window and waited for Patrick to bring back Couzens from Caerifor.

"There they are!" she cried and ran back into the kitchen to make fresh coffee so that Mr. Couzens could sit back and relax as soon as he stepped into the house. Not for years had she felt so young and so stirred as a woman; and she looked fresh, energetic, although she'd been up since seven o'clock lighting fires and tidying the little sitting-room where Couzens was to examine what he called 'the Benson-Williams archive'.

She helped him unpack the bundles wrapped away years before in exasperation and innocence. She had had no idea there were so many letters from famous people.

What he next wanted was a couple of hours with Mignon so that she could give him as much personal background as she could for his report to Matthiesen. So, that afternoon, he and Mignon shut themselves in the little sitting-room with a table between them and Couzens took down her notes on a bulky Oxford pad.

"Let me go back to the beginning, dearest, so that you get everything in perspective. It won't matter if you hear things you've heard before so long as you get the whole thing in perspective."

He nodded and lit a cigar.

"The story began last summer when my nephew, Professor

288

Lloyd-Ballantyne, the historian," Mignon began and went through the recital of events for the hundredth time. This time the recital seemed to her to be definitive, the last word, the coda and recapitulation.

"You see, I think Edward originally started the whole thing because he wanted to appear interesting to his new wife. The diaries provided something different to talk about—a sort of status symbol which his wife would appreciate. He certainly kept his promise to us. He told Heinz and Heinz sent this callow young man down who pretended all the time—you could see it—that he was living in some sort of *Château*. It was quite absurd. Then he had too narrow an approach to the diaries. I don't think he knew anything at all about the period. There were all sorts of gaps which showed that he was saying 'Rhubarb' half the time. A charming boy, in the rather girlish way so many undergraduates affect now: the long hair, the languorous eyes, the full, brooding mouth and the heavy glasses worn for effect. Eventually, my grandson, who's a casual, arrogant boy, put the young thing's back up and he went away with a low opinion of us, but not before he'd spent some days in bed reading a mountain of books he'd brought down with him as though it had been a rest cure. Priceless, dearest. Priceless."

"He must have been very stupid, your young historian."

"He was High Church and High Tory and the tenor of the diaries offended him, too. What did he expect? This house was one of the cradles of radicalism as we knew it in the 1880s."

"And the journalist?"

"The one who must have sold the letters? An amusing, witty man, full of good stories. Quick on the uptake, adaptable, on the lookout for the quick buck, as they say. He read the diaries in his own way. Undoubtedly he was looking for smut and sensation and soon lost interest when he didn't find it in the quantities or quality he desired. He and my grandson went out one evening and met a relation of ours and as far as I can make out Cappland was smitten. No one says anything, of course, in this part of the world; no one breathes a word—we're all very deep—and Rohama has never said a word to me. I don't know what he was after. It was most mysterious. He promised all sorts of things—the cruellest thing was to tell my

289

brother—who's the most unworldly person—that he would get his poems published for him and then completely let him down. And in such a sneering, contemptible way. Just like that!

"A most child-like and unworldly man," Mignon said, "the dearest person and the last one to see through such an unscrupulous fraud. But he was able to turn the tables on Mr. Jack completely."

While Mignon was talking, Couzens's mind wandered and he began to wonder about the ages of the people in the house. Mignon's remarks about the 1880s had been said with the same sort of certainty as one has saying 'yesterday' or the 'day before yesterday'. If, he was thinking, as he had seen on a document among the Benson-Williams papers, Mignon and Sir Arthur had married in 1911 she must then have been in her late twenties and the champagne-coloured-haired daughter with the marvellous, tragic eyes was in her early forties although she looked so much younger. Sir Arthur must have been several years older than his wife.

Couzens found the old woman fascinating. He especially liked her voice, which had the richness of texture and the simple eloquence of someone who might have had a position of authority in a small European court before the 1914 war. He appreciated Mignon's feeling for the balance and the beginning and end of a sentence—the carefully placed modulations and accents, the almost faultless sense of timing and effect; and all perfectly unconscious because the accents and modulations of a vanished private world that had been utterly sure of its values and intentions.

The house, the spirit of the house, had once been sure of its values and its purpose, too. It was a museum of those heavy, massive realities,—ponderous, often clumsy, but central (Couzens thought) in the British tradition,—that were out of favour at that time. The heavy earnestness, the prickly social conscience, were part of a long, sober tradition that often went with a provincial eccentricity and fervour. Bunyan, Ruskin, Beatrice Webb and Vaughan Williams seemed names in this wide tradition that had come to an end in the trivialities of the mid-century. This was the household where the social conscience of an age had been nourished. The survivors of that age, like disarmed giants, endured as best they could.

"You had two remarkable men in your life: your father and your husband. Can you tell me, Lady Benson-Williams, which of the two was the greater?"

"My father," Mignon said promptly.

"May I ask why?"

Mignon considered a moment. In the end she merely said, "Innocence. His innocence was so much greater."

"A strange choice of word for a man of the world."

"He was *never* a man of the world," Mignon said. "He never really saw the world as it was because he saw it through the filter of his own ideals. That's why my father was innocent; he only saw things as they ought to be or might be if people would only try hard enough. My husband was the second generation. The ideals had burned low; he was in the real world and saw people as they were and he wanted things my father never dreamed of. He liked power for its own sake; he liked intrigue for its own sake. My father could never have written those diaries; he would, in the old Edwardian phrase, have thought them 'not quite nice'. That was Arthur's world. But, we mustn't underestimate him or his achievements.

"My husband," said Mignon, "was born without inherited privilege of any kind except a splendid physique and good health. His family were small farmers—good, honest, even dull people. He had a remarkable mother who wanted her child to have a chance, at least, to have a different kind of life. He went to a local school, of a kind you no longer find, where all sorts of odd things were taught—more or less according to the personal tastes of the headmaster, including Latin and Greek. It was intended, originally, that he should go in for the Church; but, after winning one of the first scholarships to the University College of Wales, it became clear that the Church was not to his liking so the Professor of Classics advised him to go on to Oxford. He obtained another scholarship and did brilliantly. Then my father advised him to go into the Civil Service. In those days, the examinations lasted fourteen days and the candidates were the best brains and talents available. He got through and started in 1911, joining the Cabinet secretariat after it was formed by Lloyd George. He stayed there until he retired."

"He never wanted to do anything else?"

"Never. In fact, he had something against most other professions. Medicine he utterly despised; certain aspects of advocacy seemed to him contrary to the public good; and journalism depressed him. Architecture was the only thing he might have attempted. Later in life, he thought the fire had gone out of public service and said people were distracted by the rewards of private practice. That was the reason why he wanted to write a book about the Civil Service."

"He must have had interesting recollections of the people he met."

"True. Promotion gave us entry into interesting circles far outside the Civil Service. London was much more closely knit than now and you could meet everyone you wanted to in about six months, once you'd got the Open Sesame. There was more time for dinner parties, visiting, enjoying one another's children, sharing one another's triumphs. London life now is far more diffuse."

Couzens turned a page of his Oxford pad. "And your brother?"

Mignon explained that as a young person Freddy was considered something of an invalid and not expected to live. He went into the Church and found everything he wanted there—and in his writings.

"I wish you could get to know him. He's the only person who loves me unjudgingly; and just lately, with all this terrible worry and uncertainty, I came to realise what this loyalty means to me. Do you know, whenever I do anything wrong, or I do something he thinks unworthy, Freddy grieves over me as over a child of promise that is going astray. It's very, very touching. It's a trust and affection that never asks the price." Mignon's eyes were bright with feeling; her lip trembled a little. "It means everything to me."

*　　*　　*　　*

Couzens returned the next day with a draft of his report for Mignon to read: it was the family background needed to put the papers into perspective for the university's advanced studies board. She read it quietly and then objected to one phrase ... "and during the period since his death these papers have been guarded by his wife, whose love and faith in her husband never faltered."

Couzens was surprised. "Isn't it true?"

"It's more complex." She thought a while. "I think you ought to know the real relationship between us. It all goes back to a question of upbringing. In my young days mothers used to advise their daughters on their wedding night to lie still and think of the British Empire. I never surmounted my early formation and so never found the physical side of marriage anything but distasteful. I spent all my early married life wondering how it was possible for lovers—you know the famous ones in literature—to throw everything aside for the pleasures of being in one another's arms. I never knew physical pleasure."

Couzens drew in his breath.

"That startles you, dearest, to hear a woman of my age say such things. Well, this is something it's taken my long life to say."

She then went on to describe her husband's irritation. "At first he was patient and understanding but, gradually, I could feel an almost perpetual wall of irritation and exasperation between us. Eventually, about four years after Nesta's birth, all our relations stopped. It was a great relief. I felt I'd been released from an onerous duty. It's true. Those were my feelings. And it was years later that I realised what it cost my husband for—" and she leaned closer to Couzens—"he needed women almost to the end of his life. I didn't know it was so terrible to see this desire in old men. Wait a while. When my husband was in his fifties, the time you would have thought he could well discount all these things, he met a woman called Mrs. Benjamin on the train from Port Rydal. For years he kept her in a little flat in London and I knew nothing about it except later when he died and there was no money. They had a child. She lives just a stone's throw away now. He left her half of my father's old estate."

Couzens drew in his breath again. "But how did he get it?"

She waved the question away. "That's not important. It was an arrangement over the mortgage. Well, one day, in the middle of the winter, this woman, such a homely, simple person, came down here and told me everything."

"God in heaven!"

"Yes, she came because she'd had a quarrel with Arthur and this was her revenge. I said to her when I'd got my breath back, 'What do you want me to do?' And she said, 'You can't do nothing.' Just that. 'You can't do nothing.' She was a simple woman, who couldn't write a grammatical letter to save her life, but she gave Arthur this baby. And animal warmth. And now that both girls are grown up I see the difference in them. My own daughter is the child of duty; Rohama is the child of physical adoration. See them together and you know which is which at once. And when I see it I'm ashamed. Ashamed. I think that's why I dislike my daughter so much. And, poor thing, she can't help it. It's not her fault is it? She didn't ask to be born.

"Well, what happened to Mrs. Benjamin? I wrote to Arthur to ask him if he wanted me to divorce him and he said the decision was really mine. If his own opinion could influence my choice it was this: that even if he were free he wouldn't want to marry Mrs. Benjamin. You see, Mr. Couzens, the physical adoration had begun to pall—he was getting older, of course, and there was nothing he could do with a person like Mrs. Benjamin, who played a very Victorian role in the whole story, I can tell you. At the time, all this was a great humiliation but, in some way, I was pleased. I thought, 'Well, he's had the physical life he wanted.' And then when I saw how Mrs. Benjamin had betrayed *him* I joined ranks with him against her. We discussed the matter as though it had been a disappointment that had fallen to us both. Does that surprise you? Then you know nothing about married couples, I assure you. Mrs. Benjamin lived on; we continued to pay her money and she eventually went somewhere near Port Rydal as housekeeper to a farmer and took Rohama with her. Years passed. We didn't hear from her at all. Then, she heard that my husband was ill and she had a sudden longing to see him. So she wrote to my niece in Caerifor, the wife of an estate agent, and asked *her* whether she could arrange a meeting. Would you believe it, my niece brought her up here!" Mignon raised her hands to the sky. "Can you imagine anything more absurd? Fortunately, in some ways, I wasn't in. Nesta, who had not then married, was here, helping to nurse her father. She went

294

to the door and saw her cousin Muvvy with Mrs. Benjamin. She said, 'What do you want?' Muvvy said, 'Mrs. Benjamin heard Uncle Arthur was very ill and wants to see him.' Nesta says she brought some flowers and grapes in a basket. Nesta began to shout, 'Go away! Go away! Haven't you brought us enough unhappiness? How dare you poke your nose in here where you aren't wanted?' There was a scene on the doorstep and Mrs. Benjamin began crying and begging Nesta to be allowed to see her father. Nesta slammed the door. And when she turned back into the house there, at the top of the stairs, was her father. 'Why don't you let her in?' he asked. 'Call her back.'

" 'I won't,' Nesta said. 'I won't ever let such a woman into this place.'

" 'I tell you to let her in!'

" 'I won't.'

"And the silly man—he was within weeks of his death—tried to come down the stairs to open the door; so Nesta, right in front of him, turned the key in the lock and ran away into the back of the house. When I got home poor Arthur was sitting on a chair by the side of the bed, crying. He said, 'You've forgiven us; why can't she?' Poor pathetic old man whimpering. So I went down to Nesta and said, 'Why didn't you let Mrs. Benjamin come indoors? There's nothing left now.' "

"You did?"

"Of course. What was there left to be spiteful about? The woman had given him something I had never given. Nesta always holds this against me. The fact that I don't feel any anger or pain seems to goad her beyond belief. I don't think she ever recovered some inner balance from that morning when Mrs. Benjamin turned up and she locked the door to prevent her father going out to her."

"Well, there isn't anything I can usefully say," Couzens said.

"I don't expect you to, dearest, but don't romanticise us. That's all. Like every family we've got our griefs and they don't always get lighter with keeping. The consequences of Arthur's actions are with us to this day and this is just the period where I may be able to throw the whole thing off. Rohama wants to leave and so do I. For years I've dreamed of setting off on a new life and this is my chance."

"Where would you go?" Couzens asked.

Mignon sighed; it seemed the mere effort of thinking about an alternative was too much for her. "There are lots of things Freddy and I can do. We might buy ourselves a little house in Caerifor. It would suit us very well."

Wasn't there a possibility, he asked, that her grandson, once married, would want to farm the place; and if Rohama wanted to give up her half of the estate the whole thing would then return to the original line, as it were. Mignon shook her head in a guilty way.

"I've got to be honest with you: I can't bear Patrick. And the way he's engineering his way into the lives of those two women makes me ill."

"Surely that's not justified? They're very, very happy. That young woman is head over heels in love with the boy. When so much has happened that you've been able to forgive why do you grudge them their happiness?"

"It's not that at all. It's just that I think Patrick is a calculating and idle person. He won't do anything if he can find someone to do it for him."

"Then what can you say if the women are delighted that he's letting them do everything for him? I think you've found the ideal solution."

Unable to answer this logic Mignon fell back to shaking her head.

"You wait a while," he said. "You may come to think that their marriage was the best stroke of genius of the lot."

That day a great many things became public property: the Lewises heard from Patrick that an American university was to buy his grandfather's papers for a price yet to be finally settled; it became general knowledge that Mignon wanted to sell her half of Swanquarter at the same time as Rohama sold hers and it was even rumoured, without any basis, that Ashley Corbett was going to handle the sale.

Freddy told his friends at the Caerifor newspaper office about the diaries and the next morning Mignon received a visit from the paper's chief reporter, who told her he intended to send the story to the nationals as if, Mignon said later, "this was my apotheosis".

He was tall, intense, clear-skinned, young; a person who,

according to Freddy, might have made a name for himself as a poet if he had not gone in for writing scripts for the radio. Freddy used the word 'scripts' as though it were synonymous with rubbish.

"You must be ver-ry pr-roud," the young man said with a slight stammer on the 'r' sound. Mignon looked carefully at her hands. "When you get to my age you don't feel things quite as sharply—" then Mignon stopped; that wasn't true— "Of course, it means a tremendous lot to me and my brother. It means that all these documents will be studied carefully, properly edited and annotated and given to the world for the benefit of future historians."

"That's a kind of im-im-mortality," the man said. His eyes shone with pleasure for them all. "You'll always be on the map."

"I'd never thought of that," Mignon said, greatly surprised that such a young person should have such an idea.

"Of course, your father will always be remembered. What he did for the ordinary people was probably greater than anything your husband did, despite his eminence."

This compliment to her father touched Mignon to the bone.

"You've no idea how it pleases me to hear a person of your generation say that. Sometimes you feel these things get forgotten and you wonder whether people don't give their lives for a dream."

"I don't think so," the reporter said. "Where would we be today without such people? Somebody's got to blaze the trail."

"Memories are so short. People can't go on being grateful all the time. It's only natural, don't you feel?"

"You mean that social reformers must always be at a disadvantage because once the evils they set about eradicating are removed everyone forgets all about them."

"That's not really true, is it? On the other hand, was my father a reformer, purely and simply? I never thought of him as such. I used to think of him as a born leader of the ordinary people. He was one himself; he knew what ordinary people felt and did; he never left them. He was the perfect embodiment of the man of the people who gave back to the people their faith and belief in themselves. He was a very pure-hearted man, extremely simple-hearted in his enthusiasms and devotions. I can assure you that none of his children have quite that single-mindedness. We've temporised; we've compromised in numerous ways; we've lost that single-mindedness; our minds are ragbags of projects which never come to anything; we never see anything through wholeheartedly, partly because we're so dispersed, so shredded up into pieces by the pressures of modern life. The Giants died with my father's generation; the great, single-minded people with the courage of lions and the innocence of children. We're nothing. They seem legendary to us, I suppose, because of this purity of spirit..."

He was taking down notes as fast as he could write.

"Of course. What counts after all in life but dedication and single-mindedness, the divine simplicity which doesn't admit the possibility even of defeat. My father's generation saw things as clearly as children: there were two worlds, the rich and the poor, the haves and the have nots, the people who did nothing and drew the rents, the poor devils who worked all the hours God sent and got nothing. It was unethical, un-Christian; man had created the situation and man could cure it; and man, to a certain extent, has done so. Do you agree?"

"Entirely."

"There are abuses, of course, there are pockets of poverty and darkness; there always will be, presumably; but compared with the social realities of even my childhood these are the days of the gods, if people would only realise it. The human race in these western islands has never been so free from fear of hunger, fear of the powerful, fear of the end of plenty. If they have other fears, unknown in my time, these are the products of man's own inventiveness not his deficiencies. In some ways, the greatest period of peace and plenty the world has ever known is just beginning."

Epilogue

RECONCILIATION

ONCE the agreement was signed with the university, Mignon had to wait a little longer for the money and still longer for the university to arrange for the shipping to America of what was now known as 'The Benson-Williams Archive'. But the task was over.

Freddy and Mignon shared their triumph and bewilderment. Triumph, because the sale had been brought off, the money received; bewilderment because people's reactions were so odd. Nesta never once said she was glad. Edward never wrote; nor was there a word from Sir Ragismund Heinz or Charles Milford. Even people they had known all their lives seemed to regard the whole thing as a disgusting piece of trickery on Mignon's part—as though she had counterfeited the papers and the publicity which came after the sale. How few people could accept other people's success. The only ones who rejoiced wholeheartedly with them were Ashley and Rohama; while Mrs. Lewis sent a most friendly note over with Patrick.

At this point the curtains came down on the absurd epic of one of the last survivors of the great British Liberal tradition in her efforts to turn herself and her family into marketable objects for the consumer society of the 1960s. In a strange mid-century world, where almost every institution holds a decayed interior, Mignon was able to vindicate herself and her family.

It was remarkable that she had succeeded, for, in this society, with rare exceptions, autobiographies as an account of spiritual and moral progress are out of fashion: the genre has been discarded. The new society calls for life stories in the same way as it calls for chocolates or cigarettes or whisky, as matters for titillation—and Sir Arthur's unfinished work hardly came into this category. Mignon's main interest, once the sale had been satisfactorily arranged, was to help Rohama and Martin find the money to make their new start in Cardiff. Her first notion of selling the estate as one unit became less interesting as soon as she realised that it would involve looking for a new home. Even spiting her daughter could not justify the bother of removal elsewhere. Mignon and Freddy were too old to make radical changes, and to have sold the place at the moment when the Archive was being transported from one continent to the next, like some sacred ark, would have been a violation of sentiments. With a realist's cold, double values, Mignon knew that her duty in the few years left to her were to tend the Sacred Flame even though her eyes glittered cynically.

She enjoyed her power over her family. She liked keeping them on their toes and for days refused to say what she had in mind. She enjoyed the pleasures of being able to stay put while everyone else revolved around *her*.

Nesta and Patrick, between themselves, wondered if the old lady was going dotty and it was left to Mrs. Lewis to make a sensible approach to Freddy about the matter. She had told Rohama she was willing to buy her share of the farm for Patrick and Anne at a generous price. Mignon said she would buy Rohama out herself but was delaying because she thought this the moment to put the whole place up for sale. Back, as they say, to Square One, with Mignon saying she saw no reason why she should put herself out to help Patrick.

Then Freddy pointed out that the person who suffered was Rohama, who wanted to clear up the uncertainty. Mignon said as soon as the American money came, she would buy her out and farm the place herself. Asked how, she replied, "That's my affair. I don't want people I don't like to have it."

Freddy saw she was in another dotty, self-willed mood and by this time Mignon's obvious hatred for her grandson was becoming an embarrassment because it seemed so unreasonable. Patrick bore her ill-will well enough, urged by Mrs. Lewis to show patience. "The money has gone to her head. She's enjoying her power."

Freddy called in the faithful Ashley and asked him to use what influence he had. He warned him that Mignon had turned into a *prima donna* and was liable to fly off at tangents for the mere pleasure of watching people follow.

Ashley soon challenged her. It was not flattering to her nor in her best interests to pursue a vendetta against Patrick.

"You can't bear him yourself, dearest. What are you talking about?"

"It doesn't matter one way or another what *I* feel. He's your own flesh and blood not mine."

"He's a heartless little adventurer."

"He's just been lucky."

"Human relations are frightful. Nothing counts but power and money. For the first time in my life I've got both. It's a revelation to me to see what people will now do to get close to me."

"That's the way old Harbin from Port Rydal talks about his sons-in-law. It's not the way you should talk."

"I understand him. Very, very well."

Ashley paused. Was this a phase or had she, in fact, completely gone out of her mind?

"I've put up with enough from them. That dreary Nesta and her stupid son. I shan't ever forgive her for the way she deliberately undermined my efforts to sell the diaries. Left to her there wouldn't be any sale today."

"All I can say is this: that if, in selling your husband's papers, you got the power to damage his own daughter's interests and, through her, your own grandson, I think it's a pity the sale ever went through."

"Let's talk about something else, dearest. I'm bored. My chief concern now is helping Rohama. She's worth more than all the other members of the family put together."

* * * *

Couzens wrote. He was planning to spend Christmas in Jerusalem, a city he had last visited in the middle fifties when working for the United Nations in Beirut. Under separate cover, by way of a Christmas present, Couzens was going to send a copy of his autobiography, which had been published in New York some years before. The book turned up the next day and Mignon withdrew into her mysterious woman act holding the book to her like a sacred relic or a letter from the man she loved.

The autobiography, entitled *It wasn't all work*, was the sort of life story which almost everyone needs to write in order to create a personal pattern in a century that has none. It was a wry, amusing self-portrait filled out with lengthy descriptions of travel and books. All morning and afternoon she read the book and, by evening, had reached the pages where Couzens described his first visit to the Middle East and to Jerusalem.

"After hours of this dead-straight road from Damascus, we came to the Syrian border where everyone was drinking small cups of cardamom-scented coffee while waiting for their passports to be stamped. And then the slow descent towards the cellar of the world, the Dead Sea depression. By this time the sun was beginning to incline towards the rim of the Judaean hills.

"By this time—it was winter—it was getting towards sunset and as we crossed the Dead Sea valley—the silvery water on our left, the lights of Jericho and the refugee camps on our right, we saw two towers profiled against the red sky: the towers of Jerusalem, very far away and remote they seemed in the sunset, the outriders of the city—the Russian Orthodox convent and the Augusta Regina Hospital. From that point, whether you want to be or not, you become a pilgrim and although it may be a good half hour before you're passing through Bethany and see the first street lamps of the city, Jerusalem has cast its spell on you and, so far as I can make out, it never lets go of you."

Mignon was thinking of Couzens recovering this ground on the way southwards to Jerusalem and longed to be with him. She would have left without hesitation had he asked her to; but he had not done so and she merely sighed. She put the book away and announced importantly; "I intend to travel. I need a complete break with my old life. What do you say, Freddy?"

"What about Rohama's place first," he replied. "You've kept everyone waiting long enough. Mrs. Lewis has put off her visit to London in order to see the matter to a sensible conclusion."

"Has she?" Mignon asked absently, her thoughts elsewhere.

"Oh, Micky, that's not a reasonable way to talk. You know everyone is on tenterhooks for your decision."

"I suppose they are," Mignon replied in the same distant voice. "Suddenly, I wanted to get away from everything and see the world. Get some new ideas, new impressions ..."

"But not before you've settled Rohama's business," Freddy insisted.

"No. You're right. I've got to settle that."

"Don't let things slide too far. Can't you sit down and discuss the whole thing with everyone properly? Don't make the mistake you've always deplored in other people of holding on to the reins when it was time to let go. Remember that we're both old people. We mustn't try to stand in the way of others. Let things go on. Do so now before you think of any trip. Let things take their natural course."

"I've done my best," Mignon said as though she hadn't heard everything he had said. She was still under Couzens's spell.

"No one has done more. I agree."

"You think it's right that Patrick should have the place?"

"It's the natural thing. The right thing."

"Then he and Anne must have it."

"That's what family feeling and good sense recommend. You'll never regret it."

"What am I to do next, then?" she asked, still distant, still half-lost in her own thoughts.

"Mrs. Lewis is waiting for the word to settle with Rohama. The price has been agreed; the cheque is waiting for her signature."

"Would you like to ring her up and tell them to go ahead? I give my permission for the sale. If they want it in writing they can have it. There's no need for solicitors; they only grab a fee."

Suddenly it was all lightness, all reconciliation.

In the general excitement it went uncommented that it was the Lewis money which paid for Rohama's share of the estate. The Lewis price was, of course, extremely generous and early the next morning Rohama went across to the farm to thank Mignon for being so helpful.

"If you're happy, dearest, so am I. You were the only person I was really thinking about."

"But, Aunty Micky, aren't you glad for Patrick and Anne?"

Mignon looked ashamed of herself. "Well, of course I am. Really I am."

They had a cup of tea together sociably, like old campaigners, in front of the kitchen fire.

"You know," Mignon said, "it's much the best thing to go away: far better to begin a new life elsewhere. There are too many ghosts here. I've laid all mine. In some way everything has come out right. The same thing will happen for you. As soon as you get your new home you'll come into your own. And I know you'll succeed because Martin and yourself are united, you think as one person and that's the main thing in marriage. Wherever you go, whatever you do, Freddy and I wish you well. And later on we'll think up some suitable present for you, something towards your new life which will be our thanks to you for all you've done for us."

Rohama sat a long time without saying anything but looking into the fire regretfully. It might have happened, she was thinking, it might have happened. We might have been real friends and grown to love one another. Pity it didn't happen earlier; now it's too late. We were put into separate boxes and told never to meet and yet we needed one another. And if I'd asked them what are you so suspicious about? What harm could I have done you? Or Martin for that matter? Or both of us together? She wouldn't have had any reply. I know she wouldn't.

*　　*　　*　　*

Everyone but Nesta had cause for satisfaction; only she remained alone, with the emptiness, the solitude of people who live alone and cannot break out of themselves when they meet other people.

In those brilliantly sunlit days before Christmas, after Patrick had gone off to London with Anne and her mother, she went walking and took pleasure in turning down lanes she had never seen before, buying cigarettes in village stores and talking to people she met on the road.

It was the time of year when villagers were killing and plucking their poultry and the main subject of conversation was the unusual brightness of the weather and the greenness of the fields. It was splendid weather for walking, with the crisp wind making the berries dance in the hedges and the midwinter sun striking white radiance off distant farmhouses and the metalled roads, the stones in ploughed fields, the sea-gulls and clouds in the sky and any casually hung piece of linen drying among the cabbages of village gardens. As long as she kept walking she felt well, even happy. She took pleasure in observing small things; and in the conversations with people (many of them half aware of who she was) she went out of her way to recall herself to them as though she wanted to establish some solid existence. People could not understand why such a woman, so well-dressed, so distinguished in a wintry, abstract way, should give the impression of looking for a world that had gone.

People asked her if she would like to return to her native Caeriforshire. She could not answer. Had, say, her family been happier, had she married someone like Ashley with money and an assured local position, would she have found the life fundamentally satisfying? She could not be sure; and she wavered in her own mind about the opportunities she might have taken or the decisions she might have made. Finally, she had to confess that all the big decisions in her life had been made by other people. She had never done anything which expressed an inner conviction.

And although so much had happened in her old home that she regretted, she knew, as she returned home in the bright afternoons, that it would be impossible to cut herself off from it.

In time, she took pleasure in the coming marriage of Patrick to Anne and was sufficiently identified with her son's future happiness to be shocked when her husband, asked to advance money for a good engagement ring, cabled back, "Consider £250 a good investment in circumstances". It seemed an extra-ordinary way to refer to an only son's marriage but perhaps this was her fault in that she had devoted more space in her letters to listing the material possessions rather than discussing the real passion which united Patrick and his girl.

As for Patrick himself, he accepted everything with the good humour that comes from complete self-confidence. He had been put out by his grandmother's opposition to his having Rohama's farm but once she had allowed the sale to go through he bore her no ill-will. He did not, on the other hand,

thank her over-profusely and eventually he stood in exactly the
same relationship to his grandmother as he had always done:
he accepted people's estimates of her good qualities and her
rare virtues but he did not feel them; the gap in age and
manners was too great.

The trip to London with the Lewises finished his weaning
from his own family. He did not even wear the same clothes
when he returned. Anne bought him a sporting rifle for an
engagement present and Mrs. Lewis set him up in an expensive sheepskin coat, which seemed the sort of uniform he
ought to wear.

When he returned home he turned out immediately in the
bright weather with his new toy under his arm, his new coat
over his aggressively hunched shoulders and a new red and
black checked cap on his head. He popped away at the pigeons
with a sense of mission and destiny. His face had the hardness
and purity of the completely untried. He did not really care
whether he shot anything or not; the pleasure was in the clear
air, the glittering reaches of the frost, the berries winking in
the hedges and the marvellous sensation of having found himself.

For the first time ever, he felt he was getting exactly what he
wanted out of life and before him stretched the infinite reaches
of his own freedom as a lover and a man. Although, that day,
he walked out without his farmeress, he thought about her
most of the time and the givenness of their lives together. He
did not have a moment's doubt but that they were doing the
right thing in marrying: the only thing that made sense; and
as he walked by himself he liked thinking of the mysterious
movements that bring people together and the mysterious
forces which give them the power to recognise one another as
truth. He turned over his time with Anne as a musician
thumbs through a favourite score and he knew that their meet-
ings would always be fresh, always be unexpected and new. He
had a feeling that when people said he and Anne were children they missed the essentially childish quality in their
love for one another that turned marriage and its responsi-
bilities into a game, almost the contrivances invented by
children.

She was at the door of the house to greet him when he

returned and kissed him with the ardour and freshness of a child.

*   *   *   *

Mignon replied to Couzens:

"Dear Mr. Couzens," she wrote, "Thank you for your Christmas message and your *fascinating* book of memoirs...

"My brother and I thank you for your invitation from the bottom of our hearts. Your kindness and consideration are beyond description.

"Your letter moved us to tears of gratitude not only because you wanted us to take the wonderful offer proposed by your university but because you were so happy for us that it had been offered. And how happy it makes us that we've met such a goodhearted and disinterested person whose concern for our happiness and wellbeing is something we had no right to expect. Not only have you provided for our old age but you've been able to give us back something that money itself cannot buy: contact with the air and world of free people, the freedom of your large, generous world. We have been truly blessed.

"We were so excited at the idea of going to America but when we made enquiries in Caerifor we saw that travelling there would involve inoculations, vaccinations, injections, affidavits, assurances, security bonds—the lot—and we felt we couldn't cope with all this just at present. In addition, my brother and I feel we both need a long rest. This does not mean that we turn down the university's offer out of hand but it does mean that we won't be able to think about it until we're out of the winter and feeling that much more resilient.

"I've thought a great deal about you as you make your preparations for your trip to the Middle East and I was thinking of your first trip to Jerusalem. In my mind's eye I can see as vividly as yourself the two towers on the Judaean hills standing out so boldly against the sunset like the gateway to some wider and more meaningful existence. Freddy and I are seriously thinking of making such a trip ourselves, but we couldn't go without knowing that we can come back here. It's very warm and cosy here these days with the bright weather and the satisfaction of one's tasks accomplished.

"Bon Voyage. Do not forget,
　　"Yours sincerely,
　　　　"Mignon Benson-Williams."

There were other letters to write: to Edward and Norah Lloyd-Ballantyne keeping their unaccountable silence and, at length, to Jack Cappland.

"Dear Mr. Cappland,
　"It has been on my conscience that I never thanked you for the commission you carried out for me. The reason is that Messrs. Yoxalls and myself have had a long exchange of letters about you and your sale (on my behalf!) of the letters from my late husband's collection. Thanks to your efforts we were able to dispose of all my husband's papers to an American university for a most satisfactory price.

"And now, as the old year draws to an end, we usually thank those who have done us service during the past year: the newspaper man, the butcher, the baker, the coalman, the R.D.C. dustman—and this year, yourself. I send you 10/- herewith to buy yourself a drink with which to toast the new year which, I hope, will bring you ever more interesting travels.

"Once more, Mr. Cappland, I thank you for your work on our behalf which was all the nicer because unexpected and unforeseen.
　　　　"Very sincerely yours,
　　　　　"Mignon Benson-Williams."

Nesta saw the letter and said Cappland would think Mignon was crazy. Mignon had her reply. "He may say I'm crazy," she said, as she passed her tongue along the envelope flap, "but he'll also know he's been seen through. What's more, dearest, he'll get a funny feeling every time he goes down the Brompton Road. I'll haunt him there."

Once all this was done Mignon felt empty, drained of energy and purpose and a little like a reader of a novel in fifteen chapters and an epilogue who comes to the end and says, "Yes, but..." and does not realise that this "Yes, but..." is the soul's cry before life itself. "Yes, but..." the satisfactions are all in the mind, the values are all in the heart, the real fires which stoke our consciences are rarely seen for, all in all, only children and stallkeepers show everything on a card.

* * * *

The early morning services held before dawn on Christmas morning in areas where the old Celtic Church once held sway are known as *Pylgain* or *Plygain*. In any case, the derivation of the word is unsure and some scholars say it is a corruption of some Latin phrase meaning a religious ceremony before cock-crow. Six or seven churches in Caeriforshire maintain the old tradition and one of these churches is only about three miles from Caerifor, set on a spit of land between the open sea and the Maddau estuary, a small, compact church like a cottage, with a square tower.

It was Nesta who wanted to go, so Freddy, Anne and Patrick accompanied her. They had to leave early for the daybreak service attracts people who do not normally attend. Somehow, the dimly-lit church in the middle of the winter night creates an atmosphere such as no one experiences for the rest of the year.

So many cars jammed the narrow lane to the church that they left the Jaguar on the main road and finished the journey on foot. How cold it was! The wind came off the Atlantic—a north-west wind mountainous with salt and discomfort, and impatient for the bright, windy day that would follow. The whining sea was far out, leaving acres of black rock and seaweed glinting in the last quarter of the moon going down into a mass of black cloud. Almost hidden behind hedges turned over at right angles by the winds was the church. Candles burned in every window in special sockets garlanded with holly. Inside, the altar was brilliant with candles, holly and Christmas roses. The whole thing seemed very old and very far-away in time, like scenes remembered from tours in another country. At that time of day and in that place the sea and the wind seemed the matrices of these old, cold religions. This was the point where the missionaries of the new faith had first landed, coming tentatively out of the west, out of small boats, despite hostile pagans and the wiles of the sea currents. The little church at the edge of the world was the child of the old Celtic Church.

Its aids to devotion were of the last century: the ancient organ, the quavering vicar, the organist herself. The details of the service were mediocre, humbling. The singing was not bad but the sermon was piffling. It needed a saint to do justice to the occasion. As on so many of these religious occasions in a secular century, the service was pure anti-climax. In fact, as Anne said, the best thing on these occasions is the idea itself.

They all went back to Swanquarter and when they reached the farm Patrick parked the car in the back courtyard where the water was falling musically from the iron spout on to an iron grill. It was still dark with the last glimpse of the setting moon glittering through a break in masses of cloud over the tops of the fir plantations and the windbreaks. Here and there the first lights were appearing in farm kitchens. Everything had a cold, sub-lunar normality and reality. Patrick and Anne lingered by the side of the car until after Freddy and Nesta had climbed the stairs into the house. After a couple of long, pre-breakfast kisses they moved towards the house and were at the foot of the steps when they saw a curious shape in the courtyard itself. Was it a trick of the moonlight and some mist rising from the well or was it the figure of a woman?

Whatever-it-was rose with a flowing, fountain movement, remained poised for a moment, and then dissolved slowly in its own substance like a fountain falling back when the water supply is cut off. To have blinked would have meant missing the apparition; to have called out would have broken the enchantment. Without a word they hurried up the stairs into the kitchen where Mignon was frying bacon and eggs in the cosy way farm-women cook breakfasts early in the morning. Anne said, trying not to sound breathless, "We saw something rather extraordinary just now. Patrick and I were coming up the steps and we saw a curious white shape rising from the well."

"Yes," said Patrick, stopped short in his own disbelief, "and it disappeared as suddenly as it had come."

"You saw a kind of apparition?" Nesta asked. "What was it: a ghost?"

"A kind of, I suppose, wasn't it, Patrick?"

Patrick caught between his natural scepticism and the evidence of his senses laughed and shrugged. "It was probably a trick of the moonlight."

"But what did it look like?" his mother asked.

"Oh, it sort of rose out of the well with a curious billowy lightness, like a curtain swelling in a breeze and yet utterly graceful and feminine. That's the point: it was feminine."

"A lady ghost!"

Mignon who had been listening keenly said matter-of-factly, "You must have seen the Undine of Swanquarter."

"But I thought that was all invention to please the journalists," Patrick protested; he didn't want to be fobbed off like the others.

"I never invented it. It's a very old tradition in the family. And how right it is that you and Anne should see her. Yours is the first for a long time."

Everyone was a little staggered by the comfortable, matter-of-fact way Mignon announced this although she was smiling lopsidedly.

"I take that to be a very good omen: the finest Christmas present you could have."

"You mean, you really believe that story?"

"Of course I do. Why should *I* deny the proof of *your* eyes?"

"But did you ever see anything?"

"No. But then mine was not a happy marriage so I wouldn't see her; she didn't come to my betrothal. That she's come now means you're going to be very happy."

No one could accept this mixture of whimsy and almost detached belief: in some way they felt defrauded. Even to have put so fanciful a name to what they had seen limited them.

Mignon smiled mysteriously. "Even though you've seen something I don't expect you to believe—but later in life you'll find yourself believing: that's the beauty of it. Looking back you'll not be so troubled by the impossible but by the logic of these things. This will seem a turning-point in your lives; you'll mark certain things from this point. And that's as it should be."

Nesta went up to her mother privately and asked her whether she really meant what she was saying; she doubted whether her mother's detachment and certainty were genuine. Mignon looked up from the frying-pan and rebuked her daughter. "You're so strange, Nesta. Why not accept what I've told you? Why should it be odd I believe these things? It used to worry me that the little thing would never happen again; that worried me rather. Oh, no, dearest, you can take it that everything is as it should be."

Yes, Mignon seemed to say, we have skirted the edge of the abyss created by modern formlessness and aimlessness. When Nesta demurred by making small, grudging noises in the throat, Mignon said, "It can't be helped, dearest. You won't ever see her. I haven't seen her. That's all there is to it. Leave it at that."

Yes, Mignon seemed to say, we shan't see her and we don't deserve to. Her hatred of the bogus was as sharp as her daughter's and yet she was utterly, wholly sincere in this new role, and unshakeable in her belief that Anne and Patrick had seen 'the little thing'.

Nesta would not and she could not believe what her mother and the young people were saying. "It's true," Anne said. "It's true. We really did see it."

She led her future mother-in-law across the kitchen to the small window that looked down into the courtyard and explained again just how they had been placed when the thing had appeared. Down in the courtyard it was still dark with only the smallest lightening of the sky beyond the trees; and for a long time, after Anne had gone away to join Patrick in lighting a fire in the large sitting-room, Nesta stood at the window looking down into the courtyard and doubting, and looking still and doubting, and looking again and again and doubting until she realised that everyone else was carrying on normally and that she was the only one who was still looking back and doubting; and when she realised this she felt old and alone, as though left out of history.